BEARS BEHAVING BADLY

MARY JANICE DAVIDSON

 sourcebooks
casablanca

Published by Sourcebooks Casablanca, an imprint of Sourcebooks
P.O. Box 4410, Naperville, Illinois 60567-4410
(630) 961-3900
sourcebooks.com

Printed and bound in Canada.
MBP 10 9 8 7 6 5 4 3 2 1

For Lily Allen, who tells it like it is, and doesn't especially care if you don't like it.

And for all the good people at Godiva Chocolatier, because…well. Chocolate! (Duh.)

Chapter 1

HE TELLS HER HE WANTS HER AND PROVES IT

his hands are everywhere his hands are magic they make the world fall away

and that is just what she craves and she is desperate to do her part she is wild to make the world disappear for him

and he is easing her onto her back and filling her up with all of him and all of her knows that is fine, just fine and the only thing she wants is for this to never stop

never stop

never

oh

oh my

oh

god

"Beautiful dreamer...wake unto meeeeeee... Starlight and dewdrops...are waiting for theeeeee!"

The world was falling away—no, was *wrenched* away. And by Stephen Foster, no less. "*Nnnnnfff?*"

"Sounds of the rude world...heard in the day...lulled by the moonlight...have all passed *awaaaaaaaay!*"

"Gah." She swiped, missed, found the thing, smacked it. Opened her eyes—and her fist—and the crushed components pattered to the carpet. *Oh, hell on toast.*

Annette Garsea, twenty-seven, single, IPA caseworker in need of a shower and a new alarm clock, sat up, pawed at her blankets, and finally freed her legs. She glared at the nightstand drawer, which stayed closed more often these days than her libido liked. Especially last night, when she had gotten home so tired she'd barely had time to undress before doing a belly flop onto her (unmade) bed and succumbing immediately. And even if she *had* made the time

(note: buy replacement batteries. lots.)

it wouldn't have made much difference. She and David had just missed each other…again. And even if she'd seen him, nothing would have happened. It wouldn't have changed anything, including the fact that her sex life was barren and mornings were…yuck. It was like thinking through honey for the first ten minutes. Which wouldn't be so bad if there was actual honey, but she hadn't had a chance to go grocery shopping this week. Eggs were good several days past their expiration date, right? Right.

He tells her he wants her and proves it…

From long practice, she pushed the fantasy away, stretched, yawned, padded though her messy den toward the bathroom. Showered, shampooed, watered down her conditioner again (at this point, it was water that vaguely smelled like conditioner), hopped out, toweled, ran a comb through her shaggy locks

(note: grocery shopping and conditioner and haircut)

and dressed. Black office-appropriate slacks she could stand, sit, and run in; ditto her shoes, which were plain black rubber-soled flats. Sports bra, dark-blue turtleneck. Dad's wristwatch. Or as her partner called it, "that quaint clock you strap to your body for some reason."

Breakfast. She loved their sun-filled kitchen, with bold, black appliances (easy cleanup) and lots of counter space (room to spread out the junk mail, tape, more mail, books, pens, junk mail), and the island, which was usually Pat's domain for his project *de la semaine*. She went straight to the fridge, took inventory of the pitiful contents, and grabbed staples. She sniffed at the eggs and, satisfied, cracked three, whisked them, added the last of the half-and-half, then swirled them into the softly bubbling butter.

"Oh, *Gawd*, I can't watch."

"So don't."

"And yet," Pat whispered, round-eyed, "I cannot look away. This is what people see just before they die."

"Stop it." Annette added chopped onions, ham, tomatoes, and sprinkled half a cup of cheese over the glorious mess. She let it cook for a minute, then grabbed a rubber spatula and ran it around the edge, lifting the bubbling, thickening omelet up here and there so the raw eggs could run beneath. A minute later she plopped the thing on a paper plate

(note: dishwasher soap)

and sat across from Pat, who took one look at Annette's repast

"Want some?"

and shuddered. "You've gotta know the answer is a vehement 'Oh dear God, not even on a bet.'"

"And yet." She took a bite, relishing the overcooked bottom and the undercooked top. "It's important to start the day off right."

"Self-induced salmonella is not starting the day off right. Are you okay?" Pat was 55 percent legs, 20 percent hair, and 25 percent heart, and had a horror of people discovering the latter. So before Pat could express concern—who'd know better than her lunatic roommate that Andrea's job was dangerous?—he had to insult her breakfast. "You got in late."

"One of my kids got pinched for shoplifting. I went out to make sure they had a decent bed for him."

"Let me guess."

"Don't guess. You know I can't talk about it."

"Dev Devoss."

"What did I just saaaaay?"

"You talk about that kid in your sleep. Seriously, you yell at him in your dreams." Pat drummed his fingers on the countertop, already involved in early-morning plotting. "I've gotta meet him."

"Never happen."

"And here I was the idiot hoping you were out on a date with Donald."

She almost dropped her fork. Pat had a tendency to read her mind, and she was in no mood to be teased for her recurring fantasy, which had now invaded her dreams. "David."

"I honestly don't care, Annette. Stop playing with your food before you eat it. That's literal *and* figurative, by the way."

"I'm not following."

"Call or text Derwood—"

"David."

"Still don't care. Call him or text him or homing pigeon him and then brutally and enthusiastically shag him silly."

Oh, sure. As if it were that simple. "And then?"

Her roommate looked taken aback. "How should I know? I'm all about the setup, not what comes after. Give him cab fare? Or a wedding ring? My point is—"

"I know what your point is." She brought the flat of her butter knife down on Pat's knuckle just as the duplicitous wretch was about to snitch some ham. "Nice mani, by the way."

"Thanks. Wouldn't kill you to sit still for one, either."

"Never. If I can't read during a procedure, I won't endure it."

"God help us if you ever need surgery, then." Pat inspected his nails, which were spade-shaped and the color of glossy pink pearls. "Got an interview."

"I figured. The suit and all."

Pat was wearing one of his brother's navy-blue pin-striped suits with a crisp white shirt and a pale-blue tie dotted with poppies that looked like blood clots. Though he wouldn't leave the house, Pat was a big believer in "dress for the job you want, not the job you have." Which led to some confusion the month he wanted to be a park ranger. ("I don't care if it's five below; this is what rangers wear!") And the following month, when he wanted to be a hippotherapist. ("If you're going to do physical therapy with horses, this is what it takes!")

"I'm letting you change the subject in your clumsy and obvious way because I've said my piece—"

"Oh *God,* if only that were true."

"—and because I want you to get what this means. No longer will I be the homeless parasite suckling at your 24-acre teat!" Pat declared.

"Okay, gross." Not to mention inaccurate. Pat insisted on paying $666.66 every other month, and he was far from homeless. "You know you don't have to get another job on my account."

"This isn't about you or your account. It's about me getting a job within these four walls before I go crazy within these four walls."

"Good for you," she said, snarfing the last of her runny omelet. "And stop with the matchmaking-roommate trope."

"I'm the original, dammit! Tropes come from *me*, not the other way around. Take. That. Back."

"Nuh-uh. And good luck on your interview. Knock 'em…uh…." *Argh.* Because once upon a time, she and Pat *had* knocked 'em dead. It was why he wore his straight blond hair shoulder-length, when his preference for years had been a buzz cut. "Knock 'em good luck."

"Gosh, it's such a treat to see your razor-like mind in action."

"You wait. 'Knock 'em good luck' will be in the national lexicon within the month," she said, and stifled an eggy, hammy burp.

Chapter 2

ANNETTE WAVED AND SMILED AT THE SECOND PERSON
to cut her off (always fun to see them confused by a cheerful countenance instead of a jabbing middle finger), drove straight past the Ramsey County government building, turned left into the parking-garage ramp at the end of the block, flashed her ID, drove down three stories, flashed her ID again, and drove down one more story into the Interspecies Placement Agency, which had much in common with the State of Minnesota's standard foster-care system, except that IPA had a bigger budget and a sundae bar on Fridays.

She grabbed her purse, her case, the bakery box, and her drink, and managed to get her big butt into the elevator with minutes to spare. Minutes! Who knew, perhaps she could while away that spare time looking for David while simultaneously pretending she was not looking for David. *That's not pathetic, right? Right.*

The elevator dinged, the doors opened, and her fine mood fell away as she stepped off into chaos. The melee reminded her of the scene from *Resident Evil* when the good guys finally got the doors open, only to walk straight into a horde of slavering zombies.

Honestly, zombies couldn't be much worse.

"Where the bloody hell have you been?"

"Did you see the memo about Secret Santas? It's barely fall!"

"Hiya! Whatcha got for me today?"

"Devoss has instigated yet another debacle, and you've got a new lamb—"

"Like there isn't enough pressure with the holidays? I've gotta worry about Secret friggin' Santas—"

"Pleasebecupcakespleasebecupcakesplease—"

"—who will certainly keep you on your toes—"

"—before Halloween?"

"And the bloody server's down, so we'll have to do it the old-fashioned way, which I know you despise."

"Well, that's it. I know I say this every year, but I'm out."

"—becupcakespleasebecupcakes."

"And you owe a tenner for Helen's get-well meat tray."

"Good God," Annette muttered into her hot chocolate. She literally fought her way past the figurative horde (there were only three of them, but still), spotted the edge of her desk—*just* the edge, because she was behind on her paperwork—and dropped her purse in the middle of the maelstrom. "How can three people be a horde? Let me get my coat off."

"Hey! I'm having a Secret Santa crisis! There's no time to let you disrobe, dammit! I can't believe they didn't check with me before just…just *announcing* it."

"So get rid of the program," Annette pointed out. "End of problem."

"Beginning of migraine. Everybody loves the Secret Santa thing."

"They don't, though."

"They look forward to it all year!"

"They absolutely don't, Bob. Cross my heart and hope to, et cetera. Besides, you're the one in charge, nominally speaking. You can blitz this problem in three seconds."

"I won't squash their dreams," the agency supervisor declared, then ran away.

She turned and handed off the box to Oz Adway. "It's not cupcakes."

"No! My Monday is ruined!"

"It's Tuesday, Oz."

"Eclairs! Well. Three-point-five eclairs. This box was full when you bought it, wasn't it?"

She snickered, which was answer enough, apparently, as Oz wasted no time fleeing back to the bowels of Accounting from whence he was spawned.

That's one problem solved. Annette sighed and stared at her desk, briefly entertained the idea of turning all her paperwork into origami swans, then turned to Nadia, her facilitator-slash-colleague-slash-bane. "So. Dev Devoss and Caro Daniels?"

Nadia, who stood a foot shorter and dressed like she was the only one in the room worth looking at (which might be true), peered up at her. "How did it go?"

"What?"

"Your date with David Auberon."

Annette stared. "Why does everyone think I went out with David Auberon?"

"We don't. But speaking only for myself, I feel if I pretend it's happening, eventually you'll succumb."

Annette rolled her eyes. "How romantic."

"Oh, darling. Who said anything about romance?"

"One, it creeps me out when you call me 'darling.' Two, it also creeps me out when you decide to create an alternate reality in which you have arbitrarily decided that David Auberon and I are going out. Three, talk about work now."

Nadia shrugged elegantly, which Annette hadn't thought possible. The woman could probably clean the wax from her ears with verve and elegance. "As you like."

"Dev Devoss and Caro Daniels," Annette prompted.

"Dev got punched for shoplifting again."

"Pinched, Nadia. Not punched. Your grip on American slang is greasy at best."

"Don't slang-shame me." Nadia ruffled her hair, then settled. "Now about Dev—"

"Death by nagging—pretty sure that's his immediate future. Apparently, I yell at him in my sleep."

"It's better than strangling him. And Caro Daniels is downstairs in holding."

"My new lamb." From force of long habit, this was more murmured than spoken aloud. The adults Annette worked with didn't take it personally, but if it got back to any of her kids, the ones with a high prey drive might see it as an invitation to fight. "Did she sleep?"

"Yes. Almost immediately. And it seems to me that she's been living ralph, too."

"Living 'rough.' We *just* went over this."

"My point is that I believe she ran away."

"That would have been my guess, too. Hardly unusual." Troubled teens often bolted; that had been true for generations. But she'd noticed werewolf cubs were especially prone to it. And while she hated generalizing and stereotypes more than she hated those big puffy orange circus peanuts, more than one teenage Shifter had rebelled against the pack hierarchy, even if only for a few days. It was as if they needed to make a run for a solitary life before settling in.

She couldn't relate. At all.

"Ah. There you are." She'd rummaged through the sea of papers and come up with two files: Caro's slim one, likely just the arrest report, and Dev's vastly thicker one, which necessitated a three-inch binder. And tabs! Annette glanced through Caro's arrest report: she'd been read her rights, made no statement, did not ask for a phone call. Endured an exam, weight and height—she glanced up at Nadia. "Malnourished, underweight, small build."

"Indeed. It's rather astonishing that she came out the winner."

"That's one word for it. And she hasn't said anything?"

"Not a peep or a pip. Witnesses include David Auberon—"

"Well, *great*." Annette was well aware of the witness. It had been one of the reasons she'd been more interested than usual to get to work. "This will only feed your imagination."

"Indeed it will. And the other witness is your favorite troublemaker, Dev."

She knew that, too, and turned her attention to Dev's latest mug shot: pointed chin, wide-set green eyes, hedgehog scruffy hair, improbable "gotcha!" grin. She wanted to march into holding and smack the kit as badly as she wanted to keep him safe.

Nadia, meanwhile, was smoothing her sleek, dark hair and flicking nonexistent lint from her red suit. "Shall we? Or did you want to refill your cup o' sludge?"

"It's hot chocolate!" Annette protested.

"It's tepid water and powder. It's mock chocolate. I retract nothing."

"I've got something for you to retract," Annette muttered into her cocoa. She liked Nadia a lot—they smoothed each other's edges—but the woman was a fearful snob. She'd climbed out of her nest at 2:00 a.m. to help Annette remove a traumatized cub, but froze her out for days when Annette's Secret Santa gift was a pair of (not designer) gloves. Protests ("We're supposed to keep it under $25!") went unheeded.

Annette followed Nadia past the cheerful (mostly) disorder of desks, cubicles, and offices, while avoiding the contaminated cesspool that was the break room. So many keen noses on the floor, but no one could find the source of the smell. *O, break room, what mysteries you hold 'tween your fetid walls...*

"Hi, Annette!" One of the clerks, Taryn Wapiti, hailed her from where she'd been chatting up an attorney. (The sharp suits were always a giveaway, even if Annette could only see this one from the back.) Taryn wasn't much taller than Nadia, with sturdy legs and the characteristic broad shoulders of a were-elk. Her hair was a reddish-orange, and her dark eyes were nearly always gleaming with fun. "When are we gonna go back to the Patty Wagon?"

"Taryn, hamburgers, no matter how glorious, make you sick as a—" Hmm. *Sick as a dog* wasn't very sensitive. "As a person who shouldn't eat meat."

"Worth it," she insisted. "Plus they put a ton of vegetables on their burgers, so it evens out."

"A tomato slice, a piece of lettuce, and a small sprinkling of onions is not, by any stretch, a ton."

"Worth it," Taryn said again.

"And you understand veggie burgers exist, yes?"

"It's not the same. C'mon, Annette! I wanna gooooooooo!"

Argh, the whining. Annette sighed. "I can't go out to eat until I do some shopping. My fridge is an embarrassment. So perhaps the end of the week?"

"Done! I'm gonna destroy their V8 special."

"Something will be destroyed, but I don't think it'll be their special."

"A problem for another day. Hey, Nadia."

"Taryn, darling, surely there are less painful ways to commit gastrointestinal suicide?"

"None that I know of," Taryn replied, and with a cheerful wave went back to the lawyer.

The guard had already put Dev twelve-year-old werefox, mother incarcerated, father unknown, pack affiliation unknown—in Interview One. Caro

Daniels—sixteen-year-old female werewolf, parents unknown, pack affiliation unknown—went into Interview Three.

The girl looked up when Annette came in and shut the door. "Good morning, Ms. Daniels. My name is Annette Garsea, I'm your caseworker pro tem."

Silence.

"Would you like something to drink? Pop? Tea? Hot chocolate?"

Nothing.

"I can also offer you mock chocolate. No? All right. My understanding is that you weren't injured last night, but now that it's been a few hours, have you found you do, in fact, need medical attention?"

Nothing. So. Hopefully not.

Annette sat across from the girl and studied her as she sipped her mock chocolate. Caro Daniels had the well-scrubbed look of the werewolf next door: short black hair slicked back from a high forehead, dark skin with golden undertones, and big brown eyes an anime character would envy. She was petite and delicately made—and in dire need of several protein drinks. She was sockless in sneakers, and a navy-blue sweatshirt and sweatpants with the IPA logo on the back and sides, both size small, which dwarfed her. The clothing made sense because even if Caro didn't have a mark on her, her clothes from last night would have been ruined with copious amounts of Lund's blood. Exhibit A, as it were. Or would Lund himself be Exhibit A?

"You understand you're safe here and it's okay to talk, right? Or we could call someone for you. We'll assign you an advocate, of course, but if there's an adult you want us to contact...?"

Zip.

"I'm relieved you weren't hurt. Especially given how much bigger and stronger Mr. Lund was." *Not a peep,* Nadia had said, but Annette hadn't realized she was being literal. And that was something, wasn't it? Not a sound. Or a mark. Was she deaf? Mute? In shock? A werewolf ninja sworn to silence? "Would you like some writing materials?"

Caro shook her head. Progress! (Of a sort. They were communicating, at least.) So Caro could hear and understand, or at least read lips. Her gaze was steady, and Annette had the impression that there was a busy brain behind those luminous eyes. She made a mental note to try to get a look at the girl's school records. Of course, first they had to find her school. And her everything else.

Mental note: If Caro hasn't spoken, how do they know her name? ID? School? Driver's license? Nothing in the paperwork. Find out.

"If you change your mind, just let one of the staff know. And if you need to tell me anything, they'll know how to reach me. I'm about to go see the man you attacked last night." Unlike the other foster-care system, there was no dancing around with "allegedly attacked" at the IPA. Even if there hadn't been eyewitnesses, the spindly teenager had been covered in Lund's blood. "Are you sure there's nothing you want to tell me before I get his side of the story?"

Nothing. Not even a headshake.

"Last chance, Ms. Daniels."

Nothing.

"Well, nice talking to you, so to speak. No? Tough room. I'll be back in a bit."

Caro didn't make a sound, just watched Annette until she was on the other side of the door.

Annette let out a breath, considered her options, then stepped into the next interview room. Dev greeted her with a cheerful wave, started to rise, forgot about the lead chain, and slammed back into his seat. "Oof! Uh, hi?"

"Oh now, really?" Annette said to Jericho, the guard in charge for day shift.

The amiable werebear spread his hands, which were essentially bowling balls with knuckles. "Those are the second set of restraints. He stole the other ones. We *still* can't find them."

"Dev!"

"Frame job," the werefox replied with his trademark game grin.

"In a pig's eye. Not to insult swine." Annette kept the scowl on her face, though she noticed Jericho faking a cough so he could cover his grin. "I've got this, Jericho, thanks very much."

"You're welcome." Then to Dev, in a low rumble: "You be good."

"C'mon, Jerry!" Dev spread his hands as far as the

chain allowed. He was blinking his eyes like a startled fawn, which was as hilarious as it was annoying. "When've I *ever* misbehaved on your watch?"

"Five goddamned minutes ago," the guard muttered on his way out.

"He's way too softhearted for this job," Dev confided. "What kind of a guard hates guarding?"

"One who's made your acquaintance."

"Thanks?"

Annette stifled a sigh. "You want to tell me what happened?"

"I *did*. Frame job." He again spread his small, grimy hands as wide as the cuffs would allow, which wasn't very. "I'm *innocente, incriminado, unschuldig.*"

"Let's keep to one language, you unrepentant polyglot. Just so I understand the scam du jour—"

"Now who's bein' a polyglot?"

"—you're trying to tell me that you didn't steal two jugs of Tide—"

"With bleach alternative."

"—detergent?"

"I was gonna pay. But then I saw Caro was in trouble so I ran out to help her."

"Somehow forgetting to drop the several pounds of liquid detergent in your arms."

"I was in a rush."

"And how do you even know Caro?"

"She's my sister. I told that David guy when he grabbed me. Hey, are you guys going out?"

"What? No." Dev was in on the dating conspiracy? *Focus, woman!* Much more intriguing, Dev had been the one to ID Caro Daniels? Annette blinked, shook her head. She knew which families each of her lambs was with. And Caro was only in the system as of last night. "No, Caro's not your fos-sister. I'd know if she were."

"No, I mean my *real* sister."

No. Werefoxes were not blood relations to were-wolves. It was a paralogical impossibility. "Dev, what pile of nonsense are you trying to feed me now?"

"It's *not* nonsense." The smirk had faded, and now he just looked upset and vulnerable. The cuffs swallowing his small hands didn't help, nor the overlarge jacket he was wearing. Annette steeled herself. It would take more than Dev's big green eyes and pleading expression to get her to relent. This time. Probably. "Can I see her?"

"Not just now, Dev. Can Caro speak? Have you ever heard her talk?"

"She *can*, she just won't."

"Can you tell me why?"

"No. And I really need to see her. She needs me."

"Why?"

He gave her the *Are you stupid or just deranged?* look unique to teenagers. "Because we're family."

"How so?"

"And she's scared and doesn't feel safe."

"Understandable. She's in custody."

"No, I mean she's scared of him."

"*She's* scared? Not the werewolf she attacked?"

Dev made a face like he'd bitten into something rotten. "He wasn't a werewolf, he was a monster. Besides, she had to go for that guy."

"That guy?"

An eye roll. "Yeah, the guy she had to pounce."

"It was a little more than a pounce. She could have killed him."

"She should have. He's been trying to kill her for two years."

And, as was often the case when talking with Dev, Annette was left speechless.

Chapter 3

DAVID AUBERON LURCHED PAST THE INTAKE GANG, the guards, rando juvies, caseworkers, lawyers, stressed parents, and a UPS gal, all on his way to that which was dearest to him

"Oh, God…"

the elixir he needed as he did oxygen

"…there it is…"

and woe be-fuckin'-tide anyone who got between him and the

"Coffee!" This followed by a roar of despair: "Decaf?"

"Coming! Coming!" The guy whose name David never remembered (coffee guy? *the* coffee guy? just guy?) raced into the room and deftly filled the empty pots. "It's just that this machine is on the fritz so we're using the one downstairs and something something plus something so something else, and are you going out with Annette?"

In. His. Dreams. "No. Why do people keep asking me that?"

"Because she doesn't go out with anybody. Not anyone from here, at least."

Yeah, well. The lady had taste. She could do better than the dregs of IPA. Rather than explain this, David gulped more coffee.

After an expectant pause, Coffee Guy must've figured no gossip was forthcoming. "Well, whatever, but the good news is we're getting a new machine and something about pods and coffee something something, so it's all gonna be something."

"Okay." This while he was trying not to inhale the stuff like it was cocaine. Actually, cocaine didn't work on him, so something *like* cocaine. Carfentanil, maybe. Or a boatload of Jack. While slurping, David groped through his overcoat pockets until he found the elixir of life, put the coffee down (*you'll be back in my hands soon, gorgeous, no worries*), unscrewed the cap on his maple syrup, dumped in a couple of tablespoons, rescrewed, replaced, picked back up, drank.

"You are the second lunatic I've seen slurp down sludge in five minutes."

"Hey, Nadia." He turned and nodded at the pretty brunette in the red suit and little shiny, pointy shoes that looked like futuristic torture devices. "You're in the wrong biz if you want to watch people drink expensive shit."

"Too true, David. A pity the golden shores of my home country won't have me back."

"Yeah." Nobody knew why Nadia put the *ex* in *expatriate*. Well, the bosses probably knew, but that was it. And while plenty of people wondered, nobody wanted to ask her straight out. She might cut them to shreds for snooping. Worse, she might tell them. Theories ranged from her being a high-ranking SAS member who'd blown up a building to a billionaire lottery winner who'd fled her tax obligations. "Too bad."

"Your baritone platitudes are such a comfort."

He grunted and kept his distance. Raptors made him nervous. The littlest thing would set 'em off during a conversation, and there'd be ruffling and hand-waving and shrieking and five seconds later they were all settled again, 'til the next time. Nadia was gorgeous, sure, but too much work. Sometimes even just to talk to.

This is why you're still single, his mother whispered. Dead six years; still wouldn't leave him alone.

"Your name was prominently featured in Caro Daniels's paperwork," Nadia told him, as if he didn't know.

"Yeah, I brought her in." Christ, what a mess. Blood everywhere; his hackles had been up before he was even all the way out of the car. He hadn't wanted to take on a blood-crazy juvie werewolf; hurting a kid was a lousy way to start the week. And the guy she was savaging had already shifted back, probably due to the shock.

But she'd settled almost immediately; just dropped the guy, who hit with the sound of a raw rump roast hitting asphalt (which technically he was).

She'd also dropped her gaze—pleasant surprise—and shifted back to bipedal, followed David's curt instructions, got in the car. If he hadn't known better, he'd have thought she was a werehare, something that lived to nibble grass and hide. Not the infuriated creature who had nearly killed a werewolf in his prime. *Would* have killed, if David hadn't intervened.

And the only reason he was there to intervene was—

"Oh, that sneaky little charming, duplicitous, idiotic genius," Annette announced.

—Dev Devoss.

Nadia laughed, but Annette just shook her head and looked like she wanted to smile or bite or maybe both.

David straightened out of his slouch and fought the urge to run a hand through his hair in what would be an ultimately futile attempt to straighten it. It tended to stick up in dark spikes; he'd always been able to do the artfully moussed-to-look-mussed look without the mousse.

Being around Annette Garsea made him feel sixteen again, all hormones and hard-ons and exhilaration, followed by depression, despair, and binge-eating frozen pizza. (While still frozen, the bitter-cold bites were deeply satisfying.)

If she was just gorgeous, he'd be fine. Or if she was just charming. Or just whip-smart. Or just funny. Or just cool. Or just sexy. But she was the whole package, corny as that was, and knowing she was acres out of his league didn't stop his pulse from zooming every time he caught her plums-and-cotton scent. And it made the "Are they going out?" rumors sound like total fucking nonsense.

Besides, if he ever did settle down, it'd be with a Stable. He'd known that for over a decade.

"You won't believe this," Annette was saying, her brown eyes almost reddish in her intensity. "Dev says he knows Caro because they're—" She cut herself off and... Wait. Was that a blush? "Oh. Good morning, David."

Not a blush. Or not one for you, anyway. A blush of rage.

A rage blush. He grunted. *Oh, very charming. Why not ask her out, make the gossip real?*

"I'm glad you came in." *Jesus Christ, she's still talking to me.* "I wanted to thank you for bringing Caro Daniels in safely. And Dev."

He shrugged. "It's the job."

"Handsome *and* modest, oh dear." Nadia smirked, ice-blue eyes gleaming.

"I can't tell if you're being mean or flirting with me," he replied.

"It's adorable that you think those are two different things."

"Don't mind Nadia," Annette said pleasantly, "because she's horrible."

"I'm forced to vehemently agree," Nadia agreed.

"Lund's being released from the hospital this afternoon," he told Annette, already anxious to get the hell out of this conversation. "Wanted to ask you…"

"Yesssssss?" Nadia asked, leaning forward and blinking as though someone was shining a flashlight in her eyes.

"…if you needed an addendum to his statement."

"Yes indeed," Annette replied. "Shall we?"

"Huh?" Oh. *Oh.* She was coming with. Him. She was coming *with him.* But what did that mean? Coming with him as in following him? Coming with him in his car? At least the Razer was in decent shape; he'd had it washed just last… Wait… What year did *The Great British Baking Show* start? "Yeah, sure."

Like the blush, the fact that she seemed to be looking at him slightly too long was a figment of his overheated imagination. "Excellent. Nadia's got some more paperwork to take care of, but she'll meet us at the hospital."

"Thank you so very much for speaking for me. The good Lord knows I couldn't manage it myself." But it was reflexive snottiness; Nadia was already waving them away when Annette turned to him.

"Is it all right if I get a ride with you? I can head back with Nadia." Then a heart-stopping pause. *Here's where she backs out.* "Or you could come with me."

Okay, maybe not. "Yeah, sure."

"Which part?" she asked.

"I don't know, whatever."

"I'll just go with you, then."

"Uh-huh."

Smooooooooth!

Chapter 4

THE SAINT PAUL SKYWAY SYSTEM WAS AN ABOVE-ground labyrinth of bright corridors that connected to various shops, restaurants, office buildings, and hotels. Since the average Minnesota winter lasted approximately 304 days, it was lovely to be able to traverse buildings at any time, and the skyway had the added benefit of enormous windows and the greenhouse effect, making it warm and bright no matter what the weather.

All of which was moot, because the skyway was for the *naturae fixed*, the Stables, those poor souls who were stuck in the same shape from birth to death: *Homo sapiens* in all their stable, savage glory.

Shifters, the *naturae flex*, had to keep to the Beneath—figuratively if not literally, the ground and what was below it. If it was raining they got wet, and if it was snowing, they got snowed on, and if it was fogging, they got fogged.

Which was why she and David were not on the second floor but instead in a parking garage, after swinging by Cinnabon on the way to United Hospital. Because if she didn't have something to do with her hands and mouth, Annette was likely to jump poor unsuspecting, sexy David Auberon. Which wouldn't just be unprofessional (and possibly illegal) but would also ruin their working relationship.

What working relationship? This is the first time you've shared a case in two years.

Still chewing

(*gah, it's like eating a pillow, a wonderful cinnamon-frosted pillow*)

Annette smiled as they approached a gray Subaru. "Your car looks like—"

"A giant electric razor," David agreed. "Yeah." There was a *blip-blip!* as he hit the unlock button, and then they were getting in for the twenty-minute ride to the hospital. Two of which Annette spent finishing her second Cinnabon and casting about for something to say. Anything to say.

The fact was, she didn't know David very well. The real David, at least—she knew Dream David intimately. Real-World David wasn't IPA but a special investigator who worked with Stables as well as Shifters. He was a notorious loner, with the looks of someone right out of central casting for "mountain hermit": intimidating height and a tendency to stoop when speaking to someone shorter (which was almost everyone), bulky shoulders and long legs, a head of thick brown hair and a mouth that rarely smiled, deeply tanned skin and constant dark stubble blooming along his jawline. He favored flannels and denim—the latter matching his eye color almost exactly—with occasional daring forays into button-downs. His loafers looked a hundred years old. He spoke in as few words as possible, when he bothered using words at all.

But judging by the pile of Skittles in what was once an ashtray (How old was this car? Did they even make them with ashtrays anymore?) and the pink Starbursts in his cup holder, he had excellent taste in candy.

He saw her looking and said, "Help yourself."

"No, thanks. I had Skittles for breakfast." *Do you want to go out sometime? Kick some life into these odd rumors? Wait, I'm not sure I want to reward Nadia's insistence on an alternate reality by making it* actual *reality. Who knows what the woman might dream up next?*

Not to mention she was getting ahead of herself. For all she knew, David Auberon was married. Or seeing someone. Or gay. Or gray-A. Or not into zaftig werebears. Before she could ponder further, something caught her eye and she leaned forward. "Good God, I just realized— it's only the red ones."

"Yeah."

"That's..." *Nutty. Anal. Wasteful—where are the other flavors? Do you toss them? Give them away? Mail them to your enemies?* None of which were appropriate to ask, so she coughed to cover her confusion. He motioned to the glove compartment and she hit the button, then stared as a torrent of red Jolly Ranchers fell out. "Um..."

"There's Kleenex underneath all that. I'm pretty sure," he added in a low mutter.

"Quick! What's your favorite fruit?"

"Red?"

"Good *God.*"

"What?" He sounded defensive, which was the last emotion she wanted to elicit, but honestly.

"You're the guy who dumps maple syrup into everything."

"Not everything. Not fries. Well, once on fries," he admitted. "More an accident than design."

"Even for a werebear, your sweet tooth is ridiculous."

"Well." He seemed to consider that for a couple of seconds. "Yeah."

She laughed; she couldn't help it. Something about his bemused resignation struck her as funny. And to her surprise, he joined in, and she heard his deep, warm chuckle for the first time.

Damn. A girl could fall in love.

Not this one, though.

Too much to do.

"So, to sum up, you're fine, you're well on the road to recovery, your attempted murder was a misunderstanding, you wish your assailant all the best, and you really must be going. That about right?"

More than right, Annette thought. David had nailed it in fewer than ten seconds.

They'd bypassed the Stable floors, used their IDs to get past the security for the Shifter wing (David casting a longing look at the candy-stacked vending machines they passed), and were now watching Terry Lund limp back and forth as he tossed his few belongings and his discharge paperwork into a plastic bag. Which was tricky, since Caro had bitten off two of the fingers of his left hand. They'd found them at the scene, unsalvageable.

"This strikes me as a bad idea," Annette observed. *Cheating on your income tax bad. Jumping your unsuspecting colleague bad.*

"I'm fine." The balding redhead, who was short but powerfully built, like a fire hydrant in yesterday's suit, flapped a (whole) hand at her. "I'll be fine. I just want to put this nightmare behind me."

Annette shook her head. "I'm astonished you're not pressing charges. *Astonished.*"

"Hey, it's tough out there for troubled kids."

"She ate your fingers," David pointed out, because was it possible Lund had forgotten? Or thought they might grow back? The man was behaving like he'd been mildly inconvenienced, not mauled and nearly killed. "And crushed a couple of bones in your foot. That's a little more serious than 'these cubs today.'"

"Look, it was partly my fault. I must have provoked her. Or reminded her of someone else. You know, from her past. I mean, she's clearly had a hard life, poor cub. And no harm done. In general, I mean."

Annette glanced sideways at David to see how he was gauging this. Lund was downplaying at best, lying at worst. Lying and in a rush to leave the hospital, but not too much of a rush. Almost as though he wanted to linger long enough to assure them all was well, get his refusal to press charges on the record, then vanish. Or was she reading too much into this interview?

She cleared her throat. "We'll be in touch, of course."

"Yeah, well, I've got to get back to work. There's so

much paperwork, it's worse than a nightmare when I can't file on time."

"Falling behind in your paperwork is worse than a werewolf biting off your fingers?" *Good God. How many reams of paperwork are we talking about?*

"Well, it's not just the paperwork. I've gotta get down to the warehouse. There's customs to deal with, overseeing the quarantine facilities, clearing the charter flights for the imports..." At their blank expressions, he added, "I'm an importer and exporter of exotic pets." When they had no comment, he stood straighter and added with no small amount of pride, "Self-made man."

"Okay." From Annette.

"The paperwork's a nightmare, but the money's unbelievable."

"Okay." From David.

"So I'm sure you can see why I need to get back to it."

Annette cleared her throat. "Your work ethic is commendable, but going forward, Mr. Lund, we'll likely need your testimony. For the trial."

Lund hissed in pain; he'd tried to grab his wallet with the less-than-whole hand. "Why?" he managed. "I'm not pressing charges."

David shrugged. "Good thing we don't need your permission, then." People who watched too many *Law & Order* reruns often got the idea that if the victim wouldn't press charges, their assailant could just march; the system would have no alternative but to let him go. Fortunately, life was not run by the rules as written by Dick Wolf. (Who was Stable. Not a werewolf. Irony?)

"Well, whatever." Lund took a last look around his room. "I think that's it. Listen, it was nice meeting you both—"

"It was?" Annette would have imagined that every aspect of Lund's last fourteen hours had been wildly unpleasant.

"—and just get in touch if you need anything. Okay?"

"Okay."

"It's really not okay," Annette said, then added, "Listen, if you're signing out Against Medical Advice, do you at least have someone here to take you home? Did you want us to call your family?"

A bark of laughter. "No. They know all about it. I'll be getting shit over this for a while." At their stares, he added, "I'm kinda the black sheep. They know my business is the most important thing to me."

"All right. Well. Thanks for your time."

"Welcome." Lund gathered what was left of his belongings with what was left of his hand and marched past them. Annette obligingly stepped back as he stomped out, then glanced at David, who was staring at the slowly closing pneumatic door with an expression that likely matched her own.

"Bad guy."

She snorted. "Bad, dissembling, downplaying guy who does *not* want anyone looking into anything."

"Yeah. Like I said. Bad."

Chapter 5

"Upstanding citizens who have done nothing wrong don't generally lie about an attack that could have resulted in their grisly death. Oh, no they don't. Oh, no they *don't*. Isn't that right? Hmm?" Annette cuddled the Spencer cub a little closer. "Look how well he's healing!"

"It's weird," David agreed, remaining unmoved despite being surrounded by astonishing levels of cuteness. Took some effort, but he was up for it. And watching Annette in her maternal sweetness wasn't doing anything for him, either. Nope. Not a thing. "The Lund thing, not the healing. That could get messy," he added, because cubs weren't known for their continence. And putting a diaper on them wasn't an option. "You sure you want to keep holding him?"

"You and your silly questions. I'll risk it."

"It's your shirt." *Oh my word, seeing how maternally sweet she is just makes her sexier, DAMMIT.* "And yeah, Lund's being shady as shit. But that doesn't let Caro off the hook. She still went for him. She could've killed him. Lockup's the best place for her."

"That's your takeaway from the interview?" Annette said, inadvertently tightening her grip. The two-month-old werebear, orphaned by a fire and recovering from smoke inhalation and second-degree burns, let out a squeak. She eased up and leveled David with a glare, and he felt his heart rate pick up more than a little. "A trauma-tized teenager should stay in a cage?"

"*That* traumatized teenager, yeah." *Soft touch, even after everything she's seen. Prob'ly her only fault. That and her distractingly perfect bod.* "For now, at least. You'll recall we don't know shit yet."

"It's true. We are in a shit-free zone, knowledge-wise." She eased the cub back into the big clear box on wheels people made babies live in for some reason. The fluffy werebear—probably a subspecies of the American black were—made a faint snuffling sound of protest, then flopped over, wriggled on its belly, stuck its rump into the air, and promptly started snoring. "Caro's a blank, and Lund seems to think his assault was the equivalent of 'You kids stay off my lawn,' except with shattered bones and severed fingers."

"Jesus." David was trying to stay on track, but couldn't stop staring at the cub. Then he glanced at Annette and everything instantly got worse. "Kid sounds like he's gar-gling gravel through a megaphone. How does that much noise come out of that tiny body?"

"Focus, David."

"Right." *Good advice. So don't lose focus. Just let it be. Let. It. Be.* "You've, um. Got something."

"Pardon?"

"Your shirt." He leaned forward and brushed at the drool on her shoulder. This close, he could see the outer ring of her iris was a deep brown, and the inner ring was russet. Depending on the lighting, her eyes would gleam like banked coals. "There. I... Oh. It's not...coming off. Sorry."

She smiled. "Why apologize? You're not the one who drooled on me."

Oh God. If only. Back to business...*back to business!* "You get anything off Lund? Besides the obvious?"

She shrugged. "Well, no, but I wouldn't expect to. It's a hospital."

In other words, too many smells, too many sounds, too many people...getting a scent-read off Lund had been like trying to eavesdrop on a quiet conversation from the other side of a crowded room. She'd been able to catch some but not all of it. And what she'd heard might not be right.

"Same. I think he talked to us here on purpose. It wasn't just about letting us know he wasn't pressing charges. He's obfuscating like a motherfucker. And now he's in the wind. I'm betting if you follow up, he'll be on extended vacation somewhere out of our jurisdiction, like Mars." Silence. "Annette?"

"Sorry, I can't get over 'obfuscating like a mother-fucker.'" She snickered, then added, "But you're right. So, why?"

As they talked, the staff was quietly working around them, and one of them would occasionally catch Annette's eye with a nod or say howdy. David had never had cause to visit the peds ward before, but Annette was obviously familiar with the place. They all seemed to know her; no one had batted an eye when she'd scooped Spencer, Cub J. out of his clear box.

Before David could elaborate, a chubby RN in her mid-thirties, with curly brown hair and a lone dimple, appeared out of nowhere (was there a secret door behind the fridge full of formula and pureed meat?), went right to Annette, and handed over a small bundle of fur and a tiny bottle.

"Thanks, Sharon."

"Sure, saves me a little time. She's doing great, by the way. Probably will be discharged sometime tomorrow." The nurse nodded at David and went back to work.

David unconsciously flared his nostrils

(werefox)

as Annette cradled the small red bundle o' fluff and popped the bottle in. "I hate to harp on this, but Lund's the victim. He should be screaming for help and lawyers, not necessarily in that order, so maybe..." She eyed David while the werefox guzzled. The tiny bottle was almost empty. Before his eyes, the interior of that bottle was becoming a food desert. "Maybe you're onto something. Maybe he *is* the bad guy. Or *a* bad guy."

"Whatever he is, he's not gonna be any more help today."

She sighed. "No, that was clear. And we can't interview him again unless we want to explain the bad optics to our bosses."

"Pass."

"And unless Caro starts singing, we've only got one lead to follow right now." *We've? Oh, you're partners now? When did* that *happen? And was it before or after you went on your imaginary date?*

She sighed again, still looking down at the kit. "Dev."

"Devoss," he agreed. Which, depending on where someone stood on the "sticky-fingered scam artist who cons at a graduate level" debate, was either great news or shitty news.

Why not both? David's dead mother whispered in his ear, and he almost smiled.

Chapter 6

"WHAT ARE YOU TALKING ABOUT, GONE?"

"As in the child is no longer here. He is absent from this place. He has...gone."

"What?"

"It's an adverb, dear," Nadia explained.

"It's an adjective," Annette pointed out.

"I *beg* your pardon," Nadia sniffed, already digging out her cell phone and poking at it. "I'll have you know I have a degree in English from Oxf... Never mind."

"Adjective," Annette said again, not bothering to hide her triumph. But victory was fleeting. And a London native had a degree in English? Was that like an American having a degree in American?

Who cares? You've got more important woes. "This is not great. This is the polar opposite of great. We're the *parens familia*[1]; he's *our* kit!"

Nadia hesitated, then took the plunge. "Annette, don't be distressed—"

"I *will* be distressed. We should all be distressed! We can't keep him from getting into trouble, and when we catch him, after failing to keep him from getting into trouble, we can't fucking hang on to him!"

David raised his eyebrows. "Whoa."

---

1. "Head of the family," unique to Shifters. Stables use the term *parens patriae*, and minors in need of protection are considered wards of the state.

"*What*, David?"

"You never swear. Not even that time you pulled cubs from folks freebasing carfentanil and the mom ran you over."

"Oh, please, she barely grazed me. Then she stalled out before she could back up and try again."

"Yes, yes, the lad's a woeful handful," Nadia soothed. "One easily found. You know he's fond of you. He'll not have gone far."

"You're right!"

"I nearly always am, darling."

"He wanted to talk to Caro," Annette said with growing excitement. "He said so before we left for the hospital. But I wouldn't let him. So he must have… Is there any lock that kit can't pick? Because we should find one. And then buy them in bulk."

"Ask him," David suggested. "Maybe he'll tell you."

So off they trooped. Caro had been moved to a private cell in Juvenile Detention and seemed entirely unsurprised to see them. She sat on the edge of the bunk, crossed her legs, and waited for their questions.

"Did Dev come talk to you?"

Silence.

"Because he might be in trouble," Annette added.

"*More* trouble," Nadia elaborated.

Silence.

"Do you know him? Had you met before? He claims you're his sister."

A slow shake of her head, and the girl's expression…

Was that sadness? Without context, it was difficult to know for certain.

Annette was now even more annoyed, which she hadn't thought possible. She'd actually given credence to Dev's sibling claims. "You remember my colleague, Special Investigator David Auberon. He pulled you off the man you tried to kill."

"Hello again," he said.

Nothing. If she was intimidated by any of the three of them, Caro Daniels wasn't showing it.

Annette sighed. "Fine. You know what to do if you need to talk." On their way out, she asked, "Nadia, when's Dev's hearing?"

"Fifty-five minutes."

"Well, *great*. No idea where he is or how he got out. Nothing from Caro or Lund, adding to the great big pile of unacceptable that is this case. Nadia, I want those video feeds yesterday."

"Impossible, as I'm not a temporal-bending sorceress. But I can provide them in the next thirty minutes."

"It'll have to do."

"You're so welcome. When are you and David going out again?"

Oh, now this was too much. Teasing Annette about her nonexistent love life was one thing; doing it right in front of David was taking it too far. "Never, obviously," Annette snapped. "Drop it, will you?"

"The path of true love is never—"

"*Nadia.*" This through gritted teeth, and Annette didn't bother keeping the growl down.

"I'll see to the videos, shall I?"

As Nadia hurried away, Annette turned to David, who'd been looming over them the entire time. Not that it was his fault—you couldn't be annoyed at someone for being obscenely tall—but she was in no mood for lurking, no matter how benign. "Sorry about that."

"It's not a problem."

"It's just this dumb thing Nadia does for reasons I'm terrified to look into," Annette continued. She absently brushed the damp spot on her sweater. The baby had drooled, but David's fingers lightly grazing her shoulder was the sensation that remained. It was annoying to discover some romance tropes (burning touches, long soulful glances, pining, etc., etc., ad nauseum) were true. Annoying and maybe a little...a *very* little...exciting.

David shrugged. "It's fine."

"It's not, but you're sweet to say so."

"I'm not sweet."

She barely heard him. Well past time for a subject change. She brushed at her sweater again and mused aloud. "Now, if I were an amoral troublemaker with no regard for the system or the careers of those charged with my safety and well-being, where would I go?"

"Perkins Restaurant?"

That surprised a laugh out of her. "Not around here. But that's a good idea—Dev's always hungry." And *dammit*! Now she was feeling sorry for him again. Dev was always hungry because he'd been neglected by those who were supposed to love, protect, and *feed* him. Then he was hungry because he had to steal to feed himself. And then he was hungry when the state took him in…

You remember that all his foster homes fed him, right? Every one of them. His choice, every time, to run.

Still. Hungry cubs tweaked something inside her. In a world full of food, starving children were an abomination.

Annette spotted him the second she stepped into their vile break room, because he was the only one in there,

(obviously not hiding)

(dammit!)

and the audacious creature had the gall to greet her with "What the hell is that smell?"

"You!"

"No, it's not me. It smells like someone took a dump in here, then deep-fried it. But that can't be right." He glanced around. "Uh…can it?"

"Dev Devoss, you tricky *wretch*." Annette had to make a conscious effort not to shake her fist at him like a B-movie villain.

"What? You needed to talk to me. So here we are, talking. It's not like you… *Ow-ow-ow!*"

"The temptation to yank your ear off your skull is *so* strong," Annette confessed, tightening her grip. "I'm not sure I've got the self-control to resist."

"Aw, c'mon, not again, Garsea," David mock-groaned from the doorway. "There'll be blood everywhere and reams of paperwork. And the boss'll land on you like a disapproving motherfucker."

"Is this—*ow!*—good cop, idiot cop? Because you suck at it. Both of you."

"Never mind," David replied. "Yank away."

"Are we going to have to Hannibal Lecter you?" Annette demanded. "Strap you to a gurney and wheel you in and out of court? Where would we even get a hockey mask?"

"I've got no idea what you're talking about—*ninguna, nessuna, keine*—but I gotta say, it sounds awesome."

"Stop that. You're drawing a blank on the pop-culture reference. I get it." She let go of his ear, and he collapsed back into his chair. "Explain yourself."

"Hey, you were at the hospital again. What is it with you and para-pediatrics?" Dev leaned in and sniffed. "Who's the little punk you were holding?"

"None of your business."

"Impressive," David commented. "I don't know how you can scent anything in here."

"Thanks! And there was some Caesar-looking guy named Oz who was definitely up to no good in here—"

Oz Adway! Dammit, the man simply will NOT stay in his lane. Who leaves the sterile glory of the Accounting break room for this squalid cell? "If anyone would know what 'up to no good' looks like, it would be you, Devin Devoss."

"—and he said he's your brother, which was just weird. Why would your brother be skulking in the break room? So I told him to get bent." Dev paused. "No need to thank me."

Annette rapped on the table. "Focus, you charming

jackass. You realize you've got a hearing in a few minutes, yes?"

"I'm here, aren't I? I'm ready to go. *I* was waiting for *you*. I feel like you're not getting this."

For a second, all she could do was gnash her teeth at him. Which, given how his eyes widened, was gratifying. She silently counted to three (when she was this irked, making it to ten was impossible), then said, "Fine. And shall I suggest to His Honor that you would like to visit your mother?"

The grin fell away. "No."

"Dev…"

"*No.* What'd be the point? She can't use me anymore. It's why she's locked up." The kit's green eyes were very bright, with anger or tears or both. "*You* told me that."

"So I did." Annette lowered her voice and blessed David's silence from the doorway. "But I'm not suggesting you see her for her sake."

"You told me this already."

"I'm suggesting you do it for yours."

"You told me this already."

Annette sighed. "Fine, off we go. It's Judge Gomph, who thinks on time is late, so let's get moving."

Dev, always quick to recover his equilibrium, asked, "What the hell is a Judge Gomph?"

"Quiet, you. And you're combing your hair on the way over."

"It's supposed to stick up like this."

"Good *God.*"

"I wish you had time to change," Annette fretted as they walked through the parking garage. She and David had advised they were taking Dev to the hearing and gotten authorization for same. Not for the first time, Annette was grateful the Shifter system allowed more flexibility than the alternative. "But that would entail letting you out of my sight for more than five seconds, so that is, needless to say, off the table."

"I'll drop trou right here. I don't care," the boy declared.

"Ha!" From David, who was…cheerful? In the last three hours she'd exchanged more words with him than in the past year. Who knew he could smile? And laugh? And joke? There were rumors, of course, but nothing anyone had actually seen or heard. David's sense of humor was like the Loch Ness monster: there were passionate believers on both sides of the argument. "You don't know who Hannibal Lecter is, but you're using 'drop trou'?"

"Saw it in a movie."

"So you watch movies," Annette observed, "but you don't know who Lecter is? Because that's—" She cut herself off as a long black car suddenly swung out of a spot at the end of the row and arrowed toward them, tires squealing as the driver wrenched the wheel to make the turn. "Oh, wonderful. These are the idiots who cause pileups the first time it snows. And the second time."

"Aren't you gonna smile at them?" David asked with a smile of his own. "I thought that was your thing. You grin and it freaks people out."

"I don't *grin*. You've got me confused with a jack-o'-lantern. No, I'm polite, and if that *happens* to freak people out, I have no control…over…"—Was the thing speeding up?—"that…uh…"

Over the course of the next three seconds, many things happened. Well, four things happened. (1) Annette clamped down on Dev's collarbone and yanked, ignoring his yelp as she sent him sailing over her shoulder. (2) The car did an excellent job of trying to cream all three of them. (3) David slammed into her with the finesse of a garbage truck. (4) The car roared past and down the first ramp behind them.

"Oh my God, Net, are you okay?"

"Argh," Annette groaned. "My skeletal structure…" Then: "Net?"

"Did it hit you?" Dev cried.

"No, that was me," David said, which was especially startling since his face was less than two inches from hers. In a feat of disastrous timing, she abruptly found she loved his aftershave, which was warm and spicy, like expensive pepper. And his denim-blue eyes, inches from hers, were the sky. Which was a good trick since they were in a parking garage. "Are you okay, hon?"

Hon? Maybe he meant Hun, as in "Attila the." Have people always had nicknames for me, or is this something new everyone's trying? I want to put my arms around him. I will put my arms around him.

No. From her perspective, that is to say, from beneath him (groan), he was solid, steady warmth. Solid and sky-colored eyes and she wasn't going to hug her crush while on the floor of a filthy parking garage in the wake of their attempted murder.

Right?

Right.

"Your breath smells like Skittles. That's not a criticism. And I'm reasonably certain the car *did* hit me. Feels like it, anyway," she groaned, elbowing David off her bones. She looked up and saw Dev had landed with the inherent quickness and grace of his kind

(*generalizing's bad, but truth be told, I've never met a clumsy werefox*)

and was peering down at them while clinging to the top of a cement pillar. His eyes were so huge they dominated his small, pointed face.

"I'm fine," she said, gingerly feeling her ribs.

"Jeez, I didn't mean to hurt you." David's expression was still calm, but she could hear his distress.

"Comparatively speaking, you didn't. Sorry, nearly getting run over wreaks havoc on my manners. Thank you very much, don't mind my grumbling, I welcome the bruises because the dead don't bruise, and I am astonished and impressed by your speed." Then, louder: "Come down, Dev."

He let go and dropped to the top of a small SUV, so lightly he left no dent and made hardly any sound, then bounded back to her side. She took him by the shoulders, peered into his face, and felt his skull, which he tolerated with a minimum of squirming. "You're all right?"

"Yeah, yeah."

"Nothing scraped? Broken? Spindled? Folded?"

"I'm good. You had me flying before I had time to be scared," he said. "I bet you flipped me ten feet!"

"No betting. And…Net? What was that about?"

He blushed, which was amazing since Dev Devoss was the poster boy for shameless. "S'just somethin' we call you," he said in a voice so low she had to bend closer to hear. Under different circumstances she would have followed up, but the child was clearly distressed. Oh, and someone had just tried to kill them.

Or maybe just kill Dev. Which was worse.

She turned to David. "Thank you again." *Now! Hug him now! You're not on your back anymore. Totally appropriate time and setting!* "I should have said that first before talking about your breath."

"I understand," he replied, straight-faced.

"I like your aftershave," she said, because she was a touch-starved moron, apparently.

He smiled a little. "Thanks."

Dev was staring at them. "You guys wanna get a room?"

"Hush up, Dev." To David, in growing confusion and despair: "What is going *on*?"

"Nothing good."

Chapter 7

JUDGE GOMPH WOULD HAVE DOMINATED THE ROOM even if he wasn't seated above them on the bench. He weighed three hundred, easily, with brown skin that looked gray under unforgiving fluorescents and a wide, wrinkled face. His broad frame made it look as though someone had flung a robe over a mahogany table, and he was methodically eating salad out of what appeared to be a bucket, his big fork spearing leaves and bringing them to his mouth with such steadiness it was almost hypnotic. He was overworked, even for a juvie judge, and his stamina was legendary. When they'd lost two judges in the same month, Gomph had gone four days without sleep, wading through the jammed dockets with calm efficiency that steadied them all, from his clerk to even the smallest cubs who came through his court.

He had a reputation for never being rattled—no one had ever heard him so much as raise his voice—and this was borne out today. When they had burst into his courtroom, he had looked down at them with the eyes of a tired king, as Nadia once described them, but waited patiently for their approach. And speak of the well-dressed devil...

"Nadia, what—agh!"

Nadia's spade-shaped fingernails had sunk into Annette's biceps like a raptor on a rabbit as she leaned in to hiss, "She's gone."

"Please tell me you're not talking about Caro," Annette whispered back, knowing it was futile. That was, after all, the kind of day they were having. Were trapped in. Whatever.

"Of course I'm talking about Caro!"

"What are we whispering about?" This from Taryn, Gomph's clerk, who had crept over, probably because Annette had been too frazzled to return her wave. Annette made it a policy to return all waves, even ones to mortal enemies, which Taryn was not. "Are you guys okay?"

"You wouldn't even believe it," Annette whispered back. "I was there and I don't believe it."

"Oh. That sounds bad. Hi, David."

He nodded. "Hey, Taryn."

"Annette and I are going for burgers again," Taryn whispered. "Want to come?"

"You didn't learn your lesson last time? Meat makes you sick as shit."

"So that's a no?"

"Taryn, again: veggie burgers," Annette urged. "Seriously. Try one."

"I have. Why do you think I won't order them? Yuck, yuck, yuck."

There was some pointed throat-clearing, and they all looked up at the bench as Taryn hustled back to her spot to the left of the judge.

"Sorry!" Dev said with a grin for the impassive, massive judge. "We're sorry, Your Honor. But we almost just got creamed, so the 'adults' are freaking out."

"I heard those air quotes, you wretch," Nadia hissed. "And intelligent concern is not 'freaking out.'"

"It's not like any of you to make such a dramatic entrance," Judge Gomph rumbled.

Nadia looked up at the bench. "Then I'm clearly doing something wrong, Your Honor."

Annette cut in before Nadia could elaborate or start fishing for compliments. "I beg your pardon, Your Honor. Something unprecedented in my career has happened. I respectfully request that you clear the courtroom of everyone except you, me, Ms. Faulkner, Mr. Auberon, Ms. Wapiti, and Mr. Devoss."

As that left only five people, two of whom were dozing, the judge blinked, chewed, shrugged. "Very well." At that, Taryn surged to her feet and had the place cleared in fewer than ten seconds.

It didn't take long for Annette to explain what had happened—what was *still* happening. Gomph was about as easy to read as the *Book of Kells*, but Taryn looked gratifyingly horrified.

"Sir, I don't understand any of this, but I promise you, I will find out what is happening," Annette said. "In the meantime, we have to keep these children safe, and I'm not sure the official system is the best way to do that right now."

Munch. "Suggestions?"

She took a deep breath. "I'd like to take responsibility for Mr. Devoss as *mater Pack*, effective immediately, and once we have Ms. Daniels in custody again, I'd like to bring her before you to discuss options. We'll also be working on identifying the driver in the garage, as well as their motive, and will be following up with Mr. Lund, among other things."

He blinked at her, and if anyone else had had dark circles like that, she would assume they were getting no sleep. But Gomph's eyes always looked like that. "That's a lot to take on, Ms. Garsea."

"I'll help, Your Honor," David replied, and Annette did her best not to look astonished. *Damn. I was fool enough to forget he was there for a moment. And what's this? Volunteering?* That might be something to think about. David tended to stick to the job description, which in this case was bringing in Caro and Dev. Normally, he would have been long gone by now.

"I myself will not," Nadia announced, to the shock of precisely no one. "However, I'll continue to be Ms. Garsea's in-house liaison and research assistant, around the clock if it proves necessary. With all respect to Young Master Devoss, I wouldn't take on full responsibility for him under any circumstances. Well"—Nadia's gaze went to the ceiling as she pondered—"perhaps if I lost a bet."

"That's respectful?" Dev yelped. At Nadia's look, he added, "Okay, well. Fair."

"I'm considering it," the judge replied between bites of spinach, kale, cabbage, and romaine. Annette's stomach rumbled. *Dump a pound of grilled shrimp on that with some oil and vinegar, maybe some roasted garlic cloves, and a roll warm from the oven... Now that was* a meal. "Mr. Devoss, is there anything you'd like to tell the court?"

The kit, taken off guard, lurched to his feet. "Um. Just that I'll listen to Annette and I don't mind staying with her and I'll do everything she says, Judge."

Gomph studied him with small, kind eyes. "You understand that your reputation got here before you did, lad?"

"*Viam bonam famam habere cupis esse Studeat apparere.*"

"Brilliant, but lazy," the judge quoted back.

Dev let out a happy gasp. "Was that a Peter Parker reference?"

"No, that was an Otto Octavius reference." To Annette: "This isn't the first time you've moved to take action that under most circumstances would be considered out of your purview."

"No, sir, it is not." Was the judge referring to the seal smuggling ring, or the werehyena riot? Or the birthday fiasco? Or the other birthday fiasco? She resisted the urge to ask for clarification. Details would not make her case.

"But if memory serves—and mine always does—you have consistently held up your end. I am remanding Mr. Devoss to your custody for a period of seventy-two hours, at which time you will again come before the court to explain his status, Ms. Daniels's status, what you have found, and how you wish to proceed. Then I'll explain how we *will* proceed. Am I understood?"

"Yes, Your Honor."

"Mr. Devoss?"

Dev, who had been gaping at Annette with the air of a boy who couldn't believe what was happening, wrenched his gaze back to the bench. "Yes, Judge?"

"If you elude Ms. Garsea's custody, the consequences will be severe."

"Yes, sir, I get it. Straight to holding, do not pass Go."

"For her," Gomph clarified. "Your actions will have a direct impact on her career, among other things. It's in everyone's best interest for that impact to be positive."

"I'd never ditch Net," the boy declared. "Not like Nadia."

"Hush, you wretch."

He ignored Nadia's irritated squawk. "Not even if I lost a bet."

"Very well."

And that was that.

Chapter 8

Except that *wasn't* that.

"The video feeds all went down. Each and every one."

"Yeah."

"At the same time."

"Yes."

Taryn had been a big help, making use of her contacts to help Nadia pull whatever feeds she needed ASAP. Under ordinary circumstances, that could have taken at least a day. And if nothing else, the near-miss proved once and for all that the parking-garage security was overdue for an upgrade.

Among other changes, new cameras would be installed to take pictures of the license plate of every car that went in and out. Annette had been astonished such an upgrade was necessary, then astonished she'd been astonished. As with any regulated agency, there were ten places to put every dollar.

"And during that ninety-second blackout window," Annette continued, "someone let Caro out. Or she let herself out."

David fidgeted in the passenger seat. "Looks like."

"I know why you're both looking at me, and you can quit it right now. It wasn't me," Dev declared from the back seat. "Besides, didn't the blackout window open while we were in the parking garage? You said yourself you weren't gonna let me out of your sight. And you didn't. Y'know, after the, um, break-room thing."

All this while Annette was taking them up the driveway to her house. The hearing had been two hours ago, during which time David had determined the feeds weren't going to be any help and they verified that the silently elusive Caro wasn't anywhere on the premises.

"Dev, do you at least know why she left? Or where she would have gone?"

"No, *non, nein*. Maybe she remembered that she didn't do anything wrong and that self-defense is legal? So why stick around? That's why I would've left." Annette felt a thump as he kicked the back of her seat for emphasis.

"Or someone let her go," David pointed out.

Exactly what Annette was afraid of. "I really, really hope that's not true," she fretted. She could hear the steering wheel start to creak and forced herself to loosen her grip. "It would mean someone on the inside—one of *us*—is protecting her, or protecting Lund, or something even more sinister is going on, something we haven't yet tumbled to, and I don't like it, I don't like any of it."

"Nobody had to let me out," Dev put in. "I'll bet she let herself out. Your restraints are a joke."

"Possibly. Your amorality and skinny wrists might also be factors in play. I guess we'll just have to ask Caro when we find her."

David snorted. "Good luck."

"But don't the bad guys in the car *have* to be someone on the inside?" Dev asked. "It's not like a Stable can just roll in from Sixth Street and randomly try to run over a trio of Shifters."

Also what she was afraid of. Because of course Dev was right. No one got onto those levels by accident. Ever. And the parking-garage feeds didn't help. They showed the assault-via-vehicle attempt (and David moving faster than thought to knock her clear), but the car was nondescript and had blacked-out windows. Minnesota plates, black SUV, but the angle was bad and no one could read the plate number. If she were to bet—and she never bet—she'd guess it was a rental. If they could find it, they could follow a paper trail.

But first things first. She'd parked just outside her garage and was headed up the wide sidewalk to the broad expense of gray steps. "One problem at a time, gents. Come on."

"Holy crap. So being a caseworker is super lucrative, I guess."

"No, Dev. Do not go into this line of work if staggering wealth is your goal. My folks left me some money after they were killed, which I used for this. My roommate helped with the renovations. McMansion house, Walmart wardrobe."

"I remember!" Dev, who had been trotting at her heels, skipped ahead of her and David and was walking backward while he chattered. "The first time you caught me, you got me to come with you by saying you were in the system, too, when you were a kid."

"The first, second, and third time I caught you," she pointed out while David stifled a snort.

"What... I mean, it's none of my biz, but what happened to your folks? You don't have to say if you don't want," he added hastily.

"They were killed just outside Yosemite."

"Oh. Sorry. Poachers?" Dev hopped over one of the planters lining the walk without looking. "Stables who didn't know the difference between you guys and wild bears?"

"No. Car accident."

Dev giggled, then clapped a hand over his mouth.

"Smooth," David said, and looked amused when Annette poked him in the bicep. "Don't feel bad, kid. She gets that a lot."

"Sorry! I'm sorry. I'm not laughing 'cuz your folks died. I wouldn't laugh about that. It's—"

She smiled down at him as she opened the door and ushered them inside, past the foyer and living area. "I understand. It's what everyone assumes. No one expects the mundane explanation." Then, as her unholy trio entered the kitchen: "Pat, this is my ward pro tem, Dev Devoss, and David Auberon, one of our investigators. Dev, David, this is my roommate, Pat."

Frozen in the act of juicing what appeared to be a thousand oranges, Pat just stared at them. He'd changed out of his earlier clothing and was now in overalls and lipstick. And mascara, Annette decided after a closer look. It was criminal how men were so often blessed with long lashes. Especially men with blue eyes. Wait. Pat had hazel eyes; *David* had blue eyes. *Why am I thinking about David's eyes?*

Pat's straight blond hair was pulled back in a neat

ponytail, and he smelled like an orange grove, which was pretty wonderful. "Huh," he said after a long moment. "Welcome." To Annette: "I got excited for a second. Thought you might have a date."

"Pretty weird date," Dev commented, looking askance at David.

"Agreed," David replied. "Not to mention major-league illegal."

Annette managed to keep the aggrieved shriek behind her teeth. "This is not a date. David and I *are not dating*."

"Uh-huh." Then: "*The* Dev Devoss?" Pat grinned. "You're famous around here. I never thought I'd get to meet you."

"I am?" Delighted, he turned to Annette. "You talk about me at home?"

"I have nightmares about you at home."

"I dunno how to feel about that," the boy confessed.

"Well, ponder. Now, as I was explaining, they're going to be staying… Wait." She turned to David. "You don't have to stay here, you know."

"Disagree. People are trying to run you over."

"*Again?*" Pat yelped.

Annette ignored the interruption. "People are also trying to run *you* over."

David shrugged off the attempted vehicular homicide on his person. "And Devoss is gonna be a handful."

"A handful of sunshine, you bet!" Dev said with what he probably thought was a winning smile but mostly just showed his teeth.

"*Anyway*. Pat. It's only for a couple of days, and I'm sorry about the inconve—"

"I don't give a shit about the inconvenience. This is your house, and you can host the Timberwolves if you want, but who the hell tried to run you over?"

"That's the question."

"You didn't lose another bet, did you?" Pat asked.

"No, thank goodness."

Meanwhile, Dev had inched closer until the only thing separating him from Pat was the kitchen island, nostrils flaring as he feigned interest in all the orange carcasses. Pat enjoyed watching the boy's confusion for a few seconds, then said, "Help you with something?"

"No. No, I'm fine."

"Reeeeeeally?"

"Pat," she warned. She was fond of her eccentric roommate, but he did like to play with his food.

"It's just, uh, your scent."

Pat leaned in, blinking long eyelashes. "Yessssss? You think it's offensive?"

"No! No, I just can't figure it out is all," Dev confessed.

"Which makes you nervous."

"No." He paused and considered. "Kinda."

"No surprise. It makes adults nervous, too."

"Is that why you... Never mind. It's nobody's business."

She had to give Dev credit. She had never known the kit to deny himself a question before, even if it would land him in considerable difficulty.

Pat took pity on the deeply curious creature and replied, "Let's just say that today I'm feeling more masculine than feminine. Say about 85/15."

"I don't know what that means."

"That's all right."

"How'd your interview go?" Annette was rooting through the fridge; in all the excitement, she hadn't eaten since breakfast. *Note: go grocery shopping, dammit!*

"They'll let me know, blah-blah. In the meantime…" He produced seed packets from his overall pockets and waved them at her. "I've taken up organic gardening."

"But it's September."

"Don't try to restrain my ambitions, Annette!"

"Sorry, sorry." To Dev: "Sandwich? Leftover stir-fry? Leftover meat loaf? Leftover—no, that's far too old. I can't even remember when we had spaghetti. Perhaps a gallon of freshly squeezed orange juice? And David, I'm sorry to report we're out of Skittles *and* Starburst. I can't think how I let this happen."

"I'm good." He was staring at the litter of oranges, shaking his head and smiling. "You are juicing like a motherfucker."

"Oh, is that what I'm doing?"

David turned to Annette. "Listen, I'd like to walk your perimeter—"

"Romantic!"

"Shush." Bad enough the thought of him sleeping in her house was making her knees tremble. Worse knowing how easy it would be to show him to the guest room and then, er, initiate things. Because this was the worst time in the world to be thinking of her sexual dry spell. Her charges were in danger. David was here in a professional capacity and would not appreciate being molested. So this was no time for Pat to indulge in his shipping tendencies. But before she could elaborate—poor David was probably already ruing his impulse to remain—she heard a buzz and David turned away as he fished his phone out. "You understand that the matchmaking-roommate cliché is beyond tired, right?"

"How *dare* you call me a cliché. I'm a trope."

"Is that like a trout?" she asked. "Or tripe?"

"I won't dignify that with an answer, you harpy." To Dev: "Drink this juice."

"I dunno," the kit replied. "Are you sure there's enough?"

"I like him," Pat announced. "Let's keep him."

"He's not a stray, Pat. We can't just keep him."

"Yes I am!"

Before she could reply, David put his phone away and turned back to them. When she saw his expression, she groaned. "What? What troubling, terrible strange thing has happened now?"

"Lund's dead."

There was a silence while she digested the news. "Well, shit," she managed.

"Have some juice," Pat suggested. "You'll feel better."

Chapter 9

Never, obviously.

"I'd like to shift and take a look around. You mind?" David asked.

Drop it, will you?

Annette looked up from her grocery list, which looked long enough to be a Wiki entry. "Of course not. There's a set of sliding doors on the lower level that lead to twenty-four acres of private land and the St. Croix River."

"And if you go the other way, you'll find a Dairy Queen Grill & Chill," Pat added.

"Thanks."

Never, obviously.

Well, that was plain enough.

Just as well, his dead mother whispered. *You could only bring her pain.* He would have told his dead mom to shut it, except she was right. Blunt, as in life, but correct. Still. He wouldn't deny the sting.

He left the kitchen and headed through Annette's big, pretty house, intent on the lower level. He hadn't shifted in weeks—contrary to fiction, changing was mostly a matter of personal choice, not an irresistible paralogical imperative dictated by the lunar cycle—and he was itching for it. The Caro case was getting more fucked by the hour, and being in close proximity with Annette was distracting in all the worst ways. Which was made worse by her devastating yet honest comments to Nadia.

Never, obviously.

about the possibility of their…dating.

Drop it, will you?

Or sport fucking. Or whatever Annette wanted to do. He would've been on board with any of it.

Drop it.

There was no escaping her ripe fruit/clean cotton scent; he was surrounded by it. By contrast, the roommate's scent was barely noticeable.

The roommate. He couldn't blame the kit for being curious. The guy who took up farming (but just today, apparently) was like water: not much of a scent and it held whatever shape you dumped it in, or in Pat's case, whatever shape you felt like. And the scar was impressive, because it didn't matter how fast Shifter metabolism ran, some injuries left permanent reminders.

In Pat's case, he couldn't completely hide the seven-inch mark that started at the forehead, slashed down, narrowly missed his eye, and ended halfway down his cheek. Deep, too. David couldn't imagine the fight that had caused it.

Whatever the cause and whoever the assailant, it had been deeply personal; they'd gone for the face, not the throat, which was smooth and unmarked. And Pat kept the rest of himself covered, so no telling how extensive any other scars might be.

But David couldn't worry about that now. Lund was

unhelpful, and then he was dead. Caro was in custody, and then she wasn't. Someone tried to kill the three of them. Or just Dev. (Which was worse.) And Annette had zero interest in him as anything but a work colleague. And he wasn't even that, really; he didn't work for IPA. He was an independent contractor; IPA was just one of his clients.

"Can I come?"

The kit, right on his heels. Should've guessed. "No. I won't be gone long. Stay here." He reached for Dev's shoulder. "I mean it, kit. You...wait." Dev had flinched, then tried to cover. "Thought you said you weren't hurt."

"I'm *not*." Dev twisted away. "Not bad, I mean. It's no big deal."

"Let me see."

The young werefox sighed and stood still while David took a peek and saw deep-purple bruises blooming along the boy's shoulder and side. "From Annette tossing you," he guessed. "You smacked into something—the SUV?— before you could get back to your feet."

"Don't tell Net," he pleaded. "She'll freak, she'll... uh..."

David almost smiled. "There's not a German or Italian or French word for 'freak'?"

"I guess not," he admitted. "But please don't tell her. She'll get all upset and *verärgert* and...um...*irritato*. And I'll take bruises over getting smeared all over a parking garage pillar."

"Me, too. If it gets worse, you'll tell me? Or her?"

"Yeah."

"Eat a big supper. Couple of 'em."

Dev waved that away. "Yeah, yeah, 'sizable caloric intake with an emphasis on protein is essential for wound healing as protein is found in all cells and thus speeds up the healing process.' I've known that since I was a kid."

"Yeah, for ages and ages, I'll bet." This time David did smile. "If you were a kid way back when, what are you now? A short adult?"

Dev ignored the question. "I'll have some eggs or something. And before you say it, I won't leave the house."

"Not sure I believe you."

"That's because you and Net aren't paying attention. Why would I leave? What'd you think my endgame was?"

"Jesus, you're a kid. Why do you even *have* an endgame?"

"Hey, everybody needs a plan."

"Yeah," David pointed out, "and you've usually got half a dozen."

"All I'm saying is you don't have to worry about me leaving. This is where I've been trying to get to."

Oh, hell. The "maybe my juvenile advocate will adopt me and we'll be a perfect family" fantasy.

Not that he could blame the kit. But at least now that he knew Dev's motives, he could take him at his word (a rare and wonderful thing when dealing with Dev Devoss).

"Besides," Dev was saying, "someone should stick close to Net, doncha think? People are after her, too."

"Net?"

Shrug.

"What's up with that?"

Dev took a breath and stared up at him. "I'll tell, but only 'cuz you're helping her. It's a nickname some of us have for her."

"Ah. 'Net' like you can't escape? Because she's always scooping you off the streets and tossing your delinquent butt into lockup?"

"No," Dev replied, giving him a don't-be-a-dumbass look. "'Net' like what trapeze artists fall into while they're doing incredibly dangerous shit that could get them killed."

"That's…." *Adorable. Literally adorable.* "Don't worry, I'll take it to the grave."

"You better. Or I'll *put* you there."

"Consider me warned. You think Caro killed Lund? Broke out, tracked him, finished the job she started last night?"

Dev snorted. "Yeah, that 'I'll do an abrupt subject change and surprise the truth out of him' thing hasn't worked since I was eight."

"That's a no?"

"Totally a no."

"I'll learn some new tricks. So you don't think she did it?"

"I…don't know. I really don't," he added, anticipating David's next question. "She's capable. I mean, you saw for yourself. And I get why you might think that. But she made her point last night. I think going back would've been over-kill. No pun intended. Did I get that right? It's a pun?"

"What point was she trying to make last night?"

"That she'll put up with a lot, but there's a line, even if she's the only one who knows where it is. Cross it, and she'll fuck you up."

"Blunt," he observed.

"Accurate. Look, before last night, I hadn't seen her for a bit. I don't know why she went for Lund. But she wouldn't just, y'know, randomly attack someone. Whatever she did, she'd have a good reason." He paused, gauging David's reaction to his words. "Maybe even life or death."

Or maybe you're lying. He'd read the interview tran-scripts. Dev either didn't know anything or he did, but was being deliberately unhelpful. First he'd said Lund had been trying to kill Caro for two years, but now it was "I don't know why she went for him." First they were siblings, but Caro denied knowing him. In other words, it was classic Dev, who was scrupulously honest with kids but never hesitated to lie his little ass off to adults. And there was just no way of knowing the truth without more info.

Which David intended to get.

"Go eat," he ordered, and headed downstairs, already unbuttoning his shirt.

David smiled when he saw the downstairs setup: on the wall beside the door, about four feet up, there was a bright-yellow plastic button five inches across that could be slapped with a palm or paw, or nudged with a nose. He was willing to bet there was one on the other side, too.

Time to find out. He undressed and, mindful of colleague-guest status, folded his clothes and set them neatly aside in the guest room closest to the sliding door. Hit the button. Took a breath.

The actual physical change was the best, most terrible part. His muscles shifted and tore, his bones cracked and remade themselves, fur sprouted, teeth lengthened while his jaw reshaped itself, fingernails morphed into four-inch-long claws. His frame lengthened to seven feet. When his knees and elbows and wrists and ankles all snapped backward, forcing him to all fours, he was five feet at the shoulder. His senses sharpened with no adjustment period; for these few seconds, scents overwhelmed him and the sounds of his transformation were deafening. His mass increased to 1,200 pounds, his hind feet lengthened to fourteen inches. *Ursus actos californicus*, the California grizzly bear, with its russet fur, blond tips, and characteristic hump, has been extinct since 1922 because they couldn't adapt to Stables encroaching on their territory.

But David Auberon wasn't a Stable grizzly bear, locked into the same shape from birth to death. So that was all right.

It was the delicious agony of pulling off a scab every time. He could feel his mind receding into quasi-sentience as his senses adjusted to being ten, thirty, a hundred times stronger, as everything got *bigger* and *brighter* and *more*, as his bipedal concerns

(rent, unrequited crush, oil change, Skittles)

faded, to be replaced by other, simpler worries

(new territory, potential intruders, potential mate, protect cub, Skittles).

He heard the door slide shut behind him and promptly forgot about it and the house and Caro Daniels and the kit because *woods* and *forest* and *water* and *prey*. In five seconds, he reached the woods, forty yards away, where everything smelled like sunshine and moss and food.

And better than food, Her scent was everywhere. These were *Her* woods, and he was in them, and he'd like to be Hers, too, but it wouldn't happen, She needed no mate and it was better that they were

(safe)

snug in Her den and that was enough

(except it wasn't)

(am I sad?)

and now he could pick up the lesser scent, the

(scarface fighter)

jackal and it made him want to fight and then he remembered the jackal was in Her den so no-no-no fighting.

He prowled and swam and ate a trout

(all wriggling and shiny and tastes like summer)

and when the sun was down and he had satisfied himself they were

(safe)

alone he remembered his other self

(two legs no fur too small can't smell but can think and talk-talk-talk)

and loped back to Her and there was the door-that-moved and there She was, looking down at him from the way-up part of Her den and showing Her teeth but not to fight. Alone by choice, like him.

"Damn, David. You are *gorgeous*."

No, not to fight. And that was good; he didn't want to fight Her, he'd rather hunt for Her.

And that's something his other self could do, too.

Chapter 10

"*Nooooooo.*"

"I assure you, yes."

"A golden goddamned jackal?" Dev's delighted yelp carried all the way into the living room. "I thought you guys were extinct!"

"No," Pat replied, "we just don't use social media."

"Oh, look, a millennial joke."

"Oh, look, a millennial who instantly made it about himself."

"I'm *not* a millennial. I'm too young!" Dev insisted. "If anyone's a millennial, it's you and Annette."

"Well, what the hell are you, then?"

"I don't know! I don't think our generation has named ourselves yet."

They hadn't noticed her yet. There was still time to abort this disaster in the making. "Morning," she mumbled, stumbling into the kitchen and yawning so hard she heard something crack.

"You know who started all this generation-naming bullshit?"

"Please, Pat, no," she begged.

"The goddamned baby boomers," he declared, but since Annette had mouthed it along with him, Dev couldn't hold back a giggle. "All this shit started with them. 'Hey, let's change the world, war is bad, marijuana's good, here, have a shopping channel.' You know the thing that defined them?" Without pausing for an answer, Pat raced on. "They were born. That's it. Their parents didn't die in World War II. Instead, they came home and got laid and impregnated half the country."

"No more," Annette pleaded. "I'd rather talk about the madness unfolding before me. What are you two doing?" To be honest, it was all she could do to keep the stern expression on her face due to the high prevalence of *whaaaaaat?*

Dev, in his new jeans (on the way to her place, she, David, and Dev had swung by Super Target, where she'd stupidly forgotten to pick up a new alarm clock for herself, as well as some groceries) and one of Pat's old T-shirts ("I like coffee and maybe three people"), was floured to his elbows. Beside him, stirring chocolate chips into batter and bitching about the Greatest Generation, Pat was in his second-favorite blue tank top ("Don't follow your dreams; follow my Instagram"), black capris, and... was that...?

"But you despise lip gloss," Annette said, astounded. "You said it makes you feel like you're drooling strawberry saliva."

"I'm giving it another chance. It's called being open-minded and you should try it sometime, sunshine."

"I like it," Dev declared. "It brings out your stubble."

"*Thank* you."

"You guys, it's 7:00 a.m.! Far too early for...whatever this is."

Pat held up his phone. "Why are you talking like everyone doesn't walk around with a clock and therefore can't possibly know what time it is?"

"Morning." David shuffled past her, and it was nice to see someone else as bleary-eyed as she was. "Coffee? Please, please coffee?"

"Tea's better for you."

"Shut up, boy," he replied without malice. "Ah. There." They all watched in perplexed fascination as David poured himself half a gallon of coffee

(Is that even a go-cup? It's the size of a vase!)

with one lump of sug—no, two—no, three, no—Jesus. Followed by a splash of cream, if *splash* meant a quarter of a cup.

"Oh, lovely, now I'm living with two people who have disgusting breakfast habits."

"Back off, Pat," she warned, "or I'll force-feed you my next omelet."

"I'll die first. That's literal, by the way. Not hyperbole. My body will shut down, and you'll have a corpse on your hands in the kitchen. *Again*."

"You promised never to bring up the corpse in the kitchen." But she was actually glad it had come up. It helped her focus on something besides sleepy, scruffy David, whose other self was almost as big as hers, and possibly as dangerous. And smelled divine, like moss and warm, clean fur. And seemed completely unaware of his appeal.

No, it was good to focus on something—anything—besides how easy it would have been to slip into the guest room and wake David with mouth and hands and tongue. Which could have led to mutual orgasm but was just as likely to result in a broken nose, depending on how easily startled he was.

All this within earshot of weres who could hear a pin drop. Actual pins actually dropping—some clichés were real.

To distract herself, she went for a subtle cough

"Grraaakkk-KAW!"

and failed, given how Dev jumped. "Jesus. Are you okay?"

"Don't swear. Did you have any trouble sleeping?"

He shrugged. "Naw. And that was a huge subject change, y'know. Don't think I didn't notice."

"I also slept well, Annette," Pat intercepted with poisonous sweetness. "Thank you so much for asking."

"You're in a bit of a mood," she observed.

He sighed and set down the rubber spatula. "Yeah, sorry. It's... You're all here because someone's out to get you. *Really* get you, not 'I'll get you for throwing away my yogurt, Bob, you inconsiderate bastard' get you. And I'm glad you're all safe."

"We are, too," Dev said and smirked.

"But that's only temporary."

"Jeez. Way to bring the kitchen down."

"Dev, hush. Let Pat finish."

"You've got no idea who's after you or what they'll do next or how long it'll take to put this case to bed. So what happens now? Because as much as I like having my very own *sous-chef*… Hey!" Dev had taken advantage of Pat's inattention to covertly dump another half cup of chocolate chips into the bowl. "Ratio, Dev, we talked about ratio!"

"No, you talked about ratio. I couldn't get a word in."

Annette, meanwhile, had been giving their predicament some thought. "David, I was thinking the best place to start would be Lund's apartment."

"Yeah."

"And we'll need to check in with Nadia—we can have her meet us there so you—my *God*, you've downed half that coffee already."

"Yeah, well." David shrugged. "At least now I can see. I'll text her."

She turned back to Pat and Dev. "I know it's stressful. And I promise it's temporary—by necessity if nothing else. We've only got two more days to find Caro, give the judge some answers, and get Dev squared away safely."

"I *am* squared away safely."

"I already told you, I don't care about having these guys hang here, they're no trouble." Pat waved the spatula at Dev, who ducked. "I care about the fucko who wants to kill you."

"You'll have to narrow that down. And I don't want you or Dev to worry too much in the meantime." She really didn't. Dev's default when stressed/hurt/furious/hungry was to flee the vicinity and pop up days and miles away. Pat's was to dig in and bite harder.

"Worry too much? With *him* skulking around?" Dev

pointed a drippy whisk at David. "Didja see him last night? I knew he was gonna shift and I almost had a heart attack anyway. As long as I'm staying here, the only thing I need to worry about is a nuclear blast. *Maybe*."

Annnnnnd now she was back to thinking about jumping David Auberon with amorous intent. Before last night, she'd never seen David's other self and it was, to be equal parts blunt and accurate, astounding. She'd never seen anything like it, and she was a bear herself.

God, the *size* of him. Not to mention the confidence, which went nicely with the powerful stealth. And not that she had any intention of challenging him, but she had to wonder which of them would win a fight for dominance. He was bigger, but she thought she might be faster. Even if they never went out as a couple—she could hardly blame him if he was disinclined to make the embarrassing gossip a reality—maybe they could shift and hunt together now and again. Werebears were rare bears.

"Wait 'til the other guys hear about this guy! When it's all over, I mean," Dev added hastily. "And we're all safe again."

David was topping up his vase of coffee and managed a rueful smile. "God, kid, you act like you've never seen a bear before."

"Uh, you're downplaying a smidge."

Annette could understand Dev's fascination. Werebears weren't as numerous as werefoxes or werewolves; many Shifters went their entire lives without seeing one in the fur. Her parents were the only one of their kind they'd met, and they were in their twenties when that happened.

Was that part of her reluctance? Or, worse, David's? Not seeking out the only other bear within five hundred miles because of reverse species-ism? Or would that be actual species-ism? *Here's another werebear! Bang him and also maybe get married because you owe it to your subspecies to propagate.*

Ugh. No.

Thorny questions of duties to subspecies aside, knowing a Shifter didn't necessarily mean having seen both halves. Nadia was the only colleague who had seen Annette's other self. By contrast, just about every were Nadia knew had seen her fly.

For most, showing both halves was a matter of personal preference, and subjective issues like pride, confidence, upbringing, and even personal politics played their part. Oh, and species-ism. Mustn't forget that.

"Well, I thought it was cool. Want to see mine? I'll do it," Dev announced. "I'll do it right now. Stand back."

"Don't you *dare* get fox fur in my scone mix!"

"*Our* scone mix."

"Save me some," she ordered. Well, whined. Good God, she loved pastry, she really did. Maybe David would be amenable to swinging through a drive-through. Multiple times.

Chapter 11

As it turned out, once David had retrieved his car, he was all kinds of amenable.

"It's not just the biscuit and the egg," she explained with her mouth full. "It's the tenderness of the biscuit and the smokiness of the ham and the gooeyness of the cheese and the admittedly overcooked egg. Alone, they're insignificant. Even unpalatable, when it comes to the egg...so rubbery. But together, they're transcendent. Sorry, what was the question?"

"I wasn't talking to you. Just telling the Razer I was back." He patted the dashboard, which was so cute it was stupid. "And you're talking about Burger King chow, right?"

"Yes, but that also applies to scrambled eggs and ketchup. I don't like scrambled eggs, and I think ketchup is something you have to use when you've lost a bet. Not that I bet. But they're so good together! Don't read into that." David chuckled as she tore into her third breakfast biscuit. "I can't believe you're done eating already. Aren't you famished? You burned thousands of calories at my place last night." Then she nearly choked on the unintentional double entendre. Two in ten seconds!

"Yeah, well, I was gonna make scrambled eggs last night, but your roommate started screaming about scones and custard like I'd stabbed him."

"No, he makes a very different noise when you stab him."

"Okay, disturbing. Anyway, that's why you've got some eggs left but you're out of lunch meat and Ritz crackers. And everything on the second shelf in your fridge." David paused, thinking. "And mustard."

"We're out of mustard? How could you keep this from me?"

"I'll buy you more." He cleared his throat. "Listen, can I ask you something?"

"Something *else*, right? Because by asking if you can ask me something, you've already asked me something."

"Bad enough you're using clichés—"

"Hey!"

"—but they're Nadia's clichés. You need a new partner."

"Oh, are you volunteering?"

"...No."

She grinned. "I'm going to pass over that disconcerting pause and change the subject back to your evening stroll. I'm guessing you found nothing out of the ordinary?"

"No, just your scent everywhere. Which I expected. And Pat's, which... Actually, I thought I'd find more of it. What there was, it was really faint. Not...old, exactly. Just not as strong as yours. What's his story? Can I ask?"

"It's a standard backstory," she said. "He made a series of bad decisions, fell in with the wrong crowd, was slashed and nearly burned alive. The usual adolescent angst."

"Jesus. Where the hell did you grow up?"

"Prescott, Wisconsin," she replied. "Or was that rhetorical?"

"Why aren't you seeing anyone?"

Annette was surprised by his question (which she presumed wasn't rhetorical), but not as surprised as David, who looked startled as the color rose to his cheeks.

Ah, someone forgot to engage his filter this morning. Why do I find that so endearing?

David misinterpreted her silence, because he added, "I'm not fishing. I get that you've got no interest in…you know."

What? I know? I don't think I know. What is he talking about? Good God, this is exactly like being back in high school, which I DID NOT LOVE the first time around.

"But you're really…you know." David probably thought he was clarifying, which was as annoying as it was adorable. "So I was wondering why you're not seeing anybody."

"Why aren't you?" she countered.

He shrugged. "The job. The hours. It's hard to meet new people, and I've got no interest in Mate or Tamer or Shifter Date."

"Well, there you go. We're both in a committed relationship with a faceless government bureaucracy, and we've got little or no time to cheat on it even if we wanted to, which we don't."

He laughed. "Fair enough."

She considered ignoring everything she had learned about him and everything she had told herself and just asking him out, then reminded herself that (1) there were more important things to concentrate on, (2) his disinterest was plain, and (3) she was terrible at asking men out. It always ended up sounding like a sales pitch. And not for something vital, but something like a terrific set of mixing bowls. Something you immediately regretted purchasing, like an extended warranty on an electric toothbrush. "Oooh, here it is. Turn, turn!"

"Wonderful. I love back-seat drivers."

"David, you missed the turn!"

"I'm *making* the turn, Christ, stop screaming."

Lund lived—*had* lived—in a luxe apartment in the Layette Loft building in Saint Paul's Lowertown neighborhood. The area was justly famous for its artists' quarter, breweries, and warren of hipster lairs. "Oooh, Pazzaluna's right across the street! Excellent gnocchi and lamb chops. Maybe there'll be time after to grab a sandwich."

"It's not even 8:00 a.m. And they don't serve breakfast or lunch."

"Don't give me problems, David, give me solutions. Maybe we'll try a deli instead. See? See how I immediately found a solution? You could learn a lot from me."

"I'll never deny it," he replied, admirably straight-faced.

Traffic was annoying, which was to be expected during morning rush hour, but David quickly found a parking space out front.

"Do you have meter money? Because I don't have meter money." She snatched up her purse, rooted around. "I have four quarters. No. Six!"

"Annette, what year do you think it is?" He shut off the engine and pulled out his S metro card. It worked like any transit card in any meter in the state, but the info went into IPA's database for billing and payroll. Theoretically, they were efficient time-savers. Realistically...

"Those never work for me. Well, sometimes they don't work. Or I get it mixed up with my library card—they're the same color!"

"There's also an app."

"It's just easier to dump a bunch of quarters in a meter. Okay, okay, enough with the cross-examination!"

"I didn't—"

"Fine, you're right, I *might* have a smidge of Luddite in me. I didn't start texting until two years ago."

He smothered a laugh as they headed past the pale pillars and up the steps to Lund's building. "You know you're not being cross-examined, right?"

"I hate when you ask questions that aren't actually questions," she grumbled. "Why are you smiling? Before yesterday, I didn't know your face could do that."

"I like working with you," he replied simply, and if she wasn't careful, she'd blush like a virginal schoolgirl. Oh. Wait. She was. Blushing. Not virginal. *Virginity doesn't grow back, right? No matter how long the dry spell?* "I've been working with IPA for a while, but you and I've never had to work a case together."

"Sadly, this week your lucky streak came to an abrupt end."

"I don't see it that way. Not at all."

Aw! "Well. I like working with you, too. Now let's go visit a horrific crime scene together."

"Do we have a cover? Or should we just march in and flash IDs?"

"Who says we can't do both? Besides, I'm a fan of the classics, so…newlyweds. I'd like to measure how helpful management is when they don't know the real reason we're here." She tentatively reached out, and David's large hand more or less swallowed hers.

"After you, Mrs. Auberon."

"I kept my own name."

"Naw, I changed the marriage license when you weren't looking."

"Patriarchal bastard," she muttered. She looked up and he was right *there*, just holding her hand and smiling down at her with bright eyes, and she took a tiny step closer. She could still smell his spicy aftershave, though it was faint by now. *He's still got yesterday's stubble. I wonder what he'd do if I ran my finger from his ear to his jaw? Would he be stoic? Shiver? Would he touch me back? Lean in for a kiss? I am all for a lean-in. Yes indeed. Whatever's necessary to do the job. IPA is fortunate to have an employee willing to go to such extremes. Well, an employee and an independent contractor. I'll bet he's a terrific kisser. Except I don't bet.*

The blat of a bakery truck misfiring woke her up in time for David to open one of the double doors and escort her in, still holding hands. He was standing so close his hip nearly touched hers, which was all kinds of distracting. She caught his blue-eyed gaze. "Gotta make it look good," he whispered, then tipped her chin up with a finger and gave her a brief, sweet peck on the lips.

"Um," she replied, which was all she could manage, because *damn*. "Thank you." *What?* Idiotic. No newlywed politely thanks her new husband like he'd just handed her a napkin instead of a kiss. She'd already blitzed their cover story. Also, to hell with new batteries for the vibrator. Time to get a plug-in Hitachi ASAP.

To distract herself from what had happened one second earlier, she focused on their surroundings. The lobby was spacious, with several floor-to-ceiling windows, enough plants for a Bachman's store, and enough light for a Menard's showroom. *Note: also pick up light bulbs and basil seed packets for Pat.*

"Oh, hello!" A fair-skinned redhead had risen from behind the lobby desk and was hurrying toward them. She wore a somber dark suit, white ankle socks, saddle shoes, and a name tag which, on closer inspection, read MICHELLE: RESIDENCE ASSOCIATE. Annette assumed that was code for manager or super. "I'm so *so* sorry, we aren't giving any tours today, but I'll be glad to take your number and get back to you with an appointment time."

Annette started to reach for her ID, but David wouldn't let go of her hand. Apparently he wasn't willing to drop newlywed mode just yet, despite her blunder. Sweet? Or doggedly dedicated? "Thank you, but—"

"Have you been together long?"

Annette managed not to laugh. "A shockingly short time, actually."

"Oh! Newlyweds!"

"It's been a whirlwind romance," David deadpanned.

"I can imagine, but weddings are so *so* stressful," Michelle said, giving him a business card and a big smile. "I imagine you must be anxious to put the wedding behind you and start your married lives, and you may be in luck. One of our Franklin units has just opened up."

"Yeah, we heard."

"And I'd be delighted to give you a tour, as I said, just not today. And if your lovely bride is too busy, *you* could come. I'm happy to show you around."

Annette cleared her throat. "We just got married. Surely you noticed the hand-holding? And the brief, ordinary kiss?"

David snorted. "Thanks."

She held up their joined hands inches from the hussy's face. "You're flirting with my husband while I'm standing two feet away. What kind of bullshit bordello are you running?"

"This is what I have to put up with," David whispered to Michelle. "She redefined the term 'Bridezilla.' And don't get me started on what she did to the caterers. She was micromanaging like a motherfucker. Also, we're not married and we're here to see the dead guy's apartment."

"What?"

"It's true," Annette said, nodding. "I put the 'zilla in Bridezilla."

Michelle looked shocked. "No, I mean... This is about Mr. Lund?"

"I'm afraid so."

"So you're single?" Michelle asked, turning back to David.

"Good *God*, woman." *Don't kick her in the ankle. Don't.*

"Are these two reprobates bothering you, darling?"

Saved by Nadia. Michelle spun to face the new arrival. "I'm sorry?"

"You're flirting with my brand-new husband," Annette said before Nadia could elaborate. "You should be apologizing to *me*."

"Her jealousy," David confided, "will tear us apart."

Nadia, meanwhile, had approached and held out a hand for Michelle to shake. "Lovely to meet you, Michelle, I'm Nadia. We spoke on the phone. These are my colleagues, Inspector Auberon and Annette Garsea. Who are not married, by the way." To the busted non-newlyweds: "*What* are you two doing? You had an attack of the vapors when I teased you about dating—"

"No," David deadpanned.

"—and now this?"

"No one believes in the power of our love." Annette sighed.

"It's nice to meet you," Michelle managed, looking not a little overwhelmed.

"It always is, dear. May I have the key?"

"Yes, but…no."

Nadia arched perfectly plucked brows. "Beg pardon?"

Michelle started talking faster. "I mean I had it. I still have it, is what I'm saying. But the building's owner called just a few minutes ago and said I wasn't to show that particular unit. He was so *so* insistent. I know you're here on official business—I mean, I think you are, the married thing is confusing—"

"Not too confusing to keep you from flirting with my fake husband," Annette sniffed.

"—but I'm not authorized to hand over the key now."

Nadia shrugged. "Very well. I'm sure they've posted an officer at the late Lund's door. They can let us in when we get up there. Fourth floor, isn't it?"

"Yes, but…shouldn't I come with you?"

"Not necessary. We covered this on the phone, Michelle. But we'll certainly sing out if we need you. Come along, faux newlyweds."

The three of them said nothing until the elevator doors hissed shut.

"Wow, Nadia, you saved us. Which is something I never thought I'd say."

"We hardly needed saving," Annette pointed out. "Okay, I *was* considering scratching Michelle's eyes out. Or whatever a touchy post-wedding stressed bride would do. Who flirts with a groom when the bride is within earshot?"

"It's not nice to play with the Stables," Nadia chided.

"Fun, though." David grinned. "Sometimes."

Nadia often smoothed the way between their agency and outsiders with, among other things, attitude backed with lots of official-looking paperwork. It didn't hurt that the average American was a sucker for an upper-class

British accent. And since she always looked like she was on her way to a White House briefing and was so brittle and confident, few challenged her. On the rare occasions when a Stable or, worse, a cop decided to be recalcitrant…well, there were ways around that, too.

Lund's case was especially problematic: a Shifter, possibly murdered by another Shifter, in an apartment building that was mostly Stable. In addition to doing their own investigation, they had to placate an entirely separate government agency—Hennepin County Child Protection Services—that had no idea the IPA existed.

This entailed various employees from both agencies working, at best, parallel to one another, which was one of the reasons caseworkers were given more leeway than their Stable counterparts. Sometimes there simply wasn't time to cross every *t*.

"I know we've discussed this before…"

"Oh, hell."

"…but when will you attend to this?" Nadia had reached out, spooky quick, and tugged on a strand of Annette's thick hair. "You're too young to be going gray. Your mop is thick and healthy, and the primary color— sable, I believe—"

"Why are you talking like a Clairol spokeswoman? It's brown, by the way."

"—is nice, but the gray distracts from all that."

"My hair has been this color—colors—for twenty-five years." She smacked Nadia's hand as the woman went in for another yank. "Stop it."

"Precisely my point! It's ridiculous that you've got the face of a college cheerleader and the hair of a bingo player on a seniors' cruise. You could easily cover those grays."

"They're not gray," David snapped. "They're white. And she shouldn't change a strand."

Nadia sniffed. "It's so very odd to me that you think white is somehow better."

"Both of you, hush," Annette ordered. "There are any number of things going on here, and almost all of them are more important than my hair." As if making her point, the elevator doors whooshed open. "Now come on, both of you. And no squabbling, or I'll turn this crime scene around and go home."

The door to 4E was blocked with yellow crime-scene tape, indicating that processing was finished, but more troubling, the hallway was deserted and quiet. Nadia leaned in for a closer look. "The tape hasn't been cut. So they sealed it after they left."

"I would've thought there'd be someone on the door at least," David said. "Even if they finished processing the scene. And now that I think of it, I didn't notice any cop cars outside. No one's doing door-to-door 'did you see or hear anything' interviews? No one's come back for another walk-through?"

"Maybe they're waiting on autopsy results?" But even as Annette said it, it seemed unlikely. And before she could speculate further, their phones buzzed in unison, and there was a brief silence as they all read the incoming text, which was flagged 'Pay attention to this.' "Did either of you just now receive a 'permission rescinded, do not enter crime scene' notice, or did you get updates for your Pinterest board instead?"

"Both," Nadia said. "And I can't wait to click and find out what eyeshadow trends we can expect this fall. But this other thing is perplexing."

"I realize I've said this more than once this week—"

"If you're gonna say what I think you're gonna say, it bears repeating."

"—but what the hell is going on?" Annette cried. "Can't we go a single hour without something mysterious or puzzling or senseless happening and disrupting everything *again*? It's starting to feel like David and I have been working this for months!"

"Ouch," Nadia said, shooting David a sympathetic glance.

"I don't even work for your agency," David said. "I'm an independent contractor."

"Yes, yes," Nadia said impatiently. "It's why you *will* insist on refusing to come to the holiday party."

"No, I wouldn't go to those even if I did work there. I don't...but I've got your boss telling me to bolt."

They looked at each other, and Annette reread her text in case it had somehow changed in the last five seconds. Then she cleared her throat. "I'm not advocating that we should break any laws—"

"I am," David said. "This is bullshit." He ran a hand through his mop and looked as baffled as Annette felt. "Somebody doesn't want us to find out a goddamned thing about Lund or Caro, and I can't tell you how much that pisses me off."

"Have they never watched an American crime show?" Nadia wondered. "This is the exact tactic that makes the hero and/or heroine, heretofore a stickler for regulations, decide to disobey orders and go rogue and search for the truth no matter what."

"I wouldn't try this door," Annette said, rapping it with a knuckle. "Breaking it down—"

"Will ruin my manicure. Unlikely."

"—is messy and immediately noticeable, and we'd end up leaving a crime scene that is technically under active investigation vulnerable to anyone who wanted to walk in. Not to mention, if the door was relatively whole and still on its hinges when we were done, we'd have to put down new tape or, again, leave it vulnerable. Assuming we could get our hands on new tape."

"I literally have a trunk full of crime-scene tape," David announced.

"You're lying! It's full of red Jolly Ranchers."

"*And* tape," he insisted.

"Oh. Guess I didn't notice what with the waterfall of candy that cascaded all over my feet."

Nadia was gaping and making no effort to hide it. "What have you two been doing?"

"*However*," Annette continued, "I'll bet the sliding door to his balcony is a viable option."

Nadia saw they were both looking at her and beamed. "I won't lie, darlings. I'm flattered to be asked."

Chapter 12

FOUR MINUTES LATER, AN ELEGANT RED KITE LANDED on the railing of Lund's fourth-story balcony. The raptor, a sleek and efficient hunter, had a six-foot wing-span, a dark, reddish-brown body, and black feathers with white wing tips.

This particular predator fed on rabbits, shrews, and Restaurant Alma's roast duck special, had a grip equal to 400 psi, and a talon strike speed of 50 miles per hour.

"This isn't the first time having an extrovert for a part-ner has come in handy," Annette commented as a naked Nadia opened Lund's front door and gestured them inside with a bouncy flourish.

"I'll bet."

"You were quite right, Annette," she announced as they followed her pert backside into Lund's living room. "Locked, but you can unlock it from either side. And I heartily doubt a Stable will scale a four-story building. Not a sensible one, at least."

David snorted. "*Are* there any sensible ones?"

"Of course there are. There must be. The law of aver-ages and all that." Annette tried to give Nadia her clothes back, only to be rebuffed.

"I'll just have to disrobe again when I let you out the front, darling."

"Yes, but it's chilly in here," Annette explained. "Surely you've noticed. Your boobs certainly have."

"It's even chillier riding a downdraft from ninety feet up."

"Point."

"You guys realize we're going to get in a lot of trouble, right?" From David, who had pulled on gloves (where had he been hiding gloves?) and was now examining the bookshelves in the living room. Annette gave him points for not drooling all over Nadia's sleek curves. Nudity, like preferences about when and where and how often to shift, was defined by individual taste. Annette wasn't ashamed of her body, but she would have gotten dressed for the search. David, she'd noticed last night (and there was a lot to, um, notice), was matter-of-fact about his nudity but didn't flaunt it.

And then there was Nadia. "I daresay the aerial yoga is paying off."

"Is that something you do when you have wings," Annette asked, "or are you talking about the kind where you suspend yourself in a sheet and wriggle around for half an hour?"

"The latter. And it's a controlled wriggle. And it's a thirty-foot ribbon hung from the ceiling, not a sheet."

"Sounds exhausting."

"As for getting into trouble for our little B&E, file that under 'duh,'" Nadia said, not unkindly. "Let us hope we find something here that will mitigate the damage to our careers."

"Or we could just not get caught," David suggested.

"Both sound ideas."

The walls and much of the decor in Lund's loft were pure white, doubtless considered chic and understated by people who weren't Annette, who likened it to living inside a marshmallow. It was an open plan, with the living room, dining room, and kitchen in the same area, and the spotless gray floor shone, making the space feel chilly and unwelcoming. The large sectional sofa was also gray, and so were the armchairs flanking it. There was gray brick outlining the fireplace, which was spotless, and the matches set neatly to the side hadn't been opened. Lund was either a hell of a chimney sweep or he never used it.

All space, no life. Literally. The only items breaking the monotony were the books on the shelves and the detritus of the investigators: fingerprint dust, amido black, titanium dioxide, and the like.

"This guy's officially a psycho," David announced, examining a white bookshelf that held about a dozen books. "He's got these arranged by book spine color."

"Truly a monstrous individual," Annette agreed, and she was only half-kidding.

Stairs they were in no hurry to climb led to still more white walls and presumably the upstairs bedrooms and baths. The unvaried color was broken only by an occasional dark piece of furniture or framed landscape photograph.

"No personal photos," David mused. "No junk drawer. Nothing on the bulletin board, not even menus. Nothing on the fridge or counters. And nothing in the fridge or cupboards. Not so much as a box of crackers."

"No snacks? What kind of a monster lives like this? And for...how long has he lived here?"

"Ten months." David closed the door of the spotless, empty fridge, then stepped to his left and opened a drawer. "One set of clean cutlery." He closed it and shook his head. "Place looks like a movie set, not a home."

Upstairs there was a small alcove for a washer-dryer combo so new it still had the Best Buy stickers on it. But no detergent. No fabric softener. No lint.

The first bedroom, also blinding white, held a perfectly made bed with a white-and-gray-striped comforter, a white chest of drawers, and a white end table. Nothing on the end table, not even a box of Kleenex.

"It's clear that Lund didn't live here," Nadia ventured. "So, then, why spend a near-fortune on an apartment you rarely use but keep so sterile it could be an operating room?"

Annette could guess. "Something he didn't want anyone to find out about. Something so awful he was killed for it."

The bathrooms each had a white washcloth on a towel rack and a single toothbrush beside the spotless sink, but no toothpaste. No floss. The toilets shone. The gleaming showers were dry.

The last room. She knew it was coming, but Annette still winced when she saw the blood she'd been smelling for five minutes. The contrast after the sterile rooms was shocking. It was set up exactly as the other bedroom, except with a large circular mirror over the dresser.

And the bloodstains, of course. "Did the techs have a cause of death?" Annette asked. "Or a best guess?"

"Shot," David replied. "Probably in this room—no drag marks. Somebody walked him up here, or followed him up here, produced a gun from somewhere, emptied it into him. Then did whatever else they needed to do and left. Crime-scene guys figure he bled out in under two minutes. We'll know more once we get the ME's report. Assuming they haven't kicked us off the case by then."

"Shooting," Nadia observed, "would preclude a teen-age werewolf who likes to bite."

"Likes to bite *Lund*," Annette corrected. "We don't know a single thing about her life before Tuesday. Leaping to conclusions and tossing around assumptions—"

"You make it sound like an aerobic workout."

"—lead to errors."

David touched the bottom corners of the mirror and found out the thing slid sideways, revealing a small rectangle about eighteen inches by twelve. He took the mirror down and carefully set it aside, then lightly pressed the rectangle. There was a click, and the door swung open as though it were a medicine cabinet. "Ta-da!"

She and Nadia bumped shoulders when they leaned in for a look.

"Empty."

"And shame on us for thinking it'd be that easy." Nadia sighed.

"That little hidey-hole isn't just empty," Annette said, thinking aloud. "It's been cleaned out very carefully. There's absolutely no indication of what might have been in there."

David felt around the immaculate hiding place. "Meaning you don't think the techs emptied it and bagged the contents for evidence."

"Correct. I do not think that."

David straightened and slid the mirror back into place. "So the killer got Lund to show him his stash, shot him, grabbed his shit, and vamoosed?"

"Or Lund had enough time to move whatever-it-was from this hidey-hole before he let his killer in." *Please let it be the latter.*

Annette went back to the washer-dryer combo and opened the front-loading door. Spotless, empty, and dry.

"Hunch?"

"You said it yourself, David, this isn't a home, it's a set. Everything's a prop." She tapped the washing machine. "This is newer than anything else in here—see? It's still got the price tags. So he's been using this place for almost a year—but not really—and then a few days ago he goes to the trouble of buying a big appliance he knows he won't use?"

"Oh-ho." From Nadia. "Tricky-tricky."

Annette, who'd borrowed a pair of gloves from David—his jacket pocket bulged with them for some reason—pulled the machine toward her, out of the hidden recess that was barely noticeable until you were standing in front of it. And behind the machine

"Nice."

was another little hidey-hole, and inside this one there were stacks of files and photos.

Christ, the photos.

"Lund," David murmured, staring at a picture of a young, battered werewolf half snarling, half crouching at the camera, showing bloody flanks. "You piece of shit, I hope it hurt."

Chapter 13

THE OTHER PICTURES WERE JUST AS BAD. WOLVES, bear cubs, at least two foxes, and even a weretiger, a subspecies Annette had never seen before. All juveniles. All brutalized. And several had names scrawled across their pictures: Scout. Lambchop. Ruby. Baxter.

And then...

Jackpot.

"Caro Daniels is from Canada," David announced, holding up a battered driver's license, which Annette all but snatched out of his hands to study.

It wasn't a license; it was a learner's permit issued two years ago by the Alberta Ministry of Transportation, which Annette assumed was their version of Minnesota's Division of Driver and Vehicle Services. Caro was only fourteen in the photo—Alberta was the only Canadian province that let juveniles get a permit at that age—and her small smile and shy expression made Annette's eyes sting in a way that the worst of the abusive photos had not.

Nadia peeked over David's shoulder for a look. "That explains why the poor thing wasn't in our system. It's not international."

"Exactly. But this is a huge help. We've got something to go on. When we find her, we have to show her this." Annette tapped the Hell Folder full of hell. "When she sees what we found, she'll understand that we're on her side. Maybe she'll feel safe enough to talk."

The dozen or so Hell Folders indicated that the people behind Lund's (richly deserved) murder had been preying on vulnerable juveniles for years, snatching up homeless teens, addicts, abuse victims, and runaways. Or luring them, then keeping them. In other words, they targeted the same at-risk kids IPA was sworn to protect.

"Or it's the opposite," David pointed out. "Someone found out what Lund was up to and killed him for it. Not to protect themselves, but because they knew he was nothing but a sentient bag of guts that should be dropped off a roof."

"Urgh," Annette said, visualizing.

"Right—to avenge the children." Nadia gingerly poked through the photos with one long, perfectly man-icured fingernail. By her expression, even that minimal amount of contact was repellent. "A parent? Sibling?"

Not that Lund had obligingly left much beyond some coded notes: a page of account numbers, the kids' names, where they'd been "found," and a series of dates that could have meant anything. Birthdays? Days they'd been kidnapped? Days they were

(please not)

killed and dumped?

"Jesus Christ," David managed, dropping a pic of a bloodied werefox cringing away from the camera. He rubbed his gloved hands together as if the latex barrier wasn't nearly thick enough. "Every time I think I've seen the lowest level of fuckery... What's that sound?"

Nadia was that sound; she was gnashing her teeth in a slow, lateral grind. Annette had heard that sound fewer than half-a-dozen times in three years; it usually presaged felony-level acts of protective violence. "Nadia, do you need a min—"

"We're supposed to be better than them!" she cried, beating her small fists on the stack of folders. "Stables are the ones who foul their own nests and kill when they aren't hungry. But this, look, and look at these, all these—they're monstrous!" She shook a sheaf of photos at them. "And Lund did that to his own kind! No bloody wonder she went for him! I wish she'd severed his fingers *and* his cock!"

"Agreed." Well. Not entirely. Annette didn't think Shifters were better than Stables—both species were horrible and wonderful in their own way—but this wasn't the time to have that argument. But about the cock thing, yes. They were in absolute agreement.

She looked at the photo again. Caro's wolf was a brown so dark her fur looked black, her furiously bared teeth almost blinding white by comparison. Annette now understood the girl's watchful calm in custody: she'd survived worse. Violent captivity hadn't broken her; she likely believed the system couldn't, either.

Had Caro escaped that night with Lund on her trail? Or had she escaped two years ago, or any time in between, and just happened to run into him this week? A werewolf could pick up a scent trail from three miles away; had she gotten a whiff, then launched? It would explain why she had been docile ever since: mission accomplished. It also explained why someone would have let her out. Not out of sympathy for her plight. And not to give her freedom.

To get her out from IPA's protection, then pick her off.

Nadia's right. We're supposed to be better than this. And it's so fucking bleak when we aren't.

David was still shaking his head over the horrid photos. "Sure explains why Lund didn't want us sniffing around. But now what?"

"Now we find them and set them on fire and rip their heads off and beat them bloody and pull out their hearts and punch them in their horrid faces *so much*."

"Those are all solid ideas," Annette began. "But I think David meant what do we do with all this documented horror? Do we leave it? Take it? Hand it over to our superiors? Take it home and cry and cry and cry?"

Nadia was already shaking her head. "We mustn't hand it over. Our superiors essentially ordered us, *ordered*, not to investigate. They do not care about getting to the bottom of any of this, only closing it out. And you both know why."

Silence. Because they did know why.

"They're already edgy because there are Stables poking around. If we bring this to them, I'd wager it will all be 'lost' within the hour. Then we're suspended or fired *and* we won't have a bloody thing to show for it."

"Nadia, that sounds insane *and* impractical. Do you think it's that bad?" Annette asked quietly. *I know the department's top priority is to keep hidden, but surely in a case like this...*

"Yep." From David. "Or they'll use it as an excuse to pin everything on Lund and officially close it out. They're desperate to close this. It's why they pulled the forensics guys and sealed the crime scene. They'll slap a small bandage on a large spurting wound and call it good. We've gotta keep this shit, but first we need to make copies. And it wouldn't hurt to have a numbers guy try to do something with the account numbers."

"Okay." Removing (then concealing) evidence from a crime scene. Lying by omission to the authorities. Possible obstruction of justice. She couldn't help listing the charges in her head, not that it changed a thing. "So let's go find a UPS Store or something."

"Perhaps it's not as sinister as we think," Nadia mused. "There might well be a parallel investigation, one we're not privy to, which our supervisor can't share with us. Or..."

"It doesn't matter," Annette said. "We have to act like we think there's a superduper sinister plot—"

David shook his head. "I don't have to act. There *is* a superduper sinister plot. If anything, 'superduper sinister' is downplaying the plot. We're just not sure who all is involved."

"—because our priority here is Caro. This is a young woman who was traumatized so deeply she took refuge in selective mutism."

"Is that what it is?" Nadia asked.

"Dev indicated she could talk, she just wouldn't. And

is it any wonder? They didn't just abuse her, they documented it. Over and over and over."

Which raised another troubling detail David was quick to point out. "So clients who were into abuse porn would get pictures?"

Nadia tapped a photo of rows of cages, a third of which were empty. "This is a lot of time and trouble and expense for anyone to go to for abuse porn."

"Well, they're brutalizing these cubs for a reason," Annette replied. "And we can't rule out sex trafficking, either. Maybe Lund had clients who wanted an exotic and/or underage fuck. Which he would provide, but only after the kids had been beaten into submission."

And just like that, not one of them could stand to be in that sterile level of hell. Not for another minute. Another second.

"All right, ladies. Let's pack this shit up and get the hell gone."

"Hallelujah! I'll lock up behind you and meet you in the car park." Nadia was back on her feet and heading for the downstairs at a near-trot. "I *knew* staying naked was the right choice."

"At last!" Annette called after her. "A title for your autobiography!"

It was a silly joke, but David snorted and Nadia actually laughed, and that helped. A little.

Five minutes later, Nadia was fully dressed and they were walking toward her car, parked one row over from David's.

"All right. So." Annette shifted her grip on the Hell Folders. Even touching them was vomit-inducing. "Copies first."

"At least two sets," David added. "And we gotta stash the originals in the local equivalent of Fort Knox."

"Agreed." Though she didn't think the local FedEx would be the right choice. She could picture it: copying page after page of documented physical abuse while hunching over the files, repeatedly refusing assistance, and glaring at anyone who got too close. The police would be pulling up before they were halfway through the first folder. "As for our next step, I'll say it straight out—I have no idea what it is. They always make going rogue look so easy on TV."

"Well, we—"

Nadia stopped talking and walking so suddenly Annette almost plowed into her. Not that she could blame the woman. The three of them were upwind or they'd have caught on sooner.

Caro Daniels was sitting cross-legged on the Razer's hood.

Chapter 14

"I KNOW I KEEP SAYING THIS…"

"*What* is going *on*?" Nadia and David chorused.

"Stop it, I'm not *that* shrill!" This over her shoulder as Annette ran to Caro. "Are you okay? Are you hurt?" Thankfully, Caro shook her head. "Are you sure? How many fingers am I holding up?" In response to Annette's three fingers, Caro smirked and raised eight. "Not helpful!"

Caro was sockless, wearing the same sneakers from yesterday, black leggings, and a Hamline sweatshirt. Same penetrating gaze. Same unsettling silence.

"Do I even want to know where you got the new clothes?"

"Kid's got balls," David muttered under his breath, and Caro rolled her eyes.

Annette squashed the urge to take the girl by the shoulders and give her a shake. "Caro, why did you run? Who let you out?"

Nothing.

"And why do I keep asking you things when I know you won't answer?"

Shrug.

"We get it, darling. You're determined to cultivate an air of mystery. Pull it back a bit," Nadia advised.

"I'm glad you're okay, but do you understand we

have to take you back into custody? This isn't a TV show where a key figure vanishes, reappears, and is then whisked away to a safe place while dedicated civil servants tirelessly risk their professional reputations to get to the bottom of... Why are you two nodding?"

David shrugged. Nadia hummed and looked at the sky, doubtless calculating wind vectors. Annette turned back to Caro, who had arranged herself in *The Thinker* pose. "Are you mocking us? Never mind. We're going to do that annoying thing adults do when they talk about a youngster like they aren't well within earshot." To David and Nadia: "We have to take her to Judge Gomph." *Right? Right.* She filled their unhelpful silence with "You remember. The judge? Who ordered us to report to him with Caro's whereabouts and a progrep?"

"Tomorrow," David pointed out. "Ordered us to give him a progress report *tomorrow*."

She stared at him for a moment, then turned back to Caro. "We've found out everything. We know why you went after Lund." She gestured to the files she'd been clutching to her chest. "This changes everything for you. You're safe from Lund, he's going in the ground. You don't have to worry. And we can reach out to your family. I'm sure they've been in agony, wondering where you've been the last two years."

Caro shook her head. But at which part? Her motive? Her situation? The years of abuse? That she was safe?

That was it. Yes, Caro Daniels was safe...from Lund. But there was almost no chance that fingerless bastard had been running his own private abuse–rape club by himself and for himself. It was a syndicate with an unknown number of members, and perhaps one or more of them worked for ITA or were ITA adjacent; it would explain how Caro got out. There were more than 150 ITA employees and more than a dozen independent contractors, and they hadn't the first clue who the internal scumbag or scumbags could be. Or who *any* of Lund's accomplices were. That wouldn't change for at least a few hours.

"Did you kill him?" Nadia asked, so quietly Annette almost didn't catch it.

A tear spilled down Caro's cheek as she shook her head.

"I have to show you something awful." Annette set the folders on the hood, opened one, and showed the picture to Caro, who blinked at it and wiped away the tear. "I'm so sorry. I—I'd give anything for this not to have happened to you. But it can't be undone. What we *can* do is fix it so these duplicitous scumbags don't do it to anyone else. And I know it sounds corny, but we can't do it alone."

Nothing.

"Endearing," Nadia suggested. "Not corny."

"Thanks." Annette got ready to do something not nice. "The situation is clear. We're going to have to take Dev back in."

David and Nadia, bless them, picked up on it. "We should've done it yesterday," David snapped. "Kid *clearly* knows something. With his jacket, we could prob'ly get Gomph to okay a three-day lockdown in a max cell."

"Oh dear. I hate to do such a thing—he is so very

charming when he wants to be—but at the least, he's
obstructing justice. We'll have to hope—*Ouch!*" Nadia
rubbed her arm where Caro had leaned over and pinched
her. "Quite uncalled for, young lady."

Caro gave them all a "You guys suck at this. I'm not
falling for it" look. Annette had never met anyone whose
glares were so eloquent. She sighed and raked her fingers
through her hair. "Our options are limited."

David snorted. "Tell me. We can't take her to Gomph,
we can't leave her on her own, and we can't dump her on
a fos-fam 'til we know more."

"He didn't mean 'dump,'" Annette told Caro. "He
meant…um…gift."

"Do feel free to chime in anytime, Caro, darling." This
from a sweetly reasonable Nadia, but it had no effect on a
willfully silent teenager.

"What if we had Nadia stash her somewhere, and
we go back to IPA to let them know we've got a missing
person lead?"

Annette blinked at David's suggestion. "And…what?
Just see who shows up?"

"Pretty much."

"Stash her where, exactly? And, again, Caro, sorry to
have a discussion that directly affects you without actually discussing it with you."

The three (four?) of them thought it over, and David
was the first to break the silence. "It sucks."

"It's not…altogether terrible." Nadia ignored Caro's
snort. "However, I can't think of anything better just now."

"We can get lunch on the way and figure this out. Do we announce Caro's at my house? Or a decoy locale? Either way, I'll have to warn Pat. We've got safeguards at the house, but Pat needs to know what might be coming. He should have the option to leave."

"You think if a band of ruffians showed up at your home with lethal intent, Pat and Dev would linger?" Nadia paused. "Of course they would. I had to hear that out loud before I realized what an asinine question it was."

"Right. So let's grab some chow and work out the rough spots."

"It's all rough spots, David, darling."

"Would you like some lunch? Hamburgers? Sushi? A piping hot bowl of vengeance?" Annette asked, and was startled when Caro showed a tiny curl of a smile.

Chapter 15

"THIS IS INSANITY ON WHEELS," ANNETTE announced. "And not just figuratively."

In the short silence that followed, David considered his response. Caro couldn't have responded even if she wanted to; her cheeks were bulging with red Skittles. *Kid's got good taste in desserts.*

"I'm open to suggestions," he said mildly.

"Just a terrible, terrible idea."

"Again, happy to hear a Plan B."

"What are we thinking?" Annette fretted. "We could get in an astonishing amount of trouble. Actually, we're already in trouble. Trouble was a guarantee once Nadia let us into Lund's."

"Still waiting on your alternative."

"My complaints should make it obvious that I have none," Annette snapped. To David's surprise, he heard Caro giggle. "And *you.* Who doesn't finish a cheeseburger because they're saving room for Skittles?"

David ahem'd, because he did that all the time. Almost daily. For which he made zero apologies.

"Good *God,* you're both awful. Okay, here." Annette was leaning forward like a hound on point, fingers gripping the dashboard. "Here-here-here. Turn left right here. *Left.*"

"It's a one-way street on a bluff," David pointed out. "Where else would I turn?"

"Oh, I'm sorry! Pardon me for making sure we don't skid and die."

"You really thought if you hadn't said 'left, *left*,' I would have gone right and plunged us over a cliff?"

"You said you needed directions."

"Didn't know what I was getting into, did I?" *So! Annette has two flaws: she's a soft touch, and she's an Olympian-level back-seat driver. And her hands are small and soft, and when she stands in your space because she's pretending to be your wife, she smells like Madagascar vanilla and peaches. And her mouth is so, so sweet. Which aren't flaws. But are worth mentioning.*

David met Caro's gaze in the rearview. "This isn't as irritating as finding you was. But it's pretty close."

They'd swung through a drive-through, and between Filets-O-Fish, Annette had directed him out of Saint Paul toward Lilydale, a town on the Mississippi River that was smack in the middle of a national park. (It was always good when Shifters were on the city council; Stables were prone to asphalting woods, then complaining about the traffic).

After a five-minute drive, Annette had directed him to the older part of town, where they passed homes that were grand but aging less than gracefully. Stately home after stately home slid by, each needing a good mowing, a new paint job, or both. Nice enough, but not exactly real-estate candy. Which led him to ask…

"Is this a Shifter neighborhood?"

"Mostly. Lilydale's probably 90/10. There's one house

on the block that may or may not be cursed, but otherwise, it's all Shifter families."

"Did you say cursed?"

"No one stays in it longer than three months."

"That doesn't mean—"

"There!"

"That's the cursed house?"

"No, it's *my* house! I mean, it was. The purple house with the white trim!"

The only purple house David had ever seen, in fact. Still, something in him was moved to tease her a little. "Can you be more specific?"

"The dark-purple two-story house with white trim and the smaller, purpler bird house in front! With the Slip 'N Slide still set up even though it's September! And the attached garage, which is also purple! And last year's Christmas tree, which is smeared with peanut butter so the birds have devoured most of it by now and it's a huge fire hazard! And I'm yelling for some reason!"

He stifled a laugh. "Thanks. That narrowed it down." Christ, she was fun. If he wasn't careful, he'd get a cramp from all the grinning.

Never, obviously. Her face had been pink with embarrassment. Her tone had been angry. *Never, obviously.*

Annnnnd the grin was gone.

Just as well, his dead mother whispered. *It would have ended badly.* Argh. Why did he never hear his dead father? Or his grandmother? Or his speech coach? Wait. Mr.

Pohl wasn't dead… Regardless, why did doleful spirits never look on the bright side?

Speaking of doleful, when he glanced back at Caro he could see she was looking at the purple house with interest. Annette didn't even wait until he'd stopped the car before she popped out; she was up the sidewalk and knocking on the porch door by the time he shut the engine off. He held the back door open for Caro, then fell into step behind her.

"Oh, now look who it is. Santa's early!"

"Or criminally late," Annette said. "Mama Mac, this is—"

"Oh *my*." A tiny woman who could have been fifty or eighty was holding the door open and beckoning them all in with short, slender fingers that looked so delicate David was afraid to shake her hand. She looked like a stiff wind would tumble her across the yard and seemed to be all brown papery skin and fragile bones and twitching nose, and she smelled like cotton and coffee and freshly mowed grass. She was wearing jeans and a red sweatshirt, had a head full of tight, grayish-blond curls, a generous mouth smeared with—was that cherry ChapStick?— and pale-blue eyes bracketed by dozens of laugh lines.

While he'd been looking her over, she'd done the same. "You're a big fella! Our Nettie's never brought a beau around before."

"Your Nettie also doesn't live in the nineteenth century. And neither do you. Beau? Really? Also, Nettie?"

"Well," the older lady said reasonably, "you stopped answering to Honey Bear."

"Oh my God. Honey Bear," David murmured. "Suddenly every crappy thing that has happened in the last three days has been worth it. No offense, Caro."

Caro snickered, thankfully declining to be offended.

"If 'Honey Bear' ever comes out of your mouth again, it will be followed by your tongue. This is my foster mother," Annette added. "I lived here after my parents were killed."

"That you did, which is why I know that look. You're in it up to your neck, Nettie. Don't waste my time by denying it." The woman closed the door behind them and shooed them toward the kitchen table. "So tell me."

"I wouldn't say up to my neck, precisely. I think I'm only boob-deep."

Don't think about her boobs. Don't think about her boobs. Instead, David sidled closer to the intriguing Mama Mac, trying to subtly scent her.

Clearly an herbivore, but what type? Not a werehare. But she doesn't smell like a deer or moose, either. Giraffe? No, her build is wrong...

"Trying to figure me out?" Mama Mac asked, small eyes glittering.

"Of course not," David replied as Caro nodded.

"And this is Caro." Annette was still doing the formal intro thing, because she was either hyperpolite or a slave to appearances. "I left you a voicemail because you have repeatedly ignored my excellent advice to get a smart phone, start texting, and join us in the twenty-first century. Which I am happy to pay for!" she added, as if Caro and David were about to start yelling about Mama Mac's fixed income.

"Didn't you tell me you only started texting two years ago?"

"Shut up, David."

Mama Mac's reply was to treat them to an eye roll that looked physically painful. "I don't know when your generation decided talking on a phone was terrible and to be avoided at all costs, but I'm not playing along with any of it." She turned to Caro. "Yes, I heard you're having some troubles, m'dear. Don't worry, there weren't any specifics. Nettie doesn't tell tales out of school."

"Now that we've—"

"Not that she needed to say anything about anything," Mama Mac added.

"Argh. Can we stay on point? And not reminisce?"

"Nettie doesn't hop on over with a strange child and a tight-lipped fella in the middle of a workday if everything's peachy-perfect." Then, to Annette: "Oz came by a bit earlier. Wouldn't be surprised if you've got troubles in common. Something's on that man's mind."

"Something usually is." Annette swung open the fridge door and grabbed the cupcake box on the top left shelf. She frowned—something about the smell? the weight of the box, maybe?—and flipped it open. "Oh."

Mama Mac nodded, looking all kinds of sage. "Yup."

"He didn't touch *any* of them."

"Nope."

"Not even my favorite." She was staring at half-a-dozen

beautifully decorated red velvet cupcakes with chocolate buttercream; the other half dozen were chocolate cupcakes with salted caramel frosting. David idly wondered which was her fave. "Damn."

"Welp." Mama Mac spread her hands in a these-kits-today gesture. "He's worried about you."

"That's ridiculous," Annette snapped. "*I'm* the one who worries about *him*. It's in my job description."

"No it isn't."

"Mama, he has to keep clear of this. Whatever *this* is."

"He's a grown man, m'girl."

"It doesn't matter how old he is. Some things you stay away from whether you're five or fifty. I'm keeping him out."

Now what the hell was this? From the few interactions David had seen, Annette didn't much care for the guy. It's not like it was a secret.

She doesn't? Then why is she always slipping him food? And why is she worried about him? What could be so bad that a werewolf in his prime couldn't handle?

Great. Another mystery.

Meanwhile, the older woman had held out a small, wrinkled hand, and Caro tentatively shook it. "My name's Meredith Macropi, but everyone calls me Mama Mac. Welcome to my home."

Caro tried a tentative smile.

"Yep, she said you're a quiet one. Wait, I have…" The older woman opened a kitchen drawer, clucked her tongue at the contents, closed that drawer, opened the one beside it, mused, "So *that's* where that is now," opened the cupboard above the drawer, gasped in horror at whatever the hell was in there, slammed it shut, opened the cupboard beside it, took out a notebook and a pack of felt-tip washable pens, then handed them to the teenager. "Here's these if you feel like talking. So t'speak. Oh, I s'pose everyone makes that joke, don't they?"

"She hasn't been with us long enough for there to be a running joke. And I'm sorry again to drop in with next to no warning."

"Don't be a silly sweetie. You only do it when it's important. Or if you've skipped lunch. Or—remember that ridiculous Shift Away Stables movement?"

"Problematic for their idiotic rhetoric if nothing else," Annette muttered.

"You had to hide some kits here to prep for their testimony. Poor things stepped up, didn't they? Even though they had to testify against their folks."

They had. The SAS movement was to Shifters what the KKK was to humanity: ignorant, violent, terrible uniforms, utter hypocrites. While a segment of the Shifter population advocated for coming out, SAS wanted to take over. Violently, if necessary.

The one-percent isn't about privately held wealth, SAS insisted. It was about biology, evolution, and how Stables didn't deserve the dominance on the planet they'd enjoyed for multiple millennia. But what they really hated was that Stables classified themselves as apex predators, and their message was as simple as it was devastating: *How much more of the planet are we going to let them ruin before we take back what's ours?*

Several of the violent, murderous species-ist dumbasses were in prison, and it was safe to say they were not missed by most.

"All right, that's settled," Annette was saying. "Mama Mac, David and I have to go to IPA and do stuff I can't tell you about."

"Oh?"

"Yes. And then we have to do some other things I can't tell you about, so we can help Caro with something I can't tell you about, and then we can all do something else except I don't know what that will be just yet. So I can't tell you."

"Yes, just another Monday. Nettie, I get it."

"It's Wednesday." Annette pointed to the three-year-old calendar featuring *Deadpool*'s Blind Al hanging beside the fridge. "If you had a smart phone, you'd know the date. Since you don't, you have to actually switch these out every twelve months."

"Never!"

"You're the only person in the world who thinks Blind Al is the protagonist of the *Deadpool* franchise."

"Well, she is! That nice English bird you work with gave that to me, and I've treasured it ever since."

"She did it to mess with me and you're complicit. And the notebook and pens for Caro were thoughtful…"

Soft pens, David thought. *Tough to hurt anyone with them. Or herself.* Mama Mac had been around the block.

"…but Caro doesn't communicate. At all. With… um…"

For a good minute, the only sounds in the kitchen were the scratching of Caro's pens and the rumble of Annette's belly.

"We *just* ate."

"Shut up, David."

Finally, Caro stopped writing long enough to rip off a page and hand it to Mama Mac.

Dear Mama Mac,

I'm happy to earn my keep while staying with you, whether that's for hours or days or weeks, so if you'd be kind enough to provide a list of chores, I'll get to them ASAP.

I'm fine with indoor work like making beds, doing dishes, washing floors, scrubbing counters, sorting, washing, folding, & ironing laundry, vacuuming, and/or washing windows (both sides). I'm good at cleaning out gutters, raking, mowing, trimming weeds, gardening, weeding, mulching, & shaping hedges, but I can only make rabbits that look like balloons with pointy ears. (I'm working on that skill set.)

If it's allowed, I'd like access to a laptop or smartphone with Wi-Fi. If not, may I see whatever fiction & nonfiction books you deem appropriate?

Where do I sleep? I'm fine on any floor if you're short of beds. I don't mind the cold so the basement is also fine. Will a change of clothes be provided? If not, I can provide my own.

"Uh," Annette said, which was more than David had been able to come up with.

Caro's pen was still flying across the page, and then there was another *ri-i-i-i-p!* and another page handed off.

"Is professional speed-writing a thing?" David asked. "Because I feel like she'd be great at it."

I believe I've covered the basics but if I've omitted anything please don't hesitate to say so. Thank you for allowing me in your home.

Please know that (1) I'm not a pet, (2) I'll hurt anyone who tries to hurt me or mine.

Sincerely yours,
Caroline Daniels

"Welp, that's clear enough." Mama Mac folded Caro's first communique and tucked it away in the pocket of her jeans like it was NBD. "So. Lunch?"

Chapter 16

THEY WERE HALF A MILE AWAY WHEN DAVID SUC-cumbed to the giggles. "So there you were…"

Argh. "It was two minutes ago, David. There's no need to reminisce."

"…in the midst of explaining about our incommunicado werewolf…annnnnnd then she wrote out a chore manifesto."

Annette covered her face and groaned through her fingers. "And then just casually handed it off. My teeth almost fell out! The only saving grace is that we were the only ones present for the ritual humiliation." And *our* incommunicado werewolf? That warmed her. David often gave the impression that the kids he investigated were just pieces of paper in a file to him. But that wasn't fair. It wasn't like she'd ever sat him down and asked him about it. Any of it. *Why have I never asked this guy out for a meal? Oh. Right. Because I'm horrible at it.*

"I think fleeing the premises was the right thing to do."

"The *only* thing," she agreed.

They were both downplaying their relief at seeing Caro's capacity for clear communication, not to mention proof of what appeared to be formidable intelligence and fortitude. Should this horrifying debacle ever come to trial, she'd make a compelling witness.

David made a heroic effort to stop giggling. "And that wasn't the strangest part. I still can't believe you turned down lunch."

"Not because I wanted to. But time is not on our side in this... Oh. You're mocking me."

"Teasing you."

"I'm not sure there's a difference."

He looked at her dead-on. "If I disliked you, it'd be mockery."

"Oh."

Silence fell with an almost audible thud, which made no sense but there it was. She cast about for something to say that wasn't anything along the lines of *Do you like me, or do you LIKE-like me?* Argh. Death first.

David broke the silence (*whew!*) with a forced cough. "Not trying to tell you how to do your job or whether your family's formidable, but are you sure leaving Caro with your foster mom is safe?"

"Problem?"

"I mean...we're pretty sure Caro only attacked Lund out of self-defense and wouldn't hurt anyone else without major provocation, but... 'Pretty sure' isn't a hundred percent."

"David, we can't expect Caro to trust us if we won't trust her. And don't worry. Mama Mac is a lot more formidable than she looks. There's more than one person walking around with scars because they were dumb enough to mess with her."

"Fair enough." He sighed. "That poor kid. Could you believe that list of chores?"

"I memorized that list," she replied grimly. "And her notes are going right into her file. Don't misunderstand, I don't believe chores are proof of abuse or neglect. I mowed plenty of lawns and washed plenty of dishes—that was one of Mama Mac's rules. 'Everyone contributes to keeping our home nice.'

"But the fact that Caro instantly assumed she would be put to work, and it would be anything from making beds to mulching a quarter of an acre possibly followed by sleeping in a damp basement... I found that telling."

"Not gonna lie, now I kind of want to watch her trim a hedge into a rabbit with a balloon belly."

Annette nearly choked. "Stop it! We're headed back into the belly of the...balloon beast. We need a plan."

"The plan is we tell everyone we've got Caro safe, then go see who shows up to kill her. And stop them."

"That is a terrible plan."

"Yep."

"Also our only plan."

"Yep."

"Which, in itself, is terrible."

"Yep-yep-yep."

Television really *did* make heroically going rogue to champion the underdog look easy. Or at least organized. Because Annette had lived or worked within the same institution for all of her adult life and half of her childhood, standing on the outside was as alien as turning down lunch. It was wrong and dumb and led to irritability. The lack of paperwork alone was disorienting.

But here they were, back where the nightmare might have started for Caro. Here was the glove compartment that held a quart of Skittles and a thousand rubber gloves. Here was the parking ramp where someone tried to kill her, David, and Dev. Or just Dev. (Which was worse.)

Here was the elevator from which she stepped into madness: Nadia, the audaciously awful Oz Adway, her boss—

Boss.

"Start at the top?" she suggested while the elevator went to the bottom. "I've got the perfect icebreaker."

———————————

"Whoa. *Whoa.*" Oz was in the wrong place at the wrong time again—in this case, in her path to the boss's office. "I need to talk to you, Annette. Right now."

"Move or be moved," she growled.

He stayed planted, because he thought his good looks and her forbearance would protect him from unpleasant scenes and broken fingers. Not that he was *that* pleasing to the eye. If she ever did something so crass as to rate men on a numbered scale, Oz Adway would get a five. Well. Maybe a six. Some women didn't mind wealthy, lanky jackasses with swimmers' shoulders and green eyes and a perma-smirk. "I started going over the account numbers Nadia sent—"

"You *what.*" He'd given her such a start that Annette couldn't make it a question: behold, the flat *what* and all it implied. She remembered David saying something about getting a "numbers guy" to look at some of what they'd found and wanted to groan. Seventeen accountants in the department and Nadia picked Oz Goddamned Adway. In a week of disasters, this could make her top five. "We'll talk about it later. Will you get out of the way? I've got a meeting." A lie, technically.

"I know what you're doing, and I'm putting a stop to it right now."

"That's adorable."

"Is letting me help you *that* fucking unthinkable?" He spread his hands, which made him look charming and disarming. He used to look like that at 2:00 a.m. when he'd beat her to the leftovers.

And yes. Letting him help was *that* fucking unthinkable.

"This has nothing to do with you, Oz!"

"You keep saying that, and it's—"

"Jesus, Oz." Tired of the drama, David was shouldering his way past the werewolf with ease. "Read the room."

"I am!" He pointed at Annette. "She's the only one in the room who doesn't like me."

"Of course I like you," she snapped. "I just don't want you anywhere near my work and demand you stay away at all times." And then they were in Bob's office, closing the door on Oz's indignant face.

Now where were they? Ah. "The iron fist of your Secret Santa apartheid will unclench *now*!"

Her boss, Bob Links, actually reeled backward in his office chair. The flailing would have been spectacular in nearly every other instance. "What the hell, Annette? You said everybody loved it!"

"I have never once said that, Bob. Nor anything close to that. Not once in three years."

As a rebuttal, the agency director began indulging his repellent habit of fiddling with the hair sticking out of his ears. "Don't you get it? This is another example of The War On Christmas!"

"It's remarkable that I can actually hear the capital letters when you say it like that. And I know we go over this every year during Christmas and Easter and sometimes on the Fourth of July for some reason, but there is no war. No one is gunning for Christmas. No one is after Christmas. There's no sinister cabal holding secret meetings for the express purpose of spoiling your holiday. And I can't emphasize how deeply, *deeply* stupid it is that I have to explain this every. Single. Year."

Bob took a break from braiding his ear hair to steeple his fingers and nod in what he probably thought was a sage manner. "What's your take on this, Auberon?"

"That the whole thing is fucking dumb. If you've got this much spare time to worry about it, could you go do my laundry instead? And we found Caro Daniels."

"*Dumb?* I knew you investigator types were chilly, but that's borderline sociopathic."

David shook his head. "It really isn't, Bob."

"Also," Annette prompted, "Caro Daniels? The girl who is missing no longer? Who has beautiful penmanship and can help us blitz an abuse syndicate?"

"The Secret Santa program brings us together! C'mon, we're all overpaid and underworked—wait, that's not right… Anyway, team building! Right?"

"No." *It's not polite to disembowel your boss. It's not polite to disembowel your boss. Think of the smell.* Wait. Was that why the break room stank? Were her colleagues randomly disemboweling tiresome supervisors? She couldn't condone the behavior, though she sympathized with the motivation.

She bent at the waist until her mouth was quite close, then shouted into his tufted ear, "Caro Daniels! Has! Been found! Please! Try to! Focus! Good God!"

He flinched back, making it well worth the loss of dignity and damage to her vocal cords.

"God *damn*," David said, rubbing his own ear. "You've got lungs when you want 'em."

Her boss, meanwhile, was glaring up at her. "Your annual review's gonna be more awkward than usual."

"I'll incinerate that bridge when I come to it. Listen, David and I had to drop off the grid—"

"But you're here. I mean, right here. In the middle of the grid."

"We're working through a learning curve. Anyway, in addition to Caro—although we didn't find her so much as she allowed herself to be found, which is a smidge embarrassing when you think about it—we also found incriminating photos at Lund's loft, which I know you'll—"

At last, Bob looked alarmed about something besides

his compulsory Secret Santa initiative. "You weren't authorized to go there."

She looked at him. Said, "Ah." Pulled up a chair. Sat. Looked at him some more. "Can we talk about that? Because David and I would like to talk about that."

"You're a team now?"

"Of course."

"Aw, thanks."

"Shut up, David." To Bob: "Why did you rescind permission? IPA caseworkers and investigators visit crime scenes all the time. If it's going to be hairy, pardon the overused pun, we'll bring a Shifter police officer, or two, or however many we need. That's in our purview."

"I know. Stop narrating."

"Rude. In this case, we had a horrifying assault followed by a horrifying murder followed by the disappearance of our suspect-turned-victim by fair means or foul. We needed more information. Lund's loft was the logical choice. And yet…"

She waited, but Bob had no comment. After a few seconds, he started in his chair. "I thought you were gonna say more after that."

"Uh, no. I artfully paused to give you a chance to fill in the data." Nothing. "*Bob.*"

"I don't know what to tell you," he replied with a shrug. "Actually, I don't know why I'm explaining anything. *You* work for *me.*"

"I work for the State of Minnesota and wards of said

state as *parens familia*. You're the man who handles the paperwork and keeps clear of the mess."

"And who signs your paycheck."

"No, HR has a stamp for that. And it's not even of your name." *Easy. He's still your boss. He lets you get away with loads of lip because your work makes him look good, but there's a line.*

There's always a line.

"Look, what can I say?"

She sighed. "Something? Anything?"

"I got a call from a higher-up that the scene was to stay sealed and no one from IPA could go in without authorization. Which *also* happens all the time. So I passed it down the line."

"So you were instructed to pull us back, but not to make way for another team? Or department? Instead, nobody's working it? How can you possibly reconcile that under the circumstances?"

"Should've known that you wouldn't be able to figure out why someone would follow orders from their boss," Bob said with a smirk. "And now you're telling me you ignored it? And then went 'off the grid' for twenty minutes or whatever?"

"I think it was more like twelve hours," David piped up.

Bob glared in his direction, and for half a second Annette wanted to see David's grizzly take on Bob's lynx. The concept of so much flying fur had never been so arousing.

"Annette, you know I'm not afraid to suspend you, right?"

"Oh, Bob, of course you are," she replied pleasantly. "It makes you look bad, it increases your paperwork, and the children don't like it. You'll recall they often make their displeasure known in unsavory ways." There was the break-room food riot last spring and the cafeteria sit-in, Benny Jurg throwing a tantrum of such proportion it caused lasting property damage (adolescent wererhinos didn't always process stress as well as they should), and...

"My favorite is when they suspended you without pay for two days and Dev retaliated by stealing the lieutenant governor's sedan. Which he refused to return until they agreed to fill the trunk with pudding cups you guys could snack on during the drive to juvie processing."

"*Chocolate* pudding cups," she corrected.

He grinned. "Yeah."

"Good times." Back to the boss. "My point, Bob, is that if you're going to suspend me, then do it. But I want it on the record and I want to add my own addendum to the file. And I'll discuss it with everyone throughout the agency, purely as a method of processing the stressful situation I have found myself in, and you know I can be loquacious."

"If that means 'pain in my ass,' then yeah. You can be very goddamned loquacious."

"Which I know you don't care about, but I have friends here. And they *will* care. Well. Some of them will care. At least a third of them will care."

Bob had passed beyond scowling into full-on pout

mode. "M'not suspending you. Yet. Shouldn't have to. You're off the grid, right?"

"Right."

"Granted, we suck at it," David added.

"But maybe we should put out the word that you and I are on a leave of absence? Though I'm not sure how that would—" A thought struck her, and she turned back to Bob. "Who?"

"What?"

"Who's the 'higher-up' who told you to shut us down at the scene?"

"I didn't talk to him personally, but the order came from Judge Gomph. One minute I'm getting ready to have lunch and the next Gomph's office is yelling at me to rescind your Order of Protection ASAP."

"What you just said makes no sense."

"She's right. The call would've had to have come in before 10:00 a.m. Who's eating lunch then?"

"That's not what I meant, David, but good point. But how could it be Gomph? He knew where we were going. I told him in the hearing, and he was fine with it. Why would he do such a thing after the fact?"

"Dunno, but he's been stomping all over the place, and I'll tell you what, he's super pissed. And I'm beginning to figure out why. Hell, 'til this week, I didn't even know he had feet. I always see him sitting down." Bob had gone from horrified to put-upon to resentful to sulky to smug. None of them were good looks. "So you'd better have your shit together for the hearing today."

"What? That can't be right. We have another day! He said—"

Bob shrugged. "Changed his mind, didn't he?"

Yes.

Why?

Chapter 17

"You KNOW WHY," DAVID SAID AS HE TOOK A LEFT AT the stoplight as they headed back to Mama Mac's to pick up Caro for court.

Annette sighed. "Yes, I suppose I do. And after all that, we didn't have a chance to talk about the disgusting pictures we found."

"Waste of time. Bob's focus is on keeping his head down and staying the hell out of the field, and that's on a *good* day. He hates the job, he's scared of half his own caseworkers—"

"Oh, half." Annette waved away the exaggeration.

"Including you."

"Well, yes." *Don't preen,* she scolded herself. *That's not a compliment.* "But that's not such a trick."

"He's not gonna care," David repeated for emphasis. "He's gonna hide, and when he can't do that, he'll muddle like a motherfucker. I'm wondering if *he* didn't set Caro free. Or at least sicced the garage gang on us. It'd be up his alley, wouldn't it? Making trouble but keeping clear?"

"Hmmm." Bob wasn't a bad person, exactly, though he wasn't in danger of winning any humanitarian awards, either. He was a common enough creature: a burnout killing time until his retirement, one who put forth minimal effort. Less, if he thought no one was watching. He liked things to be quiet and uncomplicated and clean, and he was in one of the worst jobs in the world for someone who treasured such things.

"But the garage thing happened just before the hearing. So I don't think that was Gomph. He didn't know anything about Caro at that time. The hearing was for Dev." Which was awful, because that meant there were *two* moles. At least.

David's hands flexed on the steering wheel as he thought out loud. "So we grab Dev and bring him to court, but someone makes a try for us in the ramp. And someone else lets Caro free. Then we get to court, where Gomph says things in front of a court stenographer to get them on the record. But after we leave, unofficially he blocks our access to the scene. He figures we'll be like Bob, happy to have something off our plate. Or he figures even if you don't like it, you won't buck the system. And then he…what? We're missing something."

Annette snorted. "Several somethings, I've no doubt."

"Does he hear we went to the scene anyway? So he comes over to IPA to chew us out? Or worse? Which is when Bob starts paying attention, because infuriated judges make everyone nervous, especially ones who can trample you in an elevator?"

"That makes a certain sense. But…" But Gomph never so much as raised his voice. But the most upset she had ever seen him was during the kale shortage. But he'd always been an advocate for the Shifter children who came through his court. She was sure he was a good man. "It's difficult to believe."

"Annette. You're too good."

She sat back in the passenger seat and crossed her arms over her chest. *Not this nonsense again.* "I don't think there's any such thing."

"It's not a criticism. Okay, well." He shrugged. "It kinda is. Maybe 'good' wasn't the right word."

"Ah. You mean 'soft.' As in 'hearted.' Which I construe as an insult only because people *will* insist on equating compassion with weakness. Or stupidity."

"C'mon, you're famous for it. Not weakness," he added hastily. "Compassion. You let the kids run circles—no, *trapezoids* around you. You put up with Nadia's never-ending 'tude. You make it easy for Bob to hide in his office—I've seen you doing his paperwork for him. You bring Oz food for some reason. There's a pool for that, by the way, so if you tip me off and tell me what the hell that's about, we could clean up."

She had to laugh. "Some things will never be et cetera." Then she sobered, remembering what she'd found in the break room. She'd indulged a hunch and found the box of eclairs she'd brought Oz the other day.

Untouched.

Not good.

Meanwhile, the adorably clueless David was still going on about her tender heart. "And you let me stay at your place."

"Operative word *let*. You didn't force me. You were in

my home because I allowed it. Soft isn't weak or stupid. Everything I do is my choice now."

"Now?"

"Trapezoid?"

"You mean in the past it wasn't your choice?"

"You mean children run around me in a quadrilateral with only one pair of parallel sides? Left, left, *left*!"

"*I know, Annette!*"

The eggplant house loomed before them once again, and Annette was out of the car like an arrow being fired. Up the familiar steps, one-two-three, skipping the one in the middle from long force of habit

(*futile because Mama Mac always heard her charges, no matter how late they snuck in*)

and knocking on the door. She let herself in just in time to see Caro hugging Mama Mac.

"Now you hop over and see me anytime, sweetie, and think about what I said." She paused and read Caro's latest note. "Don't worry. I'll take care of it." Then she turned, beaming. "I'm sorry to see this one go, Nettie. You bring her back for a visit once everything's settled."

"Yes, well, that could be a while. And good *God*." Annette fought the urge to fan herself. "Why do you keep it like a Yellowstone geyser in here? Look, there's actually moisture on the windows!"

Rather than acknowledging her excellent point, Mama Mac went with "Are you having any luck?"

"Oh, you want to discuss the case and not your absurdly overworked thermostat. Well, I can't fault your priorities. We've had some luck. Caro, would you go wait in the car, please? Without disappearing?"

"And thank you for reorganizing my cupboards!" Mama Mac hollered after her as the door shut. "Not that I asked, but who could refuse those big brown eyes anything?"

"Someone who isn't you?" Annette guessed.

"Didn't want to watch TV, didn't want to read. Didn't really relax until she had something to do. And look!" She opened one with a flourish, like Vanna flipping letters on *Wheel of Fortune*. "Sorted by food group and then alphabetically. Plus she scrubbed out all the drawers, even the one I was scared of, and put new contact paper in. She's a treasure."

"Glad you two had fun. Could I see that?" Annette asked, reaching for the paper. "Actually, I'll need to take all her notes for my files, so if you could just—"

"No." Mama Mac held it out of reach.

"—and I wouldn't say no to a brownie or something to tide me over in the—What?"

"Can't do it, Nettie."

Annette dropped her arm and stared. She could force the older woman, but the idea was beyond unthinkable. "This is—this is really important. Her mode of communication is admissible. In some ways it's almost better than verbal communiques. I need it all."

"I understand it's important. Do you understand I won't hand them over? I promised. And I never, ever—"

"—break a promise to a child. I understand, *dammit*."

Annette started to nibble on a knuckle, only to find her hand unceremoniously slapped. "Stop that! I'm a grown woman."

"Exactly."

"Mama, if you have knowledge of illegal activity or potential illegal activity, like abuse or—or anything like that, something Caro conveyed to you in writing, shouldn't that supersede your moral code?"

"Our moral code. But it's nothing like that. She didn't indicate where she's been or what she's done or who she thinks might come for her or any of the things you're ferreting out. If anything, she was calm as a clam."

"Clams *are* pretty calm as a rule."

"She saw me hunting in the cupboards for honey—"

"There's honey?" Annette gasped. "You could be standing there obstructing me while I was eating honey?"

"—and the next thing I knew, half my cabinet contents were all over the floor and she was trying to get me to throw away the peanut butter. Guess she doesn't like the smell, even through the jar."

"This is all singularly unhelpful."

The older woman shrugged. "Not my job to make yours easier, Nettie, but days like this I wish it was. Somebody did terrible things to that poor cub, and not just this month, either. And it started before whoever-it-was got their claws in. I'll bet you everything in my junk drawer, which only has half-a-dozen things in it now."

Annette didn't bother asking Mac how she could surmise Caro's backstory; the woman had been a foster mom for decades. "Do you want to hear something strange?"

The older woman smiled. "You and your trick questions."

"Dev—he's another one of my lambs—"

"Yes, Caro mentioned him."

Annette clenched her fists so she wouldn't yank Caro's notes out of the woman's grip. "She did, huh? Well. He said Caro was his sister. Which is impossible. But now I wonder."

"You wonder if he's her brother the way I'm your mother. You're wondering if they're siblings by choice."

"I can't shake the feeling that a lot of what's happening with Caro goes back to Dev." Annette shook her head. "Too much has happened in too short a time, and I can't figure out any of it. And I assume Caro didn't write any of *that* down, either."

"No." Uh-oh. Hands were going on hips. Eyes were narrowing. "But if she did, I wouldn't give it to you."

"You made your point, Mrs. Macropi. I'll note it for the file."

"Like that, is it?"

"No." Annette took a deep, steadying breath. "No, of course not. I'm trying to tell you I understand, but I still have to do my job."

Mama Mac waved away Annette's job. "Well, your little lost cub didn't write any of that down. It was more of an impression she gave me. I think she can barely face some of it herself. There are worse things than being snatched from your family."

Annette suppressed a shiver. Her own sleuth[2] had been smashed apart when she was about Dev's age. That had defined her adolescence and set her future in bedrock. It was difficult to imagine something even more dire and dangerous.

"What could be worse than stealing her, Mama?"

"Selling her." When Annette was silent so long, Mama added, "Speaking of selling, the Curs House is for rent again."

"It's always been a problematic place." To put it mildly. The small two-story house just down the block had been for sale for over a decade. The owner occasionally took it off the market to rent it out, and the longest any tenant had remained was four months. The tenants would get a new job. Or a new spouse. Or murdered. Or there was a fire. Or the basement flooded. Or it was taken over by possums. Annette, who didn't believe in the supernatural, was reasonably certain the place was cursed. She was not the only person in the neighborhood who felt that way. "But that's a problem for another time, and for people who aren't me."

"All right, then."

"Meanwhile, regarding the case at hand, evil will be punished," Annette vowed, although that was beyond her purview. Her responsibility was her charges' safety, not vengeance. She left that to the court.

Usually.

---

2. Sleuth of bears! Like flock of ducks, or gaggle of geese. (I LOVED RESEARCHING THIS BOOK.)

Chapter 18

ALL THE WAY TO ANNETTE'S, CARO CLUTCHED THE notebook to her chest like a lifeline, which—ugh, so cheesy—it maybe was.

"I'm not going to ask if you ate. I'm sure she stuffed you like a Christmas capon."

"What the hell is a capon?" David asked.

"A castrated male chicken that gets fattened up with milk and then devoured, often with a delectable sauce on the side. And potatoes! Lots of roasted potatoes. It's *so* good, David."

Caro, meanwhile, had looked away and then slowly caught Annette's gaze in the rearview again. Like she couldn't help herself. *If I were younger, I'd wonder if she was challenging me.*

"Why are you looking at me like that? I was never going to leave you with Mama Mac for more than a couple of hours. I just wanted to see how you interacted with people who *weren't* using you for trafficking. Plus, I live in Prescott, so the round trip would have taken too long."

A small *Hmph!* sound, and Caro looked away again. But she was smiling. A little.

"Now what?" David murmured. "And if you say right-right-*right*, I'm driving us directly into a streetlight. After I unsnap my seat belt."

"Noted. And I don't know." Back home, obviously, but then what? Seek out her boss's boss? Gomph's boss? With what? A mute trafficking survivor who refused to communicate? Lund's incriminating pictures and files? Maybe. But they only proved that Lund had incriminating pictures and files in his apartment. They didn't even prove Lund was complicit; they'd been hidden, and there was no way to prove Lund knew they were there.

Recent events indicated everyone left in the abuse cabal wanted Lund to take the blame. Going to the higher-ups would likely ensure that, because with Lund dead, everything could be tied up, stowed away, and forgotten. She could already hear the spin: That poor cub, but at least justice prevailed. Now it's time for healing.

And then the rest of the scum-sucking, law-flouting troglodytes would scatter and start again somewhere else.

Unacceptable. So…

What? A tinny voice from Annette's phone had started playing "Fuck You" by Lily Allen.

"What the hell is that?" David asked over the sound of Caro's giggling. And say hey, wasn't *that* a nice sound? Caro had a light, lilting laugh, like a Disney princess. One who could rip you to pieces at any time, possibly while giggling.

"That's Lily Allen's 'Fuck You.'" Annette clawed for her ringing phone while trying to look casual so as not to alarm the others. Pat only hit the emergency button when there was a fire. Or drop-ins intent on felony assault. Or when the fridge fell on him. She held her breath and checked the screen. "Damn and triple damn. It's Pat. Do you have any cherries in this thing?"

For reply, David reached out and flipped a switch to the left of the turn signal—

"Wait! I'm not talking about red candy!"

—and red lights began rotating from the grill.

"Siren?"

"No." She had no intention of warning the soon-to-be-disemboweled that help was coming. Pat would know that and plan for it.

David stomped the accelerator. "Trouble."

"I like how you didn't say that with an upward inflection, as a question. Just a pronouncement."

"Yeah, well. Pat doesn't strike me as the kind of guy to needlessly panic."

"That," she replied, "is putting it mildly."

Chapter 19

SMALL AND STUCK. AGAIN. AND KEEPING AWAY KEEP-ing out of the way because here came whistlers their guns weren't loud they were quieter they whistled they

(*silencers*)

whispered and now the guns were on the floor now they were wolves going for the baker they wanted their teeth in

(*Pat*)

the baker who smells like vanilla except when he smells like pine trees, the baker who ordered Dev to shift and then grabbed him by the scruff

(*ow!*)

and stuffed him in the wall into a secret part of the wall and he has to stay small and slight he has to

(*"Don't come out unless it's me or Annette!"*)

listen to the baker he has to *listen* so he can stay he has to *be a good kit* so he can sleep in a bed and not a box and he will he will he can be *so* good but the baker is losing and what if the wolves hurt him, what if they rip up his snout like those other bad wolves did? The baker is smart and swift

(*like me!*)

but there's only one baker he's alone and they're hurting him and and and he was going to be *a bad kit* he was going to help the baker because now the stench of blood and predator is everywhere the smell of something with sharp sharp teeth and long long claws and and and

Who is that?

While David tore the intruders to pieces (at least that's what it sounded like) and Caro made sure Pat and Dev were all right, Annette jacked shells into her .12 gauge trench gun. Twenty-inch barrel, six-round mag, and a place to attach a bayonet, not that she'd ever felt the urge.

She eschewed buckshot; slugs had the advantage of range, greater accuracy, would shred their target at 1,800 feet per second, and could knock a full-grown werewolf off all four paws. Slugs would also, to use the technical term, incapacitate like a bastard.

Mama Mac gave the *best* presents.

Annette stepped out of the room, socked the gun to her shoulder, fired at the leaping

(sixty pounds, six-inch bite-wound radius, four feet at the shoulder, sees the gun but tries for my carotid anyway because he is a clear IDIOT)

werewolf, and moved slightly to her left as werewolf's momentum carried him another eighteen inches while the slug rearranged his coronary arteries.

To her left came a choked snarl that was chopped short. David had pulverized the werewolf's vocal cords as he went in for the final strike. While she'd run for the gun case, he had killed the other one before he'd gotten a dozen feet from the car, now parked haphazardly

(Pat's herb garden! He'll want to fight them all over again.)

at the far end of the yard.

"Oh, hell," she said, popping the safety and inhaling. Blood, cordite, fear, blood, triumph, scones. "We live to bite another day, hurrah for us, but we've killed all our fresh leads."

Welp, as Mama Mac would say, better them than us. Then she'd bake a Bundt cake.

I would love a Bundt cake.

"Pat!" she called. "Sound off!"

"I'm good, we're all good back here! Well, not 'good,' exactly, because Dev is bad, bordering on terrible, but... Oh, never mind!"

"You okay, Annette?" David asked hoarsely. "You hurt?"

She turned to see David, all six-foot-plus of him, bloodied head to heels. He wiped his face with the back of a bloody hand, which was an exercise in futility but she'd let him figure that out on his own. His dark hair was sticking up like he'd used gore for mousse, and he was all powerful arms and broad chest and long blood-spattered muscles and, um, long...long...

Feet.

Do not gape at the man like a slack-jawed yokel, you slack-jawed yokel! Shifter nudity taboos were, by necessity, far more relaxed than anything in the Stable world.

But it still wasn't polite to stare, no matter how fine the Shifter in question was. Quite the opposite: it could be construed as a challenge.

"I'm all right. Are you?" She stepped closer, and there was no way, *no* way to stop herself from reaching out. So she didn't. "Well, hell. At least one of them got his teeth into you."

"Worth it." Now *he* stepped closer. *Don't read into it. Maybe he's worried you can't hear him from two feet away. He's so considerate!* "Are you sure you're okay?"

She looked down at the spatter across her sweater. "None of this is *my* blood, David."

"That shouldn't be as hot as it is," he said, and cupped the nape of her neck and kissed her. *Neither the time nor place,* her inner Girl Scout primly pointed out, but *damn,* the man had a nice mouth. *Mmmmm...Skittles...*

Just as suddenly, he drew back, leaving her gasping. "Sorry."

"That bad?"

He shook his head. "Christ, no. But I should've asked."

"Is that an apology?"

"No."

"Well then. This serves you right." And she kissed him back. She was pressed up against him, more blood smearing all over her sweater, and he was right—it shouldn't be so exciting. But it was. It didn't matter that she'd never shifted so as to get to the guns (three cheers for opposable thumbs!). Some urges were difficult to deny. For example, the urge to slide her hands down from the small of his back to the springy muscles of his ass, because for some reason men often had the most wonderful asses and David was walking around with a top-notch booty. It wasn't fair.

He slept here last night. He'll sleep here tonight. He doesn't have to do it alone. Be bold, dammit!

She broke the kiss. "Dammit."

"Yeah, our timing sucks. And I'm glad you're okay, and you were right to go for the shotgun, but..." He trailed off, then added shyly, "I was kinda hoping to get a look at your beast."

"Next time." She took advantage of their proximity to take a closer look at his wound, while resisting the urge to stretch up and taste the spot behind his ear. "Not deep, at least. But you've definitely got more holes in you than you did this morning."

"I'm fast, not infallible."

"Noted." Fast was an understatement. It hadn't been two minutes since they'd gotten out of the car. "Let's go check on the—"

"Okay, okay! I get it. Caro, you were supposed to drag me clear of the fight. Well, fight's over, so it's okay for me to leave the room, so you can just... Oh, goddammit!"

Annette turned in time to see Pat limping into the kitchen while Caro gently clamped her teeth around his calf to hinder his momentum. Which was adorable and only slightly nerve-racking, given what she'd done to Lund's leg the other night.

"Annette, will you tell her to step off, for the love of all that's annoying?"

She went to one knee and stretched out a hand to Caro's wolf, a beast the color of midnight with eyes like hurricane lamps. *Such unusual coloring for a gray wolf Shifter.* "Thank you so much. You did exactly right. You can let him fend for himself now."

Caro dropped the bite—not that it was much of one—and made a noise that sounded suspiciously like *Hmph!*

"Pat, are you okay?" She went to her roommate, helped him up, started feeling him for injuries. "Does this hurt? Does this? How many of me can you see? Does... *Ow!*"

"I'll slap your hand again if you keep that up. You know I'm hyperticklish. Why is there blood on your face? You didn't shift. Were you so hungry you just started biting them as a biped? Because yuck and I'll have to get to work on an intervention. There's gotta be a line, Annette, and I'm the one to draw it!"

"It's just back spatter from the shotgun," she replied in her most soothing voice.

"On your face? In the shape of fingers? Like someone grabbed your face? With their fingers? And snogged you silly?"

"Don't say 'snogged' like you're British, and can we please realign our priorities?"

"You want to talk priorities? Bad enough I'm ruining my favorite apron to shield the eyes of the tender minors in our care—"

"Pat," she said, exasperated, "literally no one cares about your dick."

"My Instagram begs to differ."

"And your apron covers precisely zero percent of your ass," she continued, "so what's the point? And what is it with men having wonderful butts?"

"What the hell are you talking about?" Pat glanced around the kitchen and living area. "And speaking of butts, where's the *other* pain in our collective ass?"

A small red-and-white bundle of fur raced toward them, which was either fortuitously timely or proof that Dev knew when to make an entrance. The werefox hit Caro square in the ribs, and she let him bowl her over. The adolescent Shifters tumbled all over the floor, mock-growling while they tussled.

"Huh." From Pat, retying his "I put out (cookies for Santa)" apron. "Is it possible they know each other?"

David snorted. "Ya think?"

Dev said they were siblings. Impossible, but they're almost certainly friends. Or at least friendly. Maybe Dev wasn't kidding when he said Caro needed him.

Annette tore herself away from one of the most adorable things she'd ever seen to address one of the hottest things she'd ever seen. "Let's get those wounds cleaned up—yours, too, Pat—and figure out another terrible plan. As for you"—she stepped forward and gave Pat a hug—"thank you. Above and beyond, as always. And I'm so sorry you landed in the middle of this."

"Stop that." But he returned the hug and even blushed a little, which she would never, ever tell him, not even if she was buried alive or starved. "You knew I had it covered."

"So you did." *I knew you'd die with your enemies' blood in your mouth. I knew you'd never quit. I just didn't know if you were in a fight you could win.* "Hey! You two! Enough!"

Werefox and werewolf froze in mid-melee. One of Dev's comically large ears was in Caro's mouth. Dev twitched the other ear, then jabbed Caro with a black paw.

"Are you kidding, Dev? I'm standing right here, and I can literally see you ignoring me! 'Enough' means shift back, we have to talk. Well. Most of us have to talk. Caro can take notes. And Pat—"

"Don't worry, we can all cover up. I have eight other aprons."

"Such a relief."

Chapter 20

Twenty minutes later

No cops. No backup. No choice. Well, two choices.

"Run or dig in?"

"Run *and* dig in," Annette replied.

"I didn't know that was an option." David had no idea why Annette sounded so confident, but what the hell, he'd stick. He'd been along for the ride since the second she found his Jolly Ranchers and laughed her ass off, which got him going, and that's when he knew: the sound of their mingled laughter was the nicest sound he'd ever heard.

And her mouth. Her ripe, sweet mouth. *Jesus.*

Bad idea, his mother said dolefully. *Think of the cubs you'll force her to ruin.*

(PLEASE shut up, Mom. Go find Dad. Or something.)

"Are you all right?"

He blinked. "Why?"

Annette was studying him. "You've got an odd look on your face, did you know?"

"How would I know that?"

"Oh. Touché."

The warwolves had no ID in their clothes, no distinguishing marks (except for the wounds showing the horrific and richly deserved manner in which they died), no visible pack affiliation, no jewelry—not a wedding ring or piercing among them—and absolutely nothing anyone could use to ID them.

"Pros. Likely sent by pros."

"How do you know that?" Dev asked, skeptical but attentive.

"Go hire a professional assassin," David ordered.

"Huh?"

"Right now. How hard can it be? There's probably an app for that. So. Go get yourself a professional killer, one you know is experienced and won't burn you if he's caught. Oh, and money. You'll need loads of it. But you can get your hands on six figures in untraceable funds anytime you want, right?"

"Well, not *six* figures…" Dev nodded. "Okay, I get you."

"You know a disturbing amount about gainfully employing random hit men, David," Pat commented. "I should be more alarmed. And I hate this thing. It itches like crazy."

"Quit it!" Dev smacked Pat's hand away from the fresh bandage on his upper arm. "It won't get better if you pick at it."

"Oh, that *did not* just happen," Pat growled, hazel eyes taking on a yellowish gleam for a few seconds.

"If this was a regular case"—David paused while they all snorted—"we could run their DNA. But even then, I'm not sure these guys would show up in the system."

"Well, t'ain't a regular case, is it?" Pat declared. "So what do we do?"

"We?"

"Don't say 'we, derp,' like you're flabbergasted at the notion of me getting involved. I've *been* involved. You want to see my fucking bite marks again? Worse, they shot up my kitchen. My *kitchen*, David!"

"Hey! They also tried to kill me. Well, maybe. All right, I was probably gonna be collateral damage, but they came to kill Caro for sure!" Dev insisted, poking his friend for emphasis.

"My fruit bowl was decimated! Shards of ceramic and kiwi and grapefruit fucking everywhere, and you *know* that shit will dry all sticky and gross and cleanup will be a bitch!"

David held his hands up. *Please let me be several miles away before Pat finds out what they did to his herb garden.* "Okay, Pat. Got it. I just… I know Annette wants to keep you safe is all. I don't doubt you've got balls to spare."

"And I'd also like us to go one entire day without a discussion about my balls."

Annette covered Dev's ears so quickly the kit let out a surprised yelp. "Inappropriate!"

"But," David continued doggedly, "a sensible person would be halfway to the Manitoba woodlands by now, and maybe you should think abou—"

"Don't you *ever* imply I'm sensible again," Pat replied shortly, flicking his hair back and (inadvertently?) showing his scar for a second. David took that to mean the discussion was closed. "Besides, Annette wants to keep everybody safe all the time."

"Then she's in the wrong line of work," David replied.

"You two recall that I'm in the room, yes?"

Room was an exaggeration. They were in Pat's studio, a small structure about half a mile from the main house, one you couldn't see from ground level until you were right on top of it. After everyone had cleaned up, they'd followed Pat down the back hill, hooked a left by the river, and found the small gray dwelling shaped like a grain silo. No, wait…it *was* a grain silo.

They'd abandoned the corpses.

"Look, we're not going to be rogues forever. It's probably just through the weekend. We're pro-tem rogues. We've done nothing wrong, it was clearly self-defense. But it'll look worse for us if we try to hide the bodies or undertake any cleanup."

"I'm not getting you. At all."

"Pat, we'll eventually be able to tell the authorities everything."

David saw Caro flinch a bit at "authorities."

"Killing warwolves to keep Caro and Dev safe will fly," Annette continued, "and not calling the cops tonight will fly—the higher-ups won't like it, but they'll get it. But not if we try to cover it up."

"Good point. I can hear it now: 'If you were so sure you did nothing wrong, then why did you try to cover up your heinous gross crime, you disgusting reprobates?' 'But it wasn't a crime, it was self-defense.' 'Objection!' 'Sustained. I find the scumbag defendants guilty and sentence them to a hot date with a chamber full of nitrogen gas.'"

"Thanks for the trial recap," she replied dryly. "All right, so…we need a new plan. Once we found Caro—"

"That's some beaucoup bullshit right there." Pat waved a piece of paper in her face. "Caro said she sat on David's car and waited for you, and after an eternity—"

"Less than an hour, actually."

"—you stumbled over her. In broad daylight. Because she was waiting for you. In broad daylight."

"Oh, so Pat gets notes, too?" Annette threw up her hands. "I'm feeling somewhat excluded here, Caro."

Caro gave her a sucks-to-be-you shrug in response. David had to admit, the kid had the most expressive shrugs he'd ever seen. She could probably write a thesis with those shoulders.

To get into the repurposed grain silo, Pat had to key in a code and a thumbprint, and that only gave them access to part of the building. There were more security measures to go underground. David had been on air force bases that weren't as stringent about security. "Whoa."

Annette smirked. "Soft. Not stupid. Remember?"

"Christ, the smirk."

"I've earned this smirk."

"So you have." *You're even pretty when you're being smug, dammit.*

"Holy crap, you're Batman!" Dev murmured, goggling at the studio setup. "How much money-*dinero-argent* do you *make*?"

Family money, she'd said.

"Remember? Don't go into social services for the money."

Pat helped with the renovations, she'd said. Which was why this was Pat's studio and not "their" studio. What did the guy even do? Besides organic gardening? Which he'd started yesterday?

The building was corrugated galvanized steel on the outside, like any silo, with broad windows cut along the side, unlike any silo. The windows all faced south, keeping heating costs low (for Minnesota, at least), while the main floor had a small kitchen, a living–dining area with couch and chairs and table, and three deep cubbies in the side. Each held a twin mattress and two pillows, with a curtain that could be pulled for privacy.

The floor was crimson rubber, which was practical *and* looked nice, and the interior walls were painted tan with red accents. Virtually all the furniture was curved, and David couldn't begin to think what that must have cost. Had to be custom, and he had an idea why a steel building meant solely to store grain in bulk had been refurbished like this, then beefed up with security.

Pat led them downstairs, and the space underground was large, open, and stark: just an architect's table and some counter space (curved, of course). The first thing Pat had done was show Caro his sketch pads, easels, pens, pencils, chalks, paints, other paints, still more paints, and tons of other artist junk. "You're welcome here to talk anytime," he said, and Caro nodded and reached for a pad.

"What about me?"

"Dev, you're welcome here also. I just didn't know if you'd be into art."

"Oh. Okay."

"Plus," Pat added, "there's the fact that you can talk, so you don't have to rely on art supplies to get your point across."

"I can do art! I will art all over this place if you don't watch out."

"Stop making art a verb," Pat commanded. Meanwhile, Caro had scribbled something and showed it to him. Pat read it, reached for *his* pad, and wrote something in return.

"Why are you doing it that way?" Annette asked, puzzled. "You can talk."

Pat sighed and wrote something that got a smirk out of Caro. He showed it to Annette:

This is why bears are goddamned savages.

And out loud: "It's polite to talk to a guest in their own language. It's called class, you shaggy-haired cretin."

"I do *not* have... Well, I might be a bit overdue for a trim."

"I'd hoped my residual class would have rubbed off on you—"

"Rude."

"—but you just suck it in," Pat lamented, "like a classless black hole from which nothing can escape, including class."

"*You're* a classless black hole," she muttered like a kid getting ready to pout. David could guess what was bugging her. (Besides the stress of multiple attacks in a shockingly short time, which anyone would find off-putting.) He'd noticed over time that people liked Annette and trusted her, more or less on sight. Even the hardest, sad-dest survivors. Even the most nitpicky of supervisors. Even the most enraged of carfentanil users.

Caro, though? She was making Annette work for it.

"Well, your terrible plan worked, at least. What?" Pat asked. "Why are you looking at each other but not me?"

"Because as it turns out, our plan was moot."

"Did you tell the dead guys in our kitchen it was moot?"

"Sorry, I'll clarify. We did not get a chance to imple-ment it. We only told my boss we had Caro, but not where. We never even mentioned my house. And frankly, I would be surprised to learn that my boss retained any part of that conversation."

"So…what?"

"So only one person knew Caro was here." She turned to David. "Knows."

"Yep."

"I'm lost," Dev confessed.

"It's awful, but I guess you were right about Judge Gomph," she added, stricken. "I'm sorry I didn't give your theory any merit."

"What's a Gomph?" Pat asked.

"A guy the size of a piano with a superdeep voice who eats salad out of buckets," Dev said. "*Big* buckets. You've gotta see it to believe it."

"Judge for the juvie courts," David replied. "Looks like he might have something to do with the abuse Caro had to live through. He gave Annette permission to be *parens familia* for three days, but now it's looking like he was just isolating Caro so he could get rid of her."

Pat's eyes went big. "A fucking *judge* sent those guys?"

Before Annette could answer, the phone on the wall rang.

"Jeez, there's a cord sticking out of it and everything," Dev marveled. "That's not old school. That's prehistoric school."

"Landlines have their uses," Annette said.

"And fewer than half-a-dozen people have the number for that particular landline," Pat added. "And since my dad only calls on Labor Day, or when he needs bail or rehab, odds are it's for one or both of you two."

David could see Annette hesitate before picking up the red receiver, could almost hear her wondering *What fresh hell is this?* while she answered.

"Hello? Oh! Nadia, you won't believe what… *Ow.*" She held the phone a couple of inches away. "Nadia? Nadia? Nadia? Caaaaaaalm down… I can't understand a word you're… Can you even hear me? Nadia… I think you're going supersonic, Nadia, or would it be subsonic?"

"Who is it?" Dev asked with faux innocence.

"Nadia, I'm just going to hold the phone further away from my beleaguered ear canal… Nadia? And wait for you to finish or pass out from lack of oxygen, and we'll go from there."

Which was what happened. David was genuinely amazed: who knew Nadia could squawk and shriek an unbroken litany of complaints, reprimands, and profanity for well over three minutes? *Does Guinness keep track of stuff like this? Because they should.*

Finally: "I understand. We're on our way...: I... *Yes.* And just for the record, I'm s—annnd she hung up." She turned to David. "There's trouble at the—"

"Old mill? Lead the way, girl!"

"Kindly rot in hell, Pat. There's trouble at United. And Gomph's looking for us."

"Looking for us hard, or just ranting?"

"Both? That's when Nadia began to get especially incoherent. She said something about Oz, too. Look!" Annette held up a trembling hand. "I'm still shaking."

"Then we'd better get our rogue butts in gear." David paused and took a last look around the snug chamber. "Is this what dig in *and* run meant?"

"Of course."

"The best part is, even if it's underground, it's a lot warmer than the main house."

"Pat. We've been over this," Annette said in the tone of the long-suffering. "The main house isn't chilly."

"The thermostat up there is permanently set to sixty-three. You've basically turned your house into a satellite of the polar circles."

"I have not!"

"I am positive," Pat said to David, "that if she was wearing a sweater and I locked her in a freezer, she'd ditch the sweater."

"At least I'm not a slave to my hypothalamus." At their blank stares, she added, "The body's thermostat." Still nothing. "The cold doesn't bother me, all right? It didn't bother anyone in my family. My folks lived in Alaska for years before we came here. And the cold shouldn't bother you guys, either."

"Gotta be a werebear thing," Pat guessed. "This time of year, all her systems are telling her to load up on protein, hoard chocolate, stop shaving her legs, and get ready to hibernate beneath her Pottery Barn comforters."

"That's offensive," she snapped. "That's like me saying all werefoxes are born troublemakers. Obviously, that's a gross…" She glanced around, eyes narrowing as she realized no one was arguing the generalization. "Oh, come on!"

David cleared his throat. "I think we're getting off—"

"Dammit, if you're cold, grow fur! *We can all grow fur.*"

"Just admit you're trying to give us hypothermia! Very, very slowly. It's like the reverse of when you try to burn someone out. You're gradually freezing us out. Admit it!" Pat demanded. "You'll feel better."

She groaned, seized David's shoulder, ignored his surprised yelp, and started propelling him toward the stairs. "Enough. If the syndicate is dumb enough to send more foot soldiers, they'll never get in here in time. The big house isn't safe—"

"I'll say. It's a goddamned frigid tundra up there."

"—even if it's stuffed with snacks. Which it is. Which we can't get at." Annette sighed, no doubt wondering if her potato chip bags were still intact. "There are snacks here, but only a day's worth. So."

"Yeah, well, the big house is also stuffed with rapidly cooling corpses," Dev pointed out, "so we're good down here."

"I'm glad to hear it," Annette replied, "because you're stuck here for the duration."

"We all are," Pat said. "Trapped like bugs under a glass, slowly dying."

"That's the spirit."

Before she could elaborate, a howl from the house split the air.

"Oh shit," Dev breathed. "The dead warwolves brought reinforcements!"

"Worse," Annette said glumly. To David: "Come on. He'll just keep yelling until we come out."

Chapter 21

"THIS IS THE POLAR OPPOSITE OF STAY AWAY," ANNETTE muttered. Then, louder as they climbed the hill to the big house: "Do you hear me, Oz? Polar. Opposite!"

The werewolf up top watched them approach, so still he could've been mistaken for a statue save for the breeze ruffling his fur. He had typical *Canis rufus* coloring: reddish fur on legs and belly, fading to tawny on his flanks, face fur a pale gold, bright-green eyes standing out from the white markings around his muzzle. His ears were large and alert, ringed in red fur, and twitched as they approached.

"Jesus," David muttered. Oz's beast was lanky and lean, the tips of his furred red ears a good four inches above Annette's waist. Like a greyhound, if greyhounds had accounting degrees and could bite through femurs.

"Why are you here?" Annette had breezed past Oz and was stomping around, gathering up the man's clothes which he'd removed so quickly there were rips throughout the fabric. "Is there nothing that needs doing in Accounting? How is that possible? The end of the fiscal year is only a few months away!"

Oz growled in reply, which raised the hackles on the back of David's neck.

Don't! It's not an actual threat display! This from his late mother, sounding more panicked than usual. She was right, though David was preeeeeeetty sure he could take the wolf. Probably couldn't outrun him, though—definitely a fun fact to keep in mind.

Oz was still growling when he shifted back. "Gggggggrrrrrrreally, Annette? There's a bunch of dead guys in your house, but you wanna talk fiscal year-end? First, that's almost six months from now, and second, *dead guys in your house.*"

"I have the situation under control!" Annette punctuated her declaration by shoving Oz's ripped clothing into his arms.

Oz shoved them back. "Again, dead guys. In your house! Christ, I thought you were hurt! Or worse!"

"I'm fine. We're all fine. And the operative word is 'dead,' Oz." Another shove. "*Don't* give these back to me. This is already ridiculous beyond words."

David cleared his throat while Annette's bear went nose to nose with Oz's wolf. "Uh."

"I'm not that malnourished fourteen-year-old anymore, Annette. It's not your job to look out for me anymore. It's my job."

"I know that," she snapped back.

"Guys?"

"Except you don't know that, because you're neck deep in something—bad enough—but you seem equally engaged in keeping me clear of it, which is just dumb and shortsighted and, frankly, a little hurtful."

"*You're* dumb and shortsighted." Annette sighed, then added, "I know. Not my best comeback. Listen. It's not just the safety issues. This job will break your heart, Oz. Stay in Accounting, where everything is numbers and air-conditioning and a break room that smells like fresh bread."

"You guys?" David waited until they both looked at him. "We're doing this in the open and Oz is naked and a bunch of warwolves tried to kill us and, like Oz said… corpses. I know you don't get a lot of traffic out here, Annette, but this is just begging for trouble."

"You're right." To Oz: "Piles of corpses aside, David and I have things under control."

David nodded in semisolidarity, hoping he wore the expression of a man with everything under control.

"And so," Annette concluded with a gesture toward the house, "you can go. You can even borrow something of Pat's because you were in such a hurry to butt in where you weren't needed that you didn't take the time to disrobe properly so I'm sure you could grab a T-shirt or something but I can tell by the look on your face that you're not inclined to do any of that."

"No, you well-meaning nimrod!" Oz roared.

"Just as well. Pat would've had a fit. No one treats their clothes worse than he does, but God forbid someone *else* should accidentally—"

"Look!" David called. "I've turned around, and I'm walking back down to the studio. Where people can't see us. And even if they did, it'd take them forever to breach. See? Why don't you guys follow me? Just for fun. Just to see what happens next." He wasn't looking, but he could feel Annette roll her eyes, and

(hallelujah)

heard them fall into step behind him, Oz grumbling a bit as he stepped on a sharp rock.

"Should've kept your socks on," Annette snickered. Which was a pretty great mental image, TBH.

"Annette, I'm not here just to butt...to help. I think I found something. That's the reason I came. I wasn't even sure you'd be home."

"Technically I wasn't, Oz," she pointed out.

"But I couldn't just do nothing."

"Disagree."

"And then, the second I got out of my car I could smell blood, so..."

"So you jettisoned good sense and are fortunate you weren't killed, and then what would I tell Mama Mac?"

Oz laughed. "You've just described the week you're having. And what would *I* tell her?"

And then, behind him, a sound that was quickly becoming David's favorite thing: Annette Garsea, surprised into a giggle.

––––––––––––

"I don't know what this Lund guy was up to, but he had twenty-two bank accounts, eleven shell corporations, no attorney of record, and his favorite hobby was buying worthless property and hanging onto it, no matter how much or fast it decreased in value."

Not his favorite hobby, David thought.

"I mean, sure, you can legitimately use them for tax avoidance purposes or to get different kinds of financing—hello, Bill Gates!—but *this* guy's setup? Is weird. The methodology is *way* off. And everybody knows that it's just a hop, skip, and a pounce from tax avoidance to outright evasion, right?" Taking in their blank expressions, Oz added, "Don't worry, I'll take you through it."

"That only makes me worry *more*," Dev said.

"Aw, don't be intimidated, you guys! I know forensic accounting sounds sexy—"

Annette made a sound awfully like a snort.

"—but it's pretty straightforward. And I'm all up to date on my certified-forensic-accountant continuing ed, so don't worry about that. So! There are shell corporation and there are shell corporations—"

"I'm already lost," David admitted. Caro was, too, maybe. She'd taken one look at Oz and retreated to one of the bedroom cubbies, twitched the curtain shut for privacy, and hadn't made a peep since. *Poor cub.* David had seen such behavior before. Caro might be uneasy around unfamiliar males and/or unfamiliar werewolves for the rest of her life. He counted himself lucky that, for whatever reason, she didn't absent herself from his presence. He and Oz were different builds and different subspecies...maybe that was it.

"So, so lost." Annette reached out and gave David's hand a squeeze (assurance? sympathy?), then dropped it just as quickly. A sideways glance showed her intent on Oz's lecture. Maybe she couldn't help herself, just had to touch him, however briefly. *Yeah, right.* "So, so, so, so lost," he added.

"Hang on, I'm explaining! So this guy Lund, he had money all over the place. And shells for shelters, like I said. But the setup's all wrong. None of them are in the Caymans, for example. They're all smack in the middle of huge metropolitan areas. That's missing the point right there! And then there's his property. Warehouses, sure, but right on the floodplain? Just to insure them properly would cost more than the buildings are worth. Not to mention accounting stuff accounting stuff shell companies and more accounting jargon, and then jargon jargon, accounting stuff, and more jargon. Right?"

All this while Oz, clad in one of Pat's aprons (black, with white lettering: THIS SHIT IS GOING TO BE DELICIOUS) and nothing else, prowled around an easel holding an enormous sketch pad. He'd occasionally dart back to it and scribble more nonsense. Sometimes he would draw a box around the nonsense. And arrows pointing to the nonsense.

Annette, at least, seem to be grasping some of the lecture, thank Christ. "So you're saying Lund was exceptionally shady. To the nth degree."

"Incredibly fucking shady, yep."

"But nothing straight-up illegal. Just an occasional gray area."

"That's right." Oz sighed and capped the marker. "It's just…I can't think of a legit reason for this random guy to have twenty-two accounts and eleven shell companies."

"Okay. That's… Well, I don't know what that is. But

I'm sure it'll be helpful." There was a long, almost excruciating pause, and then Annette added, "Thank you, Oz."

"See? Toldja I could help you. Next time, let me in right away. I don't have time to chase you all over town."

"Don't spoil it, Oz."

Chapter 22

"SO WE'RE NOT GOING TO TALK ABOUT IT."

"No, we are not."

David shrugged. "Fine."

"Good."

"We've got bigger things to worry about," he added.

"Duh." Annette groaned. "Sorry. This happens when I hang around Pat and Oz too long. I'll rephrase: Oz has hidden depths, and trying to keep him out of this is looking more and more like a critical error."

"Sure. Sure. That. Yep."

"Oh." Annette blinked at him. "Oh! You were referencing our bloodlust-fueled mack session."

"Aw. It sounds super romantic when you put it like that."

"I think we've both made it clear there's nothing romantic about anything the two of us are doing right now."

Ow. "Noted. Now, about Oz—you gonna let him put his paws in now?"

"Clearly I can't keep his paws *out*," she replied dryly. "So yes." When they'd left the studio, Pat was rummaging for something besides an apron for Oz to wear out on the town, while Oz pledged to keep digging, which was great for their case. Though David hoped to God he wouldn't have to sit through another forensic accounting lecture when it was over.

"And what was Nadia squawking about?"

"Our crippling stupidity and carelessness."

"Sounds about right. Speaking of, maybe it's time for burners." He'd shut his phone off yesterday and wouldn't turn it back on anytime soon. In all the excitement, he'd forgotten to suggest Annette do the same.

"Out here, maybe," she replied, waving at the city-scape as they approached the hospital. "But cell phone signals don't work so well in Pat's studio. The chance of someone tracking us in there are beyond slim."

"And out here?"

"Well. Don't we want them to? Isn't our new terrible plan awfully like the old one? Except we're now dodging Judge Gomph? Or are we *not* dodging him?" She turned in her seat to face David, nibbling a thumbnail while she thought out loud. "Is this when we concoct a scheme to trick Gomph into incriminating himself, and then the forces of good will pounce, punish him, and exonerate us?"

"You're asking me?"

"Well, David, since we aren't discussing that devastating kiss, I guess we're back to the necessary routine of saving Caro and Dev and, subsequently, our jobs."

"Devastating, huh?"

"Don't read into it," she warned. Then, pensively: "What the hell am I supposed to say to Gomph when I see him? 'How could you?' 'Were you always evil, or is it something new you're trying?' 'It's no use protesting, you're the only one who knew where Caro was, now get the hell out and take your gavel with you and on your way out, please rot in hell forever?'"

And now, the tricky bit. He cleared his throat. "There's one other person who knew."

"Yes, but I've decided to trust you."

"That's not what I... You really thought I might be in on it?" He was equal parts hurt and pleased. *Maybe not so soft after all.*

"I considered the possibility. But you've had ample opportunities to kill all of us."

"Maybe I'm biding my time."

"Maybe you're not that stupid."

"Thanks! I think. But there's someone else who could have guessed Caro was going to your place."

Annette frowned. "Bob doesn't count. I wasn't kidding when I said I'd be astonished if he recalled anything other than the Secret Santa nonsense. He couldn't have... Dammit."

"Yeah."

He'd hated to say it, so he was relieved when she made the same leap of logic he had. If she couldn't stand the idea of Judge Gomph trafficking in brutalized kids, or, at best, abetting traffickers of brutalized kids, she'd probably vomit blood at the thought of Nadia brutalizing kids.

For his part, he wasn't sure. Nadia was a pain in the ass, yeah. A snob and a half, and high maintenance AF, but so? Plenty of people were into that. Probably.

But into what Lund was into? That was a leap. She'd helped them break into his apartment. He thought she was going to cry when she saw the photos. God knows he nearly did, and he thought he'd seen everything.

"No. David, no. We've worked together for years. And that brittle I'm-above-you-peons act of hers? Is an act. She might not love the kids, but she *hates* the abusers. She'd never countenance this. And don't forget—she's the one who reminded us that we're supposed to be better than Stables."

"Yes, it was very convincing."

Annette just looked at him. "You don't know her. Now sit down—"

"I'm driving! You can see me driving! Why wouldn't I be sitting down?"

"—and I'm going to tell you why Nadia's not the villain in this piece. See, a couple of years ago, when we first started working together—"

"Wait until I'm sitting down."

"Good heavens! There's a tiny child down there!"

Annette stepped past Nadia and squinted, but on her best day she couldn't see as well as Nadia on her worst. She could make out a flash of red among the rocks, brush, and stunted trees, but not much else. And she couldn't see any movement at all.

"Alive?" She flared her nostrils, relieved she couldn't scent any decay.

"Shall we find out?"

"That's rhetorical, I think. Because you're naked by now, aren't you? I'm going to turn around and you are going to be naked. I think that's a new speed record."

Nadia didn't reply, as she was too busy sprouting feathers and talons, and then she swooped past Annette's shoulder, climbed, circled, then folded her wings and arrowed toward the red blob. Which was amusing for several reasons, not least because the woman had just been complaining about the "unbearably frigid" fall weather (sixty degrees and sunny, or, as Annette's mother used to call it, swimsuit weather).

They'd decided to spend their lunch break at Minnehaha Park, a break they were drawing out so as to avoid the office, and Bob, and the Secret Santa madness. "It's September!" Annette had practically screamed. "Fifteenth!" This while Nadia texted lewd emoticons to everyone in the office, then pretended she hadn't hit Group Send on purpose.

Fleeing to a park had been the only sane response to such madness. And they were apparently the only ones on the grounds who weren't park employees. They hadn't seen or scented anyone else during their walk, nor had they run across anyone frantically searching for a missing child wearing something red. Which did not bode well, for unsavory reasons.

It was an unlikely place for a fall, she thought as she waited for Nadia. There were several warning signs posted along the trail, complete with a symbol of a genderless cartoon figure helplessly cartwheeling over a cliff, presumably to its death, and a slope that clearly led to a steep drop. It was also a *nasty* place for a fall. The ravine was at least forty feet deep, with unforgiving boulders and nothing to cushion a plummet but rocks and dead brush.

If someone threw a bag of puppies down there, I will be very. Fucking. Irritated. And if someone threw a... Good God, it hardly bears thinking about.

Nadia reappeared beside her and shifted back in midair, landing lightly (and nudely) on her feet, ice-blue eyes bright in her flushed face. "She's alive! Knocked about and bloody, and she's got a horrid forehead gash that will need stitching, poor darling. But she hasn't been down there long. She doesn't seem to be dehydrated, and she's no more than two or three years old, poor clumsy child."

"I'll call 9-1-1."

"And she's a Stable," Nadia warned.

"I figured." If the child had been a Shifter, she likely would have shifted from instinct if nothing else. And it was likely her other self would have been far better equipped to await rescue, or even gotten out on her own. "Should I try to get down there? Help you bring her up?"

"We don't have the appropriate equipment, and I worry we might cause her further injury. I'll keep her company so she doesn't thrash about. She thinks I'm a magical eagle who gives rides to fairies in the woods."

"Well, there's really nothing to disprove that."

"You're *so* charming when you care to take the trouble."

Nadia preened. "But you stay here. I know you're tough, Annette, but it's really quite steep and you're awfully, ah… What's the opposite of 'light on your feet'?"

"I don't know, what's the opposite of 'not condescending at all'?"

"I'm sure you can figure it out if you think about it for a bit."

"I see what you did there!" Annette hollered as Nadia shifted and swooped back down. She gathered the woman's clothes in a tidy bundle and called Emergency Services, reporting an injured minor who needed rescuing, with a possible concussion and broken bones.

Then there was little to do but wait and wonder if, on the way back, she could talk Nadia into stopping by Milkjam Creamery for Thai Tea ice cream cones. Which would only happen if they didn't have to answer too many awkward questions about how they happened to notice a girl child alive at the bottom of a ravine no one could see into or reach without mountaineering equipment.

That was the trickier side of their work and always had been. She and her kind were outnumbered thousands to one; it was a simple fact of life as well as population statistics. So when a Shifter needed an ambulance or was robbed or had to report a missing person, odds were the person or persons who came to help were going to be Stable.

So right there, they had to be careful what they said and did. Most of her kind preferred to deal privately with such problems: hire a Shifter private eye, go to a Shifter physician, hire a Shifter accountant to explain why romping through a forest at midnight was deductible.

IPA was the only all-Shifter government agency in existence, as far as she knew. Perhaps they would eventually have their own police precincts and schools. Oh, but that sounded bad, 1960s bad: separate but equal.

Except plenty of Shifters *didn't* think Stables were equal. Some of the most intelligent people she'd ever known viewed Stables with pity and condescension at best, animals at worst, locked into one shape, never evolving, just wallowing in their destructive instincts. Her own father had explained it rather crudely when she was a child: "A six-week-old puppy knows not to shit where she eats. Stables still haven't figured that one out."

And always, always hanging over their heads was the constant fear of discovery by the wider world of Stables, the most rapacious, destructive predators in the history of the planet.

One thing at a time. Focus on what's in front of you. So to speak. Good advice, and not a moment too soon. Behind her, from the south, she could hear a small group approaching. Not running or shouting, and it was too early for the paramedics. So, then: park visitors. Two males and a female.

No, she realized when all three of them blanched when they saw her. Not visitors. Or, at least, not there *just* to visit.

"Hey!" the taller man barked. "What are you doing?"

Rude. "Watching."

The taller one lowered his head and stepped forward, pushing with his shoulders like he was trying to get through a crowd. "What's going on?"

"A rescue operation," she replied pleasantly. "Isn't that good news?"

"A rescue?" The woman, small and slight, with dark-blond hair pulled into a ponytail, was cupping her elbows in both hands. "But why? There's, um, there's no one down there."

"Of course there is."

"*No*, there isn't." This from the smaller male.

"There's no need to take my word for it. Oh, and that's a lovely jailhouse tattoo. The tears aren't filled in, though. Does it signify time served, or people you tried to kill? Well, it's not important." She gestured to the edge of the ravine. "Peek for yourself."

He crossed his arms over his chest. "There's nobody down there."

"It's odd that you know that. And you're so definitive! So then, prove me wrong. How about you step over here and take a look?"

"How about you fuck the fuck off—"

"Fuck the fuck off? How would one even begin to fuck the fuck off?"

"—and mind your own business?" This from the larger, bulked-up male, who made the mistake many such men did: he assumed that hours in the gym made him an authority figure.

"I'm fine right here." She could see them more clearly now, hear them better. She was hyperaware that there was little to no wind, and that she had the sun at her back, and that the three of them smelled like fear, heavily spiked with aggression. She could feel her pulse pick up in response as she filtered the data: shocked to see her. No running or shouting. Quick to assure her that there was Nothing To See Here. Trying to drive her off with a threat display. Absolutely would not walk up to the edge.

"You dumped her, didn't you? Or she fell because you weren't paying attention, and you got the hell out so you wouldn't get in trouble. The latter, I'm guessing, given that you smell like happy hour in a dive bar and haven't brought help back with you. Chicken wings and Budweiser with just a smidge of meth. Jesus wept."

"Shut the fuck up."

"And you." She nodded at the woman who wouldn't look at her. "You talked them into coming back, didn't you? But only to reassure yourself there was no saving her. Then you could resume your life, presumably with one or both of these men, with minimal guilt."

Tell them there's an ambulance coming? One likely followed by a police unit?

No. They might run.

"They're my husband and my brother," she burst out, glancing at both men, then looking away. "We grew up together."

"Lorraine, shut the fuck *up*."

"We're family," she gasped, and fell silent beneath the larger man's glare.

"Family." *I may vomit. Yes, I really think I might. And I would hate to lose that outstanding banh mi I had for lunch.* "And your daughter?"

"She's, uh, I mean, she's mine. Not, um—"

"Oh Christ." Annette rubbed her forehead. "You got pregnant by another man while your husband was inside. Now he's out and he doesn't want any cuckoos in his nest."

"What?"

"This is your Big Test of True Love. Get rid of your daughter, and you can all go back to being the Terrible Musketeers."

Before she could elaborate, or kick someone, there was the sound of furiously beating wings as Nadia shot out of the ravine and soared above them, hoarsely screaming what Annette assumed was the red kite equivalent of "you all suck."

"Oh, look! I found my bird. That's twice! I should buy a lottery ticket. I just keep finding things. Isn't that lucky? Oh, good *God*." The two men had their heads together, while the woman stayed on the outside of their little group, studying the horizon like she'd never seen it before. "You're trying to figure out if you should toss me over the side or run away. Or both. And I'll be honest, I'm rooting for options one or three."

Their eyes widened, and she realized she was grinning at them so broadly her cheeks hurt.

("Sometimes...when you do that...you look like you have a thousand teeth." Pat, blood pouring from the six-inch slash down his face, both of them trying to keep their balance on the slick floor; he didn't pass out until she dragged him across the threshold to the ER.)

Before she could say anything else, Nadia swooped in to land. Annette obligingly stuck out her arm so Nadia wouldn't feel the need to roost on one of the men's skulls. "Gorgeous, isn't she?"

"What the fuck is *that*?"

"Stop that, you'll hurt her feelings. She's... *Ack!*" Annette brushed the feathers away from her face as Nadia displayed her six-foot wingspan. "The poor thing was a helpless, hideous bag of bones and feathers when I found... *Ow!* Dammit, Nadia! I've only worn this sweater twice!"

Q. Why didn't I wrap her skirt around my arm as a shield?

A. Because I'm an idiot.

"Jesus fucking Christ!"

Annette glanced over at the smaller man. "Oh, don't look at me like you've never seen someone in a public park using a raptor to hunt small game."

"*What?*"

Nadia's wings fluttered as she stomped up and down Annette's arm, further destroying her sweater. "Small game. Rabbits, shrews, voles, chicken nuggets. She loves 'em all. She is a fiend for shrews! And honey mustard dip. Winter's coming, she has to fatten up for... *Ow!*"

The smaller man approached, indicating true bravery or abject stupidity, and made shooing motions at a deeply unimpressed Nadia while Annette held back her snort. The larger one had chosen option one (or three) and came right for Annette, doubtless planning to punch her into compliance if the balled fists were any indication, then toss her into the ravine to keep his stepdaughter company until they died of thirst or exposure.

So she broke his jaw.

Nadia, meanwhile, had arrowed straight for the smaller one, and his shrieks were louder than hers. His arms windmilled as he tried batting her beak and talons away from his face, and Annette (almost) sympathized. A hawk didn't look like much from a distance, but in a full-on attack, all the prey can see and hear and feel are the furiously beating wings and screaming and slashing of a predator with an unbreakable grip and a beak like a razor. It was so sudden and painful and disorienting, the prey would run in any direction to get away, which is why he plunged over the edge and into the ravine.

Please God he doesn't land on the kid.

The disgruntled stepfather, meanwhile, had gotten to his feet and stood, swaying, as he considered his options while blood dripped down his jaw. He took a last look at the scene and turned away.

"Wait! Jason, don't leave me!"

"Yes, Jason." Annette kicked the back of his knee *(a fine day to wear sturdy pointed flats)* tearing his tendon and sending him to the ground.

"Don't leave her. Look at what she was willing to do for you."

Nadia let out a high-pitched cry, and though Annette didn't speak red kite, it wasn't difficult to figure out what was coming.

She sidestepped the yelping stepfather and approached Lorraine, who backed away until she tripped over a rock and sat down hard enough to bite her lip. Annette's nostrils involuntarily flared at the scent of new blood. "I...I won't say anything, I swear. About you *or* your big weird bird." Lorraine flinched as Nadia screeched a reprimand. "I'll just... We're sorry. I'm sorry. Your—your eyes are... Your eyes are all wrong. What's wrong with... I'm sorry."

"No. That's not what I'm looking for. I don't care about your apology." Annette knelt beside her. "The paramedics and the police will be in this clearing in the next sixty seconds or so. I want you to tell them everything. *Everything.* Whose idea, who pushed or abandoned her, or pushed *and* abandoned her, and whatever follow-up bullshit course you were embarking on, and I want you to finish your story with how you decided to surrender to the authorities to alleviate your crippling guilt."

She was nodding so hard her ponytail flopped. "I will! I'll tell them, I promise, you don't have to worry, okay? Okay?"

"I'm not worried. We've got your scent now. We can always find you. So please trust me when I say living in a cage for a couple of years is preferable to meeting us in the open."

"Okay. I'll... Okay. I'll do it. Don't touch me, okay? Please don't touch me. I'll do it. I swear on my life."

"You are, actually." A bit of an exaggeration, but she wasn't going to clue Lorraine in to that. Annette wasn't in the habit of running around murdering abusive Stables. No one at IPA was. Though they'd certainly been tempted. "Run along, Lorraine. But not too far. Just up to the edge. Just to see what you've done." And as Lorraine just sat there, paralyzed, Annette leaned in. "*Now.*"

She stepped aside while Lorraine scooted past her to peer into what was supposed to be her daughter's grave, as well as her brother's rest stop. Now she could see as well as hear the first responders pushing their way through the trees; in a few more seconds, they'd hit the clearing. Fortunately, Annette had been holding Nadia's clothes throughout the confrontation, so she headed down the opposite path while Nadia swooped in close

"Dammit! You've got to ruin *both* sides of my sweater?"

and perched for a ride, content to wait for the best opportunity to shift back.

"I don't know about you, but I need a vacation," Annette muttered. "That wasn't even the worst lunch break we've had this month. Which is insane. And now we have to keep an eye out for police reports and local news coverage. More obsessively than usual, I mean, in case there's a damage control issue. But first, we should fortify ourselves with ice cream. Don't glare at me, you love Milkjam as much as I do."

Rabid Bald Eagle Attacks Drunken Campers, *Star Tribune*

Toddler Found in Ravine Expected to Recover; Claims Magical Eagle Fairy Saved Her, *Star Tribune*

Man Indicted for Attempted Murder Claims 'Shaggy-Haired Crazy Bird Lady' Attacked Him with Eagle, *Pioneer Press*

Chapter 23

"THE HEADLINES WERE THE WORST PART. FOR US, I mean," Annette added. "Wrong subspecies, obviously. And do eagles even get rabies? Isn't it confined to mammals? And 'shaggy'? I'd gotten a haircut two weeks earlier!"

"'We've got your scent now'?"

"What was I supposed to say? 'If we're ever in the same restaurant, I might be able to pick up your scent but maybe not' didn't sound nearly so scary."

David snorted. "Good point. Did you tell anyone? Or get in trouble?"

"Yes. And no. We didn't go after Shifters, so Bob didn't care. Which is horrible, by the way," she added. "We should have at least been reprimanded. Or sent to our rooms without supper. Something. My point, David, is that Nadia would never be complicit in Shifter trafficking of any kind, if for no other reason than she wouldn't be able to feel superior to Stables if she was helping Shifters be just as bad."

"Okay, you make a good point about your occasionally violent partner," David admitted.

"Uh, yeah. Occasionally. That's it. She definitely doesn't make a habit of going for the eyes."

"But you have to admit, Nadia can be a little, uh, volatile. Even for a—"

Annette's eyes narrowed. "Don't generalize."

"—person who is prone to being volatile."

"Good save."

"But is it any weirder than Gomph being the culprit?" David said. "Nobody knows anything about Nadia. Not where she was born or where she went to school or if she has family—"

"Nobody knows those things about you, either."

"Stillwater, the U of M, only child, parents are dead."

"Me, too! Except for the Stillwater part. And the U of M. You're looking at a proud alumnus of St. Olaf. Wait, why am I giving you my résumé?"

David ignored her posturing, which was a relief. "Plus, nobody knows why she can't go back to the UK except the higher-ups. Which tells me that whatever she did, they didn't think it made her unemployable."

"Which would have been reassuring," Annette realized, "before this week."

"Right."

"So. Let's ask her. But we should wait until she gets the yelling out of her system."

David flinched. "You—you don't think she got it all out earlier today?"

"And to further compound your raging idiocy, you strutting morons, you came to the hospital! Where you know people are looking for you!"

"You asked us to come!"

"Exactly my point!" Nadia shrilled. "And you're late! You were to have been here thirty-five minutes ago. No, don't tell me, I can smell the bacon-and-swiss burger with mushrooms and the onion rings from here."

"It was bacon and cheddar. And we're not in the hospital!" Annette realized she was shouting and lowered her voice. "We're in the parking garage across from the hospital," she murmured. And like all parking garages, it was chilly, gloomy, and smelled like concrete, gasoline, and the scraps of discarded snacks. Parking garages always made her feel like she was in a concrete cocoon and made her crave gas and chips.

"Idiots!" (Nadia was still mad.)

"You're mad because you missed the fight, aren't you?"

"No." Sullenly, followed by "Maybe. Why didn't you call me?" She was pacing back and forth in a small circle in front of them, so frazzled she'd skipped makeup and had simply pulled her dark hair into a neat ponytail, though her deep-green suit was immaculate. "Why would you take them on by yourself, Annette?"

David pointedly cleared his throat.

"There wasn't time to take them on by myself. And I was with David." *Also, there's a teeny tiny chance you might be one of the bad guys.* She could barely think it, much less give it voice. *No. Impossible.*

"Such nonsense. As it happens, I have the perfect punishment for you."

Annette was immediately suspicious, because Nadia did not throw around words like *punishment*. Before she could ask the woman to elaborate, she heard the fire door open and, behind her, an all-too-familiar voice: "Hiya, gang!"

"Hey, you're fully dressed," David said. "Congratulations."

"Do I have to tell you to take care with Pat's clothes?" Annette asked as Oz loped over to them. "Because you need to take care. You really, really, really, really need to take care. Wait, what am I doing? I should let you find out the hard way."

"Blast," Nadia muttered. "You were supposed to be somewhat horrified. Or at least put out."

"I'm put out," Annette assured her. "I swear!"

"Naw, it's all an act, isn't it?" Oz reached out to pinch Annette's cheek, and she entertained the brief notion of a good chomp to the webbing between his thumb and forefinger. "Whoa. Your eyes are getting a little red again. Have you thought about contacts? You should get contacts. You're gonna scare someone."

"And you should get a proper change of clothes." Oz was hilariously resplendent in one of Pat's powder-blue button-downs, khaki shorts that showed off his goose-bumped legs, and brown loafers, no socks. Apparently, Pat kept his late-nineties preppie wardrobe in the studio, along with half-a-dozen aprons. "This is very...dated."

"Yeah, well." Oz shrugged, which was kind of neat, come to think of it. Here was a man who took almost as much care with his appearance as Pat did. He had clearly put Caro's investigation over the demands of fashion. "You know what they say about beggars and choosers."

"I've got no idea, actually."

"What is it with you guys?" David asked, and if it was anyone else, she'd think they sounded a little jealous. "Did you used to go out or something?"

By way of answer, Annette threw up in her mouth a little.

"Jesus Christ, *no*," Oz replied, having the gall to sound disgusted.

"Hey!" she snapped. "You could do worse."

"I don't see how. David, if I'd actually gone out with her, I wouldn't be able to spread rumors about you guys going out. Y'know, in good conscience."

Annette wanted to shriek. "*What?*"

"That was you?" David asked. "Wait. We're getting off track."

"Give me your hand, Oz," Annette growled. "I'm biting off all your fingers. I'll leave you a thumb so you can hitchhike to the hospital."

"It wasn't just him," Nadia replied. "And don't puff up and look outraged—"

"Too late."

"—because our intentions have been sublime, *sublime*. We're helping."

David blinked. "Spreading confusing gossip and making things awkward between the couple you're shipping against their will is…helping."

"David, don't try to figure it out. If you stare into the abyss that is Nadia's mind too long, the abyss stares into you." To Nadia: "You're in cahoots with my mortal enemy. Vengeance will be mine."

"Which brings me back to my question." From David. "What is it between you two?"

"Ancient history," Annette replied.

"A bet," Ox added.

"Nothing we're going into right now," Annette added.

"Which she lost," Oz finished. "Ages ago. When we were cubs."

David was eyeing them like he was watching a tennis match, one where the winner committed manslaughter with a racket and a thousand balls. "You guys knew each other when you were little?"

"We were foster sibs for a mere blink in time, and good *God*, why am I explaining any of this? Nadia, why are we here?"

"Foster sibs who fought over the fridge," Oz added, because he was annoying. "Mama Mac had about had it with all our shit so Annette and I made a bet: whoever ate the most in a day would get unlimited fridge access twenty-four seven, *and* snacks on demand if Mama Mac's fridge was out of walking distance."

"That's asinine," Nadia observed.

"The perfect word," Annette agreed.

"*That's* why you keep bringing him food?" David asked. He sounded both surprised and a bit disappointed, as though he was glad to have the mystery solved but let down because the explanation was so dumb.

"Right?" Nadia asked. To Annette: "You never bring *me* biscuits."

"Not biscuits," she replied at once. Here was an old pet peeve. "Never biscuits. They're called cookies. Biscuits are what you get at KFC. Well, you can get cookies there now, too."

Oz nodded, bouncing on his toes a little. "But I've given it some thought—"

Oh, dear God. What? What was coming?

"—and Annette, there's more to life than bringing me the odd cupcake now and again."

"Which you haven't been eating." To David: "I *told* you that was a bad sign."

"I didn't doubt you," David replied. "I genuinely have no idea what the fuck we're all talking about. It's weird and now it's starting to get a little boring."

"Who can eat eclairs when you're in trouble?" Oz asked, probably rhetorically. "Or, at least, headed for trouble. But getting back to shipping the two of you—"

Annette groaned. *This isn't happening. Waking up in 3…2…1…*

"—it occurred to me that there's more to your life than busting Dev and trying to get Pat the hell out of your house."

Not happening, this is not happening, I'm not discussing my odd life while David Auberon is standing there soaking up every last word. Pat will hear me swearing in my sleep and will wake me up any second because this is not happening.

"Or at least, there oughta be…"

Any second.

"…so Nadia and I started trying to figure out who to hook you up with, and the whole thing just sort of came to life on its own. Like Frankenstein!"

Any second. "Frankenstein's *monster* did not come to life on its own, Oz."

"We knew you'd be too stubborn to take our advice, and you'd never go on a setup—"

"Not even a setup *I* set up," Nadia added. "Which is insane, *insane*. I have exquisite taste and would find you the perfect mate."

"—so we looked around for some other sad soul who works too hard and has no life…"

"I was wondering when I was going to come into this story." David sighed. Annette had to hand it to the guy; he seemed remarkably nonhomicidal.

"And here we are!" Oz (finally) finished. He brought his hand up like he was going to give her a friendly pat, but thought better of it at the last second, which was a pity. "It's a conspiracy, sure, one with dark roots that has taken on a sinister life of its own—yeah, I'll grant you that—but you were a solitary bear when we were kids, and you still are. And we thought David could help. All the lying and meddling was done out of love and maybe a little boredom, and I'm saying all this as your loving brother."

"You were my foster brother for about ten minutes, Oz."

"One hundred and twenty-two days," he corrected.

Helpless, Annette looked at David. "I am so sorry. About everything. But especially this."

He shrugged. "Not your fault. Nice to have an explanation, though. I was starting to wonder if there were secret meetings being held that you and I weren't invited to."

"Only three," Oz said.

"No, you're forgetting the morning we went to the Salty Tart," Nadia added.

"What?" And here she had assumed the story couldn't get any more aggravating, because she was a foolish creature. "How dare you hatch plots against me in my favorite bakery without inviting me!"

"Uh. Guys? It's way past time to get back to the problem at hand. It was time to do that five minutes ago, but I got caught up in the narrative. Which happens a *lot* around here," David muttered.

When they just looked at him, David elaborated with "Lund's killer or killers? Who have tried for us twice? Don't get me wrong, the sordid details of Operation Lonely Hump are fascinating, but time and place, right?"

"It is a sad day when David Auberon is the voice of reason," Nadia said, and she probably thought that was a compliment.

"Thanks for that" was the dry reply. "So, again, what are we doing here?"

Nadia tossed her head. "Well, *David*, if you must know, Judge Gomph was looking high and low for you two."

"Was?"

"Now he's simply lying in wait for Annette. He's clever—he's picked the one place he knows Annette *must* visit."

"He's at Big Bowl? That's all the way over in Edina. It's worth the drive because the dumplings are incredible, and their homemade ginger ale is a treat, but—"

"The pediatric wing, you dim darling."

"Oh. That *is* smart," she admitted. "Because I'm definitely going there."

"No, you are not," Nadia began.

"Waste of time, Nadia," Oz said. "Waste. Of. Time."

"Oz is right." *Ow. It physically hurt me to say that out loud.* "I have to go to the peds wing. And you know that, too, or you wouldn't have called and told me Gomph was here."

"I was warning you! I didn't want you going in by yourself. David, stop clearing your throat," Nadia snapped. "You're not part of this."

"The hell I'm not! And it's either pointed throat-clearing or I just start yelling over you, and none of us wants that. Annette isn't going in by herself. I'm going with her."

"Again, you are not part of this, David."

"Again, the hell I'm not, Nadia, so get bent."

"She means because we're IPA employees, and you're an independent contractor." Annette turned to Nadia. "Right? Because in every other way, he's definitely part of this."

"Thanks, Annette."

"You're welcome, David."

"Whoa." From Oz.

"Oh, my dear Lord," Nadia breathed. "You let David get a leg over!"

"I did not!" *Yet.*

"Well, you did something."

Now Annette was doing the throat-clearing while David remained silent and gave off none-of-your-business vibes. "We're getting off-topic," she began.

"Wait, it worked?" Oz asked. "Acting like you were going out resulted in—"

"*No,*" David snapped. "It didn't happen, it will never happen, stop trying to make it happen, and Nadia, you're *not* coming with us."

"I'd like to bloody well see either of you stop me. How can you even consider leaving me out?"

"Oh, for all sorts of reasons," Annette said, because there were so. Many. Reasons. "But in this case, it's tactical, not personal. You're not looking at the trouble David and I are."

"Such bullshit." Nadia sniffed. "Of course I am."

"Annette's right," David said. "We didn't tell Bob you were with us at Lund's place. And you weren't with us when we stomped the warwolves."

"Exactly," Annette added. Perhaps ganging up was the way to verbally defeat the woman. "You're clean on this one so far, and we mean for you to stay that way. You're not the one who hid Caro at your place, and you didn't drop off the grid."

"Neither did you!" the other woman pointed out. "You're full-on trapped in the grid with the rest of us drones. Look, you're still using your phone. Give it to me."

Annette held it out of Nadia's reach. "No. That's a one-of-a-kind phone case."

"It's a Sonix Sushi case, and there are thousands of them. Give."

"Ab-so-lute-ly *not*."

"I will pull your eyes right out of your head, Annette!"

"Which, while upsetting, won't stop me from tearing you in half, Nadia!"

"*Ladies.*"

Like boxers going to their corner to take a break, they pulled back and looked at David. "What?"

"I get all that, I get what you're saying about Gomph, but why are *you* here, Nadia? Like I said, the bad guys sent by the player to be named later are no longer a threat. The—"

"Yes, about that. How many?" Nadia's eyes brightened with interest. "And what did you do? And where are the bodies? Also, good on you."

"Yeah, I'd like to get the deets on that, too," Oz said. "I just saw the gory aftermath."

Annette sniffed. "Don't say 'deets' like you're young."

"I'm twenty-five!" Oz protested.

"Hush." To Nadia: "Three. David shifted and got two, I grabbed the shotgun and got the other one." *And then I stuck my tongue down David's throat. All in all, not my worst Wednesday.*

Nadia cocked her head to one side. "Shot him? How restrained."

Annette shrugged. "I thought one of us should keep our opposable thumbs, at least for the first couple of minutes. Which is all the time it took."

"And how fares Patrick-or-Patricia?"

"It's just Pat, and he's fine. Couple of bites. The kids are fine, too. Like I said, it was quick."

"Oh. Very good."

"Why are you here, Nadia?" David asked, tenacious as a...a...something that was tenacious. A terrier? A squid? *How many times is he going to ask that question?* But Annette knew: as many times as it took to get an answer.

"I'm checking on my partner, you half-wit," she snapped. "Who disappeared? With a taciturn man no one really knows? Who pulled her off the grid but not really? And then I pulled her brother-slash-nemesis into it for reasons that now escape me?"

"Archnemesis," Oz corrected.

"And I am dismayed, *dismayed*, by what I've found so far. Except for the part where you killed the villains. And the part where Pat wasn't terribly injured. Though I'm not happy about your leave-the-corpses-where-they-lie policy. And where are Pat and Dev now? Wait! Don't tell me, not if the goal is keeping me 'clean.' Or at least granting me the power of plausible deniability."

"They're temporarily as safe as can be." And wasn't that awful? She was hiding children in her roommate's grain-silo-turned-studio because she feared they'd come to harm in IPA custody. The thought was

(it's not supposed to be like that)

as infuriating

(IT'S NOT SUPPOSED TO BE LIKE THAT)

as it was disorienting. It was almost enough to make her glad that Oz was with them, since she knew well his policies on authority figures covering up rampant child abuse.

"So now what?"

"You keep asking that, David," Nadia snapped. "Are you trying to trick me up?"

"It's 'trip you up,' and no."

"However." Nadia took a deep breath, then let it out. "Since you went to the trouble of asking ad nauseum, I think that since we're all stupid enough to be here, we might as well meet Gomph, find out what he wants, and carry on appropriately. Though I'll admit it's difficult to give him the benefit of the doubt, as he's the only one who knew Caro was staying at your house. Except for me, of course. But that's obviously not..." Nadia's eyes narrowed. "Is that what this is? Why we're having this tedious conversation? You think I've lured you here? And this wearisome dialogue is your way of... What? Tricking me into exposing myself? And here I thought it was just useless exposition."

"No, that's not what this is." *I'm pretty sure*, Annette thought. *Ninety-five percent.*

"Because if that's what you think..." To her shock, she

saw Nadia's eyes get even brighter as they filled with…
tears? She hadn't ever known Nadia to cry. Until recently,
she hadn't known the woman had tear ducts. Maybe she
was just allergic to concrete. "After what we've seen…"

"Annette doesn't think that," David said quickly. "I'm
the one who was wondering."

"Truly?"

"Yup." David stuck his hands in his pockets, wrist
deep, and rocked back and forth on his heels. "You're volatile and shrieky and snobby and you make me nervous
and nobody knows any of your backstory."

"Everything he just said is true," Oz added. "Sorry,
Nadia."

"But Annette thinks those things, too!"

*This is no time for a heated denial to try to spare her feel-
ings. Dammit.* "Yes, but I've seen you in the field, Nadia.
And I saw your face when we found Lund's pictures. I
couldn't imagine you having any part of that."

"Thank you, Annette. David, you can go straight to
hell. Oz, I'm indifferent as to where you go."

"Sounds about right," David muttered over Oz's laugh.

"Yes it does! Now," Annette said briskly, "since the
'wearisome dialogue' is over, we need to get to the pediatric unit, but not to confront Gomph. Or confess to him.
I want to check on the cubs and have a chat with the staff."

David's eyebrows shot up. "Oh-ho."

"I'm lost," Oz said, "but I assume one of you is going
to write up a memo or something to bring me up to
speed. Because the more I hear about what you're in the

middle of, the less I like it." And for once, the perpetual smirk hadn't reappeared.

"We know the abuse syndicate recruits minors from all over, right? Lund's photos and files prove it. Drug addicts, runaways, the homeless, sick and injured Shifters… That's their prey of choice, because they're cowardly fuckheads who should all die screaming. Unfortunately, by its very nature the pediatric wing is stuffed with vulnerable Shifters at all times of the day and night."

Nadia snapped her beautifully manicured fingers. "And it's the only hospital in the area for our kind."

"Right," Annette replied. "So maybe a staff member there saw something. Or sees a pattern but hasn't realized it. Or sees a pattern but doesn't know who they can talk to about it."

"Or is helping the syndicate," David suggested.

"I hope not. But either way, it's worth talking to them, at least. The more we can find out on our own, the quicker we can figure out whom to trust."

"That is hideously careless and the smallest bit brilliant."

"Nadia's half-right," David said.

"And Nadia, you have to keep keeping clear." *Wait. What? Never mind, go with it.* "You know what I'm talking about. You're the level-headed partner trying to rein me in, you had no idea what David and I have been getting up to, you're doing your best to help Judge Gomph and anyone else trying to track us down, and you're appalled—"

"*Appalled*," David added with a grin.

"—by all of it. This whole thing has you so frazzled, you had to stoop to getting my nemesis—"

"Archnemesis."

"—involved. Okay?"

"What about me?" Oz asked. "What can I do? Because it sounds like you guys are tit-deep and sinking."

"You can hover on the periphery making wisecracks while you look for an opportunity to pounce on my left-over fries."

"I can do that." Oz straightened out of his perpetual slouch, intent and serious. "I was *born* to do that."

"Yes? All right? Anyone have a better idea?" Annette paused. "I'll take that silence as a no, and the new terrible plan is as bad as the previous two terrible plans, but what the heck, it'll give us something to do until lunch."

From David: "I think you read too much into a three-second silence, Annette."

"Also, am I the only one who can't stop thinking about Big Bowl's chicken pot stickers now?"

"Yes, Annette." Nadia sighed. "The only one."

Chapter 24

"I FEEL LIKE I'M IN A SITCOM," ANNETTE FRETTED. "A dark one with an ever-increasing body count."

The four of them (she couldn't *believe* there were four of them) were doing their best to pull off nonchalant expressions as they crossed the street. David led them to the west entrance, where they passed any number of patients, visitors, and hospital employees.

"All right," David announced. "Here's where it gets tricky."

"It wasn't tricky before? Good *God*."

"Darlings, all we need to do is decide who wants to distract the guard, and who wants to—"

"Seduce distract?" Oz asked. "Or chat distract? Or stage a fake-fight distract? Dammit, I need parameters!"

"Naw, you don't," David said. "You just need to follow me."

David took a few more rights and lefts that Annette hoped weren't random, and then they were in United's newest wing, still under construction, with tarps and plastic and paint and Sheetrock and tools and builders everywhere, and David was introducing them to the man Annette assumed was in charge.

"Hey, Bri."

"Hey, Dave." Brian, if his ID was accurate, came right over to shake David's hand. His broad brown face creased into a delighted grin. "How's it goin', man? Haven't seen you since the Fourth of July."

"Work junk. Speaking of, these are my colleagues, Annette and Nadia. We're hoping you can get us to the other side for reasons none of us can go into."

"Sure. Cake."

"It's lovely to meet you, Brian, but you mustn't ever mention cake around Annette unless you have an actual cake."

"Kindly go straight to hell, Nadia." Annette took Brian's large, callused hand. It was like shaking hands with a baseball glove. "Nice to meet you. That's Oz. Feel free to ignore him. Or smack him."

All this while Brian was looking them over. To his credit, the man didn't seem especially alarmed. "Sure, c'mon. I'll take you over. So, Dave, remember that cabin we rented up north last spring? Me and some of the guys were thinking it might be fun to rent the place for the fishing opener..." Then it was time to follow David *and* Brian, take an elevator down two floors, pass through several hallways, and then step into an underground tunnel which brought them to... Wait. Were they...?

They were. Somehow Brian had led them to a virtually unused section of the Shifter side of the hospital. Even more astonishing: no guard.

No doors, either. From where they were standing, the place looked abandoned, like no one had been in this hall for at least five years. *I've been at United dozens of times—both sides!—and I've never been down here. What the blue hell?*

Brian, helpful architect/construction foreman/tour guide/cabin renter, must have seen the confusion on her face, because he elaborated. "This used to be the main entrance to the Shifter wards, right up until they put in the new walkways with the security upgrades."

"Ah, yes." Nadia nodded and did a beautiful job of pretending she knew what was happening. "New walkways. Security and such-like. Indeed."

"Nobody needed to use this part anymore—like when you build a new bridge, but you're slow to get rid of the old bridge? So everyone's just kind of forgotten about it."

"Sloppy," Nadia commented.

"Bureaucracies." Brian shrugged, unconcerned. "Anyway, it didn't pay to keep a guard way down here, so you only have to get past the key-card lock."

"Fascinating. Unfortunately, we don't have... Oh, you've pulled out a key card annnnnnd you're opening the door for us."

"Bri doesn't throw anything away," David confided. "You should see his basement."

"Anyhoo..." Brian stepped back as the door rattled open. The thing certainly sounded like no one had tended to it for years. "It'll bring you out right by the cafeteria and from there you can head up."

So straightforward. So helpful. So Stable. Oh, and because her brain thought it bore repeating: *Brian was a Stable.*

"What...is...happening?" Nadia asked, sounding as bewildered as Annette felt. "How do you—" To David: "Did you... I don't... What?"

"Eloquent and accurate, Nadia, which is why I love you."

"Do shut up, Annette."

"I'm confused," Oz announced. "Very, very confused."

"David's dad and my dad were best friends," Brian explained. "My family knows all about you guys." He shrugged. "Well. I know Dave can turn into a bear. I don't know what you guys turn into."

"David does *not* turn into a bear. We don't 'turn into' anything. We merely embrace our other selves," Nadia shrilled, because the more confused or angry she got, the higher the pitch.

"He knows?" Annette asked, flabbergasted. Stupid question; he clearly did. And such things weren't unheard of. Plenty of weres had Stable acquaintances: coworkers, bosses, friends, life coaches, dentists. Even spouses, sometimes. Shifters were vastly outnumbered; it would have been odd if they didn't have *some* Stables in their lives.

But having Stables on your periphery wasn't the same as exposing your true nature. Now here was David, completely unperturbed by the knowledge that a dangerous predator—and his entire family!—knew what David was and, thus, his weak points.

He must have scented their fear. No, wait, Stables couldn't do that… "It's okay, ladies. I'd never say anything."

"And if you plan to, Bri, you'd better hurry the hell up," David teased. "You've had years to get around to it. And a generation. You're the laziest whistle-blower I ever saw."

"Yeah, sure. My dad would come back from the grave

and kick my ass. And so would yours. Okay, well. Gotta get back to it. Nice seein' you again, Dave. Give me a buzz about the cabin. Nice meeting you guys."

"Ah…charmed…" Nadia said faintly.

"Thank you for helping us," Annette added.

"Very, very confused." (Guess who.)

Brian waved away helping Shifters avoid a judge so they could sneak around playing amateur sleuth (or, in David's case, professional sleuth), and off he went. They could hear him whistling "Mambo No. 5" all the way down the hallway.

"I don't know why you guys are so shocked," David said, which was annoying. "Did you really think we could build an entire secret wing on the back and underneath a hospital without a few Stables noticing?"

Good God, he's right. Why have I never considered this before? "When you put it that way, no," Annette admitted. How many people knew about this? Should *she* tell people? Who? Her boss? His boss? Go higher up? But how high? It wasn't like the president was a Shifter. But where did her responsibility lie?

"It could only have been a collaboration."

"Wait. Back up. Just so I understand, David, you're saying some Stables don't just know about the nature of the Shifter wing—that I could understand, though it's frightening to contemplate—but they actually assisted in the construction?"

David tapped his nose, which was also annoying, but there was no time to explore the concept further. The risk of discovery had climbed and would keep climbing until they could finish conducting their business and get the hell gone. There wasn't time to wrap her frazzled brain around a concept she had never considered until thirty seconds ago.

"This isn't over," Annette warned.

"Are you trying to sound like a clichéd movie character, or is it organic?" David asked.

"It's mostly organic. Let's go."

Then it was a matter of heading over to pediatrics, where Gomph was doubtless lying in wait, fretting over his abandoned salad and ready to stomp them into submission. Nadia agreed to seek out the judge and engage him while they headed to the peds wing.

"Just talk about how horrible it is to have a loose cannon like Annette for a partner, a maverick who plays by her own rules—"

"David, you want me to lie my elegant ass off to an officer of the court *and* use the most tired of tired clichés? Brilliant."

"I'll help, too. Um. Somehow." Oz glanced around the group. "Suggestions?"

"You're an accountant, darling. If we need you to look over someone's tax return, you'll be the first to know. In the meantime, what *can* you do?"

Annette brightened. "If Gomph indicates he's about to stomp Nadia, throw your body between them."

"Or I could have a car waiting for you guys? So you don't have to walk all the way back to the parking garage?"

"Or you could heroically allow yourself to be

trampled," Annette said again. "A life cut short, but on the upside, you'll have died a noble death."

"I'll go get the car."

And then there were two. Getting to the peds wing was easier than she thought, and thanks to Brian, the trickiest part was behind—

"Hey! You can't be here!"

Annette flinched; those words had never been directed to her in this place, and the shock of hearing them took her by surprise. Especially since she was in a part of the hospital that she knew as well as she knew her own home. Recent events had shown her she now had to question what she used to think was familiar territory, not to mention the people in it. The thought made her profoundly sad.

Sharon hurried to where they were hesitating in the doorway to the nursery. "Judge Gomph is looking for you. We have to let him or his clerk know if we see you."

"Yes, well, about th—hey."

Sharon was shaking out two sets of buttercup-yellow scrubs, complete with masks. "Put these on."

"But what if I don't want to wear a yellow pup tent?"

"You don't want to be hauled in for obstruction, either," she replied shortly. David, meanwhile, hadn't hesitated to swath himself in pastels and now resembled a sexy marshmallow Peep. With stubble.

Annette felt an invisible fist tighten around her throat. Obstruction! She'd never been in so much trouble in her life. Not even the time she refused to leave the

All-U-Can-Eat buffet to prove they were guilty of false advertising. "It's that bad?" she whispered. "What have you heard?"

"That you're up to something—nobody knows what—and it's got something to do with all the missing kids." This while Sharon effectively outfitted them to blend in with the staff as well as an Easter hunt for gigantic Easter eggs. "The last part's pretty much all we give a shit about."

"Wait, 'we'?"

"*All* the missing kids?"

"Annette!" the pediatric resident hissed from across the room. "What the hell are you doing here? You've gotta go!"

"I will, stop *nagging*. What do you mean, all the missing kids?"

"We haven't been able to find some of them."

"*What*?" Annette whisper-squawked (which, until this moment, she hadn't known she could do).

Sharon and the resident—Dr. Tilbury, who as a werewolf was so amiable she'd been mistaken for an herbivore more than once—had tugged them over to the corner, their backs to the visitor window, and they were staring down at a chart, pretending to be conferring about a patient. Which, technically, they were. "In the last couple of months, we've discharged cubs back home, or to a fosfam, or they've been released to another relative's care, but when our visiting nurses follow up, they can't find some of them. Or they'll be adopted, but then no one can find the adoptive parents. It's happened three times that we know of, but I'm betting there's more."

"Oh, fucking perfect," David muttered.

Annette had to make a deliberate effort not to walk away from their small group to scoop up the Spencer cub, or check on the female werefox she'd fed the other... Could it only be a couple of days ago?

They're supposed to be safe here. What. A. Joke.

"You say this has been going on for a couple of months?" she asked, making no effort to hide her horror.

"Yes," Sharon answered. "I told my boss, who promised to follow up and didn't, and then Tilly here told *her* boss, who promised to follow up and did. 'Paperwork snafus.' That's the party line, anyway. But before we could make more noise about it, miraculously, some of the kits turned up."

"You sound like you don't believe that," David said.

"Maybe because I don't?"

"They were found on paper," Dr. Tilbury added. "Or in the computer. Not in real life. Sharon and I haven't actually seen those kids again."

"When I went to my boss with the third one, they stalled me for a couple of days and then an investigator came to see me with all the right paperwork. 'Here they are, all snug and safe in the system, they were just misfiled, all the files are in the midst of being reorganized, not to worry, we're doing our due diligence, run along back to the ward'...like that."

Annette felt an inappropriate surge of excitement. *I was right!* Problem solving was hunting; they were all born to it. Still, it seemed wrong to be gleeful at the prospect of missing children, not to mention the ensuing cover-up.

"How has this been happening right under our snouts?" A glance at David showed he was as stunned as she was.

"You know how," Tilbury said quietly. "It's only happening to the little ones nobody cares about. That one?" She pointed to the premature werefox Annette had fed the other day. "Abandoned. No name or pack affiliation. So once she's off the oxygen therapy, into the system she goes. And we'll hope she gets adopted by a nice family and maybe she will, but…" She shrugged.

"We've all got so much work, who's got time to follow up with every single kit discharged out of here? That's exactly when we *stop* being involved, and when IPA takes point. It was a miracle we noticed the ones we did, which is a disgrace. But who can we tell?" For a moment, she looked as distressed and helpless as Annette felt. Sharon stood silently, but reached out and took her colleague's hand. "We have to keep it in-house, we can't have Stables sniffing around."

"That's what they're counting on," David muttered.

"Can you give us any names? Anything at all?"

Sharon let out a breath. "So you *are* investigating. And not just the Lund thing. You're looking into all of it." To the doctor: "That explains a lot, wouldn't you say, Tilly?"

Dr. Tilbury nodded, looking at them over the tops of her glasses. *What is it about a werewolf in spectacles that always makes me smile?* "I'd say. The word is that you're obstructing an investigation to cover your own incompetence, and that the missing kids are on you."

"On…us?" *I can't breathe. There's not enough air in here. Why are they keeping cubs in a room without enough AIR?* "They're saying it's *our* fault?"

"Keep it together," David said, giving her arm a squeeze. "It's a shitty lie, and a stupid one, because anyone who's spent more than five minutes in your company won't believe it."

"Right." *Deep breaths. In, out.* She had to keep calm, or Tilbury would start giving *her* oxygen therapy. Which, while tempting, would just slow everything down. "Right. Okay. Well, I can assure you both that we aren't trying to cover our tracks." Except for dodging Gomph. And staying mum about the dead bodies in her kitchen and living area. And not disclosing Caro's new location. Or Dev's. Or Pat's involvement and the ensuing injuries. Or Nadia stalling Gomph. Or Oz doing whatever the hell he was doing. "What's 'the Lund thing'?"

"That guy signed himself out, and the first thing he did was come up here. Tilly had to politely kick him out."

"Here? Where the babies are?" Why? Was he so desperate for new blood he was going to snatch them right out of their cribs during daylight hours? Or was he getting a head count by subspecies? Making note of the most vulnerable of the vulnerable?

And then after his head count, he went home and one of his partners killed him. And that's all. That's all we've been able to figure out. And there's so much more, and it's so much worse.

The thought made her want to bite something. Or someone.

"What about the ones who are still here?"

"That's the question," Tilbury replied. "We can't keep them indefinitely, but once word got around that you guys were looking into it, I decided my discharge plans were premature. None of these ailing cubs are going anywhere just yet. But that's just a temporary fix."

"Yeah, but they know you're watching now. And they know Annette and I are poking around. I don't think they're gonna dare snatch any kids right now. So we've got a window."

"A narrow, rapidly closing window," Annette pointed out. "Time's not on our side, either. Sharon, did you happen to keep the investigator's card?"

For the first time, Sharon smiled. "As a matter of fact, I did."

"Excellent, hand it over."

"It's on the chart you've been staring at for the last five minutes."

"Oh. Good. Sorry, being accused of kidnapping and child abuse and obstruction of justice was distracting. At least we don't have to worry about the Spencer cub for a bit. Now we've got to... *Ouch!*" David's hand had clamped down on hers, which was when she heard the telltale sound of Judge Gomph's tread. Along with the telltale sound of Nadia in crisis mode.

"…cannot imagine her doing any such thing, Judge! David Auberon, sure, one look at that reprobate and you can see he's a clear sociopath…"

"Jesus Christ," David muttered.

"—but Annette, while dangerously and stupidly naive, has too much respect for our terrible system."

Gomph must have answered, but all they heard was low muttering neither of them could quite make out.

"As you yourself know, sir, she was raised in it. And I am horrified, *horrified*, that anyone could insinuate she's involved in such repellent acts. Whomever is spreading these ugly rumors deserves a strict talking to and perhaps a kick to the seat of the pants, you'll pardon my impertinence."

Quick as thought, David and Annette dropped to all fours and scooted back until they were against the wall. They probably looked ridiculous, not that it mattered. What did matter was that Gomph could see into the room, but he couldn't see them unless he came in through the door and looked to his right and then down. And even if he did that, unless he got kissing close (or stomping close), he wouldn't be able to see them clearly; he was notoriously far-sighted.

"Not to mention, sir, that I am troubled by your seeming eagerness to believe unsavory rumors!" The closer Gomph got to their hiding place, the more high-strung Nadia sounded. Annette's eardrums throbbed in sympathy. "Yes, that's right, and I shall say it again! Unsavory! Rumors! Would you have us live in anarchy,

Judge? Because speaking for all who live in a free society, I should bloody well hope not!"

She must have looked rattled, because David leaned close and murmured, "He won't be able to scent us. Too many other odors to sort out."

"True. But how's his hearing?" she whispered back.

"Not the best. You'd think he'd be able to hear lettuce growing with those ears, but nope."

Annette stifled a giggle; it wouldn't do to waste Nadia's efforts by being overheard. *This is getting worse by the hour. Why in God's name am I laughing?*

Nadia's hectoring started to get further away as they heard Gomph plod past the window. Annette let out a relieved sigh. Prematurely, as it turned out.

"Hey! You can't be in here!"

They both flinched and looked to their left, and Annette was startled to see Taryn, Gomph's clerk, framed in the doorway, hands on hips, sturdy legs in cream-colored Uggs.

"Shit."

"The perfect word," Annette muttered. Then to Taryn: "I know you have to report us to the judge, but would you consider giving us a head start?"

"You have to get out of here! Right now!"

"People keep saying that, and I'm really beginning to hate it."

Taryn ran over, grabbed each of them by a wrist, then tugged until they were on their feet. "At best, you're going to be suspended. At worst, arrested, then fired."

"Actually, I think fired, then arrested, would be wor—"

"You have to go *right now*." She was hauling them out of the room and down the hall, and Annette was reminded that when she was inclined, Taryn could dislodge a car stuck in a snowdrift by herself. Fortunately, at this hour there was hardly anyone in the hallway, and the ones who were kept their eyes on their charts or their phones. Or deliberately turned a blind eye, which took some of the sting out of all the *You can't be here* pronouncements. "I don't know what you're into, but you need to get gone. Far, *far* away. You've got money? Passports?"

"Passports? Taryn, what—"

"We're not leaving town, much less the country," David added. "Not until we figure out—"

"Don't you understand?"

"No! Not one thing, dammit!" Annette squashed the urge to rip her hair out and make confetti out of the clumps. "In all of this!"

"They think you killed Lund," she said simply. "We just found out. The cops are bringing your arrest warrants to Judge Gomph for signature. The minute he signs, that's it. You'll both get popped for murder one. Shit!" she hissed, cocking her head to the left. "I think I hear him coming back."

And then, with very little effort, and before either of them could utter so much as a squeak of protest, Taryn yanked open the nearest supply closet door and bundled them both inside, then shut the door and left them in ammonia-scented darkness.

Chapter 25

"Well, shit."

"Well put."

She shifted against him, which gave David another whiff of her hair, and he had to tamp down a groan.

"This is unbelievable," she muttered.

"Yup."

"A closet? Really?"

"Shhhhh."

"Good *God*," she hissed. "I can't keep up with the clichés!"

The closet was tiny and Annette's wonderful ass was inches away and he mentally begged his cock to be a gentleman.

Never, obviously. That's what he needed to keep in mind. That, and strangling Oz and Nadia, whose idea of fun was apparently talking up imaginary relationships. He liked them both well enough, but the goddamned arrogance was staggering. He didn't mind so much for his sake, but Annette had to be embarrassed at best and hating it at worst.

Argh, that wonderful ass.

"You said 'that's what they're counting on.'"

Just be cool! Do you really want to be the poster boy for #NotAllShifters? "What?"

She turned her head. "When Dr. Tilbury said the missing kits were the ones nobody cared about."

Oh. The case. Gotcha. "Yeah. The syndicate or cabal or fuckstick brigade or whatever the hell they are—"

"All right, first of all, we need to make 'fuckstick brigade' the official handle for those monsters. It's just so... concisely evocative."

"Thanks. Anyway, they all count on that."

"Consciously? As in, it's part of their plan?"

"Sure," he replied, flaring his nostrils to take in more of her scent, then cursing those same nostrils. Of all the days to not have a sinus infection. "They've gotten away with this because all the caregivers and advocates have too many kids to worry about. That's been true forever, it's not something that just happened."

"So it's on us, too."

"*No.*" *Jesus. Does she really think that?* "Annette, that's not true, it's on them. You haven't done anything wrong. It's the fuckstick brigade. It's a cold, deliberate plan, and the system is set up to hamstring anyone who tumbles to it because everyone's more concerned with hiding from Stables than anything else, and they count on that, and none of that is your fault."

"But...we have to be. Concerned about the Stables, I mean. There's so many of them. It's just safer to keep to the Beneath," she murmured back. "And yes, sometimes at the expense of the few. I—I hate the phrase 'for the greater good.' Most of the time it sounds like a lazy cop-out. But now and again, that's what it is."

"That's the cage we're all in, Annette. The worst kind, the one we put *ourselves* in." Was he really giving his crush a lecture on his pet peeve while they were stuck in a closet? Yep. "And there's no reason for it. It cuts us off at the knees at every turn. How much bad shit have you had to look away from because doing something would have meant exposure? What's getting overlooked—*who's* getting overlooked—because our bosses figure the devil we know—ourselves—is better than the devil we don't?"

Silence, finally broken with "I understand that your personal experience with Stables has been positive…"

"That's underplaying it. A lot."

"Fair enough," she went on in a low voice. "But we can't put millions at risk just because your dad was friends with a nice Stable."

"And there it is. Like I said, it's the cage we put ourselves in. And since we're doing it to ourselves, I don't look for that to change anytime soon."

His speechifying was met with more silence, probably appropriately, and he sighed and shifted his weight. How long had it been? Five minutes? Seven days? He couldn't reach his phone without poking Annette (groan). Nor could he shake the sense of urgency that had been growing the moment they'd found out Caro had been set loose by a person or persons unknown. He felt like they were trapped… Well, they *were* trapped, but even before now, it was like they were stuck in some hellish game of *Beat the Clock*, where the best prize you could hope for was not getting fired. And the worst was… Well. The worst.

We have to get the holy hell out of here.

On the other hand, Annette was fragrant and wonderfully close.

Decisions.

"You were on the right track with Nadia," she said abruptly.

"Sorry, what?" *Jesus. At least pretend you're thinking about something besides her proximity, you horny jackass.*

"When you encouraged her to complain about what a trial I am. Having me as a partner is pretty horrible."

"Are you always this hard on yourself?"

"Depends on who you ask."

"Anyone who thinks you're horrible is a goddamned moron."

"That's…sweet, David. But now you're painted with the same brush. You were out of it, you could have walked away once you dropped Caro for booking the other night. You should have. But you stuck with me, and now…now…"

She buried her face in her hands and swallowed a sob.

"Hey. Hey." His hands settled around her waist and he squeezed gently. "Everybody knows it's all bullshit. Everybody. Annette, I am *not* worried about me at all, okay? Not my job or anything else—independent contractor, remember?"

"You can still get arrested. And charged. And indicted."

"Don't care."

"Well, that's insane," she said bluntly. "You should care."

"I don't regret sticking you. *With* you, sticking with you, God, sorry." *Smoooooooth!*

She giggled a little. "If you're trying to cheer me up, do better."

I could hardly do worse. "We'll find who's responsible and bounce them into a cage face-first and you'll be exonerated."

"We'll be exonerated," she corrected with a sniff.

"Sure, but I don't actually give a ripe shit about public opinion."

She snorted into her palms. "It's not just the false accusations. It's all the cubs who've been hurt over this. And the ones who *will* be hurt unless we figure this out. Alone. While hiding. In a closet."

"Be fair, we also cowered in the NICU and hung out in a grain silo."

"Point," she conceded, and shifted in his grasp. "And one of the worst parts of all this is that I'm finding you a gigantic distraction. My primary focus should be Caro and Dev, my secondary keeping Oz safe in Accounting, and…and everything else should be a distant third. Or fourth. Or not on the list at all. But that's not what's happening and I can't… Um. David?"

Too late, he realized he'd been scenting the back of her neck and nuzzling her ear. "Sorry! Sorry." He tried to take a step back, only to bump up against shelves. "Dammit!"

"Shhhh."

"Sorry." *God, you're an idiot. Get your shit together, for the love of… Oh dear God, what is she doing?*

Wriggling in his arms, that's what. Twisting and

turning while they shuffled back and forth and bumped into things, and then she was facing him and her breasts were pressed up against his chest

oh God oh God oh God oh God oh God oh God…

and she whispered, "This is what I was talking about."

…oh God oh God oh God… "Sorry, what?"

"I see I'll have to make you be quiet, you noisy thing," and then her lips were brushing his, and her clever, clever tongue was slipping past his teeth and he did his very best not to die.

It lasted for an eternity. Or ten seconds. He was never sure, after. All he could think of was her hot, soft mouth, the feel of her lush curves, her scent, the coarse glory of her hair, her low whimper as he pressed against her and wished they were anywhere anywhere *anywhere* but a closet that smelled like soap and stress.

After an age (or ten seconds), she pulled back. "Sorry," she murmured into his mouth. "Very inappropriate."

"Whuh?"

"I know you're not interested in me like that. I just… You smell *wonderful*, like linen and cloves and something else that's just you. I'm sorry."

"You're wrong," he managed, trying very hard not to gasp or unhook her bra.

"No, I'm quite certain. Linen and cloves. And a bit of pepper from your aftershave."

"No, I mean… Don't be sorry. You didn't do anything wrong."

"It's nice of you to let me off the hook. Also, if no one

has heard us by now, they never will. I think this might happen a lot around here."

"Huh?"

"People making out in closets. Ready?"

And with that, Annette wriggled

(*JESUS CHRIST*)

until she was again facing the door, and then she opened said door and stepped out. He was right on her heels; if she got too far ahead, he'd have had his nose on the tiles to follow her backtrail if he could've done it with any subtlety.

Luck was with them again; nobody noticed them. Or didn't give a shit about a panting, disheveled couple who had hidden in a closet to avoid being arrested and then made out for some reason. Annette was probably on to something: this *did* happen all the time. But even if not, it was all good.

"So you gotta know what I'm thinking," he said, his pulse rate finally coming down as he walked them back the way they came, through the Stable section of the hospital. The safer way—not that most Shifters would admit it.

"I do, huh?"

Well, some of what he was thinking. He needed to ponder the dichotomy of *Never, obviously* and *I know you're not interested in me like that*, as well as the instant, endless kiss. He foresaw much, much pondering, especially later when he was alone in his bed. He'd ponder until he was shaking and sweaty, but now wasn't the time, more was the fucking pity.

Oh, you poor idiot, his dead mother mourned.

"David? Your thinking on this?"

"We gotta talk to the investigator your hospital friends told us about. Is there an address on the card Sharon gave you?"

"She didn't give me the investigator's business card."

"Fuck."

"She gave me his business card plus files on all the missing kids. I stuffed them down the back of my pants when Taryn grabbed us."

David perked up. "Fuck!" Come to think of it, he had thought her ass felt a little flat in the closet, but he'd been too distracted by her scent and hair and voice and skin and scent to notice.

"You're cute when you're tousled and swearing."

Absurdly, this made him puff up with pleased pride.

Out of your league, his dead mom reminded him. *And worse: you'll be her end. And if she gives you cubs? You'll be their end, too. As you were mine, son. As you were mine.*

He didn't know what was more irritating: still hearing her voice, or knowing she was right.

Chapter 26

"WHAT DO YOU MEAN, THE BODIES ARE GONE?"

"The. Corpses. Ain't. There. No. More."

"Stop that," Annette scolded. "I know it's been a stressful day, but take it easy on the double negatives."

Normally at this time of the evening, she'd be plugging in a new alarm clock, padding around in her sushi slippers, and thinking about making another pan of brownies while Pat nagged her about whatever he had decided to nag her about that evening.

Not knocking on a stranger's door while discussing vanishing corpses with someone who thought the dead bodies were of less import than settling an argument with Dev.

"Look, just tell me I'm right so I can tell that insufferable monster—"

Faintly: "Hey!"

"—that he must never question me on anything pop culture-related *ever again*."

She sighed. "Yes, Pat, technically Jon Snow is 'boning his auntie' in *Game of Thrones*. Why are you discussing inappropriate adult books riddled with incest, treachery, torture, and mass murder with a minor?"

"We're not. We're discussing the show riddled with incest, treachery, torture, and mass murder. And it's because we're really, really bored."

"It's only been three hours!"

"Fine. I'll drop one of the 'really's.'"

Annette made a deliberate effort to loosen her grip on the phone. It was a burner, because David kept a box of them in his trunk for some reason. (And oh, they were going to have a chat about *that* later, thank you very much.)

She'd called the landline in Pat's studio to check on her charges and had been informed that Caro had apparently gone through three of Pat's sketch pads and Dev had found Annette's old Kindle. He was plowing his way through her online bookshelf, which was 75 percent cookbooks, 5 percent literature-themed cookbooks (current favorites were *The Little House Cookbook* and *Roald Dahl's Revolting Recipes*…ironically, given the topic under discussion, she found *A Feast of Ice and Fire* to be only so-so), and 20 percent work-related (*Stir It Up; The Lost Art of Listening*).

Oh, and sometime in the last three hours, someone had come to the main house and spirited away three dead warwolves.

"Do I even want to know how you know this?"

"You do not."

"Good God. Tell me."

"Dev, um, might have wanted to stretch his legs a bit."

She held her tongue. She had no moral high ground here. It wasn't Pat's job to keep Dev Devoss out of harm's way. It was hers.

"He wanted some room to shift and stretch, and then

he could hear cars pulling out. So he scampered up the hill—"

Faintly: "Werefoxes don't scamper! I ran. Like a predatory badass!"

"—and saw guys with sinister black cars right out of central casting clichés loading the last corpse and pulling out, because we're living in a caper movie now I guess?"

"Do you feel safe?" she asked simply. "Should we move you? I can be there in forty minutes."

"No way. To the second part, I mean. They never came near the studio. And you know it would've taken them hours to break in, assuming they even could. We're only in danger of acute boredom brought on by acute boredom because we're so acutely bored."

"Okay. We're following some new leads and won't be back tonight, which is why I called."

"Please tell me you're at least getting some nookie from Auberon out of all this."

"Um…"

"Awesome!"

"Shut up." Did kissing = nookie? She'd have to do some research. "Keep this number. David and I both shut off our cells so we'll be checking in."

"Thanks for the update, stay safe, and I might wring Dev's neck but not a jury in the world, right?"

"Try it, jackal boy!"

She cut Pat off before he could shout a rebuttal. "Pat. I'm in your debt."

"Bullshit. It's been the other way around for years. You just pretend otherwise to save my pride."

Proof (if any were needed at this point) it had been a long day/week: Pat's kind words made her want to sob. "I appreciate this more than I can say."

"You'd be a horrible person if you didn't," he replied cheerfully, and hung up.

"Sounds like business as usual."

"Except for the disappearing corpses, yes." She put the phone away and turned to David. "Why are we here?"

"Here" was the lobby of the Genesee apartment complex in Bloomington, home of the Mall of America, the Minnesota Zoo, and at least one of David's friends. It was a standard housing setup, with neutral cream-colored walls and inoffensive gray carpet. They were buzzed up in short order, and not long after, David was introducing her to a charming couple who seemed as delighted to see David as they were surprised.

"Where have you *been*?"

"Work junk. Jenn, Jim, this is my colleague, Annette."

"Hi!" Jenn exclaimed, shaking Annette's hand in an impressively strong grip. *Ow. It's like shaking hands with one of those old-fashioned laundry wringers.* "Sorry about the alliteration. I've been trying to get Jim to change his name for ten years. It's just too cute, right?"

How am I supposed to answer that?

"Annette, this is Jenn and Jim Griffith. We kind of grew up together."

"I think you can drop the 'kind of,'" Jenn said, smiling

at them both. She was tall, with a face full of freckles and short red hair that sprang from her skull in all directions, as if each hair follicle was out for itself. Her husband was six inches shorter and twenty pounds heavier, with light-brown skin, long lashes (why were those always wasted on men?), and the most melting Godiva-dark eyes Annette had ever seen. "It was the rare week when you weren't over at one of our houses for dinner at least twice."

They're Stables, like Brian. What the hell happened to David when he was a kid? Easy: one or both of his parents died. And in the resulting chaos, his neighbors opened their homes to him, found out his secret, and loved him despite his other nature. Or because of it. Which is nothing I anticipated.

In fact, she was a little ashamed at how easily she'd dismissed the man for the two years he'd been on the periphery as an IPA investigator. Nobody knew anything about him? Well, nobody bothered to ask. He kept to himself? Again: nobody reached out. In less than a day she'd discovered his intelligence, sense of humor, and sweet-tooth-fueled candy fetish.

This is odd. Two years of nothing, and suddenly…everything? Maybe it's not entirely on me. Maybe David chose to open himself up a little. And if he has, what does that mean for us?

Idiot: there is no us. David did not equivocate. It didn't happen, it will never happen, stop trying to make it happen. Remember?

Too well.

And what were you thinking, glomming onto him with

your lips? Poor guy will never consent to being stuffed into a
closet with you again. Not without a rape whistle.

She made a determined effort to stop beating herself
up and had to smile when she saw Jenn go straight to the
kitchen and pour David a cup of coffee as her husband
went for the maple syrup.

"Would you like some, Annette?"

"No, thank you, Jenn."

"Something else? Water? Milk?"

"I'd love some milk. Oh God, I can't watch." She really
couldn't; David had put so much syrup into his coffee it
was now indistinguishable from the syrup in color, smell,
and texture.

"Back off, Garsea. Do I weigh in on your nutritional
habits?"

"Frequently."

"You had a plate of raw fish for supper." To the
Griffiths: "Not sushi. Not sashimi. Literally just a big
dinner plate with a football-size pile of salmon that she
wolfed down with two ginger beers."

"Three ginger beers. May I put this in your fridge?"
She held up the doggy bag—horrible name—which held
her third helping of crème brûlée, perfect for a snack at
3:00 a.m. Or five minutes from now.

"Yes, of course. Wow, and I thought David could put
away the chow. Is that because you're like him? You're"—
Jenn's voice trailed off as her husband gave her what he
probably thought was a subtle elbow to the side—"a great
big lover of fish?" she finished weakly.

"Uh…"

"It's fine, Annette," David said, sipping and closing his eyes in bliss. You could almost see the waves of syrupy contentment coming off him. "They know all about my nature."

"So you turn into a bear?" Jenn coughed and tried to sound nonchalant, which was tough given that she was leaning so far forward she was practically looming over Annette, a good trick since she was two inches shorter. "I mean…if that's your thing. Which is none of my business. No one's business, really. It's a private thing. If it even *is* a thing. Um. We have fish sticks? If you're still hungry?"

"I'm fine." She despised fish sticks. She also wasn't sure how she felt about being so casually outed. Well, she could have denied it. David had simply handed her the chance to…not deny it. Which, she had to admit, was a novel sensation. "And I don't turn into a bear. Neither does David. We just—" She cut herself off and took a gulp of milk. Mmmm…whole milk. "It's complicated."

"I can imagine." Jim paused. "Actually, I can't. I'm sitting here trying to imagine it, and I can't make it happen in my brain."

"Don't hurt yourself, hon." Jenn snickered.

David cleared his throat. "Listen, guys, I'm sorry to just drop in like this—"

"Are you kidding?"

"It's been *ages*. How long can you stay? A week? A month?"

"—but Annette and I need a place to crash for the night."

Jim's face lit up. "Is this for one of your cases? Are bad guys after you?"

"Yep to both."

"We're actually in a great deal of danger," Annette added.

"Really?" he replied, enthralled.

"Oh yes." She had to smile at his enthusiasm. "We've stumbled across a huge conspiracy, and at least four people have been killed in fewer than ninety-six hours. There's no telling how high the body count will go, or if we'll even survive."

"That's so cool!"

"Jeez, Jim." Now Jenn was throwing elbows. "It's not cool if it's real life. Our friend's in danger. And so's his friend."

"Our friend can take on any number of assholes without ruffling his fur," Jim retorted. "And Annette probably could, too. Right, Annette?"

"Well." She shrugged modestly. "Maybe not *any* number of assholes. And we're not friends."

"No?"

"No." From David. "Definitely not."

Ow.

So it was settled. The sleeping arrangements, at least; God knew nothing else was. They'd spend the night, and not long after Annette finished all the milk, she found herself lying down in the Griffiths' spare room, in a borrowed nightgown, while Jim had made up the hide-a-bed for David, also in the spare room. David had eschewed the offer of pajamas and went to bed in his black boxer briefs, and Annette definitely didn't sneak appreciative peeks.

"There are extra blankets in the closet if you get chilly," Jenn said.

"No, thank you. I like it a little chilly."

"She keeps her house at fifty degrees," David added, sounding not unlike a third-grade tattletale.

"I do not!"

"I've been in your house, Annette. I know the truth."

"Well, the next time you're in my house, you'll see that you had it wrong. So you'd better come over. Soon!"

"Well, I will!"

"Fine!"

"Okay." Beat. "You wanna put some money on that? And no fair tipping Pat off in advance so he can turn up the therm to a balmy sixty-two degrees."

"David, you know I never gamble! Anymore."

"I thought you guys weren't friends," Jenn said, puzzled but smiling.

In unison: "We're not."

Once that issue was put to bed, and they themselves were put to bed, after assuring their hosts that they didn't require anything else, Jenn shut off the light and left them in darkness, thinking.

Well, Annette was thinking. She had no idea what David was doing.

"Are you awake?" he stage-whispered.

She snorted. "You know I am. It's been...what? Fifteen seconds since the light went out?"

"Oh. Right."

Has this case just turned into a slumber party? I think it's turned into a slumber party. Certainly Dev and Caro must think so.

"Are you sure you wouldn't rather have the bed?" She'd lost the argument, but now that David was actually trapped in the thing, he might see reason.

"No, that's okay. This is fine."

"Sure it is."

"Well, it is," he snapped.

"Where's the bar? You're lying on it, aren't you? You're lying on it right now. Admit it. Admit you're lying on the bar."

"...Yeah."

She laughed. "Your friends are nice."

"Yeah." But he sounded pleased.

"Could I ask you some personal questions?"

"Sure."

"How did you lose your parents?"

He snorted.

"If you don't want to talk—"

"It's not that. I've always thought that euphemism is just dumb, is all. I didn't misplace them. They died. My dad of cancer when I was fourteen, Mom of liver failure when I was in college."

Liver failure. Cirrhosis? Alcoholism?

"I'm sorry. I misplaced mine when I was young, too. Permanently," she added over David's chuckle. "So your father died, and you started spending time with your neighbors?"

She could hear him shifting in the sofa bed, trying to get comfortable. "Yeah. My mom had to take another job to pay the bills, and I ran a little wild."

"Roaming the countryside searching for maple syrup to dunk into your coffee?"

"Naw, back then I was all about making chocolate milk with Hershey's Syrup. You start with a cup of milk, and then you add a cup of syrup, and—"

"Good *God.* I'm getting a cavity just hearing about it."

"I've got perfect teeth, so back off."

"I'll bet," she purred, then immediately covered her face with her hands, feeling herself blush. *What the hell was that supposed to be? You sound like an amorous dentist!*

Judging by the pause, David was a bit taken aback as well. "Anyway, Jim and I were good friends, and Jenn's family had moved into the neighborhood just before my dad died, and long story short—"

"But I like long stories."

"—I was careless and Jim saw me shift. And he was half in love with Jenn already, so he told her, and…"

"Yes? And?"

"And I waited for the world to end." His voice, coming at her from the dark, was deep and amused. "The worst thing had happened, right? Even worse than my dad's death, to hear some of the adults tell it. Exposure. Potential annihilation. Everything was over—my life, my future, all gone. So I kept waiting for the government or, I dunno, assassins or evil Stable scientists or whatever to show up and kill me. Or kidnap me and vivisect me. Or put me in a zoo. Or shoot me with a silver bullet."

"Sounds like you had all the bases covered."

"And nothing happened."

"And your mother?"

"Lost it. I had to tell her—warn her—and she was furious and terrified that I had exposed us to danger. And at first I thought it'd be okay, I thought she'd settle when nothing happened to us. But she didn't relax when days and weeks and months went by and nothing happened."

"Your friends didn't do anything," Annette guessed, because obviously, "They kept your secret."

"Yeah. And probably because I was so young, I took that at face value. I didn't question it and I quit worrying about it because I trusted my friends, but she never could, because she didn't see Stables as people. She saw them as backward. Stuck. She was sure it was just a matter of time. I mean, she was *positive* that we were gonna be scooped up any day. She would have moved us, but she didn't have the money and she couldn't leave her job. Me, I thought we were just living our lives, but to her, we were trapped in a den we couldn't leave."

"I'm so sorry. That sounds unbearable."

"More for her than me."

"But hardly a picnic for you."

"Well, like I said, *I* was never worried. But she never

stopped listening for government agents or a pitchfork-waving mob. She was looking over her shoulder right up until the day she died. And that's on me. And I knew it even then."

Annette sat up in bed and had to stomp on the desire to cross the room and take him in her arms. "That's not true. I think you acquitted yourself quite well under the circumstances. You were careless—what cub isn't?—and then you were honest, and then you were vindicated over time. Living in fear… All respect to your mother, but that was her choice."

She heard him sigh and shift around. "Maybe. But she was right about one thing. We're all living on borrowed time. I don't mean in terms of life and death, but…the world's getting smaller every day, and everyone is walking around with supercomputers that double as recording studios that they occasionally use to make phone calls."

"I literally can't remember the last time I used my cell phone as a telephone," she admitted. "Oh. Wait. It was yesterday."

He laughed, then quickly sobered. "Discovery's inevitable. We *will* get busted, and the world *will* see us. We have to be ready, we have to assume that it's a certainty. Because the shocking part is that it hasn't happened yet."

"I wonder about that, too," she admitted. She and Nadia had discussed the issue more than once. Every Shifter must have. Because he was right: it was hanging over their heads all the time. Some days, she could almost hear the ticking of the countdown. "It seems like there's always another YouTube video of someone caught shifting, which prompts another round of arguments, and more and more people seem open to the possibility."

"Yeah. And eventually, something's gonna happen that people can't explain away. Wouldn't you rather get in front of the narrative? Instead of always worrying about damage control? I think it's smart to prevent the mess, instead of always running around cleaning it up after the fact."

Annette was silent. The thought of national—no, *worldwide* exposure—was terrifying. But David had a point. Maybe it *was* better to show themselves—all their selves—on their own terms. What's the worst that could happen? Besides genocide?

But first things first.

"I'm going to abruptly change the subject now."

"Yeah, I was wondering when you were gonna do that. You're not subtle."

"I'm the subtlest creature you've ever seen, so you can back right off. Now. We'll go see the investigator— Brennan? That's the name on the business card we got from Sharon. First thing tomorrow."

"Yep. No point in making an appointment." David yawned in the dark. "We don't want to tip him, and if we're in the building, we can find a way to get some face time with him, no matter what his receptionist says."

"I don't like being out of touch with Nadia."

"It's safer this way. The point was to keep her clear, right? If she's running and hiding, too, she's not much use."

"Right." Still, she fretted. Like Marge Simpson, it was her nature.

"Hell with this." David sat up. "D'you want something to drink? Or a snack? I think I'll be up for a while."

"It's the bar, isn't it?"

"It's the fucking bar," he agreed. "Every single sofa-sleeper engineer designs the bar to press right up into the middle of the sleeper's back all night long. Goddamned sadists."

She laughed. "Come over here, then."

"Really?" This in the tone of a man who couldn't believe his luck.

"Just to sleep, understand? We both need to get some... Oh hell, and here you are already climbing in. Damn. I didn't even hear you move."

"Ahhhhhh, nooooo barrrrrrr," he moaned, getting comfortable.

"Better?"

"Gobs."

"Okay. Move on your side, I want to be the big spoon."

"Sure."

"Really? There won't be a spoon-related argument?"

"Hey, I'm just happy to be here."

She laughed, her breath tickling him between his shoulder blades, making him wriggle and giggle against her. Which was adorable.

Why can't I have this?

But she knew why.

The upside: the table was all but groaning beneath her favorites: broiled rainbow trout stuffed with lemon slices, rare rib eyes, gazpacho, a platter of butter-basted morel mushrooms with thyme and parsley, a bowl of ripe raspberries and blackberries as big as her thumb, and all of them swimming in cream, Breyers vanilla fudge twirl,

(You have to special order that! It's so hard to get!)

her mother's homemade fried chicken

(even harder to get!)

scallops brushed with butter and lime juice, then skewered onto kebabs with cherry tomatoes and shallots, medium-rare venison backstrap with blackberry sauce, carbonara, fresh-squeezed lemonade, pumpkin pie, iced tea, passion-fruit pavlova, *tres leches* cake, grilled lamb chops, milk tea, and a go-cup of KFC gravy to wash it all down.

The downside: the loved ones sharing her meal were all dead—her parents, smiling at her while wearing the clothes they'd died in, her best friend from childhood, Willa Chapman, her nose in a book as she absently ate cashews, Opal Adway, whose heart shrank even as she refused food, the grandparents Annette had never met and only recognized from photos… They were all with her, which should have been comforting but wasn't.

They never spoke to her. Only to each other. And they couldn't hear her, either, because they always, always ignored her warnings. Soon enough, the food tasted like ash and one by one, each of them got up and slipped away, and she knew they wouldn't return, and it was all pointless, really, as pointless as her work. What had she been thinking?

She couldn't save Caro or Dev, she couldn't save anyone and here was the proof, and it was ridiculous that this, *this* was the one lesson she could never learn, ridiculous that she kept trying—and to make matters even more aggravating, one of them must have cranked the thermostat on the way to their death because she was roasting, she would have sold every one of them for a pitcher of Thai iced tea and no matter how much of the lemonade she drank she couldn't cool off, she could only boil in her own skin while guzzling glass after glass after glass...

...and then she was awake, quick as snapping her fingers. There was no gradual return to consciousness; one moment she was at the death banquet, and the next she was alone and trembling in the dark.

The den smells wrong! her brain screamed. Completely wrong, nothing like home, not a single familiar scent, and worse, the place was crawling with

(*predator!*)

Stables, but before she could investigate, or charge, she caught the scent of

(*David*)

another werebear

(*David*)

relaxed and snuggled close to her

(*David*)

so that was all right. She squeezed him back

"Muh?"

and got up, made straight for the kitchen, opened the fridge, seized the half gallon of skim milk

(ugh white water, but you know what they say about beggars and choosers)

drank half of it down, paused to take a deep, gulping breath, then finished it off. Set the empty container beside the sink

(note: offer to pay for that in the morning, don't forget)

turned, padded back to bed.

"Ow!" *Forgot about the sofa bed.*

"Muh? 'Nette?"

And the werebear sleeping in it. Wait, he was sleeping in the other bed. Her bed. Her temporary bed that smelled like Stables. Good. She crawled back beneath the covers and was about to give David a firm nudge to get him to scooch over

(blanket hog)

when he rolled over on his back, and his warm, sleepy scent washed over her, and for a couple of seconds he smelled like comfort and safety and sweetness, and before she knew it, she was kissing him, horrified at her utter lack of control and thrilled to be giving in to urges denied far *far* too long, and joy of joys, he was sleepily kissing her back.

Until he wasn't. "Annette? Are you all the way awake?"

"Mm-hmm."

"Because you're talking about lamb chops."

"Mmm...no. I'm callin' you a lamb chop."

"Oh."

"I really, really like lamb chops. And you too."

"Thanks. It's mutual." His hands had come up like they were going to grasp her waist, but he didn't touch her; he just lay there, holding air. "You're sure you're awake?"

"Mm-hmm." Her fingers went to skim under his T-shirt just as she remembered he was shirtless, because David Auberon was a clever, clever man. The tips of her fingers brushed over his nipples, and he sucked in a sharp breath as she leaned in to nuzzle at his collarbone.

"Oh my God. That's... Oh..."

She hummed and kissed his throat.

"Annette, are you saying 'nom-nom-nom'?"

"Uh-uh."

"And you're definitely awake."

She sat up, straddling him; her eyes had adjusted enough so she could see him blinking up at her. "Did you want to give me a field sobriety test? I'm awake! Should I stop?"

"It's not that. I just—"

"Oh. *Oh*," she said, mortified. "You're not... You don't want this." This. This was why she never did things like this. The fleeting pleasure did not outweigh the humiliation. She could feel the blood rush to her face as she started to climb off him, but he seized her by the waist and yanked her back down. "I'm sorry... Ack!"

"Dear God, no!" He lowered his voice. "Uh. I mean, I am one hundred and fifty-five percent into this, and you can do whatever the holy hell you want to me. I just wanted to make sure you... Oof! Jesus."

"That's mathematically impossible," she said, and kissed him again. "Can't be more than one hundred percent."

"Disagree," he gasped when she licked his nipple. His hand slid into her hair, careful not to pull, but as she trailed kisses lower and lower, his other hand fisted in the sheets. "Oh Christ."

"You're so sensitive here."

"Am I?" he gasped.

"And you taste so *good*," she marveled.

"Thanks," he managed. "Can I... I want to touch you, too."

She pulled back long enough to tug the borrowed nightgown over her head, then stretched out on him again, topless.

"The murder and the attempted murders are bad," he croaked, hugging her so tightly to him that she squeaked, "but this is turning into a fucking great week."

"So sweet."

"Can I... What are we... Okay, I'm down for anything you want. *Anything*." As he spoke, his hands roamed everywhere he could reach—her back, her breasts, her waist, finally cupping her ass and squeezing her still closer to him—and then he kissed her, which was excellent. "But we haven't talked about this. How far, and birth control, and...we haven't. Not even hypothetically. Since we're not dating. Not even hypothetically. I didn't think... *Ow*."

She nipped his shoulder again. "If you're coherent

and using words like 'hypothetically,' I'm doing a terrible job of seducing you."

"No. You. *Aren't*," he said fervently. "I just…I want what you want. Whatever that is. And wherever that goes. Just for tonight, obviously."

"Obviously?"

"Yeah, you don't have to worry. I don't have any. You know. Expectations."

No, of course not. A disappointment, not a surprise. But at least they both knew what they wanted from the evening. "It's fine," she said, sitting up, taking his hands and placing them on her breasts. The bitten-off gasping noise he made was deeply gratifying. "I'm not in season, but even if I was, we're staying strictly above the waist. Yes?"

"Yes. Absolutely. Whatever you want. Or don't. Anything."

She then proceeded to wring several more gratifying sounds out of him, and to her delight, she found his voice got even deeper the more she aroused him; it wasn't unlike playing a double bass. A sentient double bass who smelled divine and kept gasping her name. He returned the favor, and they kissed and teased and touched, and at one point David started to slide off the bed and she had to haul him back up, shushing his giggles, trying to stifle her own, and hoping his Stable allies were heavy sleepers with piss-poor hearing.

After a while, she had to wrench herself away from him because the urge to shred his briefs, seize his cock (which had been a hot, firm weight against her hip the

entire time they moved against each other) and unceremoniously stick it inside her was getting hard to ignore.
They both separated and lay on their backs, only their
shoulders touching, panting and staring at the ceiling.

After a while, when she could talk without begging
him to kindly fuck her already, she whispered, "It's fine
if you want to excuse yourself and, ah, use the facilities.
For whatever."

"Nope. I'm not doing anything that means leaving
this bed before morning."

"I'm quite sure it *is* morning."

"Don't care. Not moving."

"See? I told you this one was an improvement over
the sofa bed."

He snorted. "It's not the fucking bed, you gorgeous
dope. Agh," he added when she poked him.

"Thanks for indulging me."

"Anytime. That's literal, just so you know. Day or
night. Winter or summer. Upside down or right-side up.
Northern Hemisphere or Southern Hemisphere."

"David, you say the loveliest… Good God, I have
beard-burn *everywhere*," she marveled. "Even on my
elbows! How the hell did you manage that?"

He laughed. "Don't remember. I haven't made out like
that since I was a teenager."

"It's been a while for me, too."

"That's…almost impossible to believe," he confessed.

"I'm picky," she said simply. "Thanks for breaking
your I-won't-date-Annette rule." She yawned. "However

temporarily. Actually, this isn't a date. So your rule is still intact." She was sweaty and sleepy, but the intense sexual frustration was starting to ebb just a bit and she had a belly full of milk and the dead were dead, nothing would change that, but every corpse at that table would have wanted her to move on. Some days it was easier, that was all.

"Annette? What are you saying?"

"Shhhh. Sleeping."

"Okay, but I don't have a rule about—"

"Talk 'bout it t'morrow."

"Wow. You fall asleep *really* fast. But just so you know, I don't have any rules against dating you. And if I was dumb enough to have one, I'd have broken it ages ago. Okay? Annette? Oh hell…"

Chapter 27

WARM. WARM AND COMFORTABLE AND FRAGRANT AND luscious. *What kind of pillow is this? I'm buying a dozen.* Oh, it had everything; it was soft and yielding and snoring, all the things any red-blooded werebear wanted in a—

He cracked open an eye.

It was not a pillow.

It was Annette.

Which was even better.

How long can I stay like this with her? I hate to wake her up and ruin the... Ouch.

"Ten more minutes," she mumbled, then smacked him on the arm again with a small, closed fist. He had a vague memory of her saying something about needing a new alarm clock... Was it just yesterday? Christ, how many did she go through a week?

He also had a vague memory of Annette having a nightmare, going to the kitchen, guzzling something (the gulps were pretty loud), then returning and pouncing on him to initiate the hottest make-out session he'd ever had, and that included Tanya Finn the morning after senior prom. The things Annette could do with her mouth! Her ripe mouth, all soft lips hiding sharp little teeth that nibbled and kissed, and she'd had him hard and aching in about half a second, and probably not even that long.

Holding back from just picking her up, slamming her on her back, shoving her knees apart with his, and burying himself inside her sweet center had taken Olympian-level willpower.

But he'd meant what he said: she could have whatever she wanted. Even if all she wanted was nothing.

And then: back to Snoresville, population Annette. Christ, just thinking about it was enough to make him want to rip the covers off, beg her for a fuck (quick, long, mercy, hate…whatever category of fuck she was up for, though he'd have to fake hate), then doing things that would forever destroy the box spring.

None of which was on the table, not least because Annette seemed to be laboring under the laughable idea that he didn't want her. At least, that's what he thought she'd said. It had been late, they'd been horny and exhausted, and the next thing he knew, it was the crack of eight.

He reached out and gently shook her shoulder. "Annette, it's me. Uh, David. It's time to get up and go back out into the world and get disillusioned all over again."

"Don' like this brand of clock. Makes the bed shake," she whined. Then again with the fist: SMACK!

Jesus, my entire forearm just went numb. He moved out of smacking distance, like every alarm clock she'd ever had would've if they could've, and said, "Breakfast?"

She sat bolt upright, like a sexy Frankenstein's mon-ster coming to life after the electric jolt. "Nnnnnnn?" She looked around blearily and yawned. "Why does my bed smell weird? And why are you in it? And where are we? And is there bacon?"

"Ask me again when you're all the way awake, if you still have questions. We'll find the answers together," he vowed, bounding out of bed and not caring how silly he sounded. "Rise and shine!"

"Good *God*, a morning person," she moaned, and flopped back down.

"What in the name of all that's…" Annette stared at her reflection and tried not to gasp in horror. She was covered in love bites; dark-purple hickeys were dotted all across her collarbone and neck and (after a quick peek beneath the nightgown) her breasts. And as the events of last night came back to her, she'd be willing to wager David was sporting a few, too. If she ever wagered. Which she did not.

What am I going to say to him? 'Sorry about molesting you…again'? 'Please don't read into it'? 'Even though I know you're not interested, I wanted to find out what your nipples tasted like anyway'?

"It didn't happen, it will never happen, stop trying to make it happen."

Well, she'd ignored that and gone ahead anyway. So now what?

There was a polite rap on the bathroom door, and

thank goodness, because she didn't have an answer and welcomed a distraction. She could scent David on the other side. "It's open."

He stuck his head in and grinned when he saw her. "Morning."

"It is. Yes."

"How'd you—" He cut himself off as she turned to face him, then stepped inside, closed the door, then joined her at the mirror, showing off his own set of tooth-marks and love bites.

She stared at their reflection. *This is the first time we've shared a mirror. And a bathroom. And a bed.* "This will only confuse the rumormongers," she said, and she hadn't been teasing but he burst out laughing anyway, and she couldn't help smiling. If she'd overstepped, he appeared to be fine with it. Or would at least overlook it. The former was the ideal, but she'd take the latter, too. This wasn't high school. There was no time for drama. That kind of drama, anyway. They were trailing killers, or killers were trailing them, or both

(probably both)

and nothing was more important than solving the riddle of Caro.

"You okay?" David asked, tracing a finger over the darkest hickey on her neck, which sounded like the title of a romance novel.[3]

"Fine. You?"

---

3. When souls collide, danger lurks, and love is the most dangerous weapon of all, fall into… *The Darkest Hickey*. (Don't steal that, it's mine!)

"Everything's good on my end."

"Good. That's...good." *Oh my God. Reduced to single syllables. The shame of it.*

David cleared his throat, which seemed to be his way of announcing "I would like to contribute to the conversation now." Either that or he was coming down with something viral. "Listen, about—"

"If you say 'about last night,' I'll get to mark off another X on my romance-cliché bingo card."

"Regarding the events of the past evening..."

She snickered. "Nice. Listen, I'd just like to focus on the case. All right? That's got to be our priority."

"Okay." His smile faded as if someone had drawn a shade over his expression. "No problem."

"Really?"

"Of course." He nodded. "The kids come first."

"Right! They absolutely do. So let's get back to it. Please tell me that the bacon I'm smelling isn't a hallucination."

"What bacon?" he replied, and smirked at her gasp of horror.

Which was followed by another gasp of horror when Annette walked into Jim and Jenn's kitchen to see Oz Adway gently fending off Jenn's attempts to smother him with a wet washcloth, most likely because his nose was streaming blood all over her sink.

"Well, hiya," he said, his usual enthusiastic greeting muted by a good 60 percent.

"Good *God*! What happened? Your clothes are—"

"Don't talk about it," he groaned, and she knew why. Oz's bespoke navy-blue suit and crisp white dress shirt were shredded and bloodstained. He was missing a shoe, and the exposed black dress sock looked like it was on its last legs (so to speak). His monthly clothing budget was larger than her car payment. This clearly

"I've worn this shirt once. Once!"

wounded him deeply. Not to mention the actual wounds; aside from the nose, he was a mess of contusions, and there was a gash just over his ear that might need a stitch or two.

"What happened?" she cried. "Please tell me you were doing something stupid on your own—"

"No promises."

"—and this was *not* a consequence of our case."

"Again, no promises… Argh, thank you, stop it now." Oz all but yanked the washcloth from Jenn. "Look, I'll just keep the rag, okay? Bleeding's stopped. Well, mostly."

"You said you got hit by a car!" Jenn protested. "You might have a concussion!"

"Who cares? Thank God it was me and not my car."

"You're definitely concussed."

"He's not concussed," Annette interjected. "He just has a lot of feelings about his car." To Oz: "What happened?"

She'd known Oz was returning for them. He'd appointed himself their chauffeur, God knew why, and not only dropped them off at Jenn and Jim's but also promised to return the next morning.

"I got a message from my contact at Citigroup—I'd

talked to him about shell corporations. At least, I thought it was from him. Figured I'd meet with him, then come get you. But only one of those things happened."

"Let me guess," David said. He'd come up silently behind Annette and laid a hand on her waist, listening, then moved it before anyone could see. Kind of like how she'd held his hand during Oz's shell corporation lecture. She'd let go before David could get the wrong idea. Because that's what this week was: day after day of wrong ideas. "Nondescript black SUV with blacked-out windows, and you didn't get the plate number."

"Sorry. Too busy counting my cracked ribs."

Meanwhile, since Oz had spurned her rudimentary first aid efforts, Jenn, still sleep-tousled and wearing a pair of Jim's old pajamas—the size and spatula pattern gave it away—pressed a cup of milk into Annette's hand. Oh, good, she hadn't drunk it all the night before. "We were just talking with your brother."

"Nuh-uh!" Oz protested. "I barely said hello and then you tried to choke me with a wet towel that smells like onions. That's what we're doing."

"He's not my brother. He was my foster brother. Soon he'll be my *late* foster brother. Very, very soon. And very, very late." Annette rubbed her temples. "I knew it. I knew this would happen. Well. Not this exact thing. But something bad. Is it too early for a glass of orange juice and vodka and please tell me you're out of orange juice?"

Oz, for his part, was staring at her and David, nostrils flared and eyebrows arching in surprise. The bruises were hidden, but she knew he could smell David all over her and silently dared him to say something, anything, just. One. Thing. But all he did was limp to a chair and sit.

"Shouldn't we call an ambulance?" This from Jim, who had just now come upon the bloody kitchen scene.

"Why?" Oz replied. "Are you sick?"

"He'll be fine," Annette said with assurance she didn't quite feel. Oz *would* be fine if he simply dropped everything and obeyed her every command like a slavish robot programmed for compliance.

(This seemed unlikely.)

"I'm so sorry for all of this," Annette told her bewildered hosts. "It was kind of you to let us stay here. If Oz has ruined anything tangible—"

"What's that supposed to mean?" Oz asked, trying for indignant but settling for peeved. "How's tangibility a factor here?"

"—I'll of course pay to replace it."

"Don't even worry about it," Jim said at once. "The important thing is your brother wasn't killed."

"He's not my… Yes. I agree, that *is* the important thing."

Oz beamed. "Aw."

"Shut up. Gentlemen, shall we?"

"You're all welcome back anytime," Jenn added with credible sincerity, walking them to the door.

"Really?" Oz asked as he limped past her. "Why?"

"Yeah, we've gotta get going… Thanks, guys. Great seeing you again. Sorry about…" David gestured vaguely in Annette and Oz's direction, shook Jim's hand, and hugged Jenn, who still seemed inclined to fret, but fretting without impeding Annette could handle.

"The bleeding *has* stopped. And the gash by your ear—it looks smaller. How is that... Are you, uh, are you like David?" Jenn whispered, which was asinine because they were all occupying the same small room so whispering was pointless.

Oz grinned. "Naw, I'm straight. Ready, gang?"

"Huh?" From David. "Wait, I'm st—never mind, it's too early to get off track already. Let's get going. Jesus, Oz, you really are a mess."

"Yeah, but a sexy mess."

"You know what? I'm gonna let you have that one." David gave him a gentle shoulder chuck. "You *are* a sexy mess."

"And if you don't die working this case today, you're welcome to come back here tonight and crash again," Jim added, and got another elbow in the ribs from his wife for his trouble.

When the three of them were free and back on the street, they were able to settle some particulars.

"Of course I'm driving."

"Did that car knock the remaining sanity out of you? You can barely walk."

"Doesn't mean I can't drive. Otherwise, what am I here for?"

"I've asked myself that same question, Oz. Many, many, many, many, many times."

David shouldered past Annette and gave Oz a piercing

once-over. "No bullshit, pal, how are you? Hospital bad or going home and sulking and having booze for breakfast bad?"

"Honestly, it's worse than it looks. The car didn't get me head-on, just clipped me. End of the week, you'd never know I got hit. My gorgeously expensive clothes protected me, and they deserve a hero's farewell. And regardless of the state of my health, neither of you have a car here. So it's either wait for a Fubar (Shifter Uber) or let me give you a lift. So do *that*, and then I can check on the kids while you guys take the investigator."

"Do you promise to go straight home and rest after?" Annette asked, unable to keep the anxiety out of her voice. "Wait—is it even safe for you to go home? Someone set a trap for you."

"I'll rest up somewhere safe," he promised. "Cross my heart and hope to God Mama Mac never finds out about any of it."

Annette shivered. "Amen. Addendum: I hate you."

"Naw. You don't."

Once the oddly cheerful Oz had dropped them off, David asked, "Is he right?" out of nowhere.

"Sorry?" She'd been wondering how there was beard burn on the inside of her wrists, and it took a second to focus.

"Oz. He said you didn't hate him. Is he right?"

"No, no. Of course not. Is that how I come off?"

"Uh…"

"I don't hate him," she promised. "I just don't want him around me under any circumstances."

"Sure, sure." David was nodding. "Totally normal."

"Oh, stop it. If you want normal, join a book club."

"I can't tell if you're slamming me or book clubs."

"When I slam you," she warned, "there will not be a doubt in your mind."

"Got it."

"I like your friends," she said, because a subject change seemed in order. "And I'm glad they kept your secret. Though I'm not sure how much of your nature they understand. It was adorable when Jenn worried I'd accidentally bite through the toothbrush she lent me."

"Ha! I think she was messing with you."

"And if we're together in another strange bed tonight, remind me I still need to get a new alarm clock."

"Maybe more than one. Maybe a baker's dozen of alarms, if what I've experienced is any indication."

"One problem at a time," she replied. "I'll worry about the sorry state of alarm clock craftsmanship after we get through this morning. And I talked to Pat—he and the kids had a quiet night. But I have to come up with a better plan for them besides 'hide underground indefinitely with limited resources while we try to stay one step ahead of arrest warrants and hopefully Oz won't get hurt worse.'" She nibbled her lip as she stared out the window. "One way or the other, we have to take definitive action today."

"Agreed. Which is why we're on our way to see Brennan."

"Why are you narrating? I'm aware of why we're on our way to Brennan."

"And I'll bet you a metric ton of watermelon Jolly Ranchers that he'll dodge us."

"I never bet, David."

"Sure. But if you did."

"How much is a metric ton? Oh, never mind. Even if I won, what in God's name would I do with all those Jolly Ranchers? It's really... Are you *growling*?"

"No," he lied. "Just thinking about naked you and a shit-ton of unwrapped Jolly Ranchers."

"That may well be the most romantic thing you've ever said to me."

David let out a snort. "Good thing this isn't a romance, huh?"

She had no reply to that and went back to staring out the window.

Brennan greeted them with open arms. Actual open arms.

"We didn't shake on it," David muttered to Annette. "It wasn't a real bet."

"Crybaby."

If Brennan's warm welcome was an attempt to put them at ease, it flopped. Nobody should be that happy to see a scruffy PI or scruffier (they were still in yesterday's clothes) caseworker from IPA.

"Hey, it's people like you who keep the system running," he beamed when they introduced themselves, which was so dumb, David had to make a deliberate effort not to roll his eyes. "What can I help you with?"

"Thank you for seeing us without an appointment."

"No problem, no problem."

"We're tracking down some children who went missing after they were discharged from United," Annette said. "We're hoping you'll be of assistance."

Brennan plopped into his chair behind a desk that could have doubled as an oak moat: four feet wide, six feet long, and gleaming with generations of varnish. His office, located in the Hamm Building in downtown Saint Paul, was all dark, sleek wood, lush carpeting, and prints of random British people steeplechase-jumping on horseback. There was a huge globe in the corner which his family had probably lugged over on the *Mayflower*, a small fridge and wet bar beside the globe, and cubicles outside for the peons. It was like being on the set of *Wall Street*. The original, not the sequel. The only things missing were screaming brokers, shoulder pads, and frosted perms.

"Missing kids from United? If you've got my card… That's how you found me, right? So then you know I found them." He spread his hands in a *What can you do?* gesture. "So, again, what can I help you with?"

Annette studied the diplomas on the wall. "I thought you were an investigator, but you're a lawyer."

"I'm an investigator who passed the bar," Brennan corrected with a grin. "What can I say? Double threat."

Brennan was one of those Shifters who convinced David that discovery by the wider world was inevitable. Everything about the man screamed "werewolf." Even Stables probably sensed it, though they wouldn't know why he made them uneasy. When he smiled, he showed very white, very sharp teeth, with slightly elongated canines. His brown eyes were almond-shaped but under fluorescents they had a yellowish cast, and his cheekbones were so high and sharp they threw his face into shadow. He wore his dirty-blond hair slicked back to his collar, making his face seem longer. His black tailored suit showed off his lean build; his hands looked strong, and his no-polish manicured nails looked sharp. He looked like he could run a deposition or attack a flock of sheep at any moment.

"Have we met?" Annette asked suddenly, turning away from the ego wall to study Brennan's face.

"I don't think so. I'd remember someone like *you*." This, followed by a broad grin that made David want to play amateur dentist.

He cleared his throat. "The thing is, Brennan—"

Brennan's eyebrows arched, though he didn't seem put out. If anything, the smile got wider. *He likes this stuff to be out in the open. Okay.*

"—nobody's actually seen the cubs you said you found."

"*Said* I found?"

"And some people—"

"Uh-oh, 'some people.'" Brennan grinned. "That sounds bad."

"—think that you didn't actually find them. That all you did was manipulate some computer records to make it look like the kids were found."

"Wow, you think a lot of my skills. I'm flattered, man."

"No, *you* think a lot of your skills. And it's apparently justified." Annette tapped a framed diploma. "Bachelor of Science in Computer Science. And then law school." She smiled back. "That sounds exhausting."

Brennan warmed to Annette's version of yummy cop. "I don't need much sleep."

"Lucky," she replied. "Wish I could say the same."

"Yeah, well, you bears have…other nice qualities."

That's it. Before the sun sets, this guy is gonna aspirate his molars.

Annette remained admirably uncreeped out. "But you see our problem, Mr. Brennan."

"Greg, please."

"Greg. You've clearly got the skills to make it look like those children were never missing. That they're all safe and sound in various foster homes. So…how can we be sure? No offense."

"None taken, none at all," he replied promptly. "You're only doing your job."

"Well," Annette said modestly, "we *are* dedicated public servants devoted to our work."

"And this is too important to take some rando lawyer's word. That's what you're saying, right?"

"Yep." Time for grumpy cop to weigh in again. "That's exactly right, Brennan."

He glanced at David, a little irritated, then back at Annette, who got another toothy grin. "So, we'll go see them. I'll take you myself."

Annette blinked. "You will?"

"I'm in and out of depos all day today—I mean, it's kind of a miracle you were able to get in to see me at all—"

"We perform miracles on the daily," David said. "Often before lunch."

"—but I've got tomorrow morning wide open for you guys." Brennan spread his hands again, like a saint blessing the poor. Or scamming them. "We can go see all of them, if you want."

"Oh."

Yeah. Oh. Now what? They didn't have the legal authority to make him drop everything and show the kits right this minute. Worse, he was being ridiculously reasonable, so they couldn't make a fuss without drawing attention.

"That's...really nice of you," Annette said, blinking faster. David wondered if it was a tic. Only Annette could make it seem adorable. "We're going to take you up on that."

"Great! Can I get your numbers?" Grin. "Well. I really only need yours, Annette." Smirk.

She giggled. David mentally begged his stomach not to erupt all over Brennan's big-ass moat desk.

"We're sorry to interrupt your workday," Annette continued in a voice so sweet David could've used it for his coffee. "You must be so busy, being an investigator-slash-lawyer-slash-computer expert."

"Yeah, well, I've actually got a memorial service this a.m. for a former client. I'm sure you know him. Well, knew him—Lund?"

"You're Lund's investigator? Or lawyer? Or computer programmer?"

"For years." The ever-present grin finally disappeared. "*Man*, that guy was a pain in my ass. Took him on as a favor to my folks, and then I couldn't get him off my neck."

"Well, he's off it now," David pointed out.

"Thank *God*." Brennan actually spun around in his chair like a bored kid. "I know you're not supposed to speak ill of the dead, but that guy was nothing but trouble for me. And who lets a sixteen-year-old werewolf get the drop on him?"

Nice abrupt segue. One with nothing at all to do with the missing kids, as far as this guy knows. Or is supposed to know.

"He was very understanding about the attack," Annette said, her tone indicating she was also thrown by Brennan's out-of-context mention of Caro. "Especially given the digit amputations and other injuries."

"Yeah, I know. More interested in being a tough guy than paying attention. And then he gave you the brush-off, right?"

"Yes. It's a tragedy that he was murdered only a few hours later."

"Should've stayed where it was safe." Brennan shrugged and licked his lips. *Jesus. Stables must head for the hills when he does that.* "Wanted to get back to his little pet shop instead."

"Pet shop?"

"Sorry, sorry. 'Exotic pets importer and exporter.' Which he was weirdly proud of." A snort. "But, yeah. Glorified pet-shop owner."

David couldn't believe the waves of animosity coming off the guy. Was it possible Brennan could be an ally? Had he found out something unsavory about Lund but was constrained from action by attorney–client privilege? He glanced at Annette, then forced warmth into his tone. "That's the drawback to being a lawyer, man. Can't always pick your clients, even from the defense side."

"Tell me about it."

"No wonder you wanted to be an investigator, too. I don't have any fancy suits," he added, faking admiration for Brennan's wardrobe choices, "but on the other hand, I don't have to take on any client I don't want."

"Damned straight!" Brennan held up a hand, and for a second, David didn't think he'd be able to do it. *If there was any doubt this guy is a bad guy, that doubt has disappeared. Who high-fives a stranger?* David managed a listless high five. "And I'll tell you something else. Lund was a pain, but what happened to him? That was a real shame."

"Oh yes." From Annette. "Hopefully the police will be able to catch whomever did it."

"That Caro girl did it." Shrug. "At least, that's the word." Brennan popped out of his chair like a wolf-in-the-box. "Anyway. If you want to leave your contact info with my receptionist, we can meet up tomorrow. Eight o'clock okay?"

"Of course," she replied. "We appreciate you taking the time to do this."

"No prob. Nice meeting you. Both."

"You too." Annette shook his hand and smiled. David shook his hand and smiled. Brennan smiled back. Everyone looked at each other and smiled and smiled.

Chapter 28

ANNETTE INSPECTED HER PALM AS DAVID HUNG UP one of the burners and tossed it in the back seat. "There's not enough hand sanitizer in the world. And I need half-a-dozen Jolly Ranchers to get the taste out of my mouth. We only shook hands but I feel filthy."

"Not a fan, huh?"

"The opposite of a fan. Ugh, that *smile*. I'm betting the caption on his yearbook picture read Most Likely to Date Rape." She popped another red candy into her mouth. "Who'd you call?"

"Nobody," David said with a distinctly guilty look.

"You called Oz? Is he okay?"

"Seems to be. And he's checking on Caro and Dev."

"I wish we didn't have to use him like that."

"Is it using him if he's the one in a hurry to stick his head in the noose?" David cleared his throat. "I'll rephrase…"

"Please don't."

"Annette, I'm not sure if you've noticed—"

"Oh, good God. Anytime someone says that, it's always sarcastic and it always prefaces pointing out something that I have, in fact, noticed."

"—but our allies are thin on the ground. We've got Nadia running all over town for us, but she's just one person, and he wants to help. For Christ's sake, he bled for us."

"Because he is stupid! He is a stupid man who thinks he can handle real trouble, right up until the moment it whips around and gets him by the throat! And I am aware I sound heartless but I can't do anything about that right now!"

"Oooooo-kay," David added after what felt like a five-year silence. "Upside is he's had plenty of time to turn us over to Gomph and he hasn't."

"Oh, he'd never do *that*," she said at once. At David's look, she added, "All right, yes, he drives me nuts. I'm not sure if *you've* noticed, but I've got a bit of a food attachment issue—"

"No. Nope. Uh-uh. Never noticed. I don't think I've ever heard you talk about food. Or seen you eat. At all. At any time. Not once."

"—but Oz would never do anything to hurt me. On purpose, I mean. Just inconvenience me. All the damned time," she added in a mutter. "When he was staying at Mama Mac's, he'd never bust me for sneaking in late, but if I left so much as a piece of cake lying around, down his gullet it went. Half the time he wasn't even hungry, just…he'd get spite munchies. *God,* he's irritating."

"Like a little brother."

"Well. Yes."

There was another short silence, broken by David's "Aw. That's cute."

"Shut up." She sighed. "Anyway. I knew what I was getting into when I told him about the opening in Accounting last year."

David laughed.

"Again, shut up. How was I supposed to know he'd spend more time in our break room than theirs? Stop laughing. You're going to drive us into a ditch."

"It's downtown Saint Paul. There aren't any ditches."

"So he bugs you, but you helped him get a job here."

"Well, I can't let him starve to death, can I?"

"Good point. You either help Oz get a job or he starves to death. No middle ground there. And I'm gonna put it out there…"

"Ooooooh."

"…because I already pissed you off by suggesting Nadia might be the mole. But what about Oz?" When she had no comment, he plunged ahead. "He's relatively new. He bugged the shit out of you to let him help on *this* particular case. But why this one? You're always taking care of cubs in trouble. So why now?"

"Those are good points," Annette replied. Because objectively, they were. But her gut told her

(*fuck no. impossible.*)

otherwise. Also, her gut had a potty mouth. She thought about the brutality captured on film, the pain and desperation on the cubs' faces, and the fury on Caro's. She'd seen that fury before, and not just in the course of her duty.

"Oz Adway," she said slowly and carefully, "would not hurt a cub if you had him by the throat. He wouldn't abet abuse, even peripherally. And I deeply pity Lund's nasty little colleagues if Oz finds them before we do."

She thought about it. "Well, I would pity them. But not deeply."

"Where's the money come from?"

"Pardon?"

"Adway dresses like he's got a six-figure clothing budget."

"Well. He does."

"And he drives a Maserati. So why does he even work here? He's rich."

"He works here because of how he got rich. I can't go into it," she added, anticipating his question. "It's not my story to tell. I'm aware that adds to our difficulty."

There was another pause while David thought it over. "All right," he said. "But I think we can agree that there *is* a mole. So who is it? Who was helping Lund?"

"Brennan?"

"He was skeezy," David agreed, "but on the plus side, he sure didn't like Lund. So it might be a mark in his favor. D'you think he found out what Lund was doing?"

"I wondered. But if he did, there were things he could have done or said to put that across to us. And if not us, someone else from IPA. There are ways around privilege, especially when the client is dead. And where the welfare of minors is concerned. But this...his contempt for Lund felt personal. Not just a professional thing along the lines of 'Gosh, this client is such a pest!'"

"Tell you what—I've got the sudden urge to pay my respects to a dead pet importer-exporter. Think we can find out where the memorial is?"

"What a coincidence, I've got the same urge! Yes, and yes. And I'll bet Nadia can help." Annette grinned and grabbed a burner. "What's crashing a memorial compared to obstruction, anyway?"

———

I love strawberry Jolly Ranchers now! Even if they're like eating rock-hard sugar cubes steeped in artificial flavors and colors! Thanks to that glorious paean to cavities, she had David backed up against the changing-room door, her hands roaming beneath his shirt, his mouth doing wicked, astonishing things to her throat.

Also, this was all Nadia's fault. She was late. So they waited. And waited. And oops! Suddenly there was a piece of sticky candy in her hair. Just hanging there all by itself. In her hair. By accident. Which she couldn't see. Because it was in her hair. By accident. But David, ever the gentleman

"Hang on, I think you've got something—Jesus."

sprang to her assistance, and then she sprang to his, sort of, if springing meant grabbing and kissing and then *hands* everywhere and also she was very much afraid this was more than a physical attraction, more than random sex-fueled neurons firing because now she was wondering if he liked lakes or the ocean, movies or plays, salads or steaks (or both!), and that was bad, this wasn't a love story, it was…something else. And the only thing to do was to take a page from Dory's book: just keep kissing, just keep kissing, just keep kissing…

All of which came to an instant end when someone on the other side of the door hit it with enough force to rattle the thing on its hinges. They both jumped back, Annette managing to get it unlocked before more, noisier damage could be done. She knew the sound of those fists.

And there she was, rushing in, then closing and locking the door behind her. "Strip, morons." When David and Annette exchanged a glance, Nadia all but threw the clothing at them. "Now!"

"Yikes." David turned his back and began unbuckling his belt. Annette almost laughed, and hoped his erection would go down so he could get his pants off.

"You're going to a memorial to presumably fake respect for a dead fuckwit, yes? How are you going to pull that off in yesterday's rumpled clothes? Have either of you considered that? No? I thought not. Why does it smell like pheromones in here?"

"No idea," Annette lied, ignoring David's snort.

They were in the Super Target family restroom with Nadia and her bottomless bag of new clothes, which meant two werebears were trapped in a six-by-six box with an agitated raptor. Compliance was the quickest guarantee of safety. Annette kicked off her shoes, stripped off her sweater, shucked her pants, and held out her hand for...

"Dammit."

"Oh, stop it."

"I loathe salmon. The color," she clarified, looking at the dress on the hanger. "And I think you knew that."

"Beggars and choosers, darling. Besides, it's apricot, not salmon."

"And since it's a memorial," Annette continued, "shouldn't this be black?"

"Your coloring demands apricot! You have enough black. Yech. Here. No, bend forward. More. *More.* Oh, just stand still. My God. You're like a child."

"I know you are, but what am I? And any clothing I need help putting on is clothing I will never wear again," Annette warned, her voice muffled as the silky material rolled past her face.

"Do shut up, Annette." Nadia fussed with the thing, coaxing it to fall and drape wherever it was supposed to fall and drape. Annette had to admit, once it was on, it was fairly comfortable. It was an off-the-shoulder dress with a nipped-in waist and a hem that fell just below her knees. And, she realized, pivoting, it did terrific things for her big butt. Which was irrelevant, but nice.

"It's supposed to hit at mid-calf," Nadia fussed, "but you're obscenely tall. Legs too long, hair too wild, face too pale, figure too zaftig."

"You forgot about my scurvy and chronic trench mouth."

"And yet, my unerring fashion sense will be able to camouflage all of it."

"Her legs are perfect," David said, looking pretty perfect himself. "And so's her hair and her face and her zaftig. She doesn't have to change a thing."

"David, you're just too adorable sometimes."

"I thought it would itch," Annette confessed, petting the fabric.

"Yes, it's polyester, I'm *aware*, Annette. I was under considerable time constraints, and I am appalled, *appalled*, at the depth of your ingratitude."

"I meant because of the lace patchwork around the shoulders. But see?" She wriggled her (nearly bare) shoulders. "No itching."

"Oh. Very good. Now, David, *your* coloring demands embalmment. Which wasn't an option, but I did the best I could. And I'll remind you—"

"You don't have to remind us. But you will." David coughed. "A lot."

"—that my best is better than 95 percent of anyone else's best."

"Only 95 percent? It's fine." David was in black slacks, a black mock turtleneck, and a black suit jacket. "Not to sound ungrateful, but how'd you know all my sizes?"

"I have eyes, don't I?"

"It's still creepy."

Nadia sniffed and turned back to Annette, holding out a black cardigan with pearl buttons. "No, no, don't put your arms through the sleeves! That's not what they're for."

"What *are* they for?"

"To help you look breezy and relaxed," Nadia replied, exasperated.

"I'm neither. It's a memorial, not a regatta, and the sweater eventually falls off."

"Look, you demanded my help—"

"David and I called and politely asked where Lund's memorial was taking place."

"—and you're getting it. Ah! David, that's just excellent. No, leave that one unbuttoned, too. There. You two look marginally less horrifying than you did five minutes ago. I did the very best I could with the wretched material I had to work with."

"It's great," Annette said, looking down at herself and over at David. "Thank you."

"Very extremely great," David said, giving Annette an appreciative once-over.

She could feel her face getting warm because her priorities were screwed and abruptly asked, "Can we talk about what happened with Gomph yesterday?"

"He couldn't find you and was in high dudgeon. And then I left and have taken care not to be seen since."

"Nadia, the whole point was for you to stay out of trouble by pretending to try to rein us in."

"I am. My vacation started yesterday. And while I was chasing Gomph away from you like an aggrieved oxpecker—do stop laughing, David, I'm aware it's an amusing mental image but get ahold of yourself—*anyway*, I made a rather large fuss about how I refused, *refused*, to miss my flight. And Oz was at my side, appropriately and loudly sympathetic. Everyone thinks I'm in the Badlands today and thus not helping you, nor hindering the bad guys. And speaking of hindering, have you seen Oz?"

"Have you? Because he looked terrible an hour ago." David briefly explained Oz's predicament and subsequent dispatchment to the studio. "But no witnesses and no plate number."

"Why in the world would anyone want to maim an account—Oh, bugger." Nadia raised stricken eyes to Annette. "I gave him all those account numbers to sift through. Lund's wretched colleagues must be worried he's found something."

"At least we know he was on the right track." When the women had nothing to say, he added, "Subjectively, that sucks, though. Worse than you having to cancel your vacation."

Annette was still silent. Nadia's vacations were plotted and planned like an invasion into a hostile territory. (Which was entirely possible, depending on Nadia's destination that year.) Research began months in advance, as did the wardrobe dry runs. They were everything to her, and the prep work was damned entertaining to watch.

"I'm sorry. I forgot about your vacation," she confessed.

"Me, too," David added. Then: "The Badlands?"

"What?"

"I guess I figured you for… I dunno. Milan? Or Paris. Or Moscow. Or anywhere but South Dakota."

"I wanted to see how bad your so-called Badlands are. And I would like to see a buffalo."

Annette could picture Nadia soaring over Mount Rushmore, riding the thermals over 200,000 acres of wilderness with an occasional break to devour chipmunks and chicken nuggets. "I'm sorry."

"It sucks that we wrecked your vacation," David added.

"You didn't wreck anything, the dead fuckstick did. And I'm glad Oz will make a full recovery."

"A worry for another time. And maybe you'll be able to see a buffalo anyway, since..." *Buffalo. Sounds exotic. Or at least it would to someone from Great Britain, like Nadia. At least buffalo wouldn't have to be imported. But are they exported? Because that would...*

"Annette? Darling? You trailed off, and now you have a silly look on your face. Even for you."

"Exotic pets," Annette said slowly. "Lund was an importer and an exporter. We missed something."

David snorted. "No doubt. Instead of getting ahead of it—any of it—we've just been reacting. Prob'ly missed a couple of things."

"Maybe it's not about the abuse per se," Annette said. She could feel her brain trying to seize on...something. "Maybe it was his means to an end."

"Your muttering is more nonsensical than usual, dear."

Enough. It'll come to you. "I think there's a way we can get more info from Lund."

"Does it involve a séance? I would adore a séance."

"It does not. How many times do I have to tell you, no séances during work time! And your vacation might have been wrecked, but I'm pretty sure we can still arrange some entertainment."

"I'm not especially worried." Nadia shrugged. "That's what vacation insurance is for."

"There's a clause for getting your money back when you miss your flight because you're trying to keep your colleagues out of jail by distracting officers of the court?"

"There will be when I'm finished with them."

"I don't doubt it," David said, and for that he got a megawatt smile from Nadia.

"Now! The memorial starts in twenty-five minutes and it's in the next town over, so you two need to put the petal to the metal."

"It's *pedal*. With a *d*."

"Do shut up, Annette."

Chapter 29

"I never told Brennan my name. He called me Annette, but we didn't even give him our cards. We didn't want to make it easy on him to alert IPA about what we were up to."

"Jesus." David, who had been turning into the White Funeral Home, nearly went into the ditch. "I was so busy talking myself out of throwing him out the window, I didn't notice. That's fucking embarrassing."

"Don't be so hard on yourself. It's good you didn't throw him out the window."

The parking lot was half-full, which was good as well as bad; there were fewer people to keep track of, but the two of them would stand out more. Even if one of them hadn't been wearing salmon with a cardigan whose sleeves she wasn't allowed to use. "Is this a hunch? I feel like this is a hunch. A hunch is the same as desperately clutching at straws, right?"

David shrugged. "It's all we've got right now. Unless you want to go see Gomph and get arrested."

"No. But an organized mind should always have a Plan B."

David gallantly presented an elbow for her to grab and walked her up the sidewalk. It was a beautiful day, the kind Minnesota used to lure suckers into moving. *Come on over! Feel that warm sunshine, smell that crisp air! Pick apples! Go on a hayride! Stroll through jewel-colored fallen leaves! (The winters aren't that horrible.)*

"You know, David, if not for the miasma of violent death hanging over this, we could be on a date."

To her surprise, David took her seriously. "No. I'd never expect you to... I mean, obviously this isn't a date."

"Right. That's...correct." *Say something. The only thing worse than an awkward pause is a looooong awkward pause.* "I didn't actually think it was. A date, I mean."

"Good."

"It's the salmon, isn't it?" she fretted. "It makes me look jaundiced and you're turned off. Nadia won't listen. I know what looks good against my own skin tone, dammit!"

"You don't look orange."

"Oh. Relief."

"You look the opposite of orange."

"I look blue?"

"No! Beautiful. I think you look beautiful."

"Thank you. You look good, too. Are you all right? You're sweating." And it was something to see. The man hadn't been this rattled when a faceless thug tried to run him down in a parking garage.

"Fucking mock turtleneck. Be a turtleneck or don't, but what the hell is 'mock'?" He hooked a finger in the collar and yanked. "Christ, it's hot out here."

"It's sixty-five degrees out here. David, if my proximity is making you uncomfortable—"

"Of course it's making me uncomfortable!" He came to a dead stop and she nearly stumbled. "Look at you! Just standing there in all your—you-ness!"

"Sorry, what?"

"You're you—"

"You're saying 'you' a lot, seems like."

"—and I'm me, and you're smart and gorgeous and funny and everybody likes you and it's not just because you're a softie, and yeah, you're a softie, but you're a *hard* softie, so it works, and you could be with anybody and it's insane that all I want to do is take you someplace nice and feed you." He stopped, heaved a breath. "And I know that's ridiculous. You've made it perfectly clear."

"But so did you."

"What?"

"I'm sensing we've had a communication breakdown."

"What?"

Annette looked at him. Beyond the disheveled good looks and the clothing he wore like armor was a man who could have done a fade once he dropped Caro off for processing, but didn't. Who had leaped between her and a car driven with lethal intent. Who killed in defense of her cubs. Who kept to himself by choice, but didn't hesitate to throw himself snout first into danger. Who trusted her instincts and introduced her to friends who knew his deepest secret. And in return, all he asked for was…nothing.

She hadn't known any of this on Monday. He was just the guy who put maple syrup in everything on Monday. But it had all been there, all those good and noble things, like buried treasure.

"You're an idiot," she said kindly. "But I am, too. I kissed you, remember? Twice."

"I initiated the first kiss."

"Yes, and then I got even. Wait. I'll rephrase."

"It's fine, I get what you mean."

"And I'm the one who crawled into bed with you. Well. After you crawled in with me. Those are not the actions of someone who views you with disinterest." She squeezed his arm. "We're definitely going out when this is all over."

"No. We're not. That was my point."

She nearly stumbled again. This wasn't how the script in her head went. They would solve the case and go out and inhale a staggering amount of food and keep going out and perhaps fall in love, roll credits. "It was?"

"All my friends are Stables. And I won't do to you what I did to my mother. I won't have you looking over your shoulder every minute we're together."

"Maybe that's something *I* should decide?"

He ignored her, which didn't bode well. "You'd always feel pressure to share your secret because they know mine. You'd always wonder if they're going to tell anyone outside the group and how that might blow back on you. And what if we have cubs?"

"You've given this a worrisome amount of thought."

"You'd be constantly agonizing about their potential exposure. You'd probably want to move, and maybe keep moving, and you wouldn't want so many Stables in our lives. So all these thoughts and fantasies I've been having—"

"You fantasize about me?"

"Constantly."

"Oh."

"And then, last night...that just made it worse."

"Oh."

"And it's all pointless."

"Oh?"

"Because nothing's going to come of it, so it doesn't matter that you look like Aphrodite on the half shell in salmon."

"David, that's ridiculous. My hair is much, much shorter than Aphrodite's. Her hair runs past her knees in that painting."

He ignored her accurate art critique and added, "You could be with anyone. And you should be."

"Wait, *what*?" She hated when surprise made her voice squawk like that, but she had bigger problems. "You think *I* could be with anyone? *You* could be with anyone."

"That's idiotic." He made a vague gesture in her direction. "Look at you."

"Look at *you*."

He raked his fingers through his hair, and it was hilarious that his hair looked exactly as mussed after the raking as before. "I'm just saying—"

"I heard you. Are you hearing *me*?"

"Yeah, because you're shouting."

"I am not!" She lowered her voice. "I am not," she murmured.

"All right. So. We each think the other could be with anyone, and we each feel unworthy."

"Unworthy is a strong—"

"So let's just admit we both suck."

"You're damned right we suck!"

"Yelling."

"Shut up, David."

"Ah...pardon me?"

They looked. A short, chubby man in a black suit, crisp white shirt, and subtle gold name tag (Charles) had come outside and was holding the door open for them.

"Are you here for the Lund memorial? It's right this way."

Oh. Right. The murder. The missing cubs. Our impending arrests. All problems unrelated to our imaginary relationship and future mythical children.

"Yes, thank you." To David: "At least it won't be incredibly awkward now you've gotten that out of your system."

He gave her a look. "You're joking, right?"

"Also, I think you might be a little bit nuts."

"Yeah, well, I'd refute that except that it's true."

Once inside, they let their eyes adjust to the low lighting; even on the sunniest of days, funeral homes always seemed shrouded in gloom. As she'd surmised after a glance at the parking lot, not many people were there, fewer than twenty.

They stood in the small entryway, getting their bearings, and passed the guest book and a small bowl of tiny foil-wrapped candies.

"Probably inappropriate for us to sign, right?"

"Probably."

"And don't you dare go for any of that candy," she added. "Put your sweet tooth in park."

"Don't worry. Mints. Yuck."

There was no coffin, only an altar toward the front of the small nondenominational chapel on which there were several framed pictures of all sizes. The dark-clad mourners were all in mini-groups of two and three and four, murmuring to one another and shaking their heads. Annette caught several expected comments…

"Such a shame."

"Was it quick? I hope it was quick."

"His poor mother."

"I really thought he'd turned it all around."

…as well as some unexpected ones.

"Bound to happen."

"Fucking loser."

"I'll bet his family has no idea how to feel about this."

"You knew it was just a matter of time, but *this*. Yikes."

Annette grabbed David's hand, ignored his stifled hiss. "You've got a grip like an anaconda."

She hauled him to the front of the chapel for a closer look at the pictures. "Oh, now this is interesting," she said under her breath. And when David sucked in a breath, she knew he'd seen it, too.

"Annette?"

Greg Brennan had come up behind them with an older woman in tow. Literally in tow; he had her by her frail wrist and was pulling her toward them like a tugboat in a $2,000 suit.

She was spindly, her graying hair pulled back into a low bun, and her black suit was understated and elegant.

Black tights, black flats, and a little black hat with black fingertip veil (which Annette had only seen in films, never in real life—classy!) completed her chic mourning wear. She and Lund had the same eyes, brown with a narrow, yellowish cast. She looked tired and infinitely crafty.

"Hello again, Greg." Annette held out her hand. It was listlessly shaken. *Ugh, nothing makes my skin crawl more than a limp handshake. Well. Sea snakes, maybe. I am not a fan of legless reptiles that can kill a hundred men with a few milligrams of venom.* "You remember David."

"Yeah, Greg. You remember me."

"We thought we'd come by to pay our respects!" *Ugh. Tone it down. You are not going on a picnic. Ohhhhh, don't think about picnics. Don't think about cold fried chicken and potato salad and ice-cold lemonade and plates of brownies but not frosted brownies because the frosting ends up on the container and not on the brownies which is a goddamned tragedy every time.*

The older woman shuffled forward to peer up at them. "I'm sorry, who are you?"

Greg bent down to mutter, "Ma, I told you about these guys. They're looking into Terry's death."

"You're with the police?" she asked, thin voice trembling.

"No."

"Oh. Well. Thank you both for coming." Then, after a once-over: "You look lovely, dear. Very…festive."

Fucking salmon. "Our condolences," Annette said. "This must be so difficult. Especially for you, Greg. You lost a client *and* a brother."

"Half brother." Greg flushed to the eyebrows. "Different dads."

"Still." Annette gestured to the photos. Brennan was featured prominently in nearly all of them: the Good Son. Lund was shunted off to the side with a frozen grin on his face: the Unfavorite. "It must be hard. Losing a sibling. And a son. Especially when your relationship was so clearly…complex." *See? See what I did there? That pause indicates that I know more than I'm telling! And that I'm only pretending to be polite! HOW DO YOU LIKE IT, MRS. LUND OR IS IT MRS. BRENNAN?*

Greg let out a bark of laughter. "Complex. Sure. One way to put it. Fucking retarded, that's another way."

"Gregory."

"Sorry, Ma."

"You know I hate the f-word."

"I know, Ma." To Annette and David: "But he was. Sorry, I guess that's not PC or whatever."

"No, it's not PC or whatever. And—oh." *Don't gape at him like a moron. Don't gape at all. But especially not like a moron.* Which would be difficult, since things were falling into place with near-audible clicks.

Dev, that first day: *He wasn't a werewolf, he was a monster.*

Lund himself: *I'm kinda the white sheep of the family. They know my business is the most important thing to me.*

Brennan: *Lund was more interested in being a tough guy than paying attention.*

"You told us Lund was a pain," Annette said slowly. "When we were at your office, remember?"

"It was an hour and a half ago. So, yeah."

"You said what happened to him was a real shame."

"It *was* a shame," Mrs. Lund (or Brennan) agreed with a vigorous nod.

"Yeah," Greg said. "I mean, obviously."

"But you weren't talking about the attack, or even his murder," Annette said. "You meant because he was a sport."

"A what?"

"Your brother was a squib. A Shifter who couldn't shift." And before David could say anything, she added, "And don't talk to me about the Harry Potter universe and the proprietary use of the word 'squib.'"

"Nobody is talking about Harry Potter."

"Because the term 'squib' predates those books by *centuries* as a term for a firearm malfunction." At their stares, she elaborated. "When there isn't enough powder? So the bullet gets stuck in the barrel? Also known as a pop-and-no-kick?"

"It's also someone born to magicians who can't do magic." From David. "See? That's just easier. Everybody gets it right away. You don't have to explain anything. Or use phrases like 'pop-and-no-kick.'"

"I just said to leave Harry Potter out of it! J. K. Rowling does not own the rights to the word 'squib'!"

"J. K. Rowling can have the rights to any word she likes!"

"That's enough," Greg said sharply, which was timely because she and David were almost nose-to-nose.

"You're right, that's not important now." She turned

away from David's dangerous irrationality. "So here it is. Your brother—"

"Come with me."

Greg gripped Annette by the upper arm, and she let out a growl. Just a little one—it was a memorial, after all. But he let go of her like she'd grown hot. "For privacy," he elaborated, and she summoned a pleasant smile for him, because though he was a creep, they needn't put on a show for the mourners. If that's what they were.

Greg led them to an office just off the chapel, shut the door, then turned back to them. "Half brother."

"Pardon?"

"Terry was my half brother."

"As well as a Shifter who couldn't shift. And none of you ever let him forget it. Not even here. So many lovely family pictures all over the chapel! So many of them showing your other selves… It was amazing to see all those wolves.

"But not Terry Lund. He's a biped in every one. See?" She held up the photo she'd been able to snag before Greg frog-marched them into the office. "See how he tries to smile like you weren't killing him with your petty species-ist bullshit?"

Wait. Do I actually feel sorry for the late unmourned Lund? Nope.

"I'll bet if I shook your family tree, a few SAS members would fall out. Or maybe SAS-adjacent. What good is a Shifter if he's locked into one shape, right? You thought he was inferior, and you never kept it a secret."

"I'm an idiot," David groaned. "It's how Caro nearly killed him! Here's this poor cub, malnourished and weak and dehydrated, and she ripped him up. We couldn't figure it."

"Poor cub?" Mrs. Brennan (or Mrs. Lund) said sharply.

"I never saw his other self. When I rolled up, I just figure he'd shifted back from the stress of the attack. But he couldn't shift. And Caro knew it and went for him."

"That's it! That's it exactly!" Annette seized David's hands. "We figured it out!"

"We need to clutch at straws more often." David laughed.

"I know!"

"Will you two shut up?"

"Oh. Right." She cleared her throat. "Once again, our condolences." She opened her mouth to let out another platitude when the approaching sirens cut her off. "Ohhhhhh, that's not great."

Greg grinned, so any thought that it was a police siren unrelated to her present career difficulty faded. "Hear that? I don't think you're gonna be able to make our appointment tomorrow, cutie."

Which is why you suggested it.

She traded wide-eyed looks with David. She couldn't say it.

She wouldn't say it.

David said it. "Nadia's the only one who knows we're here."

Fuck.

Chapter 30

"Pat?"

"Yeah?"

"Can I ask you something?"

"You are."

"Yuck, you sound like Annette."

"That's the biggest lie you've ever told."

Dev smirked. "Wait."

"Annette sounds like me. It's *not* the other way around," Pat pointed out.

"Right." Dev slid onto the stool across from Caro, who, after a Funyuns and ginger ale break, had begun writing again. A corner of Pat's studio—well, it wasn't really a corner since the building was round—was a mini-kitchen, complete with tiny microwave, stove, and oven, and the marble island they were sitting at had cupboards stuffed with canned food, snacks, and bottles of water. Pat had reassured them that they had sufficient supplies for well over a week, unless Annette dropped by.

Dev hadn't thought it was possible, but he was getting sick of Pringles. "So. Um. The thing I wanted to ask about. Your…"

Caro looked up and shook her head. Dev exercised his prerogative as a younger brother and ignored her. "…face," he continued. "What happened? Did you know Annette back then?"

"It's how I met Annette."

"No shit?"

"Zero shit."

"What happened?"

Caro set her pencil aside and propped her chin on her palm to listen.

Pat stopped pretending to sort his nail polish art wheels. "Clichés happened."

"Yeah, I'm gonna need more than that. Please, por favor, s'il vous plaît."

"Angry loner fell in with wrong crowd, blah-blah, stupid decisions followed by something-something, which culminated in more blah-blah, which I should have seen coming but didn't, and Annette stumbled along just in time to get them off me. Literally. There was a rough chunk of sidewalk and she tripped."

"Who were they?"

"SAS."

"The species-ist guys?"

"The inbred morons who got so pissy about Stables calling themselves alpha predators that they decided genocide was a sane alternative. And this would normally be the part where I say 'Don't judge me', except joining them was monumentally stupid and hateful so judge away."

"Well." Dev, nonplussed, cast about for a positive. "We all do dumb things when we're kids."

"It was six years ago."

"Oh. When you were…"

"*Not* a kid."

A short silence, and then Caro held up her pad:

Were you scared?

"Yes."

Thought you'd die?

"Counted on it. But I consider myself lucky."

Because you lived.

"Sorry, I'll need a question mark on that."

Because you lived?

"No. Well, that's what I think *now*, but back then, I simply didn't give a shit if they killed me. Death sounded like a vacation."

Dev was shaking his head. "That's messed up, Pat. Death is detention. Forever! And you don't have anything to do and you can't talk and you can't leave your seat and the room smells like sweat and dust and there's nothing good to eat. Forever."

"Thanks for a fascinating glimpse into that bundle of neurons and synapses you call a brain, and I'm not being sarcastic. And you're right—I had a fucked-up mind-set back then. But what I mean was that fortune intervened when they decided to kill me behind an all-you-can-eat sushi restaurant. If they'd tried it behind a rice-cake manufacturer, I'd be dead."

Caro snorted, then clapped a hand over her mouth while Dev bit his lip, hard, so he wouldn't laugh.

Pat grinned. "It's fine. Even bigotry and felony assault have their lighter side. *Never* tell Annette I said that. Anyway, she saved me, we got to know each other, I moved in to recover and never left, *fin*."

"Is that why you have this silo? It's your den, like the house is Annette's?"

"Something like that. I've found since the attack that I'm...not agoraphobic, exactly. Agoraphobic-adjacent, I suppose. Apparently a near-death experience averted by a friendly stranger left me with a pile of PTSD. So I work from home, and if I feel the urge to shift, I stay on Annette's land."

"What did she do to them? The guys who hurt you?"

"Ate them" was the matter-of-fact reply.

Dev nearly toppled off of his stool. "*Ate*—you mean killed them."

"Nope." At Dev's stunned expression, he added, "Werebears are opportunistic omnivores. The apex of the apex. Why d'you think there are so few of them? The region can only support so many."

"But doesn't that... Is she a cannibal, then?"

"How does a werebear eating a werewolf make her a cannibal? Do you need a dictionary?"

"It's just... She's so... I can't even picture..." Dev shook his head. "I mean, she's so *nice*. And she never loses her temper."

"All those things can be true, Dev."

He was still shaking his head. "Uh, no. They really can't."

"She loses her temper under a very specific set of circumstances. And when that happens, it's just better to take a step back. Like, halfway across the country. And then find a bed to hide under. For a year."

"Didn't she get in trouble?"

"Nope. Clear case of coming to the rescue and then self-defense. There were three of them, after all."

"Jeez!"

"It's not against the law to defend yourself, or to eat a dead werewolf."

"This is gross and interesting and weird."

"Yes, it is."

Caro, meanwhile, had been studying Pat as if she was planning to describe him to a police sketch artist. Her steady regard was...not unpleasant, exactly. Intense. If she was a speaker, it'd be the time for her to say something dramatic.

But she wasn't a speaker. So she slapped two sketch pads down in front of Pat, who eyed them like he wasn't sure if they were snakes or snacks. Then she gestured.

Please.

Pat started to read.

Chapter 31

"OH, THAT BITCH! SHE'S DEAD! AND NOT 'DEAD TO ME' dead, but actually, biologically dead! I'm going to snuff out her life force as I stomp on her *face*."

"I was kinda hoping I wasn't right about that one," David said, taking a hard left. "Gotta wonder about her motive, though."

"And I've gotta wonder about my abysmal judge of character. Do you know how many alarm clocks the woman has bought me?"

"A hundred?"

"No goddamned wonder Caro won't speak to anyone. Random case workers and judges are literally out to get her, and I'm floundering in my own ignorance! Case in point: using flounder instead of founder!"

"I think—"

"And I'll tell you something else, I *know* I've seen Brennan before today. There's something about the set of his head. Or shoulders. It's driving me insane."

"I can tell. You haven't tried to back-seat drive at all."

"This is no time for me to stroke your driving pride," she snapped.

"Sorry."

They were minutes away from the Minneapolis warehouse district, having fled the funeral home out the back exit to avoid the cops. The family pretending to mourn

Lund didn't hinder them, which was the only nice thing she could say about them.

Annette slumped in her seat and rubbed her temples. "All right, I need to figure this out. So there were syndicate members at the memorial, yes? Had to be. And they know we've been trying to expose them."

"Couple of them must've dropped their teeth when we walked in."

"Right. They've been hoping the system—*our* system—would rubber-stamp all of it with 'case closed.' And they're desperate for Lund to take all the blame. That was the point of killing him in the first place. So they could escape detection and start over. So they can keep getting off. But Lund's motivation was different from the syndicate's. *They* were in it for their fuckstick-esque idea of fun."

"And Lund was in it for revenge."

"Lund was in it for revenge." She heard herself say the words, let her brain sift through them. This was what her brain had been trying to grasp in the Target changing room but had been too distracted by a salmon party dress and David's mock turtleneck to do so. Lund's campaign to kidnap, brutalize, and eventually dump juvenile Shifters wasn't about trafficking at all. Because the most important thing in Terry Lund's world was his work: exotic pets. He'd told them so himself.

"Caro tried to tell us," she continued. "Well, she told Mama Mac. Remember? *Please also know that I am not a pet. I will hurt anyone who tries to hurt me or mine.*"

"Oh Christ."

"Right. Those photos of abuse… He was breaking Shifter juveniles to be pets. *House*-breaking them. For syndicate members who wanted their very own pet Shifters. But perhaps also…"

"For Stables. Because what's more exotic than a were-wolf? What could be trendier? It's the sociopathic version of tropical fish or a potbellied pig."

Annette felt her gorge think about rising. *Knock it off, gorge.* "And…and that means that not only are there plenty of Stables in the world who know about us, they're also happy to subjugate us." *Every time I think this case won't get worse, it does.*

"Which suited Lund fine."

"More than fine. It's why he would have thrown himself into providing for the syndicate. Can't you picture it? Here was the perfect opportunity to show his family he wasn't worthless. Not that it worked—Brennan was still desperately ashamed of his half brother. And given some of what we overheard at the memorial, he wasn't the only family member who felt that way. So Lund grew up feeling like he wasn't one of them. Like he was a genetic joke. Worthless. *Stable.*"

"He overcompensated," David added. "Like all these scumbags do. And made his life all about punishing others for what his family did."

"And because his real motive was so well hidden—even from himself, I think—no one would guess what he was up to. Even people who routinely see abuse. We never thought 'pet store' or 'slavery.' Hell, we had photographic proof of what he was doing and we *still* couldn't connect the dots."

"The names." Scout. Lambchop.

Pet names.

"And if any Stables who weren't in the syndicate saw the photos, they'd think it was animal cruelty at worst."

Annette thought about how she'd blithely informed Caro "We've found out everything." And how the girl had just looked at her. Because they hadn't. And for all Caro knew, they never would. So while in Lund's grip she'd gone mute out of self-preservation. And out of Lund's grip, she stayed that way. Because there was no one, no one in the world she could trust. Except Dev. But how could a child—even one with Dev's, um, gifts— help her?

Even if we catch these guys, will Caro feel safe enough to speak? Ever again?

"Almost there," David warned as they crossed over into the warehouse district, and not the trendy shops and restaurants section. The dirtier, grittier, smellier section, warehouses built in the late 1880s that most of the population forgot were there.

I've gotta deal with customs, oversee the quarantine facilities, clear the charter flights for the imports...

Lund's warehouse. Because Nadia had seen it the day they found Lund's files: his apartment wasn't a home; it was an operating room. The broken-down building ahead that shielded his life's work...*that* was his home.

Oz's confusion over the accounts made sense now, too.

The methodology is way off. The setup's all wrong.

Of course it was, because profits weren't the name of the game. Secrecy was. Why else buy dilapidated warehouses in a floodplain? Why have an attorney of record when your revolting half-brother can take care of the paperwork?

I can't think of a legit reason for this random guy to have twenty-two accounts and eleven shell companies. Of course not. Because Oz was, fundamentally, a good man. Lund's polar opposite in all ways. And her foster brother's inability to sniff out sadism was one of the reasons she'd wanted him to stay in accounting. But that had backfired; Oz had just dug in. Which she should have foreseen.

Though perhaps she was underestimating him. He was clever enough to suss out some of it, after all, and leave a message for Nadia, who relayed it to them in the dressing room.

Lund was doing all this from somewhere, Annette had said, thinking aloud. *He mentioned a warehouse when we spoke with him at the hospital. I'm betting it got the same treatment his apartment did: a casual glance, and then lockdown. Can you check it out?*

Nadia had…but somewhere in that time frame, she'd also called the police.

Or had she?

Should've taken your vacation, Nadia, no matter whose side you're on. One way or the other, I think it'll be a while before you get another one.

Chapter 32

PAT PUT DOWN THE LAST PAD, ASHEN. "ANNETTE AND David don't know any of this."

Caro, who had been still as a—well, not a mouse, exactly—while he read shook her head, her grave gaze never leaving his.

"Nobody knows. Except the people who"—there was a dry click as Pat swallowed—"sold you. To the people who did those things to you."

Caro scribbled, held up the new pad:

What's going to happen to A & D?

"They're going to be arrested, Caro. But only if they're very, very lucky."

Dev had been watching the conversation for the perfect time to jump in, which he gauged was now. "Not if we help them! Well, they still might be arrested, *detenido, arrestato*, but the 'sindicate' won't be able to kill them."

"Think so?"

"We just need to buy her time. And then Annette can figure out what to do. And tell David, and, I dunno. Stuff will get done." *Sindicate*: Caro's deliberate, punny misspelling. It had seemed silly at first, a cute fuck-you from an impressively defiant teenager, but now he pictured it in his mind the way Caro had: with *sin* blackly emphasized. And it was much less cute.

Now it was Pat's turn to say nothing, which Dev could only take for a few seconds.

"Guys! Why aren't we calling for help? Or way, way better, why aren't we in your car speeding to the rescue?"

"Because to do that, Caro has to tell someone in authority where the warehouse is and all that was done there. But she'll have to break cover to do that, and if the sindicate taught her one thing in two years, it's that breaking cover can be lethal." Pat tapped his scar, baring his teeth in a humorless smile. "Take it from one who had his own teachers."

"Yeah, but—"

"And by her own word she won't speak until she's free. But as long as people like her parents and Lund are out in the world, she *isn't* free. Right, Caro?"

Scribbling.

How do I know A and/or D won't screw me over?

Pat took a breath, then slowly let it out. "You don't. I can promise you she wouldn't, and I could assume David wouldn't, and it would be the truth, but you can't know that. I'm just the random guy you met a couple days ago."

"Or random gal!" Dev piped up. "Depending on how you feel that day."

"Thanks for the validation, Dev. But…yeah. You don't know. There are no guarantees. And I wish I could tell you otherwise."

Dev had watched Pat grow paler and paler the more he read of Caro's horrible story, not that Dev blamed him. Dev already knew the story; he and Caro were siblings by choice and had no secrets. Well, no serious secrets. His stash of stolen ATM cards, his cache of lock-picks hidden all through IPA's offices, and his crush on Ariana Grande—who *had* to be a werehare—were his own business.

He and Caro were related because his mother had sold him for a week's supply of carfentanil. And because Caro's had sold her for $5,580: six months' rent, with a little left over for a nice meal at Applebee's.

He'd had options, at least. He'd been able to get away from his "owner," which was why he'd been bouncing around the system like a fuzzy Super Ball the last couple of years. And why his mother was in prison.

Caro hadn't been so lucky. No matter what they did, she wouldn't break. And no matter how she fought, she couldn't escape. Until the night she did, and crossed paths with Dev, who showed her his den on the out-skirts of one of the homeless camps, and let her stay, and decided by the end of the week that they were brother and sister and dared anyone to say otherwise.

During the weeks of her (physical) recovery, she wrote it all down for him, including the part about how she'd refused to speak to her captors, how she realized this could only be happening if the system was in on it or turning a blind eye or just didn't care, and how that led to her vow of silence. No talking until she was truly free. And no communication of *any* kind with IPA until she knew she was safe.

As promised, he burned her story while she watched.

I won't talk to IPA, Caro wrote.

"Understandable."

Or the police. Or 911. Or the fire department. Or Pet Control.

"Why the hell would I call Pet Control?"

But we can go help A&D. I know what you're gonna say, we're just cubs, we should leave it to the adults, but we can't.

"Found the keys. C'mon."

Dev whooped and leaped off his stool. "I fucking *love* hanging out here."

"Language. I don't need Annette biting my face off for teaching you bad habits. Okay, *more* bad habits."

"Literally every twelve-year-old in the world has heard 'fucking' at least once. You're not teaching me anything."

"Excellent. That's the story I expect you to stick with. We—" Pat cut himself off and tilted his head, listening. "Huh. That's Oz Adway yowling away out there again. The guy just will not knock like a civilized were."

Caro tensed and Dev asked, puzzled, "What's *he* doing here?"

"I imagine Annette sent him to check on us. Good, we can make use of him. Now go start the car while I find Mommy's shotgun."

Chapter 33

IS IT A TRAP IF WE KNOW ABOUT IT BEFOREHAND?

Annette had no idea. And no time to worry about it. She and David weren't stupid—at least, not entirely stupid. It was beyond obvious that at least two Shifters were in the warehouse with them; the stench masked a lot, but not everything.

It didn't matter. They couldn't reach out to IPA. They couldn't call for backup or for help. But they couldn't dodge the syndicate anymore or walk away, either.

We've been hares to their hounds too long.

"Are you okay?" he asked, bending close and almost whispering.

"Not at all."

He squeezed her hand and she closed her eyes, the better to shut out the sight of the place. But she couldn't shut out the smells. *I'll bet—if I hadn't sworn off betting—that David holding my hand is the only affection this squalid shithole has seen.* She let go, opened her eyes. This was business. They had work to do. She'd cry and scream and vent later.

"Well, he got some of it cleaned up," David announced, hands on his hips as he examined the scene. He was obviously sticking close to her, which she decided was adorable and only slightly irritating. "But the place still smells like piss and blood."

To be expected. There were cages, and restraints, and crates, and hoses, and collars, and prods. No clothes, though. Which made sense. Clothing was for people, not pets.

There were rows of unforgiving fluorescent lights, because all the windows were blacked out. And it was cold. Annette shivered and defied Nadia by putting her arms through her cardigan sleeves. *How about THAT, you treacherous harpy?*

David let out a hiss. "Christ. Once he broke them, he'd ship some of them overseas. No wonder the hospital couldn't find them. They must've shit themselves when Sharon and Dr. Tilbury started asking questions."

"So they brought in Brennan. And they had him 'find' the missing cubs, but only on paper. It would have been a stalling tactic while Lund tried to get those particular Shifters back from overseas. And somewhere in the middle of all of that, Caro escaped."

There were desks and file cabinets and paperwork. There were manifests to the Ukraine, Kenya, Qatar, Turkey, and the United Emirates. All in a poorly locked (David had broken in without half trying) warehouse by the river because nobody gave a shit.

The one spot that didn't seem completely terrible was a comfortable-looking twin bed made up to the left of the desk, with thick blankets and quilts, and two space heaters.

"It would appear that after a long day of torturing children, he would sometimes sleep here, too." Annette quelled the urge to spit on Lund's pillow. "*Two* space heaters for that fraudulent fucking coward. It must have made him nuts that he couldn't grow fur and they all could. Ha. Good."

"Lund must have come here straight from the hospital. Cleaned up as best he could with missing fingers and a broken foot."

"And it's not like he could have called a service. So he called the syndicate for help. But he was a liability to them at that point."

"Then he went home," David said, using a pen to sift through shipping manifests. "Got himself murdered. And whoever killed him didn't finish the cleanup."

"No, of course not." This from a new and entirely unwelcome voice. "Harder for us to pin it all on Lund if we didn't leave, y'know, evidence. The files you stole. The pictures you didn't know what to do with. And this shithole, of course."

Judge Gomph's assistant, Taryn Wapiti, stepped out of the shadows. She'd been standing beneath the stairs, watching as the two of them poked through Lund's torture chamber/business venture/nap zone. The stench had covered her scent, among others.

Annette slapped her forehead. "I. Am. An idiot."

Taryn smirked. "Lucky for us."

Annette turned to David. "Earlier this week. Taryn was talking to Brennan the morning after you brought Caro in. I only saw him from the back, which is why it took so long to place him." Back to Taryn: "You were at the memorial, weren't you?"

"Sure was. Saw you pull in. Ducked in the back office before you hit the chapel."

"And called the police. Dammit!"

"There's an upside, though," David pointed out.

"Nadia's not the mole," Annette realized. *And neither was Oz.* Good news. No, *great* news. Possibly the only great news this charnel house had seen.

Taryn came forward, dressed in a heavy brown sweater, a knee-length gray wool skirt, fleece-lined black tights, and sturdy boots. "You must be freezing in that ugly orange thing."

"It's salmon, fuck you."

"Oooooh! You almost never drop f-bombs."

"It's been a stressful week. Nice to see you're dressed appropriately for this chilly cell block. Too bad the kids weren't allowed to."

Taryn shrugged. "They had fur. They'd only be cold if they disobeyed and shifted without permission. That was against the rules. Can't be someone's pet if you're a biped. Some of 'em were quicker learners than others."

Annette had a sudden memory of Caro's letter,

(I am comfortable on any floor if you are lacking in beds. I don't mind the cold so the basement is also fine.)

felt her nails bite into her palms, forced her fists to unclench.

"You know you're not leaving here under your own power, right?" Taryn asked with off-putting gentleness. "And that sucks. I wish you hadn't followed the bread crumbs, and not just because we can't let you catch us."

"Not the 'I like you, I'd hate to kill you' speech. Murder me any way you like, but spare me that bit of trite bullshit."

"I do like you, Annette." And, ugh, the woman actually sounded sincere. "Enough to eat meat with you, even though every time we went out, I'd spend the next two days in the bathroom."

"Your depravity knows no bounds. I'm not being sarcastic, you understand. Your refusal to have a veggie burger should have tipped me off to the fact that you are a depraved monster."

"Yeah, well, I'll just have to get over that, won't I, Annette? Killing you will probably do it."

Annette waved that away. "Yes, yes, death awaits us, evil shall prevail, good shall be forever blotted out... Is it a trap if we walk in knowing you're waiting for us?"

"I'm not alone," she warned.

We're counting on it. "Why, Taryn? I know it's naive. And I know you won't have a satisfying answer. But what did those poor cubs ever do to you? How could you be a part of this?"

"Money, mostly." She shrugged. "Sooooooo much fucking money. And it's low-risk. The overhead's low, too, and it's so easy to pick up product."

"Product." David, to his credit, said that with a perfectly straight face.

"There are so few of us," Annette said in a small voice, fiddling with the buttons on her cardigan. "How could you endanger your own?"

"'So few' is open to interpretation. 'So few' compared

to Stables, sure, but that still means there are millions of juvies running around. What difference do a couple dozen here and there make? Who fucking cares? Who even notices?" The worst part: Taryn sounded genuinely puzzled. "I couldn't believe it when the med staff started asking questions. With all the work they have to do? Once the cubs are discharged, the hospital is supposed to be out of it. Fucking nosy idiots."

Annette shook her head. "I would try to explain, Taryn, but it would be a waste of everyone's time."

"God, you're such a sanctimonious shithead."

"Hey! What happened to liking my company enough to spend days on a toilet?"

"You're standing there all 'Every life is precious' when you know it's a lie." Taryn rolled her eyes. "Every life isn't precious. You only have to spend five minutes in IPA's file room to get that. Parents abuse their cubs, abandon them, kill them, and sell them, like Caro's parents did."

For a moment, Annette was back in Mama Mac's warm, welcoming kitchen.

There are worse things than being snatched from your family.

What could be worse than stealing her, Mama?

Selling her.

Annette had assumed she meant Lund selling Caro to an owner. It never occurred to her that Caro's parents would sell their own child into brutalization and permanent bondage and a denial of their very natures. For money. And probably not very much money.

I've still got so much to learn about the world. How thoroughly depressing.

Meanwhile, Taryn was still whining. "Why the fuck should I have a care for them if their own parents don't? Nobody wanted them. So we found people who did. After a few attitude adjustments. It's basically a victimless crime."

"It's the opposite of a victimless crime, you repellent twat. Tell me one thing. One thing before we get into this."

"What?"

"Is Gomph in on it?"

Taryn let out a scornful laugh. "That pussy? He's a bigger softie than you are."

"So Gomph was never after us."

"He was after you because he was worried about you. He knew something was wrong, but not what. After you left the hearing, he started thinking maybe you should all go into protective custody, or at least get a lot more backup, and I had to keep you from meeting up again."

"So you followed Nadia to the hospital, then kept us away from Gomph by saying we were going to be arrested. Hey!" She turned to David. "We're not going to be arrested! For that, anyway." Which begged the question: where was Nadia? She was one of the reasons Annette and David had run from the memorial to the warehouse in the first place.

"Believe me, you've got bigger problems than jail. Why didn't you just *go*, Annette?" Taryn shook her head so hard, her reddish-orange hair momentarily obscuring her face. "As far as you knew, you were in huge trouble. Why didn't you run?"

"Because we knew. The kids. Were in. Bigger trouble." *Not sure why I'm bothering to go over this. She will not get it.*

"You're wasting your time, Annette."

"I'm aware, David. So you and Brennan-the-IT-expert figured out how to let Caro out of IPA, and then I'm guessing Brennan was driving the car that tried to smear us all over the parking garage?"

"That was stupid," she admitted. "He was so mad about Lund's fuckup and Caro's escape, he didn't think it through."

"Yeah, no shit he didn't think it through. Because he tried the same thing with Oz this morning."

"Yep. Not arguing with you—dumb moves on Brennan's part. It put your wind up, and it got Gomph's attention. So we had to pull back *and* we had to get Caro off-site. The whole thing was a pain in the ass all the way around, and everything we did made it worse." This in the tone of someone aggrieved because their dry cleaning came back a day late.

"Meanwhile, after you killed Lund, you were a busy, bitchy bee, calling Lund's apartment manager, calling Annette's boss… You knew everything Gomph did, so we thought he was the mole."

Taryn smirked. "Not bad, right?"

"And the attack at Annette's house?"

"Would have solved a lot of problems for us. If it,

y'know, had worked. I knew Caro'd be there. But I didn't know you and Annette were bone-buddies or I'd have sent more guys."

"Saved by my slutty instincts," Annette declared. "Who were they?"

"Free soldiers from SAS. Brennan was afraid you might be able to trace them back to his family—"

"I *knew* that species-ist pack of jaded sociopaths had something to do with SAS."

"—so we had to get rid of the bodies. And don't bother asking. They're gone. Burned. The way you'll be. They'll never turn up. The way you won't turn up."

"Oh." Annette sighed. "Nice segue to our double murder, I guess."

"Aw, c'mon. I answered your questions and let you play Sherlock Holmes. I even monologued for you! Don't cry about it now."

"I never cry," Annette said hotly, "except for that time at Old Country Buffet and the first time I read *The Long Winter*."

"C'mon, you two." Brennan had joined them, flanked by five werewolves, three of whom Annette recognized from the memorial.

"Well, look who took the time to change into his murder clothes." David grinned. "Nice sweatpants."

"That suit was expensive," Brennan replied, offended. "Why *wouldn't* I change? Let's go."

"Go?" Annette sighed again. Some people yawned when they weren't breathing deeply enough; Annette sighed. "Can't you just mow us down in an unseemly display of gratuitous violence right here?"

"Oh, you'd love that. You'd be thrilled if we murdered you here, wouldn't you, Annette?"

"Uh, not really."

"You're so desperate, you'll do anything to bring more attention to what's been happening here. Forget it. We're going for a drive and dump."

"Sounds like a fast-food joint."

"Why would you make that comparison, David?" Annette complained. "Now I want fast food. A Big Mac. No! A Whopper. Two Whoppers."

"I *said*, we're going to drive you far, far away, and murder the shit out of you and dump your stupid corpses, and that'll be fucking that, *finally*."

"We appreciate you taking the time to go over the procedure with us. But we've got no incentive to come along quietly," Annette pointed out. "Now, I won't say I'm dying to be murdered in this filthy warehouse—"

David snickered. "Pun."

"That's not a pun, but I appreciate your input. Simply put, Taryn, I'm not interested in helping you murder me in a more convenient place. So. I'm staying planted. I can't speak for David, of course."

"I'm sticking with Annette."

"Thanks!"

"You'd do the same for me."

"That's right. I would. Because I'm not a worthless, gutless sociopath. That's a slam directed at *you*, Taryn. In case the subtlety escaped you. In case you have the slight-est doubt that you're a revolting jackass who only seems smart compared to your moronic coconspirators. How dare you come to the Patty Wagon and eat meat with me under false pretenses!"

"Oh my God. Too much talking." Taryn was rubbing her eyes, hard. "Brennan, shoot Annette in the kneecap."

Before Annette could protest, there was a grinding noise as the loading door rattled up to reveal another SAS merc and, parked behind him, a familiar car.

No.

"What now?" Taryn snapped. "Can *one* thing this week be easy? Just one?"

"I know precisely how you feel," Annette replied. "And I hate knowing how you feel. About anything."

"Sorry, but this car just pulled up, and the guy's got Caro Daniels with him. And some other kid." The merc looked embarrassed but resolute. "We can handle them, but they've locked the doors and they're yelling about how the cops are on the way. And Jaegar isn't answering his comm. It's probably bullshit, and we can break into the car in about two seconds. What do you want us to do?"

No.

Taryn snorted. "Caro Daniels isn't calling the cops, trust me. And Jaegar's close to useless on a good day. Why d'you think we put him on the perimeter? Half the time he forgets he's even *got* a comm."

"It's a trick. Or a decoy. Or some dumb kid's half-assed

idea of a rescue. Goddammit." Brennan turned to Taryn. "Kill 'em all, I guess?"

NO.

And there was no time, no time, and it took too long to shed the fake salmon skin so she just shifted on the spot and everything ripped and it hurt wonderfully it was pulling the tooth that was hanging by a bit of flesh it was biting nails too close to the quick it was scrubbing the dead skin of a sunburn leaving new pink, gleaming flesh beneath and she was on the

(cub killer)

were-elk she was *in* the were-elk she was *drinking* the were-elk she'd opened up the prey's throat and pulled and pulled and the other bear

(protector)

had the wolf who was still a man, a wolf too slow to change and now he'd never change and that was good

and there was a crash and a burning smell and somehow a big hot needle drilled into her shoulder but it didn't matter the cubs mattered and another bang and another needle and she surged to her hind legs and bit off the top of that bad man's head

and then two wolves hit her from behind and there were gnashing jaws and howls and yowls and she slashed at one of the wolves she knocked him away knocked his guts out they were trailing like wet ribbons and she roared as the other wolf bit down she swung she slashed she bit and told them and told them and told them

(LEAVE MY CUBS ALONE)

and everything was blood and bone and guts

(*I WILL EAT YOUR HEARTS*)

and it was terrible and it was *wonderful* because the beasts can't hurt the cubs if they're down if they're dead if their hearts stop their everything stops

and it would stop it would all stop which was good which was right because it had to stop before she could save anyone

and that was fine that was worth the drilling pain of a hundred needles, it was, it was and that good bear, that David, he was hurt, but there were only two left one for each and she turned to face the last and then heard nothing, nothing but thunder.

Chapter 34

CARNAGE, IT WAS LITERAL FRIGGIN' CARNAGE AND IT would've been cool except this was real life, so it was mostly horrifying.

Also, Dev decided that Pat was an evil genius. They hadn't roared up with guns (well, gun singular) blazing. They hadn't snuck into the warehouse for an ambush. They hadn't tried to drive over any bad guys or crash into the warehouse for a noisy distraction at the exact right time.

No, Pat had simply led them out of the studio, had a quick chat

"Fine, we'll leave your precious car here so bad guys won't scratch it and I won't accidentally pump three shotgun shells into your engine block, can we get the hell gone now?"

with Oz, who was doing a lot of yelling about warehouses and floodplains, drove them to the river, let Oz out

"Don't forget to tell Annette I wanted to leave the kids behind!"

to do whatever the hell he was gonna do (something about a perimeter?), kept going, drove up to the guard, parked, and yelled that he had Caro Daniels with him, all ready to testify to anyone who'd listen, and cops were coming and shouldn't the guard go tell his boss? Or something?

And waited. Waited while Caro and Dev traded What the hell do we do now? glances while Pat hummed under his breath, calm as a clam, and after a few seconds Caro scribbled (on the small pocket-pad Pat had given her).

He's humming the theme from the Pink Panther movies.

Because the whole thing wasn't surreal enough, apparently?

Dev should have placed the humming a lot quicker, because last night Pat had watched *The Return of the Pink Panther* and *The Pink Panther Strikes Again*, and they were old and boring as shit. Except for the fight scenes between Clouseau and Cato. Those were kinda balls-out awesome.

But anyway, so Pat was humming and waiting and he and Caro were just sitting there, also waiting, and Dev was thinking that if social work was just a bunch of parking and waiting, why was Net so tense all the time? And was he gonna have the *Pink Panther* theme in his head the rest of the day? Because that would suck to the extreme.

And when the guard didn't come back, and the roars and gunshots started up, *then* Pat had gotten out of the car and gone right into the noise and blood. No hesitation. Just *ran*. And then more noise, and the shotgun blast was *so* satisfying (provided it hit a bad guy).

"We'd better go find out," Dev said, and he and Caro wasted no time. And there was no one to stop them. All the guards had run into the warehouse. So in they went. Which was how he and Caro came to be dead center in the middle of the carnage. And there in the middle of a whole bunch of maimed/dead guys, some shifted, some not: David and Annette. David had already shifted back. He was streaked with blood and sweat and didn't care or didn't notice, because he was running his hands over Annette's fur, peering into her eyes, patting at her snout, and Dev knew why, because poor Annette was bleeding from just about everywhere. But one of the werewolves was still trying to get up and get away, and Annette wasn't having it, was growling and glaring with her red, red eyes and she was trying to get to the wolf without hurting David and it was all just a great big bloody friggin' mess.

Dev cupped his hands around his mouth. "Play dead, dumbass!" Because *duh*. The werewolf either (a) took his excellent advice or (b) died, because he quit moving. Not that she was satisfied, because the growling hadn't let up.

And Annette.

His safety Net was terrifying. Not just big. Enormous, the biggest he'd ever seen; well over a thousand pounds. Even slumped on the floor like she was, David was only a head taller, and *he* was standing upright. Her coloring was odd, too, the fur a deep russet with blond tips that were so fair they were nearly white. She had the characteristic hump of a grizzly, but with a long neck, long body, and a leaner head. He didn't know what subspecies she was; he couldn't imagine the bears that made her; he wasn't even sure, now, that he really knew anything about her. Only that he was ferociously glad she was on their side.

He managed to stop staring long enough to take another look at the

(yep, definitely the word of the day)

carnage. Blood and guts everywhere, like a movie set where the prop and makeup guys went a little crazy. The smell of blood and adrenaline was simultaneously making him gag and his mouth water. And from beneath the stairs, where there was another door he hadn't noticed, something with gleaming green eyes and a bloody muzzle came loping out, and *that's* where Oz had gotten to, he'd chomped the periphery guard, mystery solved, and—shit, was that pile of flesh and Ugg boots Taryn? Judge Gomph's clerk?

Oh.

Oh.

That's when he noticed the cages. And the stale smell of juvenile terror, and pee, and more blood, older blood. It was every horror-movie basement he'd seen on the big screen, only a hundred times worse because it was real. "We are gonna be so traumatized by this," he decided, looking around corpse valley. "Possibly. Doncha think, Caro? Maybe not. We've led pretty eventful lives so far."

To his surprise, Caro was still frozen by the doorway. He thought she'd get in there quicker than anything; he thought she'd shift and bite and bite and bite until all those bad guys were down or she was. He'd even made a mental note to keep out of her way when it happened. Unless she needed help. Then he'd get in the way, just watch.

But she wasn't, she hadn't done any of that, hadn't shifted, hadn't even moved. Just stood there breathing it all in, the smells and the blood and the shit, her home for two nightmare years. She was stuck, frozen, like someone pulled back into their worst nightmare, only it was real and she wouldn't wake up because she *was* awake.

And then Caro was running straight to Annette, throwing herself at 1,200 pounds of injured werebear, sobbing into bloody fur, and Annette's growls began to taper off like someone was slowly turning down the volume and David sat down quick, like he was worried his legs weren't gonna do the job much longer, and Dev got another whiff and realized a lot of the blood on David *was* David's.

What do I do? They're the adults, they're supposed to… I dunno. Call for help? Should I call? That's what an upside-down week this had turned into; people called the police on Dev, it was never the other way around. But his Net and David were hurt, and Caro was kind of in the middle of a breakdown and Pat was calmly reloading the shotgun while watching the exit, like he was focused on getting ready for a whole bunch of new bad guys and blocking out anything else, and Oz was prowling the interior, dead silent but eyes glaring like he'd *love* to get his teeth into another bad guy and everybody kept bleeding, so…*I guess it's up to me?* Any other day, that would have made him feel cool and grown-up.

That was when Nadia appeared out of nowhere—well, through the loading door Pat had been watching, he must've smelled them coming—with Judge Gomph and a bunch of cops in tow. And Nadia took one look around the carnage and declared, "I've brought the cavalry, darlings. Feel free to make an embarrassing amount of fuss over me."

Chapter 35

ANNETTE SLEPT BUT SHE DIDN'T MEAN TO, NOT SLEEP, not really, but she was so tired and her eyes closed by themselves but not for long and then strangers were coming strangers were *touching* her and she didn't know she couldn't remember if

(Dev? Caro?)

her cubs were safe, something had happened something deeply terrible had *just happened* and she hurt all over but here were new threats new wolves and a big stomper

(?judge?)

and she had to get up but she couldn't, she couldn't make her legs work and she couldn't see out of one eye so she swatted at the strangers, heard a curse, heard something smash, smelt fresh blood

(not her own though so good that's good)

and showed them bloody teeth

(I can still hurt you I can I can and and and where are Caro and Dev where where)

and turned toward faint voices

"…s'okay, honey, they're here to help us…"

lovely familiar voices but one she could hardly hear there were too many too many voices and smells and too many things hurt

"Wow, Net, you gotta stop clawing up the EMT guys…"

and oh oh oh *everything* hurt but she would get up again and again and again and AGAIN WHERE ARE MY

but before she could complete the thought a shrill fearsome voice cut through her cloudy confusion like claws through honeycomb

"Annette Garsea! You hirsute brute, you will shift back immediately, *immediately*, and let these paramedics help you or I will get Mama Mac down here to *make* you!"

(!!!!!!!!!!)

And then she was shrinking and getting lighter and weaker and curling into herself and she hadn't thought it possible but now everything hurt *more* and cold, ah, *God*, it was cold, and she blinked up at Nadia who was either an angel sent by the denizens of heaven

(she's glowing!)

or was simply standing with the sun at her back.

"I wrecked the salmon dress," she managed, and then everything went dark and stayed that way for who knew how long.

The upside: rainbow trout, steak, gazpacho, butter-basted morels, sugared raspberries and cream, fried chicken, shellfish kebabs, pasta, lemonade, tea, cake, and KFC gravy to wash it all down.

There didn't appear to be a downside, though. That was new.

The only dead person in the room was Opal Adway, and that was new, too. She had topped the cake with raspberries and was washing down bites of dessert with milk tea. "Well, hiya," she said in her high, piping voice, just like Oz did back then, and still did, even though his adult voice was neither high nor piping.

"Hi, Opal." Annette sat across from her long-dead friend.

She grinned, green eyes gleaming. "You lost the bet on purpose."

"Yes."

"Dummy."

"Yes." She watched Opal relishing dessert, something she'd never seen the girl do in life. "Nice to see you digging in."

"Took a while, y'know? For me to trust food again." Annette nodded, like she and the dead girl were having a sane conversation. "Oz, too. Well, he didn't trust *people*. Remember?"

Vividly. She'd been at Mama Mac's for two years by then, long enough that thoughts of her parents would sometimes make her smile, which was an improvement over the sobbing and much less exhausting, too. Twelve year-old Oz and his sister, Opal, had come to stay for a few weeks while IPA tracked down a permanent solution for them, preferably one involving competent blood relatives.

The twins had been "saved," which didn't mean what she thought it did back then. The bad guys were in cages, and lawsuits were happening, but much of the damage caused by the months of malnutrition would prove to be irreversible in Opal's case, and made worse by the fact that she no longer trusted any adult trying to feed her.

Oz's coping mechanism had been the exact reverse: he ate anything he wanted, anywhere he wanted, anytime he wanted, and if people didn't like it, too bad, and if someone decided to fight him over it, he'd go all in every time. Even if they were bigger and older. Even if it was *their* French Silk pie. Even if they won every fight, because bear versus wolf hardly ever worked out for the wolf.

So, the bet.

"I was afraid I'd hurt him eventually. He wouldn't quit. Every fight was to the pain." *Why am I explaining this to a dead girl?* But she knew why. This wasn't real. She was explaining things to herself. "That's all."

"Nuh-uh! You wanted to give him back some control. And you wanted to give him a win. So you threw the bet."

"Thanks for the nutshell summary."

"Welcome. And then I died."

"And then you died." Cardiac arrest brought on by potassium deficiency. "There's no need to narrate."

"Uh-huh! Someone's gotta remind you it's worth it, you big dummy." Opal had finished the cake and was now spooning up the sugared berries. "That's what you're *really* wondering. You think your work is pointless." When Annette opened her mouth, Opal amended her comment with "You sometimes think your work is pointless. Well, so? Sometimes going to the dentist is pointless. Shopping in the organic section. Um…buying sandals in winter. And…uh…"

"I get it," she replied dryly. "And going to the dentist is never pointless."

"What, are you shilling for the American Dental Association now? You couldn't save me, but Oz is still kicking around. You should just let him help you. You think it's a coincidence that out of all the places he could've worked, he ended up in your city, in your building, in your agency? Why was he even around for you to recommend to the Accounting department? He could've moved to any city in the world."

"I…hadn't given that much thought."

Opal snorted, but thankfully declined to comment. On that issue, at least.

"Besides, he's rich. He doesn't need to work for IPA or anyone."

"Really, Annette? You can't think why a rich abuse survivor would want to help other abused kids? Your mind's a blank? Nothing's coming to you at—"

"All right, good *God*, I understand." The civil suit against the school that had dropped the ball when it came to keeping their charges from being poisoned had netted seven figures. When Oz turned eighteen, he received his share. And Opal's, of course.

"You can't save everyone, and no one's saying otherwise," Opal said. "You'd be a huge dumbass to try. But you're not alone. Let 'em help you."

"Do you mean 'him' or 'them'?"

"It's time to wake up now."

"What?"

"Muh?"

My kingdom for a big glass of milk. Or a little glass of milk. Or a Coke. Or water. Or the blood of my enem—no, I've had enough of that.

Annette Garsea, Patient ID #FM2962–33, opened her eyes and was mildly surprised to find she was surrounded by a number of people, all of whom needed showers. *I've been here at least a day, then. Glad it wasn't a coma. Waking up to an adult Dev or an ancient David would have been unnerving.*

"One of you has a sandwich or something, right?" she croaked.

"See?" Nadia cried, triumphant. "She has regained consciousness and is now hungry and clueless, exactly as I predicted."

"Or soup. Preferably in a bread bowl. And I wouldn't say no to a gallon of iced tea, either."

David limped to her bed. Her gaze raked over him; she didn't think he'd been shot, but he had the beginnings of a glorious black eye, he was carrying himself like a man favoring cracked ribs, his wrist was heavily bandaged, and she knew there were a number of bite marks under his street clothes. Not just the little ones she gave him, either. He was in street clothes but still had his hospital bracelet, so…just discharged, then. And came to see her on his way home.

She smiled. "Sit down before you fall on me. Which I would have welcomed literally any other day but today."

Dev made a noise like a cat about to cough up a hairball. "Gross."

David took her advice and gingerly lowered himself into the chair beside her bed, manfully stifling pained groans. "When you said you needed to take definitive action yesterday, you were not fucking around."

"This wasn't quite what I had in mind," she said dryly. To Dev and Caro, huddled in the doorway: "Are you all right? You didn't get hurt?"

"We're totally fine, *bien, bene.* You, um, didn't leave anyone who was *able* to hurt us. Or walk. Or eat solid foods. Or piss without screaming."

"Oh, God, I remember now, there you were, running in at the end like bold dolts." Annette closed her eyes, appalled. "I'm so sorry you had to see that. I will kill Pat, figuratively, not literally. I recommend therapy on the hour. Starting yesterday."

"Aw, don't be like that." Dev came over and perched on the edge of her bed. He was still in yesterday's clothes as well. *Did everyone just decide to camp out in the critical care unit? Did the nurses not notice or not care?* "He promised you he wouldn't let us out of his sight. Also, closure, I guess? It was awesome. Well. Not awesome. Gross and scary and a little overwhelming. And every one of them deserved it. And I'm glad they're all maimed and dead."

"Were you yelling at them to play dead?"

"Isn't that what you're supposed to do with werebears?"

"No. Pure propaganda. It just makes us hungry." And she laughed, which hurt, but...*worth it.*

Dev sighed. "I'm just..." She realized he was huddled in one of Pat's jackets, which made him look small and vulnerable. (Only one of those impressions was accurate.) "I'm just super glad you're okay." A pointed throat-clearing from David, who had the most expressive phlegm she'd ever heard. "And you, too, Auberon."

"And a little child shall lead them." Nadia snickered, and Annette's eyes popped open as she snatched at the other woman's hand. "Gah! Some warning, please. And could you loosen your grip a smidge? I cannot shake the feeling that you've mistaken my wrist for a trout."

Annette stared up at her. "I ruined that nice cardigan you picked out for me."

"I saw."

"But first I put my arms through it. Willfully. For the purposes of warmth. Which I knew you'd hate."

Nadia patted her hand. Were her eyes brighter than normal? Was she going to weep? *Alarming.* "Well, you did almost die, so in my magnanimity, I shall overlook your spiteful sleeve appropriation."

"I'm sorry I said I was going to snuff out your life force as I stomped on your face."

"Oh? Hadn't heard that bit. I'm sorry I made you wear salmon in a fight to the death. Well. Deaths, plural."

Annette laughed, which hurt. *Worth it.* "Where were you? I kept waiting for you to spring out and try to kill us. Or spring out and try to save us. How'd you avoid getting caught?"

"Because I did not march into an abandoned warehouse I was fairly certain housed abusive fucksticks who would kill to keep their secrets?"

"So *that's* the trick," David said.

"Jeez, Nadia, do you kiss the Queen of England with that mouth?" Dev asked. "Honest question. I don't know anything about you. Like, at all."

"Quiet, you. I hid my clothes and shifted and watched from the skies, of course. When I saw Taryn arrive in the company of several armed men, all of whom looked inbred—what is it with species purists and unfortunate facial features?—it occurred to me that someone besides Gomph knew where you'd stashed Caro."

"Good for you," David said, grimacing as he shifted in the torture device disguised as a hospital chair. "We didn't figure that out until Taryn basically told us she was the bad guy."

"Yes, which is why you glorious morons were both hospitalized while I remained whole and unchomped. Once I realized who the true mole was, I thought it worth the risk to approach the judge, and so I did. And I used this, so they wasted no time."

She held something up. Annette squinted at it (her

close vision wasn't terrific) and said, "When did you lift my cell phone, you sticky-fingered shrew? Oh, don't even tell me."

"You'll want to charge that, darling."

"Later." She snatched it from Nadia and stuffed it under her pillow. "So we ended up converging where it all started."

There was a low rasp as David rubbed at his stubble, shaking his head. "Agh. Itches. It didn't start with Lund, or even Caro. It started with Dev."

Annette realized he was right and cursed herself for not seeing it earlier. Dev had found Caro, made her his sister, kept her as safe as he knew how. Protected her secrets when she was back in IPA's clutches. Stuck by her like a blond barnacle. Brought everyone together. Repeatedly.

"You've made being a pain in my ass a superpower," she realized aloud.

"Not just *your* ass," the boy said and smirked.

"Amen to that," David muttered.

"Pay attention to my exposition, Annette." Nadia managed to look elegant as she snapped her fingers, which was a good trick as she was just as rumpled and dirty as the rest of them. "As I was saying, I approached Gomph, who was most displeased. And not just with us, so that was fortunate. Apparently, he'd been harboring dark suspicions about Taryn for weeks. You're on medical leave now, but resign yourself to a series of tedious lectures by Gomph and Bob upon your return to IPA's fetid hallways. And paperwork, of course. Meters of it."

"It's nice to have something to look forward to."

"Don't worry," Dev assured her. "You're still our favorite werebear."

"Your favorite… Dev, don't *say* that," Annette replied. "It's like saying Barack Obama is your favorite black person."

"Well…"

"Just stop," she groaned.

"Speaking of werebears, and don't take this the wrong way, Net, but what the hell are you?"

"Oh. Right." Not many had seen Annette's other self. She only got the urge to shift a couple of times a month; weeks would go by while she stayed bipedal, because she had a deep love for her opposable thumbs and being able to walk into any restaurant she pleased.

"She's a polar–grizzly hybrid, you dolts."

"Those are a thing?"

Nadia shook her head in disapproval. "Have you never opened a paralogy textbook?"

"Nadia, be nice. We'd worked together for over a year before *you* figured it out. My mother was a polar were from Alaska. My father was a California grizzly were."

"Why d'you think she keeps the thermostat set at fifty degrees?"

Annette jumped. "Ack! How long have you been standing there?"

"Are you asking me, or Oz?" Pat jerked a thumb behind him, and Annette saw Oz peek around her roommate and wave.

"Hiya!"

"Good God."

"I've been here about three seconds," Pat continued. "I've got no idea how long Oz has been here." Her room-mate pushed his way past the kids.

"My goodness, Pat. A rare foray into the wider world, congratulations. And I simply adore the purple mascara. It sets off your suit to superb effect."

"Thanks, Nadia. Also, go to hell. I leave the house all the time."

Silence.

"I do, dammit! I went to the farmers market just a little while ago."

"That was the Woodbury farmers market," Annette said helpfully. "Which closed two years ago."

"I rest my case. And I'm glad you're awake. You look like shit, but not as shitty as I was expecting, so that's something."

"I'm happy to surprise you yet again. Also, the moment I'm out of this bed I'm smacking you around for an hour or so. Pat, what were you thinking, bringing the cubs to that warehouse? Oh, and Oz, I see you hovering in the doorway. You I'll be smacking around for no reason at all. Come closer." He obliged, shuffling forward, and she squinted up at him. A few scratches, but his earlier wounds from car vs. werewolf had cleared up. "You weren't hurt."

"Nope. That SAS guard never saw me coming. For a group that loves to insist they're the master race of all master races, they sure go down easy."

"Good God. And you, Pat. Again, what were you—"

"'Holy shit, Annette's gonna maybe die if we don't do something,'" Pat said. "That's what I was thinking."

"Wait. How did you even know about that w…" Annette's gaze settled on Caro, still hanging back. "Oh. My God. That took such courage, Caro, and if no one has told you, you're wonderful. Pat, Oz, you're still in for a thrashing. Give me that."

"What?" he teased.

"The *bag*, Pat. The one you're hiding behind your back for some reason."

"No, this is my bag."

"Why are you behaving like you think I won't get up out of this bed and take it from you?"

"I get off on living dangerously?" He held it out.

Annette snatched it. She knew what was in the black to-go box, but it was still lovely to behold a small pile of salmon sashimi. There were even chopsticks, which was hilarious.

"The chopsticks came with it," Pat explained. "I didn't bother explaining that you'd be double-fisting salmon into your gaping maw and small wooden sticks would only slow you down and infuriate you."

"Wise," she replied with her mouth full.

Caro chose that moment to come forward, smiling a little to see Annette's cheeks bulging with fish. The sight of her reminded Annette that there was still much to put right, that paperwork (as always) beckoned, there was more work ahead, and this wasn't a neat-and-tidy ending, because real life hardly ever worked that way. But her charges were safe, evil had been punished, and David… well. She'd have to think about that for a bit.

Caro held out her hand. "Hello. We haven't been properly introduced. My name is Caro Daniels. And it's lovely to meet you."

Chapter 36

"ARE YOU SURE YOU DON'T NEED A HAND?"

"David, step away from the bathroom door."

"I'm not sure you should be in there by yourself, is all."

"If we hadn't already slept together, I would be mortified that you're seeing me like this. Well, hearing me like this. And smelling me like this. Through a closed door. Which I'll soon have to open, so back up."

"But we have. Slept together, I mean." He squashed the urge to scratch at the door and whine.

"Away!" He stepped back as the door slid open and she limped past him. "I'm growing fond of you, David, but I have no use for a Stage 5 clinger."

"Pretty sure I've got far to go before it's that bad."

"Lovely. Something to look forward to." She sighed. "I appreciate that I'm one of many patients, but where is that doctor? He assured me I could leave in time to have lunch somewhere that wasn't here."

"No, he didn't. He was horrified that you wanted to leave and begged you to stay another night. Which you should, by the way. I'm aware I'm wasting my breath, but I wanted to just, y'know, get that comment on the record."

"That money-grubbing reprobate is padding his pockets at the expense of the good people at Blue Cross Blue Shield."

"You were shot three times!"

"One of them was just a graze." She sniffed. But she gripped his hand as she crawled back into the bed and sighed with relief when she was again settled. "You know the best part about being in the hospital?"

"Not dying?"

"The warm blankets. Did you know they have machines just for keeping the blankets warm? So they always have warm blankets on hand? Isn't that clever? It makes me forgive them for the food. Why do they think Jell-O is best at room temperature?"

"This is why we should go out," David decided, settling in the chair beside her bed. "You're really easy to please."

"I'm not, actually." She gazed at him through lowered eyelashes. She had dark circles under her eyes and the hospital gown was wildly unflattering and she had holes in her that she didn't have on Monday (and so did he) and it was all outstanding. "So what's this? I thought you were determined that we were not, in fact, going to go out."

"That was before you helped me kill the bad guys. Again."

There was more to it, of course. But he wasn't sure he could explain it. He'd known she was sexy and sweet and dedicated and dangerous. He'd known two days in that she'd kill in defense of herself or others. But he hadn't known that she'd walk into a pack of warwolves intent on her death, then basically tell them to go fuck themselves, then refuse to meekly relocate to a murder spot more convenient for said warwolves. And all that while expecting her partner to turn up any second and betray her to death. Wearing salmon. On an empty stomach.

"So that's all a woman has to do to win your heart? Bite bad guys until they bleed out?"

"No, she also has to be snarky and constantly forage for buffets and worry about her charges and go through an alarm clock every few days and back-seat drive until the person behind the wheel gives real thought to driving over a cliff."

"In what is a truly fantastic coincidence, I possess *all* those qualities. Dammit! I never did get a chance to buy a new clock…"

"Yep. So. We're going out. Will you wear salmon?" he asked. "I fucking love salmon now."

"Never again. And that's how you ask me out?"

"Initially. I'll gladly get on my knees for you, but you'll have to help me back up."

"Only if someone helps me up first." She prodded gloomily at her heavily bandaged left shoulder. "Gah, feels like the slug is still in there, roaming around and freaking out my white blood cells. What was it, a .45?"

"Yeah. Don't poke at it. It'll never get better."

"I'll poke whatever I like, thank you."

"I feel like I should come up with a sexual double entendre, but I'm really tired."

"Good instinct." And then, out of nowhere: "I was thinking about Lund in the bathroom."

He grimaced. "Why?"

"I never met a sport before," she admitted. "That I know of. It's not something people brag about."

"I went to high school with one. Most of the teachers treated him like a short-bus kid, y'know?"

"Ugh, *not* okay, David... All right, so Lund couldn't shift, but my understanding is that he enjoyed all other aspects of our paralogical physiology. The metabolism, the reflexes..."

"Yeah. Remember the Olympics scandal in '05? Guy was a werewolf who broke too many records, but he couldn't shift, so he got away with it." Until the twenty-two-year-old track star in perfect health had a fatal heart attack out of nowhere. To this day, conspiracy theories abounded. David wasn't sure he was ready to assume a secret Shifter cabal randomly poisoned the guy. On the other hand, heart attacks at that age were pretty rare...

"Right, so Lund had our metabolism... It's why he was able to leave the hospital so soon." She shook her head. "Too bad it wasn't enough for him."

"He got his."

"Yes, his downfall was almost biblical in nature. Or soap opera-ish. And that's enough talking about him. You slept here last night."

"Yeah." *I should prob'ly get used to these abrupt subject changes.*

"And the night before, and the night before that. You didn't have to."

"Disagree."

"Which is the other reason I want to get out of here. You're hindering your own recovery by sleeping in terrible hospital chairs," she said seriously, taking his hand in hers. "Also, you snore."

"I do not." Wait. Did he? He honestly had no idea. Most of his bed partners didn't spend the night.

"David, I guarantee you snore. I noticed as much the other night at your friends' house, and last night I thought someone had parked a cement mixer beside my bed."

"Nope. Just me. And while my snoring hasn't been proven—"

"It has one hundred percent been proven."

"—you *talk* in your sleep. Actually, you order food in your sleep."

"I know," she said glumly. "Pat overheard me once and took far too much delight in it. Speaking of that devil in disguise, he's gotten our charges safely back into the smothering arms of IPA?"

"Yeah, and everyone there has been brought up to speed. It helps that Gomph was there for the cleanup. He's pushing a lot of stuff through that would normally take days or weeks. He came to visit us, but you were too busy ordering prime rib in your sleep to notice."

"Ohhhhh…don't say prime rib…" she moaned.

"And Caro Daniels gave a two-hour statement."

"*Au jus* with creamy horseradish on the… She did? Wonderful! Who knew she'd be so voluble? No one," Annette answered herself. "Which was her point, I guess. It speaks to her strength of will that she was silent for so long." She sighed and scrubbed her fingers through her hair. "I want to go and I want to eat and I want to shower and I want to sleep. In that order."

"Sounds like a plan. Y'know, when you do that, it just sticks up more."

"Something we have in common" was the wry reply. "Weird, yes?"

"Yes." He reached out, tugged a white-tipped lock. "In all the best ways. So. Are you going out with me or am I getting on my knees?"

"Both of those things will happen. Just…maybe not today."

He laughed. It was hard to remember they'd worked this case together less than a week. And that three days ago he didn't want to enter into a relationship because he assumed he had to protect her from his pro-Stable… leanings? Whatever the word, the thought of having to protect Annette Garsea from anything was ridiculous. Not that he wouldn't try, if things went messy.

Maybe the biggest irony was that his mother would have been delighted. He could almost hear her: *She'll keep you and yours safe, at least. Despite yourself. You must know I only ever wanted your safety.*

Not that that was a factor in his decision. Or at least not a major one.

"Annette, I've gotta ask you something weird."

"Ooooh. Sounds promising."

"Do you ever hear your mom in your head?"

"Yes, but only when Mama Mac leaves me a blistering

voicemail. The woman simply will not text, which… Oh. You mean do I hear *dead* people in my head." When he didn't say anything, she added, "No, never, but I occasionally attend a death banquet in my sleep."

"Jesus."

"Yes, it's pretty grim. And as upsetting as it likely is for you to hear your dead mother, at least your dead talk to you. Mine sit around a big dining room table—the one in my parents' old house, which I haven't seen since my training bra days—and stare at me while I eat. And I try to warn them away from their deaths and they keep staring and the food starts to taste like mud but I keep eating it and they keep…staring…at…me."

"Jesus."

"Feel better?"

"Kind of," he admitted, ducking his head to try to hide the smile.

She reached out, took his hand. He squeezed gently, careful not to nudge the IV line. "Why are you asking, David? Are you worried you're losing your mind?"

"Annette…"

"Daaaaaaaavid…"

"God, you're like a therapist."

"Thanks! Tell me more about your mother." When he snorted, she added, "And you didn't answer my question. Are you worried you're losing your mind?"

"Sometimes," he admitted. "Mostly I wonder why she's the only one I hear."

"Because she's the one you have unfinished business

with," Annette replied promptly. "You and I haven't been close for long—"

He snorted. "Understatement."

"—but even so, I know about your mother's hopes and fears and stressors, because they were important enough to you to share with me when we were in bed. But never a word about your dad. Not one thing. I don't even know what he looked like, or what you miss about him, or what you regret about his passing. Because he's not the one on your mind, the one haunting you." She paused and considered. "For lack of a more psychologically accurate term."

He just looked at her, processing.

"You don't hear his voice because you don't feel guilty about him. It's *her*."

"Yeah?"

"Sure. And it's not even her, you know. Despite what I said two seconds ago. It's a way for your subconscious to poke at you until you make a breakthrough." Pause. "Or you're quietly going clinically insane. Or a third option that I'm too tired to think about. Hell, I'm not a therapist, even if you think I sound like one. I majored in English, for God's sake."

"None of that should've made me feel better," he confessed, "but all of it did."

"Excellent. And before my seventeenth nap, I wanted to remind you that I didn't brush my teeth just to clean them," she said, taking her hand back to flirtatiously shove a matted clump of hair out of her eyes. "Well, I did, but there's an upside to my newly cleaned teeth." She reached out a pale hand

(they pumped six pints of blood into her; he wouldn't let them touch him until she stabilized)

and tugged on his shirt until he leaned forward and kissed her. He'd meant to go for a chaste "looking forward to dating and intimate relations sometime in the future at a time and place of your choosing" peck, but she wasn't having any of that (thank God). Her mouth bloomed beneath his and she tugged him closer and her fingers were touching him everywhere she could reach and it was outstanding, so much so that he was amazed how such a simple act should be devastating in the best—

"Ouch!"

"Sorry! I'm so sorry. Here, just… There you go."

And it was fine and better than fine, and he drew her closer to him and oh, it was intoxicating, she was the predator he was and perhaps even the greater danger, which…

"Shoulder!"

"Sorry."

Was equal parts arousing and frightening and she smelled like everything good in the world, like plums and cotton and betadine and plastic tubing…

"IV! IV!"

"Wait… There, I got the kink out."

And he slipped a hand under her hospital gown, gently feeling his way up, fingertips skating past bandages and stitches and

"*Ow!*"

"Sorry! I'm so sorry. Let me just—"

"Enough," she gasped, and gently pushed him away. "To be continued when we won't hurt and/or accidentally strangle each other."

"Good call." They both looked; Sharon had come into the room, and they'd been so tangled in each other (heh) neither of them had noticed. "I'm serious. You wouldn't believe what some patients get up to, and in worse state than you two are."

"Tell us over lunch. I'd love to be regaled. Can we get prime rib? Gimme."

"You really shouldn't go home today." Sharon gave her a kind-yet-thorough once-over as she handed Annette the werecub. "Multiple GSWs and internal bleeding, for heaven's sake."

"One was just a graze, though," David pointed out with a grin.

"Yeah, not buying it." And then, to Annette: "Thank you for what you did. Tilly came down to see you when you were admitted, but you were a bit out of it."

"A bit out of it? Is that a medical term?" Annette teased, cuddling the Spencer cub, who was fat and bright-eyed and warm and smelled like milk and pureed chicken. "I don't remember. That was nice of her."

"How are *you* feeling, David?"

"Not shot, so no complaints. Annette took all the bullets, which was emasculating but also awesome. And in case you were wondering, giving us Brennan's business card along with confidential patient files worked out pretty well for people who weren't named Brennan."

"Yeah, I figured." Sharon smiled, flashing her rogue dimple. "We hoped you'd do something. We didn't know what."

"That's okay," David said. "We didn't know, either. We've basically ad-libbed the last four days."

"Yeah, I'm not surprised to hear that. Anyway, we didn't expect...whatever it was that you did. So thanks again. For whatever it was that you did. Which everyone's talking about, but not officially."

Some of the details were never going to be made public, not least because at least one IPA staff member had been in the syndicate. Annette's boss, her boss's boss, Judge Gomph (now in need of a new court clerk), and a number of others were heavily invested in damage control, and as a result, the rumor mill had cranked up almost immediately and likely wouldn't stop anytime soon. And as David had foreseen, though their bosses were determined to get to the bottom of all the awful, remaining hidden from the Stable world was still a top priority and would color every aspect of the investigation.

And that wasn't even considering the fact that, somehow, Stables had helped Shifters build their very own secret hospital wing, all without exposing their secrets. Were there more than one such hospital? Was it national? Were those Stables their own secret group? Were they formal allies that, somehow, no one knew about? How many? For how long? She needed to dig, and David's assistance would be invaluable. She suspected he would be able to show her a hidden world of Stable allies. Why else would he be so keen on their species finally coming forward?

"This one's getting fostered out today," Sharon added, indicting the cub, who was sucking on one of the ties of Annette's hospital gown and making little rumbling sounds of contentment. "We would have been scared to discharge him a few days ago. Tilly and I thought you should know."

"I'm glad," she said simply. "And thank Dr. Tilbury for taking the time to visit."

"I will. I need to get back to the ward; my break's almost up. And then you guys can get back to your incredibly ill-advised make-out session."

"It *was* ill-advised," Annette admitted.

David laughed. "I think the operative word is 'incredible.'"

"You're both deeply nuts," Sharon said, and pried the cub away from Annette. "But it appears to be working for you. So long as you discount the whole 'ending up in the hospital' aspect."

"Could you do me a quick favor?" she asked. "Would you peek in the fridge for me?"

"Sure." Sharon slung the cub over one shoulder, crossed the room, knelt, and opened the small half-fridge beside the window. "Huh. It's all takeout containers." They could hear Sharon rummaging, and then she was reading aloud. "Potstickers from Big Bowl, spicy peanut noodles from same, here's a turkey wrap, and…let's see, there's also burrata cheese from Cossetta's, some macaroons, and half of a French Silk pie. Jeez."

"And the contents are written on the containers in loopy, girlie cursive handwriting?"

"Yep."

Oz, you sneaky devil. "Thanks, Sharon."

"Should've had lunch up here. Cripes, look at all this." She shook her head and began patting the cub on the back. "Try not to tear each other's stitches, nutjobs." Exit Sharon.

"Aw, what does she know?" David asked, settling back into the uncomfortable chair.

"She was a psychiatric nurse for ten years before she switched to peds."

"Oh. So, an educated opinion."

"One we should take seriously."

"Of course."

"You're going to kiss me again now."

"Of course."

"And we're going out. To put the rumors to rest at the very least."

"I'm in," David replied. "Who knows? We might end up enjoying each other's company."

"Don't get ahead of yourself."

Chapter 37

"DEAR GOD. MAMA MAC HAS LEARNED TO, AS YOU would put it, text like a motherfucker." Annette's phone had come back to life like a tiny Frankenstein's monster, buzzing and shaking in her hand. "And I have a text from…Jenn? Of Jim and Jenn Griffith?"

"They might've heard we got hurt."

"Might have, huh?" Annette was scrolling through a river of texts. "Did they also 'might have' my phone number from an old friend?"

"Don't know anything about that," David replied. "Nope. Also you might be invited to Thanksgiving."

"I can't. Mama Mac's vengeance would be immense and far-reaching. I was hoping you'd come to *our* Thanksgiving, provided we can still stand each other come November."

"That's the spirit. And did I mention that Jim is the range chef for Loon River? He can spatchcock a turkey like a motherfucker."

"On the other hand, it's smart to cultivate goodwill with Stable allies." Annette kept scrolling past the minutia, pausing now and again to fire off a quick retort. "Thanks for bringing a charger, by the way. Though I did enjoy the screen vacation. Maybe I should get shot every few months or so."

"Sure. Way easier than just shutting off your phone, right?"

"Is that you being subtle? Because that wasn't s—left, left, *left*! What's that noise?"

"Nothing."

"I heard something, David. Coming from the driver's side. Where you are currently perched. As you drive us."

"I'm not grinding my teeth," he growled, "if that's what you're wondering."

"You did that before, too. Do you do that every time you drive?"

"Not every time."

Annette chortled as she raided the car's ashtray for another handful of Skittles. "You should mix it up a little. Less red. More everything else."

"I'm going to pretend you didn't say that." David pulled into her driveway, parked, shut the car off, unbuckled his seat belt. "Sit right there. I'm coming around to help you."

"David, you're the one with the limp. If anyone is helping anyone, it's bound to be the other way around."

"What did I *say*?" David cried as he speed-hobbled around the car, getting to Annette just in time for her to stand and close the passenger door. They reached for each other, but Annette was a bit faster as she slung an arm around his waist and started tugging him toward the front door. Her home had never looked so good, and that included the time that Pat had it painted "Homage Eggplant," as he dubbed it, after one of Mama Mac's visits.

It didn't feel like she'd only been gone a few days. It felt longer, like the house should have looked run-down

and abandoned, with peeling paint, weeds in the driveway, broken windows, and an abandoned mailbox.

She fumbled with her keys, dropped them twice…

"Wanna shift? Then tear it down with claws and
teeth? I'll help."

"Good God, no. Is that really your go-to if you don't
get a door unlocked in twenty seconds?"

"Not…all the time."

…and finally got the front door unlocked. They shuffled their way past the foyer and living room, Annette
dumping David onto one of the kitchen stools as she went
to the fridge for an ice-cold bottle of water. Midchug, she
waved another bottle at David.

"Yeah, thanks. That'd be great."

"Ahhhhhh!" Another swallow, then she slid a bottle
down the counter to him. "Remember, Dr. Tilbury said
we have to push fluids."

"It was an hour ago, Annette. I remember. And she
said *you* have to push fluids."

"And I obey. Apparently multiple gunshot wounds
wreak havoc on your system. Who knew?"

David snorted, opened his bottle, and took a few
healthy swigs. "Where's Pat?"

"He'll be recovering from the stress of the outside
world in the studio for a week or so. Which is going to
cut into his organic gardening, but it's not for me to tell
him how to spend his time."

"I feel like you probably tell him how to spend his
time all the time."

"Shut up, David." She softened the rebuke with a kiss to the top of his head. "C'mon."

David got up at once, which she liked, and followed her past the kitchen and up the stairs

("Ow. Ow. Ow. Ow.")

to her room. It was exactly as she had left it the morning after she'd seen David's bear, from the piled-up comforters and drawn shades to the… "Dammit."

"You should've stolen Jenn's alarm clock from the guest room."

"But then I wouldn't have been invited to partake of spatchcocked turkey. I'd use my phone, but…"

He started to laugh. "How many phones did you smash before you went back to alarm clocks?"

"Never mind." She held out a hand, and he crossed the room to take it, then leaned down and kissed her. "How about a nice, long, sweet, drawn-out—"

"Yes. Yes. Yes."

"—nap?"

To his credit, David didn't miss a beat. "Sounds great."

"You're adorable." She climbed into bed, and David snuggled up behind her. "Knew you were a big spoon kind of guy."

He chuckled, smoothed her hair, kissed the back of her neck. "Now you know all my secrets."

"Not hardly." But it would be fun to discover them all. Or at least interesting. She wanted to find out all his favorite foods, too. Hopefully many of them dovetailed with hers. It would be too sad if he didn't like chocolate panna cotta but did like Satan's crudité: celery. The unpleasant thought followed her

I will not have celery in this house!

into sleep.

———————————

Twenty minutes later, or five hours (stupid blinds), she came awake in the gloom and stretched. She was warm and comfy, and the painkillers had been doing their job well enough that she decided to skip that evening's dose and take it from there.

There was a rumble behind her, and she felt David nuzzling the nape of her neck. "Hate being so goddamned groggy after a midday nap."

"A small price to pay." She yawned. She wriggled until they were facing each other. "How do you feel?"

"Better n'you, hon."

Oooh, I'm a hon. "That's just ignorant. You've got no way of telling how I feel, and you certainly can't make a comparative analysis."

"I stand corrected." He smooched the tip of her nose, and when he started to pull back, she cupped the back of his neck and wriggled forward, pressing a deeper kiss to his sleep-softened mouth. He let out a pleased hum and lazily kissed her back. When they broke for air, he added, "Sorry 'bout the morning breath."

"Unless we slept over sixteen hours, it's not morning breath. And you didn't care at Jenn's house."

"Nope." He smiled at her. "Sure didn't."

She slipped her hand under his T-shirt and ran her finger in a line parallel to the waistband of his jeans, and he shivered, his taut stomach pulling back as he involuntarily tried to escape the sensation. He made a noise, some noise…

"Did you just giggle?"

"Real men don't giggle," he said with a straight face, then sabotaged himself with another giggle.

He made a decidedly *masculine* noise and caught her fingers. "Agh. Don't tell anyone I'm ticklish."

"Your shameful disgusting secret is safe with… Yeek!" His fingers trailed higher, skimmed her belly, over her ribs, then hovered just beneath her breasts. "Don't be alarmed, but I didn't bother with a bra."

"That *is* alarming," he agreed, and gently stroked the sensitive underside of her breasts. "Appreciate the warning… Oh, oh, oh God."

She'd unbuttoned his jeans and slipped her hand in, then paused. "Okay?"

He hesitated, not moving away or buttoning up, but not encouraging her, either. "We shouldn't."

"It's not about 'should,' though. Can we?"

"I think it's too soon for you," he said gently, moving his hands to the more neutral territory of her waist.

"Not your call, David. Well, it is if… This isn't more of your we-won't-date nonsense, is it?"

"No, it's multiple-gunshot-wounds-less-than-a-week-ago nonsense."

"I'm a fast healer. Half the bandages are off already. Want to help me with the other half?"

He laughed. "If you were trying to make that sound seductive, it only worked a little. 'Oooh, now that we've put down a fresh dressing, you have to keep the wound clean and dry, baby...'"

"Fine, you can help me with my shirt, pants, and panties, then. I'm keeping my socks on. Chilly in here."

"You're half-polarwere but you won't give up your socks? And, again, if you're trying to make that sound seduc... Oh." She was busily unbuttoning her blouse... Bless Nadia for bringing button-downs and easy-on, easy-off pants to the hospital. And her 'Fuck off, I'm reading' socks. "Oh, Christ, your breasts are beautiful." His hands cupped, caressed. "Perfect."

"Wait until you see my dimples of Venus and extra-long pinkie toe." She helped him ease his T-shirt over his head and dropped it on the floor. "Don't worry. We're going to have slow, careful, invalid sex."

"It's crazy that I think that's hot."

"My kind of crazy, though."

It seemed to take forever until they'd divested each other of too many clothes, and Annette knew she would have felt that way even if they were in perfect health. They weren't, but David's contusions and bruises were lighting up her neurons like the Fourth of July, working on her like a hormone shot. It was primitive

(he got those protecting cubs and protecting me; he would've fought 'til he dropped)

but undeniable. "Some of these are turning a gorgeous shade of orange-yellow," she murmured, tracing the one over his hip.

"I love that you think sickly yellowy-orange is attractive." He dipped his head and kissed her throat, her collarbone, wiggled lower and licked her nipples until they were stiff, then rubbed his stubbled cheek across them.

"Good *God!*" she gasped. "I had no idea nerves from my nipples were connected to my...other places."

"It's good that we're learning new things," he told her solemnly, then giggled when she poked his stomach, which he cut off as he realized she was working her hand lower. His cock, jutting out from a thatch of neatly trimmed dark-brown pubic hair, was thick and hot, slapping his stomach and leaving wet dabs of pre-ejaculate on his skin, and filled her hand nicely. She squeezed gently and smiled when he groaned.

"Ummm," she said. "I like this."

"I'm so glad," he managed. He seized her and kissed her, hard, but the moment she opened her mouth he gentled, licking into her mouth until she'd let go of his cock to cling to his wrists. "So. Fucking. Glad. But slow, okay, honey? Slow and steady wins the race."

"This isn't a race, you adorable idiot. Although I'll admit a worrying percentage of men seem to think so. It's the only explanation for why so many of them finish first."

"Could we talk about something besides other guys?"

"Birth control? Don't need it. I'm not in season and

I'm on the implant. STDs? We don't get them. What else is there?"

"Uh…"

"Here." She took his hand, folded the fingers back until there were only two, then drew them down until the pads of his fingers were sliding over her clit and dipping down into the wetness below.

"Oh Christ."

"Fuck slow and steady. I'm using profanity so you know I'm… Ohhhhhhh." He was slipping and sliding his fingers over and around her clit, occasionally dipping lower, spreading the slick all over her tender flesh, then popping his fingers in his mouth to lick clean, then returning to the very center of her, smiling when she let out a quiet moan and moved her hips in an unconscious bid for more friction.

"God, your scent," he groaned. "Your *taste*."

"Yes. Oh…yes… What's better for you? On your back?"

"Annette, the last thing I give a shit about right now are my ribs."

"How fortunate that one of us does, in fact, give a shit. Let's try this." She sat up, flashed a wicked grin when he whined at the loss of contact, and carefully straddled him. "Okay?"

He looked up at her, his pupils blown so wide there was only the thinnest ring of blue to be seen. "Honestly? We could be done right now and I'd consider myself damned lucky."

"Under any other circumstances I'd call that bluff."
She leaned forward, braced herself on an unbruised area
of his chest, grasped his cock, and carefully began to
lower herself onto it. The thick, plummy head slid into
place like he was made for her, and for a few seconds,
despite the aches that were starting up, she savored the
long, delicious moment before the first good slide.

"Annette...God...take your...time...but I might...
die... No pressure...though..."

She slowly eased herself onto him, her eyes slipping
shut as that hot, hard warmth filled her, soothing one
ache but awakening another. David was gripping her hips
so hard she knew she'd have new bruises to add to the
collection and did not give a ripe shit.

She rose up again until only the head was inside and
David was staying still, so still beneath her, watching her
with wide eyes, and when she dropped, harder this time,
he let out a quiet growl.

"Oh, my," she gasped, bracing her feet and beginning
to rock back and forth. "That's...quite...nice..."

"Yes. Yesyesyes. God, you taste as good as you look,
and you look fucking incredible. Are you okay? Does it
hurt?"

"A bit. Worth it," she added when he started to shift
his weight. "You stay put." She swooped down, pressed
a kiss to his nipple, then bit down lightly, feeling as well
as hearing the groan that rumbled through his chest.
"Just...like...that..."

"Can I...move a bit?"

"As long as your cock stays inside me, you can do cart-wheels." She paused. "Don't actually do cartwheels."

He snorted, tightened his grip on her waist, planted his feet, and thrust up, hard. She let out a surprised shriek.

"Are you okay?"

"Again. Do that again." She timed her rocking hips to his next thrust and they both groaned, and she laced his fingers with hers as they rocked together for the next blissful minute, and Annette could feel heat start coiling low in her belly. David forgot himself and arched to meet her, then let out a pained hiss and fell back.

"Don't hurt yourself!" she cried, and stopped moving.

That earned her another hiss. "Shit. I'm okay, I just… The way my ribs are cracked, it actually would hurt less if we… Can we try something?"

"Anything," she replied promptly. "On my back? In your lap? Should we retire to our corners, like boxers, and try again after we hydrate? Or do you want me on all…" He involuntarily tensed, and she had her answer. "Ah. I see." She smiled and leaned in. "Is that how you like it? You want me on all fours so you can take me? So all you have to do is glance down to watch yourself sliding in and out of me, all slick and sweet?"

"Annette… Christ…"

"So you can admire my ass while you're fucking me? So you can watch the muscles in my back work while I'm moving to take your cock? That position is really intense for me, David. It makes me desperate. I'll try to spread my legs for you even more than they already are, I'll try *so hard* to open myself up for you as much as I can, to give you everything I can, and it won't be enough, and I'll get loud, and I'll beg, David. You'll be able to make me beg."

"Turn over," he growled, his voice so deep it was almost unrecognizable. She obliged as fast as she could, because everything she had just said was the truth, and she wanted that thick, hot length inside her again, she wanted to feel him thrusting so hard it was like he was in her throat, she wanted to be mounted and invaded, and she didn't care if it hurt, she wanted to see the fresh bruises the next morning and blush, but not for shame.

She'd barely had time to get into position before he slammed into her so fast she had to grab for the headboard.

He pulled out and for a long, agonizing second didn't move. "Are you okay?"

"More cock, please," she managed, wriggling an invitation.

"Jesus Christ," he groaned, "your already-perfect ass is fucking heart-shaped."

"*More cock, please.* If you do it hard enough, I won't have to touch myself at all. You'll be big enough and I'll be wet enough and I'll come untouched." This was a lie, but a lie told to good effect. She'd confess later.

"I *want* you to touch yourself," he ground out, thrusting again. "I want to see you making yourself feel good. When we're both healed up, I'll be able to stroke you all over while I'm fucking you like this, just like this, but until I can manage that, until I—I—I—ah—I want you to rub your clit and pinch your nipples and push back against me. I want you to make yourself whimper. I want you to lose your mind while you're touching yourself, while you're spreading yourself for my cock with your delectable ass in the air. Do it, Annette."

Oh Jesus. Was there anything hotter than a confident man who loved watching his partner get off? She had no idea, and it was getting hard to think. It was getting hard to do anything but want to mewl and plead. Things were starting to hurt, but literally everything else her body was doing—the warnings from her nervous system, breathing, cellular mitosis, all that irrelevancy—faded before the pleasure that was swamping her brain. She reached down, found her swollen clit, rubbed lightly and moaned. *Oh, he's going to make me… I never come this fast, but he…he…*

He groaned as she shivered against him. "More, Annette. I want to see your fingers slick and shiny. I want you to forget every fucking thing in the world except how good my cock feels." She was whimpering, she knew, she was trying to speak, ask, beg, but all she could manage were little bitten-off noises as she took his cock, as he filled her and retreated and filled her again, as pleasure started to spread from her belly outward, as she met every thrust with desperate welcome. "Jesus Christ, the *sounds* you're making… Are you close, honey? Because I'm very fucking close."

"Please…David…please…please…"

"If you're not, it's okay. It might even be better that

way. I'll come and then flip you over, and then I'll touch you everywhere you want, and everywhere *I* want, and then I'll get my mouth on that sweet cunt of yours, which I have been fucking *dreaming* about for days, and I'll lick and tease your clit while I'm fingering you, you'll be so slippery with me, I'll keep you spread open for me like a feast until you're coming for me, *Christ*, I'll make you feel so good, Annette, any way you'll…let…me…"

"D-David…I'm…" Now that sweet ache was spreading everywhere, she was so close to the point of no return, desperate to reach the edge so she could plunge over. "More. Talk more."

"And I haven't even talked about what I'll do to you with whipped cream and maple syrup."

And she was gone, she was flying, pleasure thrummed through her entire body while David let out a roar behind her. She could actually feel the temperature change as he filled her, his grip on her hips tightening to the point of pain, then loosening as he collapsed against her. Thanks to the domino effect, she went down, too, flat on her belly and too sated to move.

A good minute went by while the only sounds were their panting. Finally, she managed, "You okay? How are the ribs?"

"I…have…ribs?"

"Several." She chuckled, reached out blindly, found his hand, squeezed. "My God, David. That was beyond incredible."

"Back atcha. Sorry. I know I should be saying

something flowery and sensitive, but my brain's off-line for the foreseeable future."

"How off-line can you be if you're throwing around words like 'foreseeable'? And you said plenty of flowery things. Excellent dirty talk, David. Just *superb*."

"Muh."

"David?"

"Buh."

"Getting a little hard to breathe, David."

"Oh…sorry."

After some careful wriggling, they were on their backs, looking at the ceiling. "You're staying over, right?"

He groped, found her hand, clasped it, kissed her palm. "Absolutely."

"Excellent." She paused, thinking. "Thank you for this week."

"Pretty sure my line is 'No, thank *you*.'"

"I'm not just talking about the sex. I mean all of it. You could've been hurt. Worse than you were, I mean. Or killed. But you never quit."

"Neither did you," he pointed out.

"I guess we're both awfully heroic," she said with faux modesty, and he laughed. She turned until she was on her side, studying his profile.

He was still holding her hand as his breathing steadied, and he turned his head to smile at her. "I'm going to stay just like this for now. I'm afraid if I try to get on my side, I'll puncture a lung. But ask me if I give a shit."

"I try not to ask questions I know the answers to."

Then she sobered. "I was so blind. You were right there. You were under my nose for two years, and I never saw. I never saw. Not your bravery or kindness or disturbingly strong sweet tooth…"

"I've been crushing on you for over a year and never did anything about it. So, the opposite of brave."

"There are different types, I suppose." Then: "Really? A year?"

"Don't get smug."

"Too late!" She began to stretch, then groaned. "I think I might give the painkillers one more night."

"Good call."

"But imagine how the sex will be when we can bring our A game."

He groaned. "You'll kill me."

"Too late to chicken out now," she said, and kissed his knuckles.

Chapter 38

"I said I was sorry!"

"You didn't, actually." Mama Mac swiped at her with the dish towel again. "Worse, I had to hear about it from that nice bird you work with."

"I can't decide if you're calling Nadia a bird because she's British or because she's a raptor. The first one's okay, but the second could be considered—*ack!* That hurts almost as much as the bullets did."

"Well, the towel's damp." But Mama Mac backed off, which validated Annette's decision to pretend the annoying, half-hearted towel whaps hurt more than they did. "And here. This is what you came for."

Annette took Lund's original files back. "It's one of the things I came for. Do I want to know where you stashed these?"

"You don't, Nettie. And well done, you. For all of it. Except the part where you forgot to tell me you were attacked and hospitalized with multiple gunshot wounds."

"Let's not dwell on the past," she replied as Mama Mac brandished the towel again. "That was days ago. We're living in the present, which means I've got to follow a judge's order to turn these in to IPA, and then I'm meeting David for lunch."

Caro yawned as she slouched into the kitchen,

scribbled on her pad, then handed Annette a note and tucked the pad back into her pajama pocket:

Lunch? It's 8:30 in the morning, Net.

"I know, I'm running late. And oh, goody, you're starting with the Net stuff, too." What was up with that silly nickname? Laziness? Was it *that* hard to pronounce both syllables of her name? How much time could it possibly take?

But it was gratifying to see Caro again. She was still painfully thin (which Mama Mac was combatting with several small meals a day, plus protein shakes with pureed beef, and brownies, lots of brownies), but was clean and well rested in flannel pajamas and bare feet.

Mama Mac pushed a bowl of savory oatmeal toward her

"Ooooh!"

and past her to Caro, who fell to like she was starving. Which made sense.

"Oh."

Mama Mac rolled her eyes and slid over another bowl. Annette had been doubtful about the savory oatmeal trend—she preferred hers with loads of cream and brown sugar—but there was something to be said for steel-cut oats with a fried egg, a slice of pork belly, sautéed mushrooms, and chives. "Yay!"

Caro snorted.

"What can I say?" Annette replied with her mouth full. "I take joy in the simple things."

"And you always have, m'dear. As for you, Caroline Daniels, what have I told you about sleeping in the basement?"

Caro fixed Mama with one of her eloquent expressions. *Not to?*

"Not to." Mama softened her tone. "There are plenty of beds, m'dear. Even with Dev coming to stay for a bit."

Caro shrugged and scribbled. She was lightning fast, like a court stenographer.

Room's too warm & bright. It's like trying to sleep on a giant marshmallow under operating room lights.

"That does sound off-putting," Annette admitted. "Mama, am I seeing things, or did they rent out the Curs house again?"

"Second time this month. The last tenants didn't even stay 'til the 15th."

"Unbelievable. They should just raze it and build...I don't know, a playground or something."

"I'm finished," Caro said aloud. "Thank you."

"Good God," Annette said, awed. "Did you chew? At all?"

That earned her a look every teenager had mastered by their fourteenth birthday: *Are you stupid?*

"All right, I get it. Technically, you don't have to chew oatmeal. You can just slurp it straight down, like a duck. I guess we should be glad it wasn't granola."

"I won't have granola in this house," Mama Mac declared, slinging the dreaded dish towel over her shoulder.

"Yes, I remember. And speaking of remembering, you'll all recall that this"—Annette gestured to the kitchen, the table, the fridge, Mama Mac—"isn't permanent. I'll push to get you and Dev fostered here long-term, but it's a process. Bureaucracy is everywhere and swallows everything. Even the paranormal."

"Nothing's permanent. Disaster can strike any time," Caro said. After two years of self-enforced silence, she still preferred to write notes, even when she felt perfectly safe. No one was pressuring her to speak, because recovery took time; actual real-world psychological issues were hardly ever wrapped up in a neat bow. Still, Annette was warmed every time Caro said something aloud to her. "Got it, you glass-is-half-empty bureaucrat."

Well. Warmed most of the time. "That wasn't quite what I was trying to put across."

MM, more milk?

"Of course, m'girl." Mama Mac handed Caro what looked like a vase full of whole milk. "And *you*—you're seeing that David? Officially? Going together or whatever the current phrase is?"

"We have begun to mate and will do so again," Annette said solemnly, then snickered when Caro wrote-screamed *GROSS!!!* and Mama rolled her eyes. "He had to be talked into it, but yes."

"If he had to be talked into it, he's a fool."

"Well, at first he wasn't going to go out with me for my own good, if that makes a difference."

Mama's voice rose. "I *said*, he's a fool."

"I don't expect you to be objective. His dead mom was entirely against it, but then he figured out that she was against it out of thwarted concern, not any real dislike. Then we boned."

GROSS!!!

"Wow, you took up the whole piece of paper that time." Annette pushed back from the table. "Thank you for the oatmeal."

"You're welcome, you're always welcome. Come for supper. We're having pork roast—"

"Wonderful. What time?"

"—and Oz is coming, too."

"So sorry, something just came up," she teased.

"Oh, stop it."

"I have! He's transferring from Accounting. Wants to be in the field more, God help me. So now I'll be worrying about my lambs, his lambs, and *him*."

Caro passed her a note.

Or you could acknowledge he's a grown man who can take care of himself and calm down already.

"Zip it, Caro. Anyway, David and I—"

"When are you seeing him?" Mama asked.

"In about ninety seconds. He lost the coin toss, so he had to give Dev a ride over here. The alternative was to let that duplicitous kit steal a car and wait for the inevitable police report."

"You were always in over your head with him," Caro pointed out with a sorry-not-sorry grin.

"I'd love to hotly refute that, but since it's the complete truth, I'm going to ignore it instead and pretend that I'm in control of absolutely everything. Cue door knock."

At David's knock, Mama Mac opened the door, only to be gently moved aside as Caro went to Dev and hugged him hard enough to lift him off his feet.

Dev let out a pained squeak. "Missed you, too."

"You'll like it here," Caro said, setting him down. "She's nice and there are lots of beds and if you sneak food at midnight she notices but she doesn't say anything until the next morning which is when she'll lecture you. There are a lot of those. But that's the worst of it. Well, that and the 'no screens allowed after 10:00 p.m.' rule." Caro let out a long breath, as if talking was physically taxing. Which it probably was, after so little practice. It was, as far as she knew, Caro's longest verbal speech to date.

"Little tip?" Annette suggested. "If you only take one or two small things to eat in the wee hours, she won't get up later and check again. So the second time, you can really empty that thing out and she won't find out for hours."

"That would have been helpful if she hadn't been standing there hearing every word."

"Enjoy my childhood, kids." To David: "Hello, you."

"Hi." He pulled her in for a kiss and handed her a CVS bag. "I'm taking you up on your invitation for tonight."

She opened the bag and burst out laughing. "You're the third person to give me an alarm clock in two days."

"Excellent, it's good you'll have a supply on hand. Wait. Who else thinks they get to sleep with you?"

"Gross," Dev said as Caro handed him a note. "They're

mating? Who uses that word in the twenty-first century? Double, triple, quadruple gross."

"Quite right. Hello, Dev Devoss. I'm Mama Mac, and I've heard a lot about you."

"Thanks for letting me stay anyway," he replied, grinning his irresistible grin. "Since you raised Annette, does this mean Net and I are sisters?"

"Good *God*."

"Of course," Mama replied seriously. "Those are the very best families, the ones you reach out for and make for yourself."

"Corny," he replied. "Really, really corny."

"Ooooh. Am I the only one who wants corn on the cob now?"

Author's Note

I express my love of the graphic novel/movie *The Losers* through my characters and make no apologies for it.

Annette is right to fear sea snakes. Some of them have venom so potent just a few milligrams can kill you. I'm sharing this with you so I don't have to be terrified by myself.

Pazzaluna has excellent gnocchi and lamb chops and Annette is right to want to eat there all the time.

Polar–grizzly hybrids are real. They've been seen in the wild as well as in captivity. They're also referred to as grolar bears, or pizzly bears. Which is pretty wonderful.

About the Author

MaryJanice Davidson is the *New York Times* and *USA Today* bestselling author of several novels and is published across multiple genres, including the UNDEAD series and the Tropes Trilogy. Her books have been published in over a dozen languages and have been on bestseller lists all over the world. She has published books, novellas, articles, short stories, recipes, reviews, and rants, and writes a biweekly column for *USA Today*. A former model and medical test subject (two jobs that aren't as far apart as you'd think), she has been sentenced to live in Saint Paul, Minnesota, with her husband, children, and dogs. You can track her down (wait, that came out wrong…) at twitter.com/MaryJaniceD, facebook.com/maryjanicedavidson, instagram.com/maryjanicedavidson, and maryjanicedavidson.org.